FIRST KISS

Sarah looked out over the prairie, then slowly turned in a circle, seeming to delight in what she saw. Her gaze rested on Orion and her face lit up in a luminous smile.

"I love this place, Mr. Beaudine." Sarah flung her arms out in a gesture of exuberance. "Thank you for bringing me here."

"I'm probably going to regret this," Orion whispered, taking Sarah's face gently between his hands. Her eyes widened with surprise, and that was the last thing he saw before his own eyes closed and his lips descended to hers. He kissed her softly at first, with the reverence demanded by the place she had called sacred, but when she gasped and clutched his forearms with her hands, he was lost. Her lips trembled under his tender onslaught, then opened to him. His hands tangled in her hair as if he were a man grasping a lifeline, which he felt he was.

Sarah was the lifeline.

Finally, he dragged his mouth from hers and held her tightly, breathing in the scent of her hair, treasuring the feel of her arms once again around him, this time face-to-face.

Books by Jessica Wulf

THE IRISH ROSE
THE MOUNTAIN ROSE
THE WILD ROSE
HUNTER'S BRIDE

Published by Zebra Books

HUNTER'S BRIDE

Jessica Wulf

Zebra Books
Kensington Publishing Corp.
http://www.zebrabooks.com

ZEBRA BOOKS are published by

Kensington Publishing Corp.
850 Third Avenue
New York, NY 10022

Zebra and the Z logo Reg. U.S. Pat. & TM Off. The Lovegram
logo is a trademark of Kensington Publishing Corp.

First Printing: November, 1996
10 9 8 7 6 5 4 3 2 1

Printed in the United States of America

for Sundance

the gentlest and most loving spirit
I have ever known, in any lifetime.
I will love you forever.

♥

Prologue

Her mother was dying.

Sarah Hancock stared out through the frost-covered window with unseeing, tear-filled eyes. The truth could no longer be denied. Her dear, gentle mother was going to die, as her father had nine years earlier, and she would be left alone in the world. Sarah's cold hand clutched the plain woolen curtain in a tight grip as an agony of grief and fear flooded through her.

"Sarah." Her mother's raspy voice called to her.

Determinedly, Sarah blinked the tears away and turned to face her mother. A new spasm of coughing wracked Grace Hancock's thin form, a spasm that was noticeably weaker than the one before. Even under the thick pile of blankets, Sarah could see the fever-induced trembling of her mother's body. She hurried to sit on the edge of the bed, taking Grace's hand in hers.

"I'm here, Mama." She smoothed strands of gray hair away from her mother's damp forehead.

"You must listen to me, child. There's not much time."

At the look of resignation in Grace's eyes, Sarah's instinctive protest died on her tongue. Her shoulders slumped. "No, Mama, there isn't."

"You mustn't worry about me, daughter. I'll soon be with your father, and out of this sick and aching body. It is yourself you must be concerned about. I'm ready to go, but God knows I hate leaving you alone." A worried frown creased Grace's forehead.

"Please, Mama, don't trouble yourself. I'm twenty-three years old, soon to be twenty-four, a woman grown and capable of supporting myself, thanks to the education you and Papa gave me. I'll continue on as you and I have done since Papa died. Students will always need tutoring in French and dance, and women will always need dresses." Sarah patted her mother's hand, resolved to ignore the fear that coiled around in her belly.

Grace's talent as a dressmaker had always brought in more income than Sarah's tutoring had, and there was no possible way Sarah could take her mother's place in that respect. She was handy enough with a needle, but she had not inherited Grace's natural genius with dress design, nor the speed of her fingers. Those gifted fingers now tightened on Sarah's.

"I am frightened for you, Sarah. The world is a hard place for a woman alone. Please accept Adam Rutledge's offer of marriage. I will die in peace if I know you are to wed your dear friend. He cares deeply for you, and will be good to you. You and he can make a fine life together." Grace turned her face toward the pillow as another bout of coughing came upon her.

The knot in Sarah's stomach tightened. Her mother had long been urging her to marry Adam, as had his mother, Cornelia, their neighbor and Grace's closest friend.

Sarah and Adam had grown up together. Although he was a few years older than she, he had been her best friend throughout her childhood. Adam had gone on to West Point, graduating near the top of his class. Later he had distinguished himself in the war with Mexico, and it seemed that young Captain Rutledge had a promising future with the Army. He had recently written to her from Washington, D.C., telling her that he was soon to leave for his new post on the western frontier, and had again begged her to join him, to build a life with him. Sarah found the idea of a new life in the West appealing, but she wasn't as intrigued by the thought of becoming Adam's wife. She had simply never viewed him as a lover or husband, and so had not yet responded to his letter, for she knew her answer would disappoint him.

"Mama," Sarah began gently, "I do care for Adam; indeed, I love him. But I do not feel the depth nor the type of love I hope to feel for the man I marry." She covered their joined hands with her free one. "I want what you and Papa had, which was much more than the love of friendship. You had adoration, and fascination, and passion for each other. I want that, with all my heart." Her voice took on an urgent note.

Grace smiled in understanding. "Henry and I shared something rare, it's true. But, darling daughter, you must see that friendship is the foundation for all good relationships. Passion is exciting, even intoxicating, yet without a basis in friendship, without a deep, abiding respect for the other person as he or she is, the passion will one day blow out like a candle in the wind. You and Adam have that necessary, fundamental friendship. The rest will come."

"Truly, Mama?"

Grace smiled, a weary, gentle smile. "Truly, daughter."

Sarah wanted to believe her mother. She knew that Grace believed the words she spoke.

"Sarah?"

"Yes, Mama?"

"Is there someone else? Someone I don't know about?"

Sarah's heart flooded with love for her parent. "Do you think I could have kept such a thing from you?" she chided with an affectionate smile. "You would have known the moment I met him, just by looking at me."

Grace nodded, her own tired features moving in an answering smile. "I do know you well, child."

"You do," Sarah agreed softly.

Grace closed her eyes. Her breathing seemed more labored now.

What to do? She stroked her mother's alarmingly frail hand. Sarah had handled the finances since her father's death, and knew she could not keep their humble apartment on her earnings alone. Not only was she facing the loss of her beloved mother, but she would lose her home, the place where she had been born, where she and her parents had lived quite comfortably on her father's income as a professor of philosophy at nearby Yale College, where she and Grace had managed to hang on after Henry's death.

Sarah was also very pragmatic about what she had to offer a potential mate. True, she was well educated, but she had no dowry to speak of, and she was old enough to be considered a spinster in some circles. In addition, her rather ordinary physical appearance had not so far enticed eligible young men to line up at her door. Nondescript brown hair, plain features, and an average figure, along with her modest wardrobe, had not sent out a siren's call. Without a trace of bitterness, Sarah had no illusions about her prospects in the marriage market.

She again considered Adam's last letter. He had told her that President Polk's confirmation a month earlier that gold had been discovered in the faraway territory of California had triggered a frenzy in the United States. The newspapers backed him up; every day the reports told more of the mass migration to the Promised Land that was sure to happen when spring came.

Sarah knew there were only two ways to get to California: by sea—an unappealing voyage of some three to four months' duration that included an anxiety-ridden and potentially deadly passage through the Straits of Magellan—and by land. The tedious trip by land also took months, and passed through the Great American Desert in the middle of the continent, which unfortunately included Indian Territory. And, Adam had written, where there were Indians, there was trouble. The Army was to set up a series of forts along the Oregon Trail in order to offer some measure of protection to the passing emigrants, and he would be part of it. *Join me. Marry me, dear Sarah. Please.*

She looked down on her mother's pale face. "Mama."

Grace's eyes fluttered open. "Yes, my dear?"

"I will accept Adam's offer."

Her mother's relief was palpable. "You won't regret it, Sarah."

"And if I do?" Sarah blurted out, mortified that she could not keep the unsettling words inside.

Grace met her gaze, unblinking. "His uncle and aunt have agreed to act as chaperone if you come. Go to him. Society dictates that you wait one year after my death before you wed. Take that year, Sarah. Get to know Adam again, for he has been gone for a long time. You will see that I am right."

"I swear to you that I will do everything in my power to honor the marriage agreement." Sarah glanced down at her hands. "But what if, in the end, I decide we will not suit as spouses?"

"There is nothing to fear, daughter. I am certain you and Adam will suit famously," Grace assured her.

Sarah looked at her dying mother's beloved, hopeful face and ignored the doubt in her own heart.

"Then I will go, Mama. Be at peace."

One

*Near Fort St. Charles, U.S. Indian Territory
Mid-September, 1849*

Someone, or some thing, was watching her.

Sarah Hancock could feel it. She brushed a tear from her cheek, her apprehension growing when her bay mare—whom she called Star for the white mark on its forehead—nickered nervously and tossed her head, straining against the reins that tethered her to a nearby tree. Sarah's gaze darted around the lovely, peaceful clearing that had become a sanctuary to her, a place she had visited many times before. When she felt overwhelmed by grief for her parents, when she and Adam, her fiancé, had a disagreement, like today, or when she simply needed to be alone, it was to this clearing she would come. It was a place where she had always felt safe.

Until now.

She saw nothing out of the ordinary, heard nothing except the whisper of the wind as it danced over the tops of the tall grasses and played through the boughs of the encircling pine trees.

Still, it was time to go.

Sarah stood up and shook pieces of grass and pine needles from her full skirt. Perhaps some creature of the wild had come to drink at the pond just over the rise to the west, and had caught her scent. That would explain Star's nervousness,

a nervousness Sarah understood perfectly. She certainly had
no desire to meet a cougar or a bear.

Just as she snatched up the broad-brimmed straw hat that
lay close to her booted foot, Star let out a scream of terror.
Sarah jumped, stifling a scream of her own, and grabbed for
the reins. The mare jerked its head with enough force to break
the small branch around which the reins were looped and,
with another frightened whinny, whirled about and raced
away.

"Star, no!" Sarah cried, taking a few instinctive and futile
steps after the horse. Her pounding heart seemed to keep time
with the rapidly receding hoofbeats. Now genuinely scared,
Sarah again searched the clearing, and this time she found
what she was looking for. Her breath caught in her throat at
the sight of a wolf emerging from the trees on the far side of
the clearing. The animal stopped and stared at her.

Sarah crushed the hat to her chest and stared back. What
did one do when faced with a wolf? She tried desperately to
recall any words of advice her friend Jubal Sage may have
given her regarding wolves. But she could conjure up no
memory of any words of wisdom from the aging mountain
man, at least none pertaining to the current situation. Except
that somehow she knew not to run.

The wolf lifted its head to sniff the air. Sarah waited,
breathless. Perhaps Adam had been right when he had
warned her against riding alone. Actually, her fiancé had
forbidden her to ride alone, and she had defied him. He
would truly be furious with her if she were injured because
of that defiance. She would be annoyed, too, because she
would never hear the end of it.

The wolf looked back over its shoulder. Sarah followed
the animal's gaze and was startled to see a man materialize
from the shadows of the trees. Her feelings of relief warred
with renewed fear at the sight of long legs encased within
fringed buckskin trousers, the broad expanse of a naked chest
upon which rested a beaded necklace, and long dark hair. A

rifle was clutched in one strong hand. When he stepped into the sunlight, Sarah saw that the lower half of his face was covered with several days' growth of dark beard. She'd never seen an Indian with a beard, nor one wearing tall black boots, so presumably he was a white man. He said something to the wolf, and, to Sarah's amazement, the animal trotted to the man's side. Then both man and beast started across the clearing toward her.

Never would Sarah forget the sight.

He moved with the same powerful grace as the wolf. The early afternoon sunlight glinted off of tanned skin and dark brown hair that she now realized were wet, perhaps from bathing in the distant pond. His green eyes remained on her, and it was as if she could feel their heat on her face, on her body through the material of her dress. Again she was breathless. They came to her, the man and the wolf, like something out of a dream. A wild, wonderful dream.

"Are you alone?" the man demanded as he rapidly closed the distance between them. The hint of a pleasing accent was overshadowed by his harsh, almost angry tone.

Piqued that he would speak to her so, Sarah straightened her shoulders and lifted her chin. This glorious, half-naked man of the forest would not intimidate her. "Yes, now that your wolf has frightened my horse away." She struggled to keep her eyes on the man's face. Having never been so close to a man's naked chest before, the urge to look was powerful.

"I'm sorry for that." The man's tone had softened somewhat. "Dancer would not have hurt the horse."

"Dancer?"

"My wolf." He gestured toward the animal.

Sarah glanced down at the wolf, who was watching her with odd golden eyes.

"He won't hurt you, either."

"I'm relieved to hear that."

His gaze wandered over her, and Sarah stiffened under his perusal. Her chin went up another notch.

He spoke again. "I assume you're from the fort."

"Yes."

"Colonel Rutledge allowed you to ride out alone?"

"I do not ask for, nor do I need, Colonel Rutledge's permission to ride alone, sir." Sarah did the best she could to smooth out her crushed hat, then plopped the sorry-looking thing on her head and tied the blue bow under her chin. "Now, if you'll excuse me, I must be on my way. I have a long walk ahead of me." She looked pointedly at the wolf before she turned away.

"I'll take you back." His statement was more a command than an offer.

Sarah did not slow her stride. "Do not trouble yourself."

"No, miss, I insist."

Her upper arm was taken in a strong hold. Sarah stopped abruptly and spun around to face him. "Unhand me, sir," she ordered through clenched teeth. To her surprise, he obeyed.

"My horse is at the pond, as are some of my things. We'll collect them, and I'll take you to the fort." Without waiting for her reply, he headed back across the clearing.

Mutinously, Sarah crossed her arms over her chest and watched him go. Then she realized the wolf had not followed him. She found the animal standing behind her, watching her. When she took a step in the direction of the fort, Dancer moved in front of her. Sarah gave up and turned in the direction of the pond, not surprised that the wolf stayed close to her heels.

She made her way through a stand of trees and came out on the bank of the pond. The man had pulled a fringed buckskin shirt over his head and was now strapping around his waist a belt that held a beaded sheath, in which nestled a long knife. The flash of disappointment Sarah felt because he had covered his chest irritated her.

"What is your name?" he asked. He did not look at her

as he retrieved a leather pouch from the ground and tied it to the horn of his saddle.

As his tone was calm now, Sarah decided to answer him. "I am Miss Sarah Hancock, recently arrived from Connecticut."

The man turned from his horse. "And I am Orion Beaudine, scout and frontiersman, also known as the Hunter, at your service." He executed a courtly bow, a movement that seemed ridiculously out of place for both the wild-looking man and the wild surroundings.

Yet, without thinking, Sarah dropped a slight curtsy in response. She caught herself and glanced away, disconcerted. "Are you called the Hunter because of your mythological name, or are you famous for your skill as a hunter?" she asked.

"Both, I guess, but I hunt animals only when necessary, and even then, I don't relish the killing. The name was bestowed upon me by the Cheyenne for my ability to track and read sign."

Now she looked at him again. "Read sign?"

"Follow a trail, tell what happened, and how long ago."

"You can do that?"

"Yes, ma'am."

Sarah was impressed. "I believe you can, Mr. Beaudine."

"Why did you come out here, alone, to this place?" Orion asked.

She glanced at him. He was now tying a blanket behind the saddle. Surprising herself, she answered him honestly. "Sometimes I need to be alone." She looked out across the small expanse of clear water.

"I think most people prefer to cry alone."

Sarah jerked her head around to look at him. He was watching her now, his green eyes burning with intensity.

"I wasn't—" she began hotly, then stopped when he reached out and gently brushed his thumb over the lashes of her right eye.

"There's no shame in crying, Miss Sarah Hancock," he said softly.

His kind words caused the tears to threaten again, and she turned away to once more stare out over the pond.

Orion watched her shoulders rise slightly, then fall as she sighed. Of course she had been crying. Not only had the tears sparkled on her eyelashes, but her large eyes had seemed very blue, the color heightened as a side effect of recent tears. What had brought this interesting woman out into the wilderness, alone? What—or who—had made her cry?

He studied her slender form. She carried herself with a natural, easy grace very common with Indian women, but unusual among white women. That in itself was intriguing. The plain gray dress she wore was made of a serviceable material, which was neatly tailored to her back and narrow waist. Under the full skirt she obviously wore a few petticoats, but no hoops. Of course, hoops were impractical when riding a horse, and Orion had the feeling that Miss Sarah Hancock was usually very practical, her dangerous solitary ride notwithstanding. Her dark hair was pulled into a simple chignon at the back of her head, showing off her neck below and the absurd crushed hat above. The blue ribbon on the hat did not match the gray dress, indicating either a poor sense of color coordination, or haste in leaving for her ride. Orion suspected the latter. Again he wondered what had made her seek the solitude in which to indulge her need to cry.

"We'd best be on our way, Miss Hancock," he said in a carefully neutral tone.

She nodded and turned to face him.

Orion vaulted into the saddle, then held his hand down to her. "Put your foot in the stirrup, and when I pull, jump up behind me."

Sarah gave him her gloved hand, gathered her skirts with the other hand, and placed her foot in the stirrup. He pulled, and she landed behind him with a little gasp. She took a moment to arrange her skirts over her legs, then clutched the rim of the saddle seat with both hands.

"Put your arms around me, Miss Hancock, or you'll slide right off."

After a moment's hesitation, she did as he instructed, but only her hands touched him. She held herself away from his body. Orion smiled, knowing that wouldn't last long. He nudged the horse into a walk, then a trot, then a lope, and sure enough, Miss Sarah Hancock tightened her hold on him and pressed herself against his back. He caught the faint scent of lavender. It was very pleasing, as was the feel of her soft breasts against him.

He wondered how long she had been at the fort, and what she was doing there. An unmarried white woman would be fighting men off, unless one had already staked a claim on her. He frowned at the thought, then pondered his reaction. He hardly knew the woman. He shook his head at his own foolishness. He'd eventually learn more about her, but bouncing along on a horse was not the time for a chat. They rode some distance in silence.

Sarah estimated it would take at least a half hour to reach the fort. It was frightening to ride with no stirrups for her feet; it did feel as if she would slide off except for her hold on Orion. She clung to him and tried to concentrate on following the rhythm of the horse, determined that she would not fall off, for surely she would die of embarrassment if she did. But it was hard to concentrate on anything except the feel of the powerful man within the circle of her arms. She was forced to rest her cheek against his shoulder blade, and could not help but notice the faint smoky scent of his buckskin shirt, the clean scent of his long, drying hair that flew around her in the wind created by the movement of the horse. He was a tall man, and strong, and confident. Sarah had no doubt that he knew how to use the wicked-looking knife in the sheath on his hip, that he was proficient with the rifle now in its scabbard tied to the saddle horn. She sensed that Orion Beaudine was a man to count on in times of trouble or danger.

He slowed the horse to a walk.

"Is something wrong?" Sarah asked.

"No. I don't want to wind him."

Sarah relaxed her hold slightly and moved her cheek away from Orion's back. "Where is Dancer?"

"He's close by."

Sarah glanced around, but saw no sign of the wolf. "I take it you've been to the fort before," she commented.

"Many times."

"Is it your home?"

"No. This is my home." Orion waved an arm to encompass the surrounding land.

Sarah could think of no response to that puzzling statement.

"You're a long way from Connecticut, Miss Hancock. How long have you been here?"

"About two months. I came across the plains to Fort Laramie with Colonel Mackay and his detachment in July, then made the journey to Fort St. Charles a few weeks later."

"Why are you here?"

"I am promised to marry Captain Adam Rutledge." Was it Sarah's imagination or had Orion's body stiffened somewhat? Surely not, for why would he care who she was promised to?

"Ah, the good captain."

She was not imagining the sudden chill in Orion's tone. "Do you know him?"

"I know him."

There was a definite curtness to his tone now. "Adam and I have known each other since childhood," Sarah said, wondering why she felt the urge to explain. "We became engaged shortly before my mother's death last January, and I am staying with Colonel and Mrs. Rutledge—who are, of course, Adam's uncle and aunt—until the mourning period has passed. We are to be married in the spring." She had the uncomfortable feeling that she sounded like a chattering twit.

"I'm sorry for the loss of your mother," Orion said.

Sarah was surprised he would choose that to comment on. "Thank you. We were very close, and it has been difficult." She swallowed around a sudden lump in her throat.

"What of your father?"

"He died over nine years ago."

"Again, I'm sorry." Orion paused, then asked, "Any brothers or sisters?"

"I am alone in the world, Mr. Beaudine."

"Except for your childhood friend, Captain Adam Rutledge."

The strange, almost derisive note had come into his voice again. Sarah bristled defensively, but before she could speak, Orion drew the horse to a stop.

"Speak of the devil," he muttered.

The sound of approaching hoofbeats reached Sarah's ears. She peered around Orion's shoulder and saw Adam bearing down on them at a lope, followed by a detachment of four soldiers. A sigh of disappointment escaped her lips. Then she straightened her spine and waited. Even from a distance, Adam made a striking figure. Blonde and handsome, with blue eyes and a neatly trimmed beard, he turned many a woman's head, especially when in uniform. Usually Sarah was happy to see him; she wasn't now, and that troubled her.

Orion heard the sigh. He also noticed that she had not removed her arms from around his waist. This could prove to be an interesting meeting. He nudged the horse sideways so that Sarah had a clear view of the approaching soldiers.

"Sarah!" The look of relief on Adam Rutledge's face was quickly replaced with anger. "When your horse came back without you, I feared the worst. How many times have I told you not to ride alone?"

Orion felt her stiffen.

"Please guide me down, Mr. Beaudine." Her tone was quiet, but Orion knew she was angry.

He held his arm out, which she grasped, and she slid off the horse. She glared up at Adam as she brushed the wrinkles from her skirt. "I felt the need to be alone, Adam, and I'm sorry if that upsets you. There was no trouble. My mare was startled and ran off, that is all. Mr. Beaudine happened along and generously offered to bring me back." She turned to face Orion. "Thank you for your kindness, Mr. Beaudine. It was a pleasure to meet you. Perhaps we will see each other again."

"I hope so, Miss Hancock," Orion said, aware that his words, although honestly spoken, would annoy Captain Rutledge. He wondered why she didn't mention that his wolf had been responsible for the untimely departure of her horse. "Good day."

"Good day." With that, Sarah spun on her heel and marched off in the direction of the fort.

Fighting a smile, Orion watched her go. Her anger was apparent in every tense line of her slender body. He glanced at Rutledge and found the man staring at him, obviously furious. He said nothing, nor did Rutledge. After a moment, Rutledge turned his horse's head around and ordered his men to return to the fort. They obeyed, giving Sarah a wide berth as they rode by. Adam followed Sarah, coming to a halt at her side. He held down a hand to her.

"Come, Sarah. You'll ride with me."

Sarah glanced up at him. "Thank you, but I prefer to walk." She continued on her proud way.

Even from a distance, Orion felt that he could see the anger flashing in Sarah's large eyes. This time he could not stop the smile that curved his lips. Rutledge would have his hands full with her. Any man would.

"Suit yourself." With gritted teeth and a flushed face, Captain Rutledge kept his horse at a slow walk just behind her.

Orion watched until they disappeared over a slight rise. He suspected the twenty-minute walk to the fort was going to seem long to both Sarah and Rutledge. There was obviously trouble between them; how serious was it? Had Rutledge been the cause of Sarah's earlier tears?

"Why do you care?" he muttered to himself as he turned his horse's head. It was none of his business. Still, he didn't like Adam Rutledge, and in contrast, he did like Sarah, the little he knew of her. The thought of Rutledge upsetting her to the point of tears angered him, but again, it was none of his business.

Orion urged the horse to a gallop. As he had originally planned, he would retrieve his packhorse and break camp, then head back to the fort. By sundown, he'd be there, maybe a little before. And she would be there. He was disturbed by his eagerness to again see a woman who was promised to another man.

Sarah maintained her rapid pace until she reached the porch of Colonel Rutledge's neat log house, paying no attention to the stares she earned from the soldiers working on the slowly expanding stockade wall. Dismayed to see Harriet Rutledge waiting on one of the two chairs—with a disapproving look on her stern face—Sarah climbed the steps and turned around to face Adam. "Was my horse seen to?"

"Yes." The clipped anger in Adam's voice caused her stomach to tighten.

"Thank you." She turned toward the door and was reaching for the handle when Adam spoke again.

"Sarah."

She turned to face him. "What is it?"

"I will not have you disobeying my orders, nor will you again humiliate me in front of others." His pale blue eyes seemed to spark with the fury she knew raged in him.

With jerky movements, Sarah loosened the tie on the ruined hat and pulled it from her head as she stepped close to the edge of the porch. She kept her voice low. "You will not order me about as if I were one of your soldiers, Adam; I'll not tolerate it. If my refusal to ride back with you embarrassed you in front of Mr. Beaudine, I apologize. That was not my intention. I felt it was better to leave some distance between us for a while. And I think we should discuss this later." She glanced meaningfully at Harriet, who was taking obvious interest in their conversation. "When we have both calmed down, we'll talk again, in private. Now, if you'll excuse me, I need to wash up."

Adam did not respond. He turned his horse's head and rode into the original compound, his jaw clenched, his back ramrod-straight.

Sarah watched him go, her own anger burning out and leaving a weary, troubled sadness in its place. This was not the first such argument they'd had since her arrival at Fort St. Charles. She nodded a silent greeting to Harriet and entered the house, making her way to her tiny bedroom off the dining room.

It still hurt that Adam had taken Harriet's side that morning when the older woman had scolded Sarah, and over such a petty thing.

"Surely you do not intend to wear that gown, Sarah. You are still in mourning for your dear mother."

"It has been well over six months, Mrs. Rutledge. Gray is an acceptable color, as is violet. I am showing no disrespect."

A self-righteous sniff. "Were it my mother, I would wear black the entire year of mourning. Don't you agree, Adam?"

And he had.

Feeling betrayed, and unable to bear Harriet's look of triumph, Sarah had left the table, snatched up the first hat she could find, and left for her ride.

Now she plopped down on her narrow cot, overwhelmed with discouragement. It seemed that both Adam and his aunt had very definite ideas of the type of behavior that she should exhibit as the future wife of an Army officer. Actually, although he had never discussed it with her, she suspected that

Adam had given her over to his aunt's care with the hope, or perhaps even the understanding, that Harriet would turn Sarah into a proper wife. Gone was the easy camaraderie she had shared with Adam prior to her arrival in the West. Sarah was beginning to wonder if they would ever recapture it.

Adam had changed, as her mother had warned her could happen. He was so driven now, so intense about his career. And from all Sarah could see, he was an excellent officer; conscientious, efficient, trusted by his superiors, respected by his men. It was obvious that Adam had found his niche in the world. Sarah just wasn't certain there was room in it for her.

Two

The late afternoon shadows stretched across the dirt yard in front of Colonel Rutledge's log house. Sarah sat motionless on an uncomfortable straight-back chair on the shaded porch, the petticoat she was mending forgotten in her lap. Some minutes earlier, much to Sarah's relief, Harriet Rutledge had come to the end of her tedious lecture on the vulgarity of having cross words with others in public and the necessity of submitting to one's husband. Harriet seemed to have forgotten that Adam had in fact started the "cross" discussion, and that he was not yet Sarah's husband. The older woman now rocked ceaselessly, fanning herself with a lace fan, every now and then shouting out a terse order to Lucy, the Rutledges' Negro servant, who was toiling in the kitchen with supper preparations.

Harriet often treated Lucy rudely, but Sarah knew she was proud of having acquired Lucy's services. Not only was the free woman an excellent housekeeper and cook, but because she was Negro, there was no danger of losing her to marriage, as always happened with white servants. Sarah just wished Harriet would be nicer to Lucy.

In an effort to get her mind off of both Harriet's unkindness and the distressing argument with Adam, Sarah let her gaze wander around the bustling compound. Vast changes had been made in the two months she had been here, thanks to the hard work of the small detachment of soldiers stationed there. Ten years earlier, Fort St. Charles had begun its life as a crude trading post perched on a rise to the east of the junction of the Laramie and North Laramie Rivers, and over the years the post had gradually been expanded. Now, with the rush of immigrants to the west coast, the Army was examining several sites for a planned series of forts. Another trading post, to the north at the junction of the Laramie and North Platte rivers, had been purchased by the Army and named Fort Laramie. There was some doubt that Fort St. Charles would stay manned for long, due to its location so far south of the Oregon Trail, but as it was situated on a route that stretched between the Oregon Trail to the north and the Overland Trail to the south, it might offer some value. In what Sarah now knew to be typical Army fashion, the improvements made to Fort St. Charles would continue until a decision was made, even if it meant that all the hard work of the soldiers was for naught.

The original trading post building was surrounded by a stout wall of upended logs. Because the enclosed compound was not nearly big enough to meet the needs of the thirty-man detachment now posted there, construction of a much larger enclosure was underway. Colonel Rutledge's house had been one of the first new buildings put up, then a stable, and now a barracks was nearing completion. The enlisted men would be happy to pack away the tents in which they had been living, for winter was fast approaching and even now the nights were cold. Adam lived in a small, crude cabin near the headquarters building, where he would stay until formal officers' quarters could be built.

As with all Army installations, a smattering of various types of structures surrounded the area, structures that would not be enclosed within the protective circle of the almost-finished outer walls. The odd assortment of buildings included a few abandoned cabins in various states of disrepair and the snug adobe houses of three Mexican families who had come up from the south years earlier with Miles Breen, the trader who had built the original post and who now enjoyed success as the fort's sutler.

All in all, Fort St. Charles painted a primitive, perhaps even dismal picture, and many of the people forced to live there—like Harriet Rutledge and most of the soldiers—found it very disagreeable. Sarah did not really mind the rustic way of life. The progress made so far had been speedy, and to her mind, impressive. Life at the little fort offered a fascinating contrast to her protected life in the East. She welcomed all of it.

She was startled out of her reverie by the sight of a tall man on horseback entering the compound, leading a packhorse. There was something familiar about him, but she could not make out his face, which was hidden in the shadows of his broad-brimmed hat. Then the man turned his horse in her direction, and Sarah's breath caught when she recognized Orion Beaudine. To see him on horseback from a distance, rather than riding behind him, gave her the chance to appreciate what a skillful rider he was. He rode with graceful ease, which did not surprise her, as he had come to her across the meadow in the same manner. Mrs. Rutledge's rocking chair ceased its movement when he drew the horse to a halt in front of the house.

He took his hat off. "Hello, Mrs. Colonel Rutledge. How nice to see you again, Miss Hancock."

Sarah felt an absurd blush heating her cheeks. Why had his polite greeting caused such a reaction when molding her body so intimately to his back earlier had not? Her fingers tightened on the petticoat in her lap. "Hello, Mr. Beaudine."

"Is there something I can do for you, sir?" Harriet demanded in a disapproving tone.

"I've come to speak with Colonel Rutledge. I bring dispatches from Fort Laramie."

"The colonel is out with a scouting party and is not expected back until tomorrow. You'll have to come back then."

Harriet pushed herself out of the chair and moved toward the door. "Come, Sarah."

Now Sarah blushed in earnest, appalled at Harriet's rudeness. Would she not even offer the man refreshment? Colonel Rutledge would have invited him to supper. Sarah stood up, clutching the petticoat, and felt a new wave of embarrassment when it dawned on her that she was holding a piece of intimate apparel in full view. "I'll be right in, Mrs. Rutledge," she said over her shoulder, squashing the petticoat into as small a bundle as she could.

Harriet's mouth tightened in an angry line. "Remember what I said about observing the rules of propriety and submission, Sarah. I doubt you would respond to Adam in this way had he made the request."

Sarah stiffened. "Yes, Mrs. Rutledge, I would have," she said, her own mouth tight now. "Mr. Beaudine is my friend, and I am certain Adam would have no objection to me speaking with one of my friends."

"Perhaps you should choose your friends with greater care," Harriet said sharply. "You may rest assured that Adam will hear of this." She stormed into the house.

"I will speak to him myself, madam," Sarah snapped, just as Harriet slammed the door. She bit her lip, willing herself to calm down, then turned to face Orion. "It seems I am always arguing with someone in front of you, doesn't it, Mr. Beaudine? How tiresome you must find it. I do apologize.

"There is no need, Miss Hancock."

"You are very kind. However, there is a real need to apologize for Mrs. Rutledge's rudeness; I must confess that I am astonished at her behavior. She usually reserves that tone for Lucy . . ." Sarah's voice dropped off when she realized she was putting Orion in the same class as a servant. "Or me," she hastily added.

"Mrs. Rutledge has made her opinion of me very clear on previous occasions." He leaned forward in the saddle, his voice dropping conspiratorially. "She would be mortified to know that, to me, her opinion does not matter in the least."

Sarah smiled. "She would be horrified, I'm sure." Her smile faded. "I would invite you in for some refreshment, but the circumstances are awkward."

"I understand. Don't trouble yourself." He straightened. "Where is Dancer?"

"Out there." Orion waved a hand in the direction of the hills across the river. "But he won't come near the fort. He's wary around most people to begin with, and crowds make him even more nervous."

"Oh." For the life of her, Sarah could not think of anything else to say.

"I will see you again, Miss Hancock."

"That sounds like a promise, sir," she teased.

Orion put his hat back on. "It is." He stared at her for a moment, his eyes alight with intensity, then he touched the brim of his hat and turned his horse's head away.

As she watched him ride off, a warm feeling of pleasure rushed through Sarah, followed quickly by a powerful pang of guilt. What was wrong with her? She was promised to another man, a good man, a man she had loved since childhood, albeit as a brother. And there were problems between them, serious problems which needed to be addressed. Soon. She wondered if Adam would be joining them for supper. She hoped so; the feeling of unfinished business was uncomfortable. Sarah hated arguing with Adam, and never felt at ease until they straightened things out. Perhaps she would send Lucy to ask him for supper.

She also hated to be out of sorts with Harriet, although that seemed to be happening more and more often. The woman was impossible to please. Sarah was beginning to wonder if Harriet totally approved of the match.

Sarah sighed and went into the house. She desperately craved an evening of peace. And she felt the need to get Orion Beaudine out of her mind. Her thoughts were scattered as it was. She certainly did not need to remind herself again and again of the picture the scout had made, crossing the meadow with the sun shining off his powerful body, his magnificent wolf at his side—which was exactly what she had been doing all afternoon. She needed to focus on mending fences with her betrothed. Adam. She needed to think of him, and of their future together.

Adam refused the invitation to supper, informing Lucy that he had reports to write. Sarah knew it for the rejection it was. Adam wrote reports almost every night, but he also ate supper every night, often at the colonel's house. The rejection stung. How were they to mend fences if he would not speak to her?

Due to Colonel Rutledge's absence, supper was an unpleasant affair. After several minutes of stilted silence, Harriet set her fork down with an ominous thump.

"I *simply* cannot imagine what possessed you to defy me in front of that . . . that *mountain man,* Sarah. What were you thinking? And how did one such as Hunter Beaudine become your 'friend'? Surely Adam does not approve. He *simply* cannot approve. I wish you will explain yourself." She took a deep, self-righteous breath and stared at Sarah, her dark eyes glittering in the light of the whale oil lamp.

Sarah set her own fork down with far more calm than she felt. "Harriet, I did not set out to defy you, and it grieves me to see you so upset." She raised her eyes to the formidable woman. "I appreciate your concern, but I must tell you that I can allow no one to dictate whom I call friend, and that includes Adam. Thus far he has not attempted to do so." Her gentle chiding apparently hit its mark, for Harriet's eyes narrowed in anger. Sarah continued. "I only met Mr. Beaudine today, when he rescued me from a predicament. He was very kind and went out of his way to assist me. Adam knows all about it."

She wondered at her reluctance to reveal—even to Adam—that Orion's wolf had caused her predicament in the first place; that she had seen him half-naked; that he had practically forced her to accompany him back toward the fort; that she had clung to his strong body in a very inappropriate manner. "Please don't worry so," she finished. Sarah meant those last words; Harriet Rutledge's worry was bothersome, indeed.

"Hunter Beaudine is nothing but trouble, Sarah, not worthy to be in the same room with ladies of gentle breeding, and I am certain Adam will back me in this. That man and his brothers—one is a *half-breed*—" she spat out the word as she would a bite of bad meat, "carry on with the Indians, call them friends, live with them at times, speak their language, just as their disreputable father did. Why, I heard that Jedediah Beaudine had *three* wives, one of whom was a Cheyenne squaw, although no true Christian would call such a heathen union a marriage." Her tone softened curiously. "Stay away from all of them, the whole clan. They will only bring you grief. And I would not see my beloved nephew hurt, especially through you, his fiancée and friend."

Sarah stared at her, incredulous. "How can my friendship with Mr. Beaudine bring Adam hurt?"

"You can make him look bad, Sarah, in the eyes of his superiors, in the eyes of his men. I have tried to impress that upon you these last two months, to no avail. If Adam cannot command his own wife and be obeyed, how is he to command his men and expect them to obey?"

It was becoming more and more difficult for Sarah to control her anger. "I am not an enlisted man or a servant to be ordered about, Harriet," she said stiffly. "I will be Adam's wife, his life's partner, and, God willing, the mother of his children, and shall be the best wife, partner, and mother I can possibly be. I fail to understand why my occasional need for a solitary ride must cause so much trouble, both with Adam and with you."

Harriet drew herself up, seeming to tower over the table even from a sitting position. "If you cannot understand, then you are either selfish or unrealistic. Adam is very clear about his career goals, and has the talent and the dedication to reach them. He needs a woman at his side who is willing to be a helpmate to him, to sacrifice her wishes if need be for his sake, just as I did for Colonel Rutledge."

Sarah set her napkin on the table. Although her plate was still half full, she no longer had an appetite. "My idea of marriage is an equal partnership for both rather than the subjugation of one." Her quiet tone belied the force of her conviction.

"You are looking at it all wrong," Harriet argued. "You will not be subjugated. By sacrificing your petty wishes for the sake of your husband's career, you will become a good and dutiful wife, one of whom Adam will be very proud. He will come to depend on you, as Colonel Rutledge does me." She leaned forward over the table. "Forgo your solitary rides. Choose your friends carefully, always thinking of how a friendship can hurt or help your husband's career. Devote yourself to Adam. You will be amazed at how fulfilling it is."

"Of what good am I to Adam if I lose the very essence of who I am through such sacrifice?" Sarah asked softly. "Is that what you think he expects of me? Does he care so little?"

Harriet shook her head in somber disappointment. "I have grave doubts that you have what it takes to be a military wife, Sarah. Grave doubts, indeed."

"Adam will make that determination." Sarah stood up, pushing her chair back. "Please excuse me." She took her plate and carried it into the small, rustic kitchen at the back of the house.

"I have repeatedly asked that you let Lucy clear the table, as is her duty," Harriet called out sharply.

Sarah stuck her head back around the door. "Please indulge me in this, Harriet, for I am merely trying to be practical. Adam and I will not have the luxury of domestic help when we are wed, at least not at first. I feel that, as a loving wife, I should know how to clean my own kitchen." She did not add that because she and her mother had been unable to afford domestic help after her father died, she had cleaned her own house and cooked her own meals for many years. Nor did she add that her insistence upon helping Lucy with chores, as well as the small luxuries she purchased for the household out of her meager funds—such as imported tea and scented soap—were a desperate attempt to lighten the weight of debt she felt she owed the colonel and his wife for taking her in.

Harriet's only response was an angry tightening of her mouth. She pushed back from the table and stomped into the parlor. Sarah returned to the table and gathered up more dishes.

"It does you no good to rile her, Miss Sarah," Lucy softly said with a warning shake of her scarf-covered head.

"I know," Sarah said tiredly. She flashed the tall, slender woman a small smile. "Just as I know I am beholden to her for allowing me to live here, and therefore should hold my tongue. But sometimes I simply don't agree with her, and, perhaps unfortunately, my parents raised me to speak my mind, to stand up for my beliefs. I've never been good at keeping my mouth shut, even when it would make things easier for me."

"Just be sure you don't pick battles you can't win."

"I won't. And remember—I have Adam on my side."

"If you say so."

Sarah looked up from the plate she was scraping, a frown drawing her eyebrows together. "What do you mean by that?"

The shuttered look that Lucy always wore in Harriet's presence came over her attractive dark face. "Not a thing, Miss Sarah. Not a thing." She moved into the dining room.

Sarah knew it was useless to try to pry anything out of Lucy when she shut herself away like that. *Is that what Har-*

riet expects me to do, to become? A silent, biddable servant like Lucy? Is that what Adam expects of me?

Deeply troubled, Sarah set the rest of the dishes next to the basin of hot, soapy water Lucy had waiting. Lucy returned to the kitchen with the linen tablecloth and napkins. Since the floorboards had finally been installed a month ago, at great personal financial cost to Colonel Rutledge, Harriet had insisted—impractically, Sarah thought, considering how much work it took to keep them washed and ironed—upon using linen tablecloths and napkins and serving a formal supper each evening. It was a woman's duty to introduce elements of civilization even under the most uncivilized of circumstances, she had intoned with righteous fervor. It was a woman's duty to make a comfortable home for her husband, a home of which he could be proud. Sarah had so far been able to resist the powerful urge to add that it was certainly easier to put up a good front when one had a servant like Lucy doing a good deal of the work.

"You look done in, miss," Lucy said sternly. "Get yourself ready for bed. I've got wash water heating for you and will bring it directly. And thank you for your help," she added.

Sarah knew she had been dismissed as surely as if Lucy had ordered her from the room. With a tired sigh, she gave in. Perhaps retiring early was just what she needed. After a good night's sleep, she would be prepared to meet with Adam, to talk things out. "I think you're right, Lucy," she admitted. "I'll take the wash water, so you needn't bother. Thank you for a wonderful meal, and for everything you do around here. Whatever Colonel Rutledge pays you, it isn't enough." She poured water from a large cast iron tea kettle into a plain ceramic pitcher.

Lucy stared at her, clearly startled. "G-good night, miss," she finally stammered.

"Good night." Sarah took up the pitcher and left the room.

* * *

But it was not a good night. Sarah had trouble falling asleep, because her mind refused to stop rehashing the scenes of her disagreements with Adam. There had been three that day—the one over the color of her dress, the one over her refusal to ride with him, and the one on the porch in front of Harriet. Growing up together, they had never argued so often, nor over such small things. But Adam had not been in the military then. Nor had she, Sarah thought wryly. Perhaps it was a simple matter of pressure and stress; both she and Adam had experienced plenty of each in the last two months. Surely things would settle down when the fort was completed, when life fell into some kind of a routine, when she and Adam were married and lived in their own house, away from the prying and critical eye of Harriet Rutledge.

Sarah felt a surge of hope. She and Adam would work things out. As her mother had told her, they had the basis of a deep and affectionate friendship. That was more than many marriages had. They would make it.

Adam. Dear Adam. His image filled her mind—tall and blonde, so handsome in the uniform he wore with such pride, and he was intelligent and capable, determined to succeed. He was a man any woman would be proud to call husband; she was lucky he had chosen her.

Sarah nestled deeper into the pillow, determined to sleep, determined to ignore the tiny, gnawing seed of doubt. She would sleep, and dream of Adam, and their future together.

But when she did at last fall into a troubled sleep, it was not Adam who filled her dreams. Instead, Sarah dreamed of a frontiersman with long dark hair and kind eyes, of a beautiful wolf, of the wild and majestic mountains she had come to love in such a short time. The traitorous dream was lovely, but hardly restful.

Too soon, the discordant bugle announcing reveille awakened her in the predawn darkness. The chill in the tiny, unheated room caused Sarah to snuggle farther under the blankets, while the pleasant dream that still teased the corners of her mind enticed her to keep her eyes closed. But she heard Lucy moving about the kitchen, and the need to speak with Adam returned with guilty urgency.

The last remaining vestiges of the dream faded like an early morning mist. Sarah threw back the blankets and scrambled out of bed, ignoring the shock of cold air. The meeting with Adam could not be put off, for she would not feel comfortable until things were once more right between them.

Three

Sarah fidgeted as she waited in Colonel Rutledge's small headquarters office, where Adam had agreed—somewhat coldly, she thought—to meet her when he was finished with inspection. Absentmindedly she smoothed her hand over the soft material of her violet skirt. She had dressed with great care that morning, and a certain amount of defiance, choosing the richly colored gown over the somber black Harriet had pressed her to wear. Violet had been her mother's favorite color, and Sarah felt the need for some of her mother's strength. Her hair was neatly styled and covered with a charming hat of the same shade of violet and accented with a wide black ribbon, which was tied in a bow under her chin. A black shawl completed her ensemble.

She was reasonably confident about her appearance, but a strong underlying sense of tension disturbed Sarah. In all of their lives together, never had she felt so nervous about talking to Adam.

Her dearest friend.

Or so she had thought.

Sarah jumped at the sound of the door behind her opening, then fought for some semblance of calm. Rather than take the chair next to her, Adam came around the crude table that served as a desk and, with ramrod stiffness, sat in the chair behind it. Sarah didn't like that the table was between them; it made her feel like an unruly student about to be disciplined.

The thought stiffened her own spine. She had a right to voice her concerns and opinions to her betrothed.

"What is it, Sarah?" Adam demanded. "I am very busy."

Sarah stared at him. "How can you ask me that? There is unfinished business between us, which surely causes you discomfort, just as it does me. I would see it resolved."

Adam relaxed a little. "As would I. I don't like arguing with you."

Relief rushed through her. "I hate it," she admitted. Adam did not respond with anything more than a nod. He seemed to be waiting for her to continue, so she did. "I am deeply concerned by what is happening between us, Adam," she said gently. "We seem to be bickering all the time, and I am astonished by it. We have always been such good friends. Why, the worst argument we ever had before I came out here was over who truly won that game of marbles when I was twelve. Now it seems that we would argue over whether the sky was blue."

"I know." Adam sighed, then leaned forward over the table, his weight resting on his elbows, his fingers intertwined. "Things have changed, Sarah. *I* have changed. I am determined to make a successful career for myself in the Army, and in order to do so, there are rules and regulations which I must follow, appearances which must be upheld. I had hoped that Aunt Harriet would help prepare you for the role you will undertake as my wife, but that does not seem to have worked. You don't get along with her."

"I think it is more a case of her not getting along with me," Sarah protested. "I have tried to please her, truly I have, but she is unreasonable in her demands. Why, she told me last night that, as a dutiful Army wife, it was expected of me—that *you* would expect me—to happily and without complaint give up all thoughts of my own wishes and goals for the sake of your career. My argument of marriage as a loving partnership fell on deaf ears." She looked into his blue eyes. "In which do you believe, Adam? Equal partnership for both or the sub-jugation of one for the benefit of the other?"

Adam shifted uncomfortably. "Subjugation is a strong word, too strong for this circumstance. My career with the Army will demand sacrifices from both of us. We will have no say in where we will live. I could be transferred at a moment's notice. We will have to make the best of whatever living conditions are provided us, which, as you have learned here, can be rustic if not downright uncomfortable. There may be times of separation, for weeks or months at a time." His gaze met hers. "I thought I made all of this clear before you came out here."

"You did, and I have no trouble with any of what you just said." Sarah leaned forward herself and laid one of her hands on his still entwined ones. "I will go with you, gladly, to any post, to the farthest reaches of the earth. I will live with you in a tent or a shanty or a palace, and do my best to make it into a home. If you must go on campaign and leave me behind, I will wait for you and storm heaven with my prayers for your safe return." She released his hands and straightened. "But I will not allow you to dictate what opinions I may have, the color of clothes I wear, or when I may ride alone. No one will dictate my thoughts, or my friends. I am prepared to compro-mise on some issues and, if warranted, sacrifice on others. I am prepared—no, eager—to work with you to make this mar-riage a happy one. Will that be enough for you?"

He did not answer her.

Her heart grabbed with deep misgiving. "Adam, this is Sarah," she said softly. "Your Sarah. Your friend. Do you not trust me?"

"Of course I do," he said tiredly.

A troublesome thought forced its way to the front of Sarah's mind, and the words popped out before she consid-ered the wisdom of saying them. "Your aunt fears that I may not be proper material for an Army wife, that I will hinder your career."

Again Adam said nothing in response. His eyes darted around the small room as if he could not face her.

"Do you feel that way?"

Silence.

"Adam, you must tell me." Sarah twisted her hands in her lap. "Please."

Adam jumped up from the chair to pace the floor in front of the crude stone fireplace, his hands clasped behind him. "You are still grieving your mother, and I have tried to be patient. Life here is a world away from the sedate, comfortable life you knew in New Haven. But I must admit I have been concerned. I had hoped you would adapt more easily."

Stung, Sarah asked, "Are you certain you don't mean that you hoped I would *submit* more easily?"

"Don't put words in my mouth," Adam snapped, turning to glare at her. "As both Aunt and I have tried to explain, in the military, things are done a certain way, there are certain appearances and standards which must be upheld. You do not seem to appreciate the importance of that."

Sarah's mouth suddenly felt very dry, and she had to swallow before she could speak. "In which areas do you find me lacking?"

"Please, Sarah, it is not my wish to hurt you."

"Nor is it mine to hurt you, but evidently I have done so. You must be honest with me."

Adam resumed his pacing, and when he spoke, it was with obvious reluctance. "You defy me in front of my aunt, in front of my men. Aunt Harriet tells me you defy her, as well. You insist upon riding alone when, for your own safety, I have requested that you do not, I have pleaded with you, I have even forbidden you. And you humiliated me yesterday when you refused to accept my hand and ride back with me."

Sarah stared at him, fighting a sick feeling in her stomach. "You are disappointed in me."

"No."

"Yes, you are."

He faced her. "Surely you can see all that needs to be done just to make this sorry excuse for a post liveable. I am under tremendous pressure to perform a difficult if not impossible job. I did not expect, nor do I appreciate, trouble from you as well."

Disbelief warred with hurt inside her, for never had Adam spoken to her in such a way. "I came out here too soon, didn't I?" she asked quietly. "I am only in your way."

Adam sighed, and his expression softened. "No, you're not. I promised to look after you, and I shall. There was bound to be a period of adjustment for us. We need to work out our differences; it's that simple."

"Do you think it will be simple?"

"Perhaps not, but we must try. Let's start with your riding alone. Surely you can understand that my concern is for you. It is dangerous for you—for anyone—to be alone in the wilderness."

Not for Orion Beaudine. He is at home in the wilderness.

Sarah did not give voice to those argumentative and pointless thoughts. She looked down at her clasped hands. Could she bear to give up her solitary, comforting rides, which she took only occasionally anyway? In all honesty, she could see Adam's point about safety concerns, for she herself had known a moment's trepidation when Orion Beaudine had started across the field toward her. Not all men were gentlemen, and she *was* in Indian Territory. Sarah raised her eyes to her betrothed.

"I wish you could understand that sometimes I need to be alone, Adam. Sometimes, all of this—the Army, your aunt, the strain between you and me—is overwhelming, and I find a quiet, solitary ride soothing to my spirit. I am not afraid of the wilderness and so am comfortable riding alone." She paused. "But I have no wish to upset you. Therefore, I will no longer ride alone." She wondered why she felt that she was betraying some deep part of her soul.

"No, you will not," Adam agreed, not unkindly. "I have

issued orders that your horse is not to be saddled unless you have an escort. Unlike you, dear Sarah, my men obey me."

Sarah stiffened. She had just sacrificed something deeply important to her for his sake, and he threw the gift back in her face. Wounded anew, she rose out of her chair. "As I told you yesterday, it was not my intention to humiliate you when I refused to ride with you, and I regret that I apparently did so. Please accept my apologies; it will not happen again."

"Thank you." Adam did not seem to notice her tight tone of voice.

She raised her chin and continued. "I realize I am beholden to your uncle and aunt for allowing me to stay with them until our marriage, but I do not think that I should be required to endure petty criticism. I will hear nothing more on the color of my clothing, from you or from your aunt. There is no disrespect to my mother in my wearing violet or grey." Sarah fingered her skirt. "Mama liked violet; I do her more honor wearing this."

He nodded. "Very well."

"There is one more thing, Adam."

He waited for her to continue.

"No one will dictate whom I shall call my friend." She steadily met his gaze. "No one."

"I have not done so."

"No, but your aunt has, and I will tolerate it no longer. Mrs. Rutledge can compromise as well as I can."

"I will speak to her."

"Thank you. I feel strongly about this; if you don't tell her, I will."

"It would be better if I did, and I will." Adam stepped toward her, his hands held out in invitation. "Come now. Let us kiss and make up." An entreating smile lit his handsome face.

Sarah allowed him to draw her into his arms, wrapping her own arms around his waist.

"I know Aunt Harriet can be difficult," he said. "It's only because she cares so much."

She cares about you, Adam, but not about me. "I'm certain she does."

"I didn't realize things had gotten so uncomfortable between you and her. I will speak to her today, and later, I'll join you for supper." He patted her shoulder.

"That would be nice." Sarah tightened her arms around him, wishing he would hold her closer, but instead he set her back.

"Run along now." He kissed her cheek, then guided her toward the door. "I have work to do."

"Very well." She looked up at him with an uncertain smile. "Good day, Adam."

"Good day, Sarah."

She lifted her chin in the hope that he would kiss her mouth, but he did not seem to notice her unspoken invitation. He opened the door, and she stepped outside, blinking against the sunlight. She turned back one more time, but Adam had already closed the door. Sarah pulled her shawl more tightly around her shoulders and stood there for a moment, trying to decide what to do, trying to gauge her feelings. She could not bear the thought of facing Harriet Rutledge right now, and the consolation offered by a solitary ride had been taken from her. The idea of an escorted ride held no appeal, for Sarah always felt self-conscious being followed by a bored soldier. It also seemed a selfish imposition to ask a soldier to leave his duties, considering the amount of work still to be done on the fort. It never occurred to her that perhaps the soldiers would welcome the chance for a respite from their back-breaking labors.

She needed to be alone for a while, to think through the many things she and Adam had said to each other. On the surface, they had mended their fences, but she was still left with a deep-seated sense of dissatisfaction.

Perhaps a walk would help; surely Adam would not protest

a short walk along the river. Sarah crossed the bustling compound, acknowledging the polite greetings called to her, and set off to the northeast, along the bank of the Laramie River. A few minutes later, she rounded a bend, and the fort disappeared from view. She could still hear the sounds made by the toiling soldiers, which meant they could hear her if she had to call for help. Even Adam would think her safe here.

She found a place where a large, dry, and mostly flat rock jutted out into the river. With care, she stepped out onto the rock, then sat down. Her hoops collapsed as she lowered herself, allowing her skirts to pool around her hips, and she let the shawl fall from her shoulders. The warmth of both the sun above her and the rock beneath her felt good.

The bow under her chin scratched, and Sarah pulled the bonnet off, annoyed that one of her hairpins was caught in the ruffle. Her impatient tugging only succeeded in causing her eyes to tear, for the pin would not come loose from either her hair or the bonnet. In exasperation, she pulled all the pins from her hair, finally releasing the troublesome bonnet. She tossed the offending article aside, set the pins next to it, and used her fingers to comb out the worst of the tangles and to massage her aching scalp, uttering a silent prayer that Harriet Rutledge did not see her with her hair down. The last thing she needed was another lecture. She rested her chin on her drawn knees and stared into the clear, flowing water.

What had happened to her since she had arrived in the West? On one hand, she felt that she had, at last, come home. She loved the wild beauty of this majestic place, the power she could sense in the untamed land. Everything about it she found fascinating, from the seemingly endless prairies to the towering mountains, from the muddy, lazy, yet treacherous waters of the North Platte River to the clear, sparkling lakes in the high country, from the widely varied plants to the familiar and not-so-familiar animals. She was even drawn to the few Indians she had seen so far, respecting the fact that those interesting if daunting people had lived and thrived on this unforgiving land for generations.

Yet, on the other hand, she felt more unsure of herself than she ever had in her life. Her parents had raised her with what Sarah had always felt was a good, practical, realistic head on her shoulders, but now she was beginning to doubt herself in ways she never had before. Over the color of her gown? Sarah shook her head in dismay. The feeling of self-doubt was decidedly uncomfortable—no, it was more than that. It was disturbing, deeply so. Who else could she depend upon if not herself?

She had never had trouble getting along with people, yet it seemed there was no way she could please Harriet Rutledge. And, unfortunately, Harriet was not a person she could ignore. Not only was she living in the woman's house, and therefore beholden to her, but Harriet was important to Adam, beloved by him, and would one day be a member of her—Sarah's—extended family. One could not discard annoying family members as one could unpleasant acquaintances.

Then there was Adam. He had indeed changed, dramatically so, from the friendly, easygoing youth she remembered and loved. And he denied it, but she *was* in his way. Her betrothed had no time for her now. He was driven, devoted to his career, stiff in more ways than just his military bearing, expecting and needing things from her that she wasn't sure she could give.

How could she feel so at home with the land, and at the same time feel so out of place with the people surrounding her?

Sarah raised her head, suddenly on edge. She was no longer alone; she could feel it. She looked around, searching, listening; she heard the lively gurgle of the water as it tumbled over the rocks, heard the wind rustle the dying leaves of the towering cottonwoods over her head, heard the muted shouts of the laboring soldiers at the distant fort.

She saw nothing.

Then she did. The wolf stepped out of the shadows of the trees across the river, gracefully, silently. As before, he stopped and stood, staring at her, motionless.

Sarah was struck anew by the beauty of the beast's unusual golden eyes, by the markings of his noble face.

"Hello, Dancer," she said softly. After a moment, she held out her hand. "Come here, boy." She wiggled her fingers in invitation and waited. The wolf did not move.

"Please come," she begged. "I need a friend."

Still, the wolf did not move; he did not so much as blink.

In her present emotional state, Sarah felt the rejection keenly. Her outstretched hand dropped to her side and her eyes filled with tears.

From his vantage point behind her, Orion Beaudine heard Sarah's pleading words to Dancer, saw the weary set of her shoulders. He had seen her slip from the compound, and had not been able to resist the temptation to follow her. He felt like a spy when she let her hair down, yet he had been mesmerized by the long, dark locks falling over her shoulders and down her back to the rock. He could not have turned away if he had wanted to. And now, the sight of the independent, spirited Miss Sarah Hancock drooped so disconsolately on the sun-warmed rock distressed him. What had brought her to such a state? Or who? The same reason—or person—that yesterday had sent her dangerously alone into the wilderness to cry? "I'll be your friend," he said quietly.

Sarah jerked her head around to look at him, while one slender hand hurriedly wiped over her tear-brightened eyes. He could not tell if the pink tinge on her cheeks was from a flush of embarrassment or the beginnings of a sunburn. Obviously self-conscious, she gathered her waist-length hair to pull it forward over one shoulder, and swallowed before she spoke.

"Mr. Beaudine. I did not hear your approach." She waved in the direction of the wolf. "I suppose I should not be surprised to see you, though. After all, the two of you are companions."

She turned away and straightened her spine as well as her shoulders. "How unfortunate that you heard my self-pitying remark," she said without looking at him. "Please forgive me for expressing such dreary sentiment."

To Orion, the sunlight seemed to shine on her hair with the same brilliance that it did on the rushing water, bringing out the same sparkling highlights. "There is nothing to forgive, Miss Hancock."

She glanced back over her shoulder. "Would you care to join me?"

"Thank you; I would." He crossed the distance between them in a few long strides and dropped to a cross-legged sitting position next to her, careful to avoid her skirts. Across the river, Dancer lay down in the thick, yellowing grass, resting his muzzle on his paws, his eyes open and alert.

The silence between them reigned for several comfortable minutes, broken only by the sounds of the river and the occasional cry of a circling hawk.

Finally, Orion spoke. "I'll listen if you'd like to talk about what's troubling you."

Sarah did not respond for a long moment, and when she did, she did not look at him. "Thank you, but I must work this out on my own." She rested her chin on her drawn-up knees. "I heard your father was a frontiersman, and that he had three wives."

Orion smiled, both at her deliberate change of the subject and her innocent-sounding comment about his father. He was certain she had heard more about Jedediah Beaudine than what she had stated, and most likely, depending on who was doing the telling, little of it had been flattering. "Yes. In 1819 he came out here from Virginia to make his fortune. He met my mother along the way and married her in St. Louis. My brother Joseph was born a year later, and I the year after that."

"And you were named Orion. It is an interesting name. One doesn't hear it often."

"No. There's a story behind my name, behind all of our names. Perhaps I'll tell you sometime."

Now—at last—she looked at him, with her pretty blue eyes. "I hope you will," she murmured. Then her brow furrowed. "So you lost your mother, too. I'm sorry, Mr. Beaudine."

He shrugged. "She died when I was very young. I don't remember much of her. But I remember both of my stepmothers."

"Then tell me about them." Sarah rested her cheek rather than her chin on her knees this time, and watched him. Her eyes seemed incredibly blue.

Because Orion sensed that she needed to get her mind off her worries, he obliged her, surprising himself, for he did not discuss his family with many people.

"After my mother died, my father brought Joseph and me out here. We lived with the Cheyenne, and after awhile, Jedediah married a woman named Morning Sky. To them my brother Gray Eagle was born." Orion looked up the river without seeing it. "Those were good days," he said softly.

"How were they good?" Sarah asked.

He looked at her then, saw that she was watching him intently. When he was younger, and less experienced in the ways of feminine wiles, women had asked him of his life among the Cheyenne with an almost morbid interest, or they shuddered in revulsion and begged him not to talk about it. But there was nothing more than honest curiosity in Sarah's expression.

"The Cheyenne were free then, and life was good. It was a wonderful life for a boy. There were troubles, of course; the same difficulties with life that all people face—finding enough to eat, surviving the harsh winters, fending off our enemies."

"You mean the white man?"

"No, not then. The Pawnee, and the Sioux. Then, as now,

the Indians fought each other. Only recently has the white man started to present the same problems to the Cheyenne that he did to the Eastern Indians when he arrived on their shores. And more trouble will come."

"Because more white men will come," Sarah commented.

Orion looked at her, surprised by her insight. "Yes."

"What happened to Morning Star?"

"She died giving birth to a still-born daughter. Jedediah was devastated—we all were. He took us back to St. Louis."

"Even Gray Eagle?"

Orion nodded. "Jedediah treated us all equally, educated us all equally. He taught us himself, and he was a very educated man, a graduate of Oxford. Gray Eagle learned to speak English, to read and write; Joseph and I learned the language and the ways of the Cheyenne. We were more welcomed by the Cheyenne than Gray Eagle was by the whites."

"That doesn't surprise me," Sarah said wryly. "I've never understood the arrogance of the white race, that so many of them think the color of their skin and their religious beliefs alone makes them superior to other peoples." She raised an eyebrow. "So who became Jedediah's third wife?"

"My aunt Florrie, my mother's younger sister. She had lived with my mother and father from the time of their marriage, and had taken care of Jedediah's house in St. Louis all the years we were gone. Jedediah decided to stay in St. Louis that first winter after Morning Star's death, and late the next spring, he and Florrie were married. My sisters Juliet and Cora were born of that union."

"You have a large family," Sarah commented, with a wistful touch to her tone. "I wish I did."

"You'll have a family again when you marry." Orion meant the words to be consoling, but Sarah did not appear to be comforted.

"Yes," she whispered. She faced him with a smile that seemed forced. "Why won't Dancer come to me?"

"He won't come to many people, sometimes not even to

me. Don't take it personally." Orion stood up and stepped
back off the rock. He didn't mention that Dancer let only a
handful of people near him, and that privileged group was
restricted to himself, his two brothers, and Jubal Sage, an
old mountain man and scout who had been a close friend of
Jedediah's. For reasons Orion did not understand, the wolf
had never let a woman touch him. He caught the wolf's eye
and pointed to the ground at his feet.

After a long minute, Dancer rose and majestically
stretched, then, at a leisurely pace, crossed the shallow river.
He stopped at Orion's side, looked up at him, and shook,
sending a shower of fine drops all over Orion. Sarah giggled.

"Thank you so much," Orion said sarcastically to the un-
repentant wolf. "Now, I'd like you to say hello to my friend.
This is Miss Sarah Hancock, Dancer. You may call her Miss
Hancock."

Sarah scrambled around on the rock to a kneeling position
facing them and sat back on her heels. She held one hand
out to the wolf.

Dancer stared at her with his usual motionless stance.
Sarah invited him closer by wiggling her fingers, then
waited. "Come here, Dancer," she crooned.

To Orion's astonishment, his stomach and loins tightened
in response to the enticing tone of her soft voice. If Sarah
Hancock ever held out her hand to him and invited him
closer, he'd move a lot quicker than Dancer was now moving,
which was not at all.

Orion's hands clenched into fists and his jaw tightened.
She is promised to another man.

But the sight of her in that shimmering violet gown, kneeling in the sunlight like some goddess of the river, with her
shining hair unbound and her blue eyes alight with the hope
that his cautious wolf would come closer, did something to
him. The temptation to push Dancer out of the way and take
Sarah in his arms, to soothe away the unhappiness and con-

fusion he had seen in her eyes, was so strong that Orion was left shaking.

If he were smart, he'd walk away right now.

And he would have, except Dancer took a few steps toward Sarah. Orion couldn't believe what he was seeing.

"Come here, darling." Sarah's sweet voice washed over him, and apparently over the wolf as well, for Dancer moved closer yet. Orion had the strange sensation that he was watching a beautiful dream unfold before his eyes.

Sarah seemed to hold her breath as she allowed Dancer to sniff her outstretched hand. She slowly brought her other hand up and scratched behind his ears, then both her hands wandered down his furry neck. An expression of wonder came over her pretty face as she and the wolf stared into each other's eyes.

Realization dawned, and Orion's heart slammed against his ribs.

Sarah Hancock understood the Power of the Wolf.

He knew as surely as he drew breath that she had felt it just now, was feeling it still. He was stunned.

Dancer licked Sarah's cheek, breaking the spell. She smiled and scratched his head again, then the wolf sauntered off down to the water and drank.

"He's incredible," she whispered. A soft joy seemed to light up her features.

So are you. The words shouted in Orion's brain, but he refused to give them voice. She would run like a scared rabbit if he started talking like that. He merely stepped forward and held out his hand. She took it and scrambled to her feet, then stumbled against him. His free arm snaked around her narrow waist as he steadied her.

"Are you all right?" he asked. Her warm, womanly body and the faint scent of lavender teased his senses, and he briefly closed his eyes.

"Yes, thank you. My legs are just a little stiff. They're not used to that position." She moved away from him and shaded her eyes against the midday sun, watching as Dancer splashed back across the creek and disappeared into the trees. "Where does he go?"

"I don't know for sure." Orion leaned down to take up her shawl and bonnet from the rock and gather the hairpins. "Not far, though. He's always close by." He straightened and saw that she was weaving her hair into a thick plait. When she was finished, he held out the bonnet.

"Thank you," she said.

Orion noticed that her braid had begun to unravel. "You have no ribbon for your hair."

"No." Sarah tied the bow under her chin. "But I'll go straight home. It will be all right."

Orion reached down and broke a piece of fringe off his pant leg, then held it out to her. "Use this."

She hesitated only a moment before taking the offered bit of buckskin. "Thank you." She tied the end of the braid.

He stepped close to her and draped the shawl around her shoulders, not able to see her eyes under the short brim of the bonnet, for she was looking down. But he could see the sweet curve of her cheeks, and he would swear they were pink again. He fought the urge to caress that inviting skin and stepped back, still holding the hairpins tightly clenched in one hand.

"I'll escort you back," he said.

"Thank you."

They walked in silence for a time, then Sarah spoke. "I'm not sure Dancer is a good name for your wolf."

Her words startled him, but there was a pensive note to her voice rather than a critical one. "No?" he asked.

Sarah shook her head, flashing him a mischievous grin. "Perhaps you should give him a name like Thundercloud, one that fits the land of his birth. After all, he did shake water all over you."

Now Orion laughed out loud. "Actually, I named my horse Thunder. And there is a reason I call him Dancer."

"What is it?"

Orion shrugged, feeling a little foolish. "Sometimes he dances."

Apparently Sarah found nothing foolish in his remark. "I'd like to see that," was all she said. She fell silent again, not speaking until they approached Colonel Rutledge's house. Then the words came softly. "Thank you, Mr. Beaudine. I needed a friend, and you were there, you and Dancer."

Orion guided her up the porch steps with a hand at her elbow. "We were happy to be of assistance." He was tempted to delay her disappearance through the door, but he had seen the curtain at the window pull back, then fall into place. Sarah needed no further trouble from Mrs. Colonel Rutledge on his account. "Good day, Miss Hancock. Both Dancer and I hope to see you again soon."

"I would like that. Good day." Sarah's smile reached her eyes this time, and Orion knew she meant what she said. He turned and walked away, before he made a fool of himself. It was only later that he realized he still held her hairpins in his hand.

Sarah watched him go. He strode tall and graceful across the compound, his long hair laying over his shoulders, his buckskin shirt moving with the fluid motion of his muscular back, the fringe that clung to the sides of his long legs waving in time to his movements. She touched the thin strip of buckskin that held her hair in its braid and remembered how he had looked when she turned to find him beside her on the rock. He had shaved, and his long hair was neatly brushed.

To her, as he stood on the rock in the sunshine, Orion Beaudine had been beautiful. So much so that it had been difficult for her to find her voice, which she hoped he hadn't noticed.

His striking eyes had reflected the green of the few nearby pine trees, and something else. Interest, perhaps? Sarah quickly dismissed the thought. A man such as he would have no interest in a woman such as her. Besides, he was aware that she was promised to Adam, and even though she knew little of Orion, she knew he was an honorable man. If she had glimpsed a spark of interest in his eyes, she could trust him not to act on it.

Most importantly, he was her friend. The thought gave her comfort, and helped her overcome her reluctance to turn and open the door, for she knew Harriet Rutledge waited inside.

Four

Surprisingly, Harriet did not comment on Sarah's untidy braid, nor on the fact that Sarah had once again been in the company of Orion Beaudine. In fact, Harriet hardly said a word to her for the remainder of the afternoon. Sarah wondered if Adam had spoken to his aunt already; she suspected he had.

Colonel Rutledge returned from his reconnaissance mission shortly after the sun slid behind the mountains. He stopped for a few minutes in order to greet Harriet and tell her that they would be having guests for supper. He apologized for the short notice, but said he was certain she would make him proud, just as she always did.

Harriet had preened under his praise. Sarah had to admit that there seemed to be a genuine affection between the tall, efficient colonel and his rigidly proper wife. After an affectionate greeting to Sarah, which she had returned with equal feeling, the colonel left for a meeting with his officers and, presumably, Orion Beaudine. She couldn't help but wonder if, once he delivered his messages to Colonel Rutledge, Orion would be leaving. The thought distressed her, even though she knew she had no business feeling anything about the handsome scout.

Sarah dressed with care that night. She even asked Lucy to arrange her hair. Adam would be at supper, and she wanted to make him feel as proud of her as Colonel Rutledge was of Harriet. For that reason, she chose to wear a black gown, so that no fault could be found with her, from any quarter. When she heard Harriet's strident voice in the kitchen, she slipped into the Rutledges' bedroom off the parlor to check her appearance in Harriet's prized mahogany-framed standing mirror. Sarah was pleased with what she saw.

The black gown, under which she wore a modest set of hoops, fit her well, although she wondered if it, combined with her dark hair, didn't cause her face to appear too pale. The dress was several years old, having been one of her mother's mourning gowns when Sarah's father had died, but after her mother's death, Sarah had been able to remake it into a respectable if not fashionable gown. She had removed the high collar and lowered the neckline in front to a plunging vee that coordinated with the vee at the waist, then filled in the neckline vee with a panel of burgundy brocade in order to lend some relief to the unrelenting black. Daringly, she had also added a narrow burgundy ruffle at the cuffs of the long puffed sleeves. Lucy had arranged her hair in an up-swept style and coaxed three strands into ringlets that lay demurely on the back of her neck, then added a small, curling black feather as adornment. For a finishing touch, Sarah had hooked her mother's dangling garnet earrings in her earlobes. The effect, as Sarah now saw in the mirror, was satisfying. She looked properly refined. Surely both Adam and Harriet would be pleased.

She could only assume that they were, for neither commented on her costume when they gathered in the parlor before supper. In addition to Adam and Harriet, Major Benton Dillard and Lieutenants Roger Fielding and Callahan Roe had joined the party. Adam had once explained to her that the unusually high ratio of officers to enlisted men was only temporary because Lieutenant Fielding was on special assignment and would soon be ordered to another post. Colonel Rutledge had not yet made his appearance.

"I must say, Miss Hancock, that you look stunning to-night," Major Dillard said gallantly.

"You certainly do," Lieutenant Roe added with enthusiasm.

"Thank you, gentlemen." An annoying blush heated Sarah's cheeks, even though she did not believe either man's words. She would allow that she looked nice, but "stunning" was going too far. She had not yet become accustomed to the flattery Adam's fellow officers constantly showered upon her, which Harriet had assured her was normal. Due to the dearth of women at any post, flirtation—guided by strict and apparently unspoken rules—was rampant. Sarah thought it odd that men would flirt, sometimes outrageously, with other men's wives or fiancées, often when the husband or soon-to-be husband was in the same room.

"How are your wife and children?" she asked the major, knowing that his family waited at Fort Laramie until Fort St. Charles was deemed ready to house families. She also knew Major Dillard was devoted to his family and loved to talk about them.

"Just fine, just fine. Penelope sent a letter along with that scout, that Orion Beaudine; she doesn't care much for the rough accommodations at Fort Laramie and hopes to join me soon, although accommodations will probably be no better here."

Relieved that the conversation had been turned from her, Sarah listened only halfheartedly while the major droned on about the accomplishments of his young son. As her gaze wandered around the small room, she caught Lieutenant Fielding's eye. He was in conversation with Adam and Harriet Rutledge, yet he stared at her with a calculating, almost predatory expression on his face. Sarah looked away, suddenly uncomfortable. He had never been out of line in his manner toward her, but for some reason Lieutenant Fielding disturbed her. Hoping that Harriet did not seat her next to the man at supper, she made an attempt to follow what Major Dillard was saying.

Just then, the door opened to admit Colonel Rutledge and, much to Sarah's surprise, Orion Beaudine. Harriet was obviously surprised as well, and not pleasantly so. She made her way to the colonel's side, her blue satin skirts rustling, her lips curved in a forced smile. "Hello, Colonel." She glanced pointedly at Orion, who removed his hat. "You have brought another guest." There was no hint of welcome in her voice.

"Yes, I have."

Sarah could not keep a smile from her own lips when Orion nodded a greeting to her from across the room. He still wore his buckskin pants and black boots, but he had exchanged his buckskin shirt for one of white cotton, over which he wore a beautifully finished fringed buckskin jacket. He looked out of place in a room full of uniformed officers and formally dressed ladies. To Sarah's eye, he also looked very handsome. After murmuring her excuses to Major Dillard and Lieutenant Roe, she crossed the room to Orion's side. Colonel and Mrs. Rutledge moved away, heading in the direction of the dining room, deeply involved in what appeared to be a tense conversation.

"How nice to see you again, Mr. Beaudine." Sarah held her hand out, and Orion took it.

"The pleasure is mine," he said, then leaned toward her and added, for her ears alone, "I told you we would meet again."

Sarah arched an eyebrow at him. "So you did, sir."

His intense gaze roamed over her, coming back to rest on her face. "You look lovely tonight, Miss Hancock. The gown suits you, as does the style of your hair."

At his compliment, Sarah blushed again, but this time it was due to the note of sincerity in his voice. Orion Beaudine meant what he said.

"Thank you." Shyly, she smiled at him, then blurted out,

"I think you look wonderful, too." Suddenly, she really blushed, the full, red-faced flush of mortification, and dropped her gaze to the floor. Why had she said that? He would think her terribly forward, and perhaps even out of line, since she was an engaged woman. And she had said "wonderful." What a stupid thing to say to a man! Even if she did think it was the truth. "I apologize, Mr. Beaudine, for my forwardness. You must think me ill-mannered."

"That depends, Miss Hancock." There was a teasing quality to Orion's tone, and Sarah finally looked up at him.

"On what?"

"On whether you meant what you said."

"I did," she admitted. For the life of her, she could not pull her gaze away from his face.

"Then there is nothing to apologize for. Had you been exaggerating, or lying, I would consider that ill-mannered, but I doubt you are capable of telling a falsehood. So I thank you for the compliment. I am flattered. I also want to return these." He held out his hand, on which laid some of her hairpins.

There was a warmth in Orion's green eyes that Sarah felt herself drowning in. Why did this man wreak such havoc with her senses? She blinked, then scooped the pins from his hand, her fingers tingling from the contact with his warm skin. "Thank you," she managed to murmur. "Have you met all of our guests?"

Orion looked around the small room. "Yes, I know them all."

"Then I will leave you to greet them while I fetch you some sherry."

"Thank you, Miss Hancock."

Sarah moved away, over to the upended stacked wooden boxes that served as a temporary sideboard until the rest of Harriet's furnishings arrived from Fort Kearny. A lovely tablecloth edged with fine lace covered the rough boxes, upon which rested a crystal decanter and two remaining cordial glasses from the set of eight. She could hear muted voices coming from the dining room and wondered if Harriet was actually going to challenge the colonel over Orion's presence. Did the woman expect her husband to ask Orion to leave? Such an action would be unpardonably rude. Sarah set her hairpins down at the back of the makeshift table and reached for the decanter, puzzled at Harriet's continued and blatant hostility toward Orion Beaudine. What had he ever done to her?

She filled a glass with sherry and added a little more to her own, then returned to Orion's side and handed him the fresh glass. Major Dillard and Lieutenant Roe were questioning him on conditions at Fort Laramie, while Adam and Lieutenant Fielding carried on a conversation a short distance away. Sarah was content to sip her sherry and listen to the men discuss what they felt the future held for their tiny garrison, especially whether or not the Army commanders would leave Fort St. Charles manned.

"I think it's doubtful," Orion commented. "Fort St. Charles is too far south of the Oregon Trail."

"But it is still situated in a crucial position," Major Dillard argued.

Orion clearly did not agree, but before anything more could be said, Harriet Rutledge appeared at the door to the dining room and announced that supper was served. She spoke politely, yet her mouth was tight with tension and her eyes fairly snapped with anger.

Sarah knew Orion would be staying for supper.

Colonel Rutledge directed the seating himself. He and Harriet each took one end of the table, while Sarah was seated next to the colonel, with Orion at her other side and Lieutenant Fielding across from her. Adam sat next to his aunt, opposite Major Dillard, leaving Lieutenant Roe between Adam and Fielding.

Lucy came from the kitchen with wonderful-smelling platters of food, and the meal began pleasantly enough. Sarah spoke little, not only listening to and absorbing what was said, but observing how everyone acted. If Harriet was still upset over Orion's presence at her table, she did a masterful job of hiding her feelings. But she never addressed Orion directly, nor did she look at him. Neither did Adam or Lieutenant Fielding. Sarah had the sense that powerful undercurrents were at play and she was on the shore watching, yet not seeing. She was certain Orion was being insulted, but it was done so subtly that nothing was obvious to the casual observer. Sarah glanced at Orion. Had he noticed? He did not seem to have, for he was speaking to the colonel with the same friendly ease he always used. Then, as if he felt her eyes on him, he turned to her and smiled.

Her breath caught. The expression on his handsome face bespoke of genuine affection for her, and that warm look, combined with the nearness of his powerful male presence, set her heart to hammering. She was staring at him, and he at her, and if she did not break eye contact soon, everyone at the table would notice.

Adam unintentionally broke the spell with his next words. "Sarah has agreed to forgo her solitary rides," he announced.

Sarah bristled at the curious note of triumph in his tone, but said nothing. She merely dropped her gaze to her plate.

Adam continued. "I have at last persuaded her of the danger of riding with no escort."

"I am relieved to hear it, Sarah," Harriet said. "One never knows what . . . beasts . . . may lurk in the wilderness. A lady simply cannot go roaming about unescorted."

Sarah's head snapped up. The remark about beasts was meant as a gibe toward Orion; she knew it. It appeared she was right, because, for the first time, Harriet was staring directly at him. Glaring, actually, as if she were daring him to respond. Orion calmly met her gaze, but said nothing.

"You are so right, Mrs. Rutledge," Sarah said sweetly, although she was seething with anger. "Heaven only knows what would have become of me had Mr. Beaudine not come to my rescue yesterday."

"What happened yesterday?" Colonel Rutledge demanded.

"I went riding alone," Sarah explained. "My horse bolted and left me stranded. Mr. Beaudine found me and offered his protection until Adam came along."

"I agree with Adam," the colonel said. "You must not ride alone. I know Adam's duties as my adjutant keep him busy, but I'm certain any of the other officers would be glad to escort you."

"Absolutely, Miss Hancock," Lieutenant Roe inserted.

"Glad to, Miss Hancock," Major Dillard said, "at least until my dear Penelope and the children arrive."

"Thank you, gentlemen." Sarah smiled at each man in turn. Lieutenant Fielding stared at her with that odd calculating expression before he spoke.

"You'll ride with me in the morning, Miss Hancock." Fielding spoke as if he were issuing an order.

Was it Sarah's imagination or did Orion stiffen? She was about to refuse Lieutenant Fielding's offer when Orion spoke.

"Perhaps Miss Hancock does not *wish* to ride in the morning, Lieutenant."

Fielding glared at him; the enmity between the two men was palpable. Before either said anything further, Adam stepped in. "Colonel Rutledge will need the assistance of all of his officers in preparing the dispatches for Fort Laramie, Lieutenant Fielding. None of us will have time for a pleasure ride in the morning. I'm certain Miss Hancock understands."

"Of course I do," Sarah assured him, wanting to add that she had never asked to ride in the morning. She looked at Adam and was bewildered to find him eyeing Fielding with a troubled gaze. What was going on? It seemed that neither

Adam nor Orion wanted her to ride with Fielding anymore than she herself did.

"The captain is correct," Colonel Rutledge said. "Even with all of the officers working on them, we won't have the reports and dispatches ready until noon." He turned to Orion. "Perhaps you would be willing to escort Miss Hancock in the morning."

Orion nodded. "It would be my pleasure, if Captain Rutledge has no objections."

Sarah watched Adam carefully, trying to gauge his reaction.

He seemed calm, almost relieved. "I have no objections. I'm certain Miss Hancock will be safe in your capable hands." He turned to Major Dillard and asked him about one of the topographical reports he was working on, effectively drawing the attention away from Sarah, for which she was very thankful.

Orion leaned closer to Sarah. "Would you like to join me for a ride in the morning?"

Sarah wondered why she suddenly felt like nervous butterflies were aswarm in her belly. It wasn't proper that she should feel such anticipation about seeing any man other than Adam, but she did. After a moment's hesitation, she answered him honestly. "Yes, I would."

"I'll call for you a half hour after reveille."

"Very well." She glanced at her fiancé, wondering if he truly had no objections, but he was still involved in his discussion with Major Dillard. Harriet's lips were pressed into the thin, disapproving line Sarah now recognized so well, making clear her opinion on the matter. The burning anger evident in Lieutenant Fielding's eyes made Sarah look away. Suddenly she was very grateful that Adam and Orion had saved her from having to refuse Fielding's offer. He would not have taken it well, she suspected.

The rest of the meal passed in relative peace. The two

lieutenants and Major Dillard took their leave, and a few minutes later Sarah walked Orion out to the lantern-lit porch.

"I will see you in the morning, Mr. Beaudine. Thank you for agreeing to escort me." Sarah held out her hand.

Orion took it, but instead of giving her hand a little shake, as was customary, he held it warmly in his. "My pleasure, Miss Hancock." His voice dropped to a lower tone. "Captain Rutledge is right to be concerned about Fielding. Don't ever allow him to escort you unless someone else is with you."

Sarah looked up at him. "What do you know about him?"

"Too much. Please just trust me." Orion squeezed her hand, then released her. "I'll see you in the morning." He stepped off the porch.

"Good night, Mr. Beaudine," Sarah called after him.

"Good night." Orion disappeared into the shadows just as Adam came out the door to join her.

"I must be off, Sarah," he said. "I want to get started on those reports tonight."

Sarah watched him in the dim light. "I'm proud of your dedication to your work," she said in all sincerity.

Adam looked at her strangely, twisting his hat in his hands. "I hope you always feel that way. If I'm to be successful in the Army, if I'm to ever get back to Washington, to get a post away from this godforsaken frontier, my dedication must never waver. You must be prepared for that. The Army will come before all else, including my wife."

Sarah was astounded at the resentment in his voice. Was it directed at her? "I am prepared," she said softly. She laid a hand on his forearm. "Adam, I thought you liked serving on the frontier."

"Of course I do." Adam made a disgusted sound. "I like to endure searing heat and freezing cold in substandard quarters, just as I like to eat rice and beans day after day, and drill idiotic enlisted men in either mud or dust. I especially enjoy supervising the construction of latrines."

Sarah flinched at the heavy sarcasm.

Adam crammed his Army-issue hat on his head. "I am a strategist and a fighter, Sarah. At least give me some Indians to kill."

She stared at him, appalled. "I had no idea you felt this way. Have you considered resigning your commission?"

"Of course not, nor will I ever." Adam stared out over the half-finished compound. "The Army gave me a chance to make something of myself—a real chance. And by God, I will. But an officer cannot make a name for himself on the frontier unless there is a war. I won't get promoted for wet-nursing a bunch of foolhardy immigrants across the Great American Desert." As suddenly as he had erupted, he calmed down. "Good night, my dear. Enjoy your ride tomorrow." He planted a chaste kiss on her cheek, then stepped off the porch and disappeared into the night.

Sarah stared after him, deeply troubled. Had he meant what he'd said about killing Indians? Adam rarely spoke of his service in the Mexican War, yet he had been promoted to captain for bravery on the field of battle. Had he developed a taste for killing? Would he welcome the chance to kill—under the guise of war—for another promotion?

Adam had indeed changed, perhaps in ways Sarah would not be able to accept.

Five

Even before reveille sounded the next morning, Sarah was awake. At the call of the bugle, she scrambled out of bed, ignoring the chill of the tiny room, and dressed hurriedly in her dark gray riding habit. Surely Harriet would not find fault with the white bodice she wore under the close-fitting jacket, and the gray broad-brimmed hat was decorated with a black scarf. Sarah pulled a pair of black leather gloves on her cold hands and let herself out the front door without speaking to anyone, even though she could hear Lucy moving about in the kitchen, and a low murmur of voices came from the Rutledges' bedroom. As she did not want to give Harriet a chance to make any trouble, she would wait for Mr. Beaudine on the porch.

Her breath was visible in little puffs of white. Sarah suppressed a shiver; winter was on its way, and she had heard terrible stories of winter on the western plains. She hoped the little fort would be ready in time to withstand the punishment and privation of the coming months.

The eastern sky was painted with brilliant shades of red, gold, and purple, indicating that the sun would soon haul itself over the horizon. Sarah never tired of watching the sun rise over the prairies, for it seemed she could see to the very ends of the earth. This morning was no different. So caught up was she in the unfolding spectacle of daybreak that she did not hear Orion approach, even though he led two saddled horses.

He stopped, the reins held tightly in his gloved hand, and studied her profile. On the porch she stood, waiting for him, her arms wrapped around herself, staring with rapt attention at the rapidly lightening eastern sky. She held herself straight and tall, wearing a well-tailored riding habit, her hair pulled up under a brimmed hat which was decorated with a long, black gauze scarf tied around the crown. The tails of the filmy material rode gracefully on the early morning breeze.

To Orion's eye, in that moment Sarah presented a calm and noble picture, almost as if she were a figurehead on the prow of one of those magnificent clipper ships he had once seen a drawing of. She was the type of woman who would offer her man a port in the stormy seas of life. Sarah Hancock's man would be able to rest his head against the softness of her breasts and know that whatever happened, she would be at his side. He could not help but wonder if Captain Adam Rutledge knew how lucky he was. Orion doubted it. With fierce determination, he banished the thought of Captain Rutledge from his mind and refocused on Captain Rutledge's intended bride.

"Good morning," he called softly.

She turned with a smile that lit up her face as surely as the climbing sun lit up the eastern skies. "Good morning, Mr. Beaudine."

I want you to call me Orion. Instead, he said, "Are you ready?" knowing full well that she was.

"Yes."

She took the hand he held out to her as she descended the steps. Did he only imagine that her fingers tightened on his before she released him?

"The soldier at the stables told me there are no sidesaddles," he said, feeling apologetic, even though she had ridden astride just two days ago, with her legs nestled next to his.

"No," Sarah responded. "I don't have my own saddle, and

Mrs. Colonel Rutledge does not ride. As we are the only two Army women here yet, I had to learn to ride astride if I was to ride at all. Adam, uh, Captain Rutledge was very busy with his duties, so Mr. Jubal Sage taught me."

Lucky Jubal. "I'll help you up," Orion said, making a cup of his hands.

"Thank you."

Sarah gathered her skirts and placed her booted foot in his hands. Orion was impressed with how easily she found her seat when he boosted her up.

"Do you know Mr. Sage?" she asked as Orion adjusted the length of the stirrups to her legs.

"Yes; I've known him all of my life. He and my father were close friends."

Sarah accepted the reins he handed her. "I like him very much," she said. "He is a fascinating man to talk to, and very wise in the ways of nature. But he never mentioned what to do when confronted with a wolf. For that omission, I shall have to take him to task when next I see him."

Caught off guard by her words, wondering if she was teasing, Orion landed in his saddle more forcefully than normal. He drew a sharp breath. "A wolf?" he managed to ask.

"Yes. When Dancer approached me that first time, I wracked my brain trying to think of what Mr. Sage might have told me about wolves. I could remember nothing, except that I knew not to run, which is a caution one must take with dogs. Of course, I suppose dogs and wolves are to be considered distant relatives."

"Of course." Orion positioned his reins. "Why didn't you tell Rutledge, or anyone, for that matter, that Dancer caused your horse to bolt?"

Sarah shrugged. "No one needs to know. It isn't important." She smiled at him, causing his stomach to tighten. "Well, lead on, Mr. Beaudine. Since this glorious land is your home, I shall trust you to show me something wonderful this morning."

She belongs to another man.

His jaw clenched, Orion led her out of the compound.

He took her across the river to a high hill that overlooked the fort and the confluence of the two Laramie rivers. Judging from the look of awe on her face, Sarah Hancock was duly impressed.

Orion steadied her as she climbed down from the saddle, then he stood at her side, seeing what she saw with the wonder of newly reawakened eyes.

Behind them and to the north, in a gentle protective curve, stretched the arms of the Laramie Mountains, capped by the splendor of Laramie Peak. Before them, the land rolled away, first in rounded hills and large outcroppings of tumbled rock, both of which were kissed here and there with pine trees, then in increasingly smooth-looking acres—no, miles—of prairie land. The distant shoulder-high grasses seemed fluid, bending and flowing at the command of the relentless and never-ending wind. The two rivers appeared to be ribbons of molten silver, coming together near the small dark forms that comprised Fort St. Charles. And over it all rose the sun at last, blinding in its glory as it broke free of the horizon.

The black gauze of Sarah's hat scarf teased Orion's cheek with soft, tantalizing caresses, carrying the elusive scent of lavender. At the sound of her contented sigh, his heart lurched, never again to find its proper place unless Sarah Hancock was near. He tore his gaze from the sight of wonder before him to the sight of the woman next to him, and his breath stopped.

He could see it in her eyes, in her expression, could feel it in her bated breath and the pulse he saw in her lovely neck. She understood the Power of the Land, just as she had understood the Power of the Wolf.

She was his woman, as surely as the sun had risen.

She belongs to another man.

"Are you hungry?" he rasped.

A frown creased her brow, only for a second, as she shook free of the spell that had caught her. "Yes," she whispered.

Orion guided her to a rock and indicated with a wave of his hand that she should sit. Without a word, Sarah followed his lead, sinking to the rock with her skirts pooling about her. Her gaze once more locked on the view before her, and Orion led the horses away, content to let her rest while he made a small fire and set out the food he had brought in his saddlebags.

A short time later he joined her, bearing two tin cups of steaming black coffee in one hand, a bundle of bread and cheeses wrapped in a clean towel in the other. She had taken off her hat and gloves and laid them aside. She looked up at him when he held the cups down to her, one of which she accepted.

"Do you come here often?" she asked quietly.

"Every chance I get, which hasn't been often enough lately. With all the immigrants crossing the plains last summer, and the coming rush next summer, the Army has kept me busy." Orion sat at her side, setting his cup on the rock, and unwrapped the food.

"It's so quiet," Sarah marveled. "I feel as if I can hear the spirits of the four winds whispering to each other, or perhaps it is the very earth I hear, breathing and sighing."

"Perhaps it is. I hear it, too." Orion held a piece of bread out to her.

"I believe you do, Orion Beaudine." Her eyes met his as she reached blindly for the bread. Their hands touched.

Then Sarah blinked. "I feel him," she whispered.

Alarmed, Orion looked around. "Who?"

"Dancer."

Orion could only stare at her. A moment later, Dancer materialized from a thicket of scrub oak and daintily picked his way to Sarah's side. "Of course he appears when there's food to be had," Orion said lightly, but inside he was shaken. She could truly feel Dancer's presence? Dancer was now sitting at Sarah's side, this wolf who had let no woman touch him?

"Where did you get him?" Sarah asked as she scratched the wolf's ears.

"I found him near death, huddled next to his mother's body when he was no more than a little ball of fur." Orion looked out over the awakening land. "She'd been caught in a trap, and a bear or something got to her before she could chew her foot off to escape." He tried to keep his voice neutral against the anger swelling up inside him as it always did at the memory. "I don't hold with trapping, even though my own father did a fair amount in his life. If you have to kill an animal, make the kill quick and clean, and thank the animal for giving its life so you can eat." Then he caught himself and glanced at Sarah. One slender hand covered her mouth while the other maintained its hold on Dancer. Once again, her eyes were very blue with unshed tears.

Damn.

"I'm sorry, Miss Hancock. I didn't mean to upset you."

She shook her head. "Don't ever apologize for telling the truth, Mr. Beaudine." She faced him. "In fact, I shall always expect nothing but the truth from you. Friends are honest with each other."

"Yes, ma'am." He took a bite of bread, still angry with himself for going into such unnecessary detail.

Sarah broke her bread in two and offered half to Dancer, who, after sniffing the offering quite closely, accepted it. Sarah took a bite, then sipped from her cup. "Tell me the story behind your name," she invited.

"All right." Orion handed her a piece of yellow cheese. "My father came from an old Virginia family, the youngest of four sons, and the last to inherit, so he made his way out here to seek his own fortune. He met my mother somewhere along the Natchez Trace; she and her sister were living in squalor with their drunken father. Jedediah stepped in when the man started beating on the girls, and he took them with him, marrying Ellie, the older one, when they reached St. Louis. He taught my mother to read before he headed west that first time, and he left her carrying my older brother. While he was gone, she read the Bible from cover to cover, and when my brother was born, she named him Joseph."

"Ah," Sarah said with a smile. "And she was reading Greek mythology while carrying you."

Orion nodded. "She taught her sister Florrie to read, and when Jedediah married Florrie years later, Florrie continued the tradition to honor Ellie's memory."

"No doubt your sister Juliet was named during the Shakespeare phase."

"No doubt."

"And Cora?"

"After Cora Munro in *The Last of the Mohicans*."

"The James Fenimore Cooper stage." Sarah frowned. "Cora died in that book."

"Yes, but Florrie always thought she shouldn't have. 'Cora was the strong one,' she always says. 'A much more appealing character than that Alice, who lived. Cora should have ended up with Nathaniel, because he was strong, too.' " Orion shrugged. "She wanted to rewrite the book."

Sarah pursed her lips thoughtfully before speaking. "I agree with her, Mr. Beaudine. Cora was the strong one. But Juliet died, too."

"For love."

"And Orion was killed by Artemis, or by his beloved Diana, who was tricked into killing him, depending on which version you follow."

"He died for love, also."

"Still, they all died." There was a sad quality to her voice.

Orion faced her. "We all die, Miss Hancock, sooner or later. Even the father of Jesus died. We're all named after dead people, and in the end, the names aren't important. What's important is what we do before we die, the choices

we make, the people we love, the principles we are willing
to fight for, maybe even die for."

Sarah returned her gaze to the vista spread before them.
"You're right." Her voice had dropped to a whisper.

They spent a long time in companionable silence, with
Dancer stretched out on the rock at Sarah's side. Finally,
Orion stood up.

"We'd best head back," he said reluctantly.

"I suppose so." She squinted up at him. "Thank you for
bringing me here, Mr. Beaudine. I will treasure the memory
of this time with you, in this sacred place."

Sacred. That was a good word for it. This was indeed a
sacred place, especially now that it had been touched by
Sarah's presence, by her spirit. Orion knew he would never
again be able to come here and not think of her. "I'll see to
the fire," he said, and, after taking up the cups and the towel,
turned away.

He poured the bitter-smelling remains of the coffee from
the small, dented enamel pot over the embers of the fire he
had made, then covered the hissing, steaming coals with
rocks. When all was packed in his saddlebags, he turned
again to the woman and the wolf on the rock.

She stood now, as did Dancer. Both looked out over the
prairie far below, then Sarah slowly turned in a circle, seeming to delight in what she saw. Her gaze rested on him, and
her face lit up in a luminous smile.

"I love this place, Mr. Beaudine." She flung her arms out
in a gesture of exuberance. "Thank you for bringing me
here."

Seemingly of their own accord, his feet took him to her
side, for later he could not recall making the decision to
move. "I'm probably going to regret this," he muttered, taking Sarah's face gently between his hands. Her eyes widened
with surprise, and that was the last thing he saw before his
own eyes closed and his lips descended to hers. He kissed
her softly at first, with the reverence demanded by the place

she had called sacred, but when she gasped and clutched his forearms with her hands, he was lost. Her lips trembled under his tender onslaught, then opened to him. His hands tangled in her hair as if he were a drowning man grasping a lifeline, which he felt he was.

And Sarah was the lifeline.

Finally, he dragged his mouth from hers and held her tightly, breathing in the scent of her hair, treasuring the feel of her arms once again around him, this time face-to-face. Her heart pounded against his; he was certain of it. After a long moment, he stepped back, steadying her with a firm grip on her upper arms.

She used a shaking hand to push a wayward lock of hair away from her face, then met his gaze. "Do you truly regret kissing me?" she whispered.

Orion blinked, then shook his head. "No, ma'am, but I probably should. Under the circumstances, it wasn't right."

"No, I don't suppose it was."

"I'd best get you back, before I make an even bigger fool of myself." Orion gathered her hat and gloves from the rock, then took Sarah's elbow and propelled her toward her horse.

"Wait, please. Let me fix my hair."

He waited, and watched as she pulled the pins from her hair, then deftly twisted the long mass into a chignon at the back of her head. A few pins secured it there, and Sarah accepted her hat from him, then her gloves. He boosted her into the saddle, handed her the reins, then vaulted onto his own horse. They rode in silence for some time, with Orion leading the way.

The fort was in view when Sarah spoke. "Mr. Beaudine."

Orion pulled up as she came alongside him.

"Under the circumstances, I, too, should regret what happened between us." Her cheeks flamed red, and she looked directly at him. "But I don't, and I'm not sure why. Perhaps it's not wise, but I would like us to remain friends."

He found her honesty touching. "I would like that, too, Miss Hancock."

They fell into silence once more as they approached the steadily growing stockade wall of the compound. The spell had been broken.

Orion delivered her to the Rutledges' front door, Sarah politely thanked him for a pleasant outing, and he rode away, leading her horse toward the stables. Now he was with Colonel Rutledge, receiving his final instructions before he left for Fort Laramie, which was almost forty miles away. When would she see him again? she wondered, knowing it would be best if the answer to that question was "never." Friend though she wanted him to be, Orion Beaudine was dangerous to her peace of mind.

Sarah stripped off her hat and gloves, then the tailored jacket. She pulled the pins from her untidy hair and let the long locks fall down her back. Then she caught sight of herself in the little hand mirror that hung from a nail in the wall of her bedroom. Would her flushed cheeks ever return to their normal color? She answered her own question. Not as long as she kept thinking about kissing Orion Beaudine. She plopped down on the bed and pressed her hands to her warm cheeks.

She had never been kissed like that.

Adam had kissed her, but always chastely. Their relationship was still one of friendship more than anything else. There was no passion between them, and Sarah could only assume—hope—that would develop with time, as her mother had promised her.

Not so with Orion. The moment his lips touched hers, it was as if a bolt of lightning had shot through her, weakening her knees and leaving her breathless. The feel of his hands in her hair, of his strong arms around her, had filled her with wonder and a strange sense of longing. Shamelessly she had pressed her body to his, and it had felt right.

How could that be, when she was betrothed to Adam? How could she feel such things about another man?

If she were to be honest with herself, Sarah had to admit that her fascination for Orion Beaudine had not started with that kiss; it had started from the first moment she saw him, striding toward her across the sun-drenched meadow. Just as she had known she would never forget the picture the man and the wolf had made that day, she had also known he would touch, even impact her life. If only he had not impacted it so powerfully!

Sarah needed to talk to her mother. Tears of loneliness and confusion filled her eyes as she lay back on the neatly made cot and curled into a fetal position. There was no one to whom she could turn, no older, understanding woman who could explain what was happening, why she could feel so drawn to a man she had known for only two days when she was engaged to another man, one she had known and cared for all of her life. Harriet would accuse her of possessing a weakness of character, of being untrustworthy, perhaps even unfaithful, and part of Sarah would agree with her.

Ironically, the one person she had been able to talk to about anything was Adam. However, her feelings of confusion and guilt over her clandestine kiss shared with Orion Beaudine was not a topic she cared to bring up with her fiancé. She would have to work this one out on her own. The whole situation brought home to Sarah how truly alone she was. It was a terrifying and deeply saddening realization.

She fell into a restless doze, then, perhaps an hour later, came awake with a start.

He was leaving. Orion was leaving.

She had to see him, to tell him farewell, to urge him to be careful.

To be careful? Where had that come from?

Sarah hastily ran a brush through her hair, then tied it with a black ribbon at the back of her neck. Under normal circumstances she would never venture outside without at least braiding her hair, but there was no time. The urgency to see Orion was overwhelming, and he could already be gone. She snatched her shawl from its nail and hurried out of the cabin.

Orion was astride his horse outside the rough headquarters building, evidently ready to depart. Colonel Rutledge stood next to him, as did the other officers, milling about, speaking to him, and to each other. Lieutenant Fielding stood in the open door of the headquarters office, his arms folded across his chest, a look of arrogant disdain on his face. The look did not change when his gaze fell upon Sarah. She decided against joining the group at the building.

She crossed the compound and waited near what would one day—when the fortified wall was complete—be the main gate. A trail from there followed the eastern bank of the Laramie River and north toward the North Platte River and Fort Laramie.

He came a few minutes later, slowing his horse from a trot to a stop. Sarah wondered where his packhorse was. He took off his hat, allowing his long hair to blow in the wind. A smile lit his handsome face.

"Hello, Miss Hancock. I wasn't sure you'd want me to stop by the Rutledge cabin and say goodbye, so I asked the colonel to give you my best."

Sarah lifted her chin. "As long as I live there, you are welcome to stop by whenever you wish, Mr. Beaudine. It is not my house, so I may not be able to invite you in, but you can certainly stop by."

"I don't want to cause problems for you with Mrs. Colonel Rutledge."

"Thank you for your concern, but please do not trouble yourself about it. There were problems between us long before I met you. She and I will have to work it out."

"Yes, especially if you are to be related."

Sarah's voice faltered, and she looked away from him. "Yes."

After a moment of silence, Orion spoke again, softly. "I like your hair down like that."

Stricken, Sarah looked back up at him. "You mustn't say such things."

A shuttered look fell over his face. "No, I suppose not."

Impulsively, Sarah reached up to him. "We must take care with each other, Mr. Beaudine, or we will only cause each other pain."

He caught her hand in his and leaned down toward her. "I know, sweet woman. I won't hurt you."

At the tenderness on his face, her heart pounded so strongly that Sarah was certain he could hear it. "I wanted to tell you farewell," she said, her voice not much more than a whisper. "And to be careful."

"I'm always careful." He smiled again. "Don't look so worried, Miss Hancock. I can take care of myself. It's only a two-day journey; I'll be there by nightfall tomorrow."

That explained the absence of his packhorse. Sarah chewed on her lower lip, wondering if she should ask the question on her mind. She did. "Will I see you again?"

"Do you want to?"

"I shouldn't want to, but I do."

"As long as you live out here, on the frontier, you'll see me from time to time. Remember: this is my home."

Sarah nodded. "I remember." She gave him a shy smile.

His fingers tightened on hers as he brought her hand to his mouth and kissed it. "Fare you well while I'm gone, Miss Sarah Hancock." He released her.

"I will." Sarah pulled the shawl more tightly around her shoulders. The wind had taken on a chill.

"And stay away from Fielding."

Oddly enough, the commanding tone to his voice did not offend Sarah, even though he had no business telling her what to do. Wasn't Orion Beaudine dictating the company she kept as surely as Harriet Rutledge had? Yet this was different. Harriet had spoken out of her concern for appearances. Orion spoke out of his concern for her.

"I will. There is something disturbing about him."

Orion nodded approvingly as he repositioned his hat on his head. "You have good instincts, Miss Hancock. Trust them."

"I will." Sarah stepped away from the horse.

"I hope so," he whispered, a strange sadness filling his green eyes. "Goodbye." He touched his heels to the horse's side, and the animal lunged to a trot.

"Take care of Dancer!" Sarah cried.

Orion waved in response and urged his horse to a canter. Sarah watched until the dust stirred up by his horse's hooves had settled once again to earth, then she trudged back to the cabin, feeling more lonely than before. She let herself into the parlor, dismayed to find both Harriet and Adam there.

"You went out with your hair down, and without a hat?" Harriet demanded.

Wearily, Sarah replied, "Yes, Harriet, I did."

"Aunt Harriet," Adam warned, rising from his chair.

Harriet closed her mouth on whatever remark she had been about to make and, a moment later, said instead, "Very well, Adam. You speak to her. Perhaps she will listen to you. Lord knows she won't listen to me." She stuffed her mending in the basket at her feet and stormed out of the room. Sarah felt a pang of guilt for the angry note in Harriet's voice as she bellowed for Lucy.

"Sarah, are you well?"

Startled by the concern in Adam's tone, Sarah looked at him. "Of course. Why do you ask?"

Adam approached her and took her hands in his. "You've seemed unhappy lately, and I know I've been neglecting you since you arrived." He pulled her into his arms.

A sob caught in Sarah's throat as she put her own arms

around his waist. It seemed like it had been a long time since Adam had just held her. Dear Adam.

"Things are difficult for both of us right now," Adam said soothingly. He stroked her shoulder with one hand. "But they will get better."

"I know." Sarah's voice was muffled against his blue uniform coat.

"Aunt Harriet means well, Sarah. She's not always tactful, but her heart is in the right place."

Sarah silently rebelled against that for a moment, then she sighed. "She only wants what is best for you. She loves you very much."

"She loves you, too."

Sarah pulled back far enough to be able to look into his eyes. "No, she doesn't." She spoke without rancor. "Perhaps one day she will, though. I hope she and I can become close friends, for your sake if for no other reason. After all, we both love you."

"That's my girl." Adam kissed her forehead. "Did you enjoy your ride this morning?"

"Yes, I did." Sarah tried to ignore the guilt that suddenly knotted her stomach.

"The colonel ordered me to get away every so often and escort you myself, and I must obey orders." There was a teasing note to his voice as well as a smile on his handsome, bearded face. "I know how you love to ride, my dear. And I thank you for agreeing to my wishes about not riding alone."

Sarah tried to hide her astonishment. What had happened to Adam? Perhaps she had Colonel Rutledge to thank for this sudden change in the behavior of her betrothed.

"I must go now. I'll be dining with you tonight, so I'll see you then." Adam kissed her cheek this time and moved toward the door. His voice dropped to a whisper. "And it probably would be best if you put your hair up before you leave the house."

Another pang of guilt assailed Sarah. If she hadn't been in such a hurry to see Orion Beaudine off, she would have taken the time to fix her hair, and the latest upset with Harriet would have been prevented.

"Very well, Adam," Sarah said meekly. "It will be nice to see you tonight," she added.

"Until then." The door closed and he was gone, leaving Sarah feeling more confused than ever.

Six

True to his word, Orion rode into Fort Laramie the next day just as the sun disappeared behind the mountains to the west. Like Fort St. Charles, Fort Laramie was built at the confluence of two rivers, in this case the North Platte and the Laramie. Most distinctive about Fort Laramie was the large whitewashed adobe structure that dominated the site. Called Fort John until the U.S. Army bought the site earlier that year, the old fort was in a serious state of disrepair, and the decision had been made to build an entirely new installation rather than shore up the crumbling walls of the old one.

Much had been accomplished in the four months since the site passed into the Army's hands. Even a small sawmill was up and operating near the Laramie River, cutting the logs which were dragged from the mountains twelve miles away on specially rigged wagon beds. Mrs. Colonel Rutledge had the hardworking soldiers of Fort Laramie to thank for the plank floor in her modest cabin at Fort St. Charles, but Orion doubted she would ever express her thanks to the men who deserved it.

The post commander's headquarters were currently housed in a room of what used to be the old fur traders' post. Orion slowed his horse to a walk, heading in that general direction, then was forced to circumvent the large, rough parade ground because the retreat dress parade, performed each day at sundown, had just started. It was an impressive sight to see close to one hundred uniformed men march in relatively tight formation, the event ended by the solemn lowering of the flag. At least Fort Laramie had a small band, unlike Fort St. Charles' lone bugler. The music was nice to hear.

The ceremony ended as Orion reached the door of the headquarters building. A tall officer moved away from the breaking ranks of soldiers and hurried toward him.

"Hey, you long-haired mountain man!" the officer called. He reached Orion's horse and literally pulled him out of the saddle. "How the hell are you, little brother?"

With a broad grin, Orion pounded his brother on the back. "Damn, Joseph, it's good to see you! When did you get here?"

"Came with a small contingent just last week. They sent some lieutenant fresh from West Point out to help the engineer design this place. They've also posted any soldier who can communicate with the Indians to the frontier."

"Well, with your fluency in Cheyenne and sign language, you would have been first on their list." Orion looked at his brother with affection. The two men were of equal height and build, and Orion knew it would be clear to any onlooker that they were brothers, so closely did they resemble each other. The only real differences between them, in addition to their style of dress, were the color of their eyes—Orion had inherited the green eyes of their father, while Joseph had the deep brown eyes of their mother; the length of their hair, although Joseph's had grown longer than his collar—long for an Army officer, Orion thought—and Joseph sported a thick, neatly trimmed mustache, while Orion was clean shaven—relatively. He ran a hand over the two-day stubble covering his chin. "I need to report to Colonel Mackay and deliver these dispatches from Fort St. Charles. Then give me a chance to get cleaned up, and I'll join you for supper."

"I'd like that, Orion. How long has it been since we've seen each other? Over a year, hasn't it?"

Orion nodded as he took in the bars on his brother's shoulders. "Captain Beaudine now, huh?"

Joseph shrugged. "Yeah."

Orion looked thoughtfully at Joseph's inscrutable face. Tension had formed lines in his forehead, and there seemed to be a shadow of restlessness or sadness in his brown eyes. Something was going on with his older brother, but now was not the time to ask him about it. He reached for his saddlebags. "Did you stop in St. Louis on the way out and see Ma and the girls?"

"Sure did. They said you were back last spring, but since the immigrant trains started you've been busy."

"I have been. How was everyone?"

"Just fine, as always. I'll tell you all about it at supper. Do you still have that wolf?"

"Yes. He's out there somewhere." Orion waved toward the hills in the distance. "He still doesn't care much for crowds."

Joseph smiled. "Can't say as I blame him. I hope I get to see him."

"We'll ride out and find him," Orion promised.

"Good." Joseph nodded with satisfaction. "I'll see to your horse while you deliver your dispatches."

"Thanks." Orion handed him the reins. "His name is Thunder."

Joseph ran his hand over Thunder's forehead and down to the animal's nose. "Hello, Thunder." He spoke in a gentle tone, one that for some reason reminded Orion of Sarah Hancock and the way she had spoken to Dancer. A pang of loneliness for her jolted through him, catching him by surprise. He had no business missing another man's woman. But he did. It took him a moment to realize Joseph was still speaking.

"He's beautiful, Orion. Where'd you get him?"

"From Gray Eagle. He said there's some crazy old white man living up in the mountains, raising the most incredible horses. He breeds the wild mustangs with thoroughbreds, or some such thing. The result is a bigger horse with the speed and endurance of a mustang. He also does a great job of training the horses before he sells them."

"You can see the Spanish bloodlines passed down from the mustangs," Joseph said admiringly. His expression turned thoughtful. "I wonder who the man is—an old trapper, do you suppose? The Indian tribes wouldn't let just anybody homestead up there."

Orion draped the saddlebags over one shoulder. "I don't know. We'll have to ask Gray Eagle."

"It'll be good to see him again. Where is his band going to winter?"

"Farther south, somewhere along Elk Tooth Creek, near that heated mineral pool, I think. He promised he'd send word. I'm thinking I'd like to winter with them. There won't be much going on around here in terms of scouting until spring."

A wistful look came over Joseph's face. "That does sound good."

Orion moved toward the headquarters door. "You can always resign your commission," he teased over his shoulder.

"Yes, I could."

There was no answering hint of jest in Joseph's tone. Orion stared as his brother led Thunder away. Joseph had been so anxious to join the Army all those years ago. He had taken their uncle—their father's brother—up on his offer of a commission to West Point with great enthusiasm, and over the last ten years had spent most of his time in the East—with the exception of a year fighting the Mexicans in that recent war—while Orion had never been farther east than St. Louis, and was perfectly content to keep it that way. He always thought Joseph enjoyed his life in the military, but that did not seem true now. Something was definitely troubling his older brother, and Orion intended to find out what it was.

* * *

It wasn't until after supper was finished—Colonel Mackay had insisted that both brothers dine with him—that they had a chance to talk in private. They were in Joseph's cramped quarters, which consisted of one small room that boasted a narrow bed, a small stove which Orion feared would be next to useless when winter really set in, and one chair to go with the battered wooden table that also served as a desk. He had taken the chair, while Joseph sat on the edge of the bed. They each held a handleless clay cup, from which they periodically took swallows of the smooth whiskey Joseph had brought with him from their uncle's plantation in Virginia.

"Ma doesn't ever seem to age," Joseph said. "And I swear, Juliet gets more beautiful each time I see her; it's hard to believe she's near twenty years old now. And Cora—what a spirited little thing."

Orion laughed, his mind filled with the images of his two pretty sisters. "She'll be a handful when she grows up, that's for certain."

"She's grown up now, Orion. It was sort of spooky, seeing our little girls as lovely, grown women. I wish Jedediah was still alive to keep an eye on them. There's far too many men sniffing around their skirts for my liking." Joseph lifted his cup to his lips.

"Mama Florrie isn't going to let anyone hurt her girls," Orion assured him. "Juliet and Cora will be lucky if she lets a man near them before they turn thirty."

"I suppose you're right. Still, I don't like the family being so split up. With Jedediah gone, we're the men of the family—it seems one of us should be back there with the womenfolk."

Orion was silent for a minute as conflicting feelings warred within him. He agreed with Joseph—the women should have a man to look after them, even though both their mother and now their stepmother had done quite well on their own the many months Jedediah had been away each year. But the idea of living in a city chilled him to the bone. "Could you live in St. Louis?" he finally asked.

Joseph shrugged. "Maybe for a while."

"Well, I'd suffocate," Orion stated flatly. "And so would Gray Eagle, if the good citizens of the city didn't string him up first, just for being an Indian. And after a while, you'd suffocate, too, big brother. Maybe that's what's eating at you—now that you're back, you're realizing that you've been gone from home too long."

Joseph only stared at him.

"Hell, Joe, look around." Orion waved a hand to indicate the crude fort beyond the walls of the small room. "This place'll be civilized before we know it. Maybe we can bring Ma and the girls out here come spring."

"Maybe we can. I hadn't thought of that." Joseph visibly brightened. "Do you think they'd come?"

"Who knows? There's no telling with women."

"That's for certain. They might be willing, they might not. Of course, we could each put our foot down, you know, *insist.*"

Orion snorted. "Sure." He eyed his brother over the rim of his cup. "You've definitely been away too long if you think we can insist that Ma do anything she doesn't have a mind to do, and the same can be said for our 'spirited' sisters. Not even Jedediah could get Florrie to budge once she'd set her mind to something."

"You're right." Joseph reached for the whiskey bottle. "Maybe I have been gone too long," he said softly.

"Talk to me," Orion invited, shaking his head when Joseph held the bottle up questioningly.

Joseph poured a small amount into his cup and set the bottle down. He hooked a boot heel on the edge of the bed and leaned back across the thin mattress until his shoulders rested against the wall. "Things have changed since the end of the war with Mexico, Orion."

"Things in the Army have changed?"

"No, not really. And maybe that's part of the problem. I've changed, and the Army hasn't. The whole purpose behind all we are taught, all we train for, is to more effectively and efficiently fight a war. War is glorified in the teachings of the Army." A fleeting look of regret, or even sorrow, flashed across Joseph's face. "But I didn't find it much to my liking."

Orion looked down at his almost-empty cup. "It never appealed to me. I just don't enjoy killing, not even animals when it's necessary to eat."

"Me, neither. And we weren't fighting animals, although some felt that way. We were fighting Mexicans, who believed the United States had designs on their northern provinces, which we did. I don't know if the situation ever would have led to war had the Mexicans not started it, and I do believe President Polk did all he could to avoid war. But still, war came. And it isn't glorious." Joseph shook his head, and his voice softened when he spoke again. "The worst was the final march into *Ciudad de Mexico*. Those people were fighting for their homes, for their families, in some cases on their own front porches, in their own front rooms."

"At least now the land along the Rio Grande is no longer in dispute," Orion said dryly.

"No, we once again succeeded in taking land that belonged to someone else first, just as the white man has done in this country since he landed at Jamestown." Joseph pushed away from the wall and stood up to pace the dirt floor. One hand tightened around his cup while the other raked his dark hair.

"Is that what's bothering you?" Orion asked. "You regret your part in that war?"

"Yes, I do, but what's done is done." Joseph whirled around to face his brother, his dark eyes intense. "It's going to happen again, Orion. That's what's bothering me. It's going to happen here. And this time it will be our brothers—the Cheyenne and the Arapaho, as well as the Sioux, the Blackfeet, and all the other tribes—who will be fighting for their homes and their families on their own front porches."

Fear knotted Orion's stomach, a fear he resolutely forced down. "Come on, Joe. No white man wants this land. It's too inhospitable for their little crops and their farm animals. They're just passing through on their way to Oregon and California, and a few Mormons are trying to turn the arid valley of the Great Salt Lake into their Promised Land because they want to be left in peace. No one's going to stay here."

"You don't understand." Joseph set his empty cup down on the table. "You've never been back East. You don't know how many white men there are. Or how many of them believe in that Manifest Destiny the politicians are all espousing."

"Manifest Destiny?"

"The belief that God Himself has ordained that the light of democracy shall shine from the Atlantic to the Pacific. The Americans are His Chosen People, the ones to carry that torch of democracy into the far reaches of the land, regardless of the wishes of the people who already inhabit some of those territories. People like the Mexicans who lived in California, people like the Cheyenne who live here." Joseph pointed a finger at Orion. "Mark my word, brother. The day is coming when some of the immigrants rushing through this land will stop and look around. And when they do, they'll see what we see: a beautiful land of plenty. But they won't be content to use the land as it is, to take what it so freely offers, as the Cheyenne do. The whites will want to tame the land, to fence it and tear it up, as they did in the East. And they'll want the Indians gone, just as they wanted the Mexicans gone from Texas and the Rio Grande and California, just as they wanted the Indians gone from the North, and the East, and the South."

Orion stared at Joseph, horrified, unable to think of anything to say.

Joseph's shoulders slumped in abject weariness, a weariness that Orion could tell reached to his brother's soul. Joseph *had* changed, drastically and tragically so.

"It's only a matter of time," Joseph said tiredly as he rubbed his eyes. "These forts are the beginning, and I want no part of it. That is the reason I am seriously considering resigning my commission. I will not raise my sword against my Cheyenne brothers."

"What will you do?" Orion set his cup next to Joseph's.

"I don't know yet." Joseph sank back down on the bed. "There's no standing against a tidal wave. And that's what it will be—a tidal wave of farmers, or, God forbid, miners, if gold is ever found anywhere out here. Maybe it won't happen for another twenty, thirty years, but the wave is coming. I'd like to do something to ease the transition, maybe to act as a mediator between the red world and the white. I just have to figure out the best way to do it."

"We'll think of something."

Joseph looked at him. "We?"

"I wish I could say your vision of the future is wrong, Joseph, but the knot in my gut tells me you're right. I'll play no role in driving the Cheyenne from their land. We'll work together with Gray Eagle. The Beaudine brothers are a force to be reckoned with." He held out his hand.

Joseph grabbed Orion's forearm near his elbow and the men clutched each other. "No one else understands, Orion. I'm glad you do."

"I do, brother. You are not alone." Orion was pleased to see some of the tension leave his brother's face. "It's good you've come home."

Orion stayed at Fort Laramie for over a week. He bunked down in Joseph's quarters, sleeping on a pallet they fashioned in one corner. He treasured the time with his older brother, for they had always been close; indeed, all of the five Beaudine siblings were close. Orion kept his promise and took Joseph riding one afternoon. Within the hour, Dancer appeared, running alongside the horses. The brothers spent an enjoyable afternoon on top of a hill, sharing a cold lunch with Dancer.

To help fill his time while he waited for dispatches expected to arrive from the East any day, Orion wrote long letters to each of his sisters and to his stepmother. He had to stop himself from mentioning Sarah Hancock in those letters, and was surprised that he had felt the urge to tell his sisters about her. Why had she had such an impact on him? He had known her for only three days, and yet it felt like much longer than that. In some ways, he felt that he had known her forever, almost as if there were a mystical bond between them. But, as she had said, they were friends. Only friends. And come spring, she would marry another man.

The awaited dispatches arrived, and, as Colonel Mackay had anticipated, some were for Colonel Rutledge. Orion would leave the next day for Fort St. Charles. That night, he and Joseph again shared the fine whiskey while they talked.

"Have you given any more thought to resigning?" Orion asked.

"I'm sure I'll resign," Joseph answered, swirling the whiskey around in the clay cup. "The longer I'm here, the more obvious it becomes to me that I will. I just don't know when yet."

"Where do you think you'll settle down?"

Joseph flashed him a grin. "Who said anything about settling down? I've given a lot of thought to moving Ma and the sisters out here, and I like the idea. Then maybe I'll do like you—hire on with the Army as a scout. At least that way I can keep on top of what's happening."

"Do you have any trustworthy contacts in the Army who'll feed you information once you've resigned?"

"Maybe. I served with a Major Rutledge for a while; now I hear he's a colonel and commanding Fort St. Charles down south of here."

Orion nodded. "He has spoken of you. He seems like a good man, one whose word can be trusted."

"He is," Joseph assured him. "I heard there were two women down there, too, following their men. One has to be the colonel's wife. She always insisted upon following him to every post."

"You're right. Mrs. Colonel Rutledge is there, demanding plank floors for the cabin and serving supper on white linen tablecloths. She's a character."

"You're being kind, Orion, unless she's changed since I knew her. She was a martinet, making life miserable for the enlisted men unfortunate enough to be assigned to seeing to her needs. Everything had to be perfect, and she never thought it was, despite their best efforts. And she doesn't think much of any white man who would leave his own kind to live with the Indians."

Orion smiled. "She's made that very clear, while Colonel Rutledge treats me with nothing but respect. They're an odd match, and yet their marriage seems to work. I really believe they are devoted to each other."

Joseph nodded his agreement. "Strange, isn't it?"

Orion could not help but think of another odd match—Captain Adam Rutledge and Miss Sarah Hancock. If ever two people were not suited for each other, it was them. He could not stop the next question from escaping his lips. "Do you know Colonel Rutledge's nephew? Captain Adam Rutledge?"

"I met him once, when he was just out of West Point. Why do you ask?"

"No real reason," Orion answered with a nonchalant shrug. "He's posted to Fort St. Charles as well. I was just curious what you thought of him."

"I heard he distinguished himself in the Mexican War, got promoted. Seemed like a nice enough fellow—very correct and dedicated. He should go far in the Army." Joseph's eyes narrowed in thought. "Is the second woman his wife?"

"She's not his wife," Orion snapped. "She's his fiancée."

Joseph stared at him. "Didn't mean to set you off, little

brother." One eyebrow rose. "You seem awful touchy about this woman. What is she to you?"

Orion reached for the bottle. "She's my friend, that's all. She's a nice lady."

"And you think she deserves better than Captain Adam Rutledge."

After a long moment, Orion looked up at Joseph. He wasn't really surprised by his brother's astute observation. Joseph knew him well. "Yes, I do," he finally answered.

"What does the lady think?"

Suddenly very uncomfortable with the conversation, Orion took a drink before he answered. "I guess she thinks he'll do. She agreed to marry him, and Miss Sarah Hancock is no one's fool."

"Sarah Hancock," Joseph repeated softly. "A nice name for a nice lady."

Orion glared at him. "Don't tease me about this."

"Well, you told me she was nice." Joseph peered at his brother, all traces of humor gone. "She's important to you."

After another long moment, Orion spoke, quietly and soberly. "She understands the Power of the Wolf, Joseph. And of the land. She heard the spirits of the four winds."

Joseph let his breath out in a long sigh. "That is rare, especially in a white woman." He paused before he spoke, and when he did, he seemed to be choosing his words with great care. "For what my advice is worth, stay out of it. Let her make up her own mind." Another pause. "And it sounds to me like she has," he finished gently.

"She agreed to marry him before she knew me."

"And you think you'll make her change her mind? Is that what you hope? If she does, then what? You'll marry her? And live where? How will your Miss Sarah Hancock feel about spending the winter in a tipi on the banks of Elk Tooth Creek, surrounded by the Cheyenne?"

"I don't know," Orion said, somewhat defensively, slumping down in his chair. "I don't know what I want. I just know

I don't want her to marry Rutledge." He looked at Joseph. "He'll break her spirit."

"Then be her friend, Orion. But be careful. Let her make the calls. The situation could blow up in your face."

"That I do know," Orion said glumly.

The eastern sky was only beginning to lighten when Orion climbed into the saddle. Thunder was restless after the days of inactivity, and ready to run. He tossed his head and danced with impatience.

"Be careful, little brother." Joseph stood next to the horse, holding his hand up. Orion took it, and the men shook hands.

"I always am." Orion repeated the same words he had said to Sarah ten days earlier. Why was everyone cautioning him to be careful?

Joseph released his hand. "There was some information in one of the dispatches about a few wagons being harassed between here and Fort Kearny on the Platte River Road. The freighters swore it was Indians."

"Could have been, although there've been reports of some white men causing trouble, too," Orion said. "You know people will prey on their own kind. But there's been no trouble to the south, where I'm headed. It's too far off the beaten path." He settled his hat more firmly on his head. "The rush through here last summer was unbelievable, Joseph, and there were sporadic attacks, mostly to steal. I know the number of immigrants alone made some of the tribes nervous. And the rush will start again come spring, because people go crazy with the desire to find gold. I just hope nothing flares out of control."

"Me, too. But then, that's why the Army is here—to make sure that doesn't happen." A note of sarcasm had slipped into Joseph's tone. He stepped back. "Best be on your way, brother. Daylight's wasting." He raised his hand in farewell. "Watch your back."

Orion held the eager Thunder in check. "It's not like you to worry about me, Joe. Do you have a bad feeling?"

Joseph shrugged. "Maybe I do. Just be careful."

"I will." Orion finally gave Thunder his head, and the stallion jumped to a run, crossing the empty parade ground just as the sleepy soldiers were lining up for the reveille roll call. The notes of the bugle sounded clear in the chilled early morning air. Orion was glad to be leaving the fort, glad to be heading into his beloved wilderness again. And, he admitted to himself with reluctant honesty, he was glad that with every step, Thunder took him one step closer to Sarah Hancock.

Seven

Sarah straightened from the tub of steaming laundry water over which she was leaning, and put a hand to her aching back. The October day had seemed cool when she and Lucy had pulled the heavy washtubs out near the fire that one of the soldiers built for them a short distance from the back of the Rutledges' cabin. It did not seem cool any longer. She would be glad when the Army made their decision about Fort St. Charles, for more than one reason. Until a decision was reached about whether or not to keep the little outpost manned, no laundresses would be sent from Fort Laramie. The officers and a few of the men had been fortunate enough to enlist the aid of the three Mexican women who lived nearby, but most of the enlisted men had to make do with washing their uniforms themselves.

Lucy, of course, saw to the colonel's uniforms and had also taken care of Adam's, but in her renewed determination to be a good wife, Sarah now insisted upon doing Adam's uniforms herself, at least until the laundresses arrived. She had found the task not much to her liking.

"Lord have mercy, Lucy," Sarah said, wiping a thin sheen of perspiration off her forehead with the hem of her apron. "How do the laundresses do this all the time?"

"It's a hard job, that's for sure. But it pays, and the women get to be with their menfolk. Guess it's worth it to them."

Sarah knew that most of the Army laundresses were married to enlisted men, and the few who remained single did so by their own choice rather than from a lack of suitors. "I can understand that," she said. "I'd want to stay with my man, even if it took being a laundress to do it."

"You won't have to be a laundress to stay with the captain," Lucy assured her.

"No." *Just a perfect Army wife.* Sarah glanced at Lucy, then returned to her task with renewed vigor. "You work so quickly, Lucy," she said, feeling both admiration and envy. "I can't believe you're finished with the colonel's uniforms already."

Lucy shrugged. "Speed comes with practice. You'll get faster, Miss Sarah." She turned to the basket of soiled table linens that awaited her attention.

Sarah still felt that Harriet's insistence on using fresh table linens every night was impractical, and she was angered by the extra work the woman's extravagance made for Lucy. "I don't know what Mrs. Colonel Rutledge would do without you," she commented. "She sure wouldn't have the luxury of clean table linens every night."

"Yes, she would," Lucy calmly replied. "She'd wash and iron them her own self. She has done so in the past."

"You must be joking. Somehow I can't see Mrs. Colonel Rutledge bending over a laundry caldron, or a heavy iron."

"The Mrs. Colonel will do whatever is necessary to make the colonel's home a pleasant and proper one, Miss Sarah, be that home a cabin or a tent. She stakes her pride on it." Lucy paused before correcting herself. "No, it would not be too much to say that it is her main reason for living, especially since she and the colonel lost their son. She must find an outlet for her energies. That is also why she dotes so on Captain Rutledge, and expects so much from you." The woman's large dark eyes softened with patient understanding. "Perhaps if you can see those things about her, you can forgive her other occasional unkindnesses."

Sarah focused on the wool shirt she had just dropped in

the soapy water, suddenly ashamed. She knew the Rutledges had lost their son and only child several years earlier, and that he had been a soldier like his father, but she knew none of the details. Was it possible that Harriet had never completely recovered from her son's death? If she hadn't, that would explain much about her frustrated personality. Sarah felt a pang of sympathy for the woman. "Perhaps I have been hasty in my judgment of her."

"Oh, don't be hard on yourself, miss. She's made it difficult for you to see her in a more compassionate light."

With a smile, Sarah looked up at Lucy. "Thank you," she said softly. "I don't think you're much older than I, but you are much wiser. I appreciate your gentle teachings."

Lucy seemed taken aback. "Fiddlesticks, Miss Sarah." She turned away, but not before Sarah saw a pleased smile lift the corners of Lucy's mouth. She felt a rush of affection for the woman.

"Lucy, I wish you would drop the 'miss' you insist upon putting before my name," she said impulsively. "Please just call me Sarah."

"No, miss. Wouldn't be proper. Besides, the Mrs. Colonel would have my head."

"Not even when it's just the two of us, like now?"

"No." Lucy punctuated the word with a determined shake of her head.

"But we are both free women, and therefore free to address each other as we see fit."

At that, Lucy turned around, her hands at her hips. Sarah saw, with a sinking feeling, that the shuttered expression had come over Lucy's face again.

"We may both be free, Miss Sarah, but we ain't equal, and we never will be. Free or not, I am a servant, and I will always be someone's servant, while you will soon be an officer's wife, ordering your own servants around just like the Mrs. Colonel does. There is a natural order to things, and

that order shouldn't be messed with. Ladies and their servants are not friends."

"But you're not my servant," Sarah protested, knowing
she was wasting her breath.

"Don't matter." Lucy's fierce expression softened. "I
know you're lonesome somewhat, but soon the other women
will come, and things will be better."

Stung by the implication of Lucy's words, Sarah said, "I
don't want your friendship simply because I'm lonely. It's
because of who you are. I think we can be friends, Lucy."

A look of sadness came over Lucy's face. "Maybe in a
perfect world, Miss Sarah. But not in this one."

"Lucy!" Harriet's strident voice came from the cabin.

"Coming, ma'am," Lucy called. She hurried toward the
back door, pausing before she stepped inside to look at Sarah.
Then she disappeared inside.

Sarah sank down onto a log near the fire and again wiped
her face. "I hope I didn't offend her," she whispered to herself, but she feared she had. She didn't seem to be able to
do anything right, to say anything right, to anyone.

Except Orion Beaudine.

Almost against her will, her gaze turned again toward the
nearly completed gate. Since his departure for Fort Laramie
over a week ago, she had caught herself looking for him,
several times a day. He seemed to understand her, and she,
him. Even though she had no business doing so, she missed
him.

She was also worried about him, and she didn't know why.
Ever since she watched Orion ride away, she had fought a
nagging fear that he was in some kind of danger. The fear
would not be laid to rest until she saw him again, safe. Perhaps that was why she watched for him. She just wanted to
see him safe.

Liar.

Yes, she wanted to see him safe, but she also wanted to
see *him.* She wanted to go riding with him. She wanted to

talk with him, or not talk with him, for she was just as comfortable with him in silence. She longed for the easy acceptance and friendship he offered her. *And his kiss, which had shaken her world.*

Sarah clenched her fists in determination. She would not think of the handsome scout. She would think instead of her handsome captain. With conscious effort, she banished the image of Orion Beaudine from her mind and replaced him with Adam Rutledge.

Things had been better between them lately, and Adam had been very attentive, at least in terms of how often he came to see her. Each night he joined her and the Rutledges for supper, and once he had astonished her by calling on her at midday, just to say hello. Twice he had taken her riding, but both excursions had been of disappointingly short duration, and Adam did not seem to really enjoy them. Although he was always pleasant during their time together, Sarah often had the feeling his thoughts were elsewhere. Once Lieutenant Fielding had offered to take her riding, but Sarah had refused, pleading a headache. She would be glad when he returned to Fort Laramie.

Sarah's reverie was broken by the sound of a rifle shot, then another. Excited shouting followed, then more shots. Sarah's heart pounded. Were they under attack? If so, she, Harriet, and Lucy needed to get to the old stockade at once.

She jumped to her feet and started toward the cabin, glancing back over her shoulder. Although more soldiers had grabbed their rifles, they were not taking cover. Some actually laughed. Curious now rather than frightened, Sarah changed her direction and hurried to the gate.

"What is it?" she asked the first soldier she came upon.

The young man did not turn around. "Damned if I know." Then he looked at her, and his eyes widened, as if he had just realized who he was speaking to. "Uh, ma'am. Sorry, ma'am. Heard one of the boys say it was a wolf or something, ma'am."

Sarah's heart started pounding again. "A wolf?"

"Ma'am, there's no need to be afraid," the young soldier said reassuringly. "We won't let it hurt you. It'll be dead in no time." Another round of shots filled the air. "Maybe it is now," he added helpfully.

"Oh, no," she moaned. A sickness roiled around in her stomach. *Dancer.*

Sarah ran out to the line of men who were shooting across the river. "What are you shooting at?" she cried.

Lieutenant Fielding approached and took her elbow in a firm grip, pulling her back. "They're shooting at a wolf, Miss Hancock. Perhaps they will present you with the tail, as they do after a fox hunt."

Sarah glared up at him through narrowed eyes. "Order them to stop shooting."

Fielding laughed. "And spoil their sport? I think not."

"Then I will." Sarah jerked her arm from his grasp, whirled about, and marched back to the line of men. She grabbed the sleeve of the closest soldier and pulled, hard. "Lower your weapon, sir," she commanded. The surprised soldier did as she said.

Fielding hurried to once again take her arm, this time in a bruising grip. There was no sign of a smile on his face now. "I shall have to escort you away from here, Miss Hancock. It's dangerous." His tone was fierce rather than concerned.

"Take your hand off me, Lieutenant." Sarah trembled from the force of her anger. "Now."

Fielding stared at her, his fury making his eyes almost glow. "Don't defy me, Miss Hancock," he warned.

Deep inside, Sarah felt a pang of warning, of fear, but she ignored it. "It is not your place to order me about," she answered in a dangerously soft tone. "Do not make me send for Captain Rutledge." She noticed the shooting had stopped. The afternoon was suddenly very quiet.

"You will regret this," Fielding whispered. His fingers

tightened on her arm even more, then he released her and strode away.

Sarah willed herself not to grab her aching arm, for the instinctive gesture would not keep the bruise she knew she would have from forming. She took a deep, steadying breath, then turned to face the group of silent soldiers.

"Were you indeed shooting at a wolf?" she asked.

"Yes, ma'am," a young, red-haired man answered. "Don't know that we got it, though. It was pretty fast."

"But it's unusual for a wolf to come so close to the fort, ma'am, at least in daylight," another soldier offered encouragingly. "It shouldn't happen again."

"I sure hope we didn't frighten you with our shenanigans, ma'am," another said.

"No," Sarah responded. "Will one of you please point out to me where it was?"

The red-haired soldier offered his arm to her. "I will, ma'am."

She laid her hand on his arm and allowed him to lead her to the bank of the river.

"It was over there, near that stand of trees, ma'am."

"Thank you." Sarah moved away from the soldier and walked a few feet up the river. When he started to follow her, she waved him back. "Please stay there, sir."

The soldier nervously glanced back at his friends. "Uh, ma'am, please don't go far. The captain'll skin me alive if anything happens to you. He'll skin all of us."

"Nothing will happen to me," Sarah promised. "I won't leave your sight." She walked a little farther, then stopped and shaded her eyes with her hand, searching the far bank for any sign of movement. There was none except that of the wind, whispering across the dead grasses. "Dancer," she whispered sorrowfully. She could feel his presence, just as she always could. She prayed it was not his departed spirit she felt now.

"What are you looking for, ma'am?" the soldier called. "Maybe we can help you."

"You can't help, sir." Sarah struggled to keep the fear and anger she felt out of her voice. Even if the soldiers had succeeded in killing the wolf, could she really blame them? Ingrained beliefs and old habits died hard. Wolves, coyotes, bears, cougars—all were considered fair game on sight, at least by most people.

Across the river, something moved.

Or was it her imagination? Sarah squinted against the harsh afternoon sunlight, struggling to see into the shadows of the distant trees. "Dancer." This time she called his name.

"Dancer?" the soldier behind her repeated disbelievingly. "Ma'am, are you calling to that wolf?"

"Yes, she is, soldier. Hush up."

Sarah whirled around at the sound of that rough, familiar voice. "Mr. Sage!" she cried happily. Her glad eyes took in the sight of a tall, lanky man with long gray hair and a bushy beard, dressed in colorfully and elaborately beaded buckskins. One eagle feather decorated the fur cap atop his head, while another, tied to the barrel of the Hawken rifle he cradled in his arms, danced in the wind.

"Miss Hancock." Jubal Sage nodded at her. "Is that Hunter Beaudine's wolf you're callin' for?"

"Yes, sir," Sarah answered. "These men were shooting at a wolf; Dancer is the only one I know. I thought it might be him."

"It just might be." Jubal pointed across the river with his rifle.

Sarah whirled again. Her heart soared to see a wolf cautiously peering from the trees. "Dancer!"

The animal's ears pricked up. Sarah remembered how Orion had stood, on the banks of that very river, and pointed to the ground at his feet. Dancer had come then. Would he come now? She straightened, again took a steadying breath, and pointed to the ground. In case it would help, she added a silent prayer.

She would never know if the prayer was what did it.

The wolf came. Slowly. Warily. He paused at the edge of the water.

Sarah's stomach knotted when she saw a red smear along the animal's side. He had been hit. Her eyes filled with tears, but she rapidly blinked them away. Now was not the time to cry.

Dancer picked his way across the shallow river and came to stand in front of her. She dropped to her knees and was reaching for him when the sound of a rifle being cocked echoed in the eerie silence of the afternoon. Without a moment's hesitation, Sarah threw her arms around the wolf, shielding him with her body.

"Move away from the wolf, Miss Hancock." Lieutenant Roger Fielding's arrogant, angry voice sounded across the clearing.

Instead, Sarah tightened her hold on Dancer, a part of her surprised that the wolf didn't try to escape. When a second cocking sound reached her ears, she looked back over her shoulder.

Lieutenant Fielding stood braced on the bank near the group of soldiers, a rifle at his shoulder. Jubal Sage still sat his horse, but now the Hawken he had carried so nonchalantly was poised and aimed at Fielding.

"Lower the weapon, Lieutenant."

"Don't interfere in a military matter, old man." Fielding's voice was heavy with scorn. "A military dependent is in imminent danger. I shall see to her safety." His rifle did not waver.

"The only danger Miss Hancock is in right now is from you, Fielding, and I mean to see that she comes to no harm."

"I won't miss the wolf, damn you."

"I don't know that, now do I? I've never seen you shoot," Jubal said conversationally. "I do know that I won't miss you."

He raised the Hawken to his shoulder and took aim. "If your trigger finger so much as trembles, you're a dead man."

Sarah stared at the two men, horrified. As if he had struck her with a flaming sword, she felt the hot force of Roger Fielding's hate, even across the distance that separated them. She did not trust that he wouldn't shoot.

"What in hell is going on here?" Colonel Rutledge's authoritative voice boomed over the area. "Lieutenant, lower your weapon."

"Yes, sir!" Fielding shouted.

"You, too, Mr. Sage," the colonel said. "There'll be no shooting here, at least not until I figure out what is going on. Then I might decide to shoot someone myself."

Sarah closed her eyes and buried her face in Dancer's sun-warmed fur. Her body trembled. The wolf whined and licked her arm. Then she remembered his wound. Fearful that she might hurt him, she gently ran her hand over the blood smeared on his side; it was dry and stiff, and had matted Dancer's fur. A quick examination showed no wound beneath. The blood wasn't his. Then whose was it?

Orion.

A wave of terror welled up in Sarah's heart. "Where is he, Dancer?" she whispered, her voice cracking. "Where is Orion?" His name rolled off her tongue easily. Sometime in the past week he had ceased being Mr. Beaudine. Now he was simply Orion.

As if he understood her, Dancer pulled away from her and ran across the river. He stopped and looked at her, then whined again.

Sarah scrambled to her feet and hurried back to Jubal Sage. "He wants us to follow him, Mr. Sage."

"Looks that way, don't it?"

"I'll get my horse," Sarah said breathlessly. She nodded at the colonel and was about to rush off toward the stables when Adam approached. Every line of his rigid body gave evidence of his mood. She met his angry glare, then glanced beyond him, to the other soldiers. They were watching her in awe, looking from her to the wolf across the river, and back again.

"What is going on, Sarah?" Adam demanded. "Lieutenant Fielding said something about you being endangered by a wolf. And why do you need your horse?"

"The only danger I was in came from the lieutenant," she said. "Mr. Sage kept me from harm. I need my horse because Mr. Sage and I are going to follow the wolf."

Adam stared at her as if she had lost her mind. "You're going to follow the wolf? What are you talking about?"

"Or—Mr. Beaudine is in trouble, Adam. We really don't have time to talk." She pushed by him.

"Sarah, wait!" Adam spun around and grabbed her arm. "How do you know Beaudine is in trouble?"

Sarah winced as Adam's fingers tightened on the bruises Lieutenant Fielding had given her. "Dancer made it very clear. Please let me go."

Looking more confused than ever, Adam released her. "Who is Dancer?"

"The wolf," Sarah explained impatiently. "Now come. I need you to help me saddle my horse. There is no time to lose."

Adam grabbed her again, now by her hand. "Let me get this straight. You and Sage are going to follow the wolf because the animal somehow conveyed to you that Beaudine is hurt?"

Sarah looked at him. For the first time, she realized how her words must sound to other people. Even the colonel was staring at her. Only Jubal Sage seemed comfortable. "Yes," she finally said, firmly.

"The hell you are," Adam said through gritted teeth. "You are going home this instant."

Sarah pulled away from him. "No. Mr. Beaudine is in trouble, Adam. Please come with us. We may need help."

"An escort isn't a bad idea," said Jubal calmly.

Colonel Rutledge stepped forward. "Mr. Sage, do you agree with what Miss Hancock is saying?"

"Yes, sir, I do. That's Beaudine's wolf, all right, and the two ain't never far apart. For the wolf to approach the fort, feelin' like he does about most folks, somethin' has to be wrong." He shifted his rifle. "I suggest we stop jawin' and get on the trail."

"Captain, ready a detachment of six men and accompany Mr. Sage. See what you can find."

"Yes, sir." The tic in Adam's jaw muscle indicated his displeasure.

"The rest of you men get back to work." Colonel Rutledge disappeared into the compound.

Dancer howled.

"I'm going, too," Sarah said quietly.

"No, you're not," Adam snapped. His voice dropped. "Don't argue with me, Sarah, not here, not in front of others."

Although a strong pang of guilt assaulted her, she remained firm. "I'm sorry, but I must do this. The wolf came for me; I can understand him."

"I will not allow your horse to be saddled. My men will obey me, even if you won't."

Sarah grabbed his arm. "I'm begging you, Adam. You must let me come."

"Absolutely not. Go home." The cold fury in his eyes frightened Sarah. He shook her hand off and turned away.

"I'm gonna get started, Captain," Jubal called out. "Catch up as soon as you can."

"Fine." Adam marched into the compound.

Sarah fought tears of frustration and fear as she stared across the river at Dancer. The wolf howled again. "I *must* go," she whispered.

"Are you married to the captain yet?" Jubal asked casually. She shook her head.

"Then you don't have to do like he says, not unless you want to, Miss Hancock. You ain't in the Army yet."

Sarah looked up at him, her heart suddenly alive with hope. Did she dare do as Jubal was suggesting? "He will be angry."

"Reckon so. Reckon he'll get over it. Reckon it won't be the last time in his life he gets angry."

Sarah smiled. "I reckon not. I'll get my hat and shawl if you'll get my horse."

"There's no time." Jubal took his battered hat off and leaned down from the saddle to plop the thing on Sarah's head. "Now you have a hat, and one of my extra blankets will work as a shawl, when you want it." He held his hand down to her.

With a broad grin, Sarah grabbed it and swung up behind him, very grateful that because she had been doing laundry, she wore no hoops. "You were just coming in, Mr. Sage. Aren't your horses tired?" She glanced back over her shoulder at the patient packhorse.

"They'll live. If we don't get a move on, our friend, Mr. Beaudine, may not." He urged the horse into the river, and the packhorse followed.

Jubal's words had a sobering effect on Sarah. She put her arms around the wiry mountain man's waist and held on, saying a silent prayer for her friend, Mr. Beaudine. *Orion.*

Eight

After two hours of hard riding, during which time Adam and his detachment did not catch up to them, Dancer led Jubal and Sarah to a small hill overlooking the Laramie River. Jubal approached the area slowly, cautiously, his rifle cocked and ready. Then he pulled the horse to a stop and waited, listening, even sniffing the air. Sarah knew to remain quiet.

After what seemed like a long time to her, he lifted one leg over the front of the saddle and slipped to the ground.

"Get into the saddle, girl," he ordered in a low tone. "If I tell you to, ride, and I mean ride for your life."

Sarah did as she was told. She lifted herself over the cantle and took the reins Jubal handed her. As much as she hated the idea of leaving before they found Orion, the thought of arguing with Jubal Sage never crossed her mind. Mr. Sage was not a man to argue with; in addition, he did not issue commands without having a good reason for doing so. Her stomach knotted, and for the first time in her life, she experienced the dry, metallic taste of fear she had once heard Adam describe; she was afraid for herself, for Jubal, and terribly afraid for Orion. She prayed they were in time.

Dancer climbed the hill and disappeared into a jumbled formation of rocks. A moment later, he emitted a series of excited yips. Jubal crossed the remaining distance to the rocks, and when he reached them, motioned over his shoulder for Sarah to come ahead. She urged the horse forward, then stopped at the base of the hill and dismounted. Without hesitation, she scrambled up the hill after Jubal.

They found Orion wedged into a small space formed by the meeting of two rocks, in a half-sitting position, his long knife clutched in one hand.

"It's about damn time you got here, Jubal." Orion's voice sounded raspy and alarmingly weak, but it was one of the sweetest sounds Sarah had ever heard.

Jubal snorted. "Don't get lippy with me, Orion Beaudine. You're just lucky I was around to pull you out of this mess you got yourself into. Miss Hancock is here, too, so watch your mouth."

"Sarah." Orion whispered her name as he closed his eyes and leaned his head back against the rock.

Sarah peered around Jubal's shoulder to study Orion's un-moving form. Intense relief and gladness filled her at the sight of him, as well as horror and an overwhelming fear. An arrow, with the shaft broken, protruded from his right thigh, and another from his left shoulder. Very little of the original golden color of his buckskin shirt remained on the blood-soaked left side. The late afternoon wind blew a strand of his long hair over one stubble-covered cheek, the hair appearing very dark against the unnatural paleness of his skin. There was no sign of his hat, or of his horse, now that she thought about it.

"Hold this." Jubal's terse words snapped Sarah out of her troubled daze, and she accepted the heavy rifle he held out to her. He stared at her for a minute, as if he were assessing her state.

"I'm fine, Mr. Sage," she said quietly.

He nodded in approval. "Figured you would be; just makin' sure. It's a hard sight to see, one of your friends all hurt like this." He turned back to Orion. "Come on, son; let's get you down to some flat ground." He pried the knife out of Orion's hand and gave that to Sarah as well, then draped Orion's arm over his own shoulders.

"I could use some water, Jubal." Orion grimaced when Jubal pulled him to his feet.

"I know. We'll get you some soon as you're settled."

Sarah led the way the short distance down the hill to where the horses waited. Dancer followed them, staying close to Orion's heels. The horses did not seem to mind that a wolf was in their midst. With care, Jubal guided Orion to a sitting position on the grass.

"I'll get you some fresh water," he said, and took off at a trot for the packhorse, then for the river. Sarah moved to Orion's side and dropped to her knees, laying the rifle and knife aside, while Dancer sat down at his other side. A strange whining whimper escaped the wolf.

"Dancer," Orion breathed. He did not seem to have the strength to say more.

"Why don't you lie down?" Sarah struggled to keep the fear from her voice. She gave into the need to touch him and lightly patted his unwounded shoulder.

"After the water," he mumbled, his chin dropping to his chest.

Jubal returned with a tin cup of water and a blanket, which he placed around Orion's shoulders. He pressed the cup into Orion's hand, then supported his shoulders while Orion drank. "You can have more later," Jubal promised when the cup was empty. "Now lay back and rest while we get ready to do some doctorin'."

Orion obeyed. Jubal supported him as he lay down, and when his head rested on the ground, he sighed and closed his eyes.

"It's gettin' late to be headin' to the fort," Jubal said. "And my horses are tired. We'll stay here tonight."

Sarah nodded her agreement. "What can I do?"

"We have to get those arrows out of him, and more water and some food into him." Jubal squinted as he surveyed the area. "I'd sure like a chance to look around, see if I can figure out what happened here, before it gets too dark or those soldiers come and trample all the sign."

Sarah had forgotten that Adam was on their trail and would probably show up very soon. She did not want to see him, for an ugly scene would surely follow when he discovered that she had disobeyed him.

"We'll need hot water," she said, forcing the thought of Adam from her mind. "Do you have anything to use as washing cloths and bandages?"

"I was thinkin' that your apron would do nicely," Jubal answered, nodding at the article tied around her waist.

"Of course." Sarah immediately untied the strings. "It was clean this morning."

"I'll build a fire first thing." Jubal hauled himself to his feet. "We'll get water on to boil, then I'll scout around a bit. There's no tellin' when those soldiers will come." He headed toward a stand of trees a short distance away. Sarah watched him go, then at last responded to the urge to brush the hair away from Orion's face. "Orion." She whispered his name. He turned his head toward her, and his lips curved in a faint smile, but he did not open his eyes. Sarah's own eyes filled with tears, which she tried in vain to blink away. She took Jubal's hat off and laid it next to the rifle. After laying her hand gently on Orion's forehead for a moment, she rolled up her sleeves and set to work.

In short order, a fire was hungrily devouring the pile of sticks and small logs Jubal had set within a circle of river stones. A battered coffeepot and a cast-iron stew pot, both filled with water from the nearby river, sat over the flames on an ingenious collapsible grate Jubal had retrieved from his packhorse. While Jubal prowled the surrounding area on astonishingly silent feet, Sarah busied herself with cutting her apron into long strips, using Orion's knife. It sickened her to see where the broken shaft of the embedded arrow kept the blanket from laying on Orion's shoulder. She fought the powerful urge to grab the hateful thing and wrench it from his body, as well as the one in his leg. They would go into the fire as soon as Orion was free of them, she vowed.

Jubal returned to her side. "They were waitin' for him over there, four of them." He pointed to a stand of trees at the far edge of the hill. "I think he got at least two of 'em, though, judgin' from where the grass was flattened and stained with blood."

"I did," Orion mumbled.

Sarah shuddered at the thought of four armed men lying in wait for a single man. The treachery and cowardice of the attack sickened her. "Did they take his horse?"

"I don't think so. I know Thunder's track, and he headed north. One followed him, but gave up the chase at the river. Dancer was involved in the battle, too. His tracks are all over the place. Scared the hell outta their horses." Jubal suddenly ducked his head. "Beg pardon, Miss Sarah, for my swearin'."

"It's all right," Sarah said softly. She laid a hand on Jubal's forearm. "The water is hot. We need to see to Mr. Beaudine now."

Jubal nodded and rose, then went to the packhorse. He returned in a few minutes with his arms full. Sarah helped him arrange the articles he brought.

"We'll make him a bed over here, close enough to the fire for a little warmth, but not so close that he can be seen from a distance come dark." He spread a buffalo robe on the ground, then turned to Orion. "Gotta move you one more time, Hunter," he said gently.

Orion struggled to push himself to a sitting position. Sarah and Jubal helped him to his feet and together they crossed the short distance to the robe. Orion sank down on it with a sigh of relief. Again, Sarah brushed the hair away from his face. Jubal held his own knife in the fire for a minute, then grabbed the pot of water and a dented washbasin and returned to Orion's side. "Hold him down if he struggles, girl."

Jubal's rough tone told Sarah that he did not relish what

he was about to do. Sarah nodded, swallowing against the bile that threatened to come up from her stomach. She closed her eyes and said a quick prayer for all of them—that Orion would survive, that Jubal's hand would be steady, that she would not embarrass herself by crying, fainting, or, worst of all, throwing up.

Orion survived, Jubal's hand was steady, and Sarah amazed herself by how calm she remained through the ordeal. It was surprisingly easy to stay calm, she found, when she focused all of her attention and concern on Orion. All that mattered was his well-being.

She helped pull away the ruined shirt when Jubal cut it off him, and moved the intriguing beaded necklace around Orion's neck to one side. She kept a section of the apron warm and rinsed as best she could, ready to catch the blood that seeped from around the arrow and would no doubt gush when Jubal pulled the arrow out. Orion didn't struggle, but he did hold Sarah's hand in a grip that gradually—and painfully—tightened. When at last Orion's shoulder was free of the bloody arrow, Sarah's hand ached from the crushing strength of Orion's hand, her lower lip bled where she bit it while watching Orion's face contort with pain, and Orion was unconscious, the pain, the loss of blood, and dehydration finally catching up to him. His loss of consciousness was a blessing, one Jubal took quick advantage of.

"I'll pull that arrow from his leg while he's out. You hold this here cloth over the shoulder wound and wash him off as best you can." He stood up and came around to her side. "I'll take that necklace off him and put it in my pack, so's it won't be in your way." He took Sarah's arm and helped her to her feet. "I know this is hard on you—you've prob'ly never seen so much blood. You're doin' just fine, girl."

"Thank you, Mr. Sage," Sarah said, although she didn't think she was doing fine at all. The terror that Orion might die had formed a knot in her stomach that made her feel ill, and her heart ached for the pain he was suffering. As she knelt at his side, she looked at the broad, muscular, and bloody expanse of his naked chest. He was breathing, but he was also so still!

Already the blood had saturated the piece of cloth over the wound. Sarah quickly rinsed the cloth in the now red-tinged water and reapplied it to the wound, then tossed the water away and poured more from the pot into the basin. "I've used all the water in the coffeepot," she said.

Jubal nodded, his head bent as he concentrated on his task. "I'll fetch the stew pot in a minute. Just to warn you, I'm cuttin' these here pants off him, too. They're ruined anyways, and I need to get at that damned arrow. Sorry for my swearin'."

Sarah turned her head, taken aback by Jubal's frank words. She understood the medical necessity of removing Orion's clothes, but the last thing she needed to think about was Orion Beaudine naked under that blanket. She snatched up a clean piece of the dismembered apron and dropped it in the steaming basin, then gingerly pulled it out, holding the cloth in the rapidly cooling air for a minute before she squeezed out the excess water. With care, she cleaned the blood from around the shoulder wound. A quick glance under the cloth covering it assured her that the bleeding had slowed. She eased her compression of the cloth and set to work cleaning the dried blood from Orion's chest and left arm, resolutely keeping her gaze above his waist.

"The bleeding has slowed," she reported quietly.

"Good. Watch for any bits of buckskin washin' out. A good-sized piece came out with the arrowhead, but there could be more." Jubal paused, then continued in a conversational tone. "That's why the Indians always go into battle near naked. If they do get hit, there's less chance of infection settin' in if there ain't no cloth stuck in the wound."

Sarah shuddered.

"Come on to me, honey."

Her head snapped up. "I beg your pardon?"

"I'm talkin' to this here arrow—gotcha!" Jubal held up the second bloody arrow in triumph. "Hand me one of those cloths, girl."

Sarah complied, and a minute later, Jubal stood and went to get the other pot of water.

As she continued with her gentle washing, a strange mood came over Sarah. Wrong as it was, she had wanted to touch Orion, and now that she had the chance—no, the obligation—to touch him, regret filled her for the horrible circumstances under which her guilty wish had been granted. Yet, she also found the experience incredible, even wondrous, for she had never touched a man's naked chest before.

He was so warm, and powerful! The soft black hair that covered Orion's upper chest and tapered down intriguingly to disappear beneath the blanket Jubal had pulled up to his hips felt both alien and wonderful to Sarah. When her hand covered his heart, tears filled her eyes. The beating of his heart was a song to her, a testament to the vitality of his very being. He was such a beautiful, alive man. It would be a sin against the heavens if that strong heart were to be silenced now, while Orion was in the prime of his life.

"Please live," she whispered. A single tear ran down one cheek.

"I reckon he will," Jubal said quietly as he returned to Orion's side carrying the stew pot filled with hot water. "He's young and strong. If we can keep the infection at bay, he'll come through just fine, and have a few more scars to brag about to his grandkids someday."

A new terror grabbed Sarah's heart. "Do you think the wounds will infect?"

"They almost always do. Infection kills more men than actual wounds do. And it ain't a pleasant way to go. There ain't no surgeon at Fort St. Charles yet, and the Hunter's gonna need some nursin'."

"I'll nurse him." The words came impulsively, but with

fierce determination. Orion Beaudine would not die, at least
not now, not if she had anything to do with it.

Jubal raised an eyebrow. "We're talkin' about maybe real
personal nursin', Miss Sarah."

"I nursed my dying mother for months, Mr. Sage. I have
experience."

"Still, I don't think your captain is gonna like the idea
much. Maybe the Mrs. Colonel will help, you know, to keep
things respectable."

Sarah shook her head. "I doubt it. She hates Or—uh, Mr.
Beaudine, and I don't know why." She chewed thoughtfully
on her swollen lower lip. "But I'm sure Lucy will help."

"That woman does have a good heart, as well as a good
head on her shoulders," Jubal said approvingly. "And I'll be
there for a spell. Between us, we'll manage."

With a nod, Sarah looked down at Orion's still form.
"Shouldn't we get these wounds bandaged?" She lost the
struggle to keep the note of worry out of her voice.

"Not yet. But keep them covered. I want to lay in a supply
of horsetail weed, in case either one of them holes starts
bleedin' again, and before we bandage the wounds I want to
lay on a paste of wild onion. It seems to help keep the infection down. Garlic is good for that, too, and I know them
Mexicans back at the fort planted some. Don't you worry
none, missy. We'll keep the man goin'."

Sarah nodded again. "What can I do?"

"Just keep the fire up, but not so high as to draw attention.
I'll be bringing supper back with me. I was hungry 'fore I
even got to the fort, and now I'm starvin'." Jubal shook his
shaggy gray head as he picked up the rifle that lay on the
ground near Sarah. "Shows what this man means to me, I'd
miss my luncheon for him. Must be gettin' soft." He shook
his head again, then held out a pistol, butt first. "Take this.
I don't wanna leave you unarmed. Know how to use it?"

"No." Sarah's hand trembled as she accepted the weapon
from Jubal.

"She's all primed and ready. Just point her and shoot, but pull back on the trigger kinda gentle-like. Like some women I know, she's sorta touchy."

"Do you expect trouble?"

"No, and I won't be that far away if there is any. It just ain't a good idea to be unarmed."

"I have this, too." Sarah held up Orion's knife. "And Dancer."

"He's the best watchdog you could have. Sit tight, girl. I'll be back shortly." Jubal disappeared into the lengthening shadows, again with the speed and silence that was almost unnerving. It seemed like one minute he was there and the next he wasn't, and if her life had depended on it, Sarah could not have told anyone in which direction the old mountain man had gone.

She turned her attention back to Orion. He shifted and moaned, but his eyes did not open, even when she softly said his name. Perhaps it was best, she reasoned. As long as he was unconscious, he would not feel the pain his wounds must be causing him, although from the frown on his handsome face, she knew he was at the least uncomfortable, unconscious or not. Again, her heart—and her stomach—grabbed as the memories of another time, and another sick person, washed over her. From nursing her mother during that final illness, Sarah was intimately familiar with the devastating sense of helplessness she now felt. Surely one of the cruelest of all of life's trials was to watch a friend or a loved one suffer, and be powerless to alleviate that suffering.

"I would take the pain from you if I could," she whispered sadly.

As if he understood her words, Dancer lifted his head from its resting place on his paws and whimpered.

"You would, too, wouldn't you, boy?" Sarah asked.

Dancer yipped in response, and Sarah felt that they were truly communicating. "You could use some cleaning yourself," she said. She took another small piece of apron and wetted it, then moved to the animal's side and washed the dried blood from his fur. "There." Sarah scratched the wolf's ears as she looked around the eerily quiet clearing.

The hill rose up behind them to the east, to the north the stand of trees trailed from the hill to the river, the river formed a boundary to the west, and to the south—the direction from which they had come—an expanse of prairie filled the darkening horizon. Other than the muted whisperings of the nearby river, the only sounds were those of the crackling fire, and the ever present wind, which had taken on a definite chill now that the sun had gone down behind the mountains. Sarah suppressed a shiver. Where was Adam and the detachment of soldiers? Surely they should have been here by now. She was very grateful for Dancer's presence, and hoped that Jubal would not be much longer.

"Sarah."

The soft sound of Orion's whisper touched her as gently as the wind. She slowly turned to look at him. His beautiful eyes were open now, and his hand reached for her. Of its own accord, her hand caught his. His fingers tightened on hers.

"I was afraid I had dreamed you."

She smiled. Suddenly the intimacy of calling him by his first name was too much to bear, especially combined with the knowledge that he was naked under the blanket. Especially knowing that Adam would be riding in any minute. She had to put some barrier between them, even one as flimsy as his formal name. "No, Mr. Beaudine, I'm here."

Disappointment flashed in his eyes, quickly replaced by a grimace of pain. He shifted under the blanket. "Are the arrow heads out?"

"Yes, but please don't move too much." Sarah laid her free hand on his uninjured shoulder. "The wounds are not yet bandaged. Jubal wants to put a poultice on them first, and so is out hunting for horsetail weed, wild onions, and supper. He shouldn't be much longer."

As if to demonstrate her words, a gunshot sounded in the distance.

"Let's hope that's supper and not more trouble," Orion murmured.

Fighting down a chill of fear, Sarah asked, "Are you hungry?"

"No, but I am thirsty."

"I'll get you some water."

"Thanks," Orion said, but he seemed reluctant to release her hand. "Why did you come?" he whispered.

"I had to. Dancer came for me. I couldn't bear the thought of you out here alone and hurt."

His fingers tightened on hers again. "How did you know I was hurt?"

Sarah could not look away from his eyes, for they appeared to glow in the fading light, so intense was his gaze. Her answer seemed terribly important to him. "I just knew. Maybe Dancer told me. Maybe I knew all along something would happen. I had a bad feeling the day you left Fort St. Charles and it didn't go away until . . . until now, now that I know you're alive."

"Joseph had a feeling, too."

"Joseph? You mean your brother? Did you see him at Fort Laramie?"

Orion nodded, his eyes now wearily closing.

"I'm tiring you; please forgive me," Sarah said. "I'll get you some water."

This time Orion let her go. She took up the cup and hurried to the river to fill it, taking the time to put another couple of pieces of wood from the pile Jubal had collected on the fire as she passed.

Orion had pushed himself up on one elbow. Sarah hurried to his side, for it looked like he wouldn't be able to support himself for very long. She fell to her knees behind him. "Lean against me," she urged. He obeyed her, and she braced his back with her body, holding the cup to his lips from behind. His hand covered hers around the cup as he drank, then he leaned his head back against her, exhausted.

"Thank you." His eyes drifted closed.

Sarah tossed the empty cup aside and wrapped both her arms around him. His heart beat strongly against her forearm, and she laid her cheek on his dark head for just a moment before she reluctantly eased him to the ground. After checking the two wounds to make certain that the bleeding had not started again—which it hadn't—she settled next to him, and could not resist once more taking his hand in hers. His fingers tightened on hers briefly, then he relaxed into a deep sleep.

She waited there, without moving, as the sky darkened, letting her thoughts roam, content to hold Orion's hand. The fire was a beacon of warmth and light, comforting in its cheerful sounds. Perhaps a half hour later, Jubal returned, cautiously entering the circle of firelight, the hind leg of a deer or antelope in one hand, the rifle in the other. A bunch of greens was tied to his belt. Sarah felt almost weak with relief.

"How is he?" Jubal asked.

Sarah glanced down at Orion. "As well as can be expected, I guess. He drank another cup of water and seems to be sleeping now."

Jubal nodded in satisfaction. "Any sign of that detachment?"

"No. Isn't that strange? Do you think the same men who attacked Orion attacked them?"

"No. I think they was slow in leavin' the fort, and now they're havin' trouble followin' our track since the light is about gone." He shook his head in disgust. "Damned fools— uh, sorry. Let's get the Hunter bandaged up and some supper on the fire. Then I'll take the horse and go get the rest of this antelope, and if them soldiers still ain't here, I'll go find 'em and bring 'em on in. I swear, some folks couldn't find their way to the privy without a map."

Sarah fought a smile. "What can I do to help?"

"Nothin' just yet. Won't take me but a couple of shakes

to get these wild onions mashed up and get the haunch clean and roasting. You keep an eye on the Hunter." He looked over at her, eyeing her hand entwined with Orion's.

"It seems to offer him comfort," she said defensively.

"I'm sure it does, Miss Sarah." He studied her a minute longer, then marched over to the packhorse. A moment later he draped a blanket around her shoulders. "Should've said something about bein' cold," he scolded.

"Thank you," she murmured. The wool blanket felt heavy and warm. She watched as Jubal moved around the makeshift camp, awed by his efficiency. There were no wasted movements, and in a matter of minutes, it seemed, he had the packhorse unloaded, brushed, and hobbled in a patch of thick, yellowing grass, the onion paste warming in a frying pan, the antelope haunch skinned and roasting, and a pot of broth heating for Orion, flavored with a little onion, some meat shavings, and some fat. Finally, Jubal grabbed the frying pan and brought it over to where she waited.

"I'll slap some of this on those wounds, and we'll get him bandaged up," he said.

Between them, they made short work of it, although the shoulder wound was in such a place that it was awkward to bandage. Orion awakened and helped as much as he could. Sarah tried not to stare at the long, naked expanse of his muscular leg when he bent it at the knee to facilitate the wrapping of the bandage around his upper thigh. They had just finished, and Sarah was arranging the blanket over Orion when Dancer sounded a warning growl. She froze as Jubal faded back from the firelight into the dark and Dancer took a protective stand at her side. In the sudden silence she could hear the faint sound of horses, and of men talking. Relief warred with anxiety within Sarah. The detachment—and Adam—had found them.

Nine

As Orion watched, Sarah took a deep breath, then straightened her spine and waited.

"The detachment is here," he commented quietly.

"Yes."

Gritting his teeth against the pain the movement cost him, Orion reached out from under the blanket and laid a hand on her arm. "I regret causing you trouble with Captain Rutledge."

She looked down at him. "You aren't the cause of the trouble. This has been brewing ever since I arrived at the fort. I tried to avoid it, tried to be what he expects me to be, but I have failed. This was inevitable." She stared off in the direction of the yet-unseen approaching soldiers. When she spoke again, her voice was filled with confusion and a deep sadness. "All of our lives, he and I have been wonderful friends. But so far we have been terrible mates."

Mates? Sarah's word choice shook him. Had Adam Rutledge already taken her as a lover? Orion's stomach knotted as jealousy ripped through him, a jealousy he knew he had no right to feel. Still, he felt it. Powerfully.

He struggled to compose himself, because the silence between them was growing long and he felt compelled to say something. Only minutes remained before the soldiers rode into the camp, and his time to speak privately with her would end. "Friendship is a good beginning for a marriage," he said lamely. The words sounded pat and clichéd, even to his ear.

"So I've been told." Sarah spoke somewhat sharply. "I agree that it is a necessary ingredient, but I wish for more than that."

"You wish for passion." His words were barely above a whisper, but her head jerked around and she stared at him, her beautiful eyes wide with astonishment. *Oh, Sarah,* he thought longingly. *I can show you passion.*

But there was no more time for private words. The soldiers rode into the camp, led by Captain Rutledge and Lieutenant Fielding.

Jubal materialized out of the darkness, his long rifle cradled in his arms.

Dancer growled low in his throat.

Sarah again settled herself and waited, her head held high.

Orion moved his hand from her arm, suddenly very troubled. Everything in him cried out to defend Sarah if necessary, to protect her from whatever angry words or actions Rutledge might use against her. At the same time, he also knew it was not his place to say anything. As Joseph had told him, Sarah had to work this out herself. But Orion suspected that staying out of it was going to be one of the hardest things he ever had to do.

"Evenin', Captain Rutledge," Jubal called out. "Was thinkin' I'd have to go find you."

"You won't," Rutledge said harshly. He waved a gauntleted hand in the direction of the makeshift bed. "I see you found him." If he saw Sarah sitting there—he couldn't have missed seeing her—he gave no sign of it.

"Sure did. Miss Hancock was right in thinkin' he was hurt."

"Well, let's get him on a horse, Mr. Sage," Rutledge commanded with no trace of sympathy or concern in his voice. "At this rate, we'll be lucky to get back to the fort before midnight."

Orion saw Sarah stiffen. She was about to say something, but Jubal spoke first, and firmly.

"No, sir. We pulled two arrows outta Mr. Beaudine, and he ain't well enough to ride."

At the mention of the arrows, the five enlisted men looked around nervously. Both Rutledge and Fielding seemed unconcerned about a potential problem with Indians. Jubal continued.

"Even if Mr. Beaudine could ride, my horses are wore out. We're stayin' here tonight, and in the mornin' I'm buildin' a travois. You all can head on back if you want to. Miss Hancock and I, we done just fine on our own so far. We can get Mr. Beaudine back to the fort by our own selves."

Orion had to smile. Jubal had just made it very clear that Sarah would be returning to the fort with him, whether Rutledge and the detachment left tonight or not. Rutledge's frustration was evident in the way his grip tightened on the reins, causing his horse to sidestep.

"I brung down an antelope a bit ago and was just about to go get the rest of it," Jubal said in a friendly tone. "Send one of your men along to help me and I'll share. We'll have us a good supper, and a night's rest, and head back in the mornin'."

Orion shook his head in admiration. Jubal was not known as a master negotiator for nothing. He had settled disputes between warring Indian tribes with no bloodshed. On more than one occasion he had successfully traded with an Indian tribe for the life of a white captive. And he had just persuaded an angry, arrogant officer to get off his high horse and yet still allowed the fool to save face in front of his men.

"Very well, Mr. Sage," Rutledge snapped. "Troop, dismount! Except for you, Private Wilson. Accompany Mr. Sage on his excursion to retrieve our supper."

"Yes, sir," one of the soldiers answered.

Rutledge stepped down from the saddle as Jubal swung up into his.

"One of you men keep turnin' that haunch that's a-cookin'," Jubal ordered. "I hate burned antelope."

"You're certain you can find the remains of that animal in the dark, Sage?" Fielding called out derisively.

Jubal glanced back over his shoulder as he rode out of the firelight. "Better'n you can find your ass with both hands, Fielding. Beg pardon, Miss Sarah." He and the soldier following him disappeared.

Orion stifled a laugh, and saw that Sarah's lips had curved in a smile. Her smile quickly faded, though, as Rutledge approached. Dancer growled again. Orion placed a calming hand on the wolf's head.

"How badly is he injured, Sarah?" The captain's voice was cold with anger.

If Sarah was nervous about facing the captain, it didn't show. She answered him clearly and firmly. "You heard Mr. Sage, Adam. Mr. Beaudine has two serious wounds. Both bled profusely, and we must not risk breaking them open again. He has already lost too much blood."

Evidently Rutledge was not satisfied with her answer, for he focused on Orion. "If we have to escort a travois, it will take at least half a day to get back to the fort, Beaudine. I want you to ride tomorrow."

"Adam!" Sarah gasped.

Orion held up his hand to silence her. "Jubal is the doctor, Captain, and Miss Hancock is the nurse. They call the tune. They'll skin me alive if I argue with them, which I have no intention of doing. Like Jubal said, you go back whenever you have a mind to." He paused. "But then, Colonel Rutledge sent you to escort us back, didn't he?" Orion was baiting the man on purpose, and was perversely pleased when Rutledge bit, as was evidenced by the man's tightened jaw and flaring eyes.

"Don't push me, Beaudine. I've been pushed about as far as I'm going to go." He turned his fierce gaze on Sarah.

Orion held his tongue, suddenly furious with himself. His

jealousy had goaded him into making a mistake; he had pushed the captain into a corner, leaving the man no choice but to lash out. Orion had figured Rutledge would lash out at him. In fact, he had counted on it. Even in his weakened state, even if it was only a battle of words, he would relish a battle with Adam Rutledge. But instead, Rutledge just might turn on Sarah.

"I will speak to you later, Sarah," Rutledge barked. "We have much to discuss." He turned and marched away without waiting for her reply.

"Yes, we do, Adam," she called after him, obviously embarrassed. Again, she visibly gathered herself, straightening her shoulders and taking a slow breath. Then she faced Orion. "I apologize for Adam's rudeness, Mr. Beaudine. As you can see, there is tension between him and me. My only regret is that he took it out on you."

"Don't fool yourself, Sarah." Again, her Christian name slipped out. "His attitude toward me isn't your fault. He's angry with me, too."

"But you haven't done anything," she protested.

"I got hurt, which is the direct cause of your rebellion against his orders. He blames me."

"He'll get over it, just like Mr. Sage said. And that's enough of this nonsense. You don't need to be dragged into the problems between Adam and me. You need to rest." She laid a gentle hand on his forehead. "So far no sign of fever. Thank God." Her voice trailed off to a whisper.

Orion closed his eyes, suddenly overcome with physical pain and both physical and mental weariness. His wounds had begun to throb, and it seemed that his whole body was on fire. He loved the touch of Sarah's cool hand on him, and wished he could just go to sleep. But he would not rest until Jubal returned to watch over her.

"I'll get you some broth," she said. "And more water."

He opened his eyes and watched as she stood up. One of the soldiers had built up the fire, and in the heightened light, it now registered that she was wearing the same gray dress she had worn the first day they met. Her hair was pulled back into a chignon at her neck, but several dark strands had escaped the simple arrangement. One teased her cheek, moving in time with the night wind. The firelight played off her fair skin and sparkled in her eyes. She looked beautiful to him.

"Shall I feed Dancer?" she asked.

"No. I'll give him a treat once in a while, but for the most part, he takes care of himself."

"Then I'll be right back." She pulled the blanket around her shoulders like a shawl, or perhaps a shield.

"Stay away from Fielding," he warned. "Jubal's remark upset him."

"Jubal's remark was justified," Sarah answered. "But don't worry—I'll stay away from the lieutenant. He was angry with me earlier."

Orion's stomach grabbed. "What happened?" he demanded, concern making his tone more harsh than he intended.

Sarah shrugged. "Back at the fort . . . he wanted to kill Dancer, and didn't appreciate my interference."

"If he laid a hand on you . . ." Orion struggled to sit up, hating the weakness that washed over him.

At once she was on her knees at his side. "No, no, calm yourself, Orion. Nothing happened. Others were there." She placed her hands on his shoulders, avoiding the bandage covering his wound. Her touch warmed him, calmed him. He fell back against the softness of the buffalo robe. *She had called him Orion.*

"You must rest," she whispered.

He nodded.

"I won't be long." Her voice was as soothing as her touch.

"I know," he said.

She smiled at that. "You know everything, don't you, Orion Beaudine? How annoying you are."

He smiled, too. "Go, woman. Hurry back. I'm hungry."

Her smile widened, and Orion felt that if death were to claim him at that moment, he would die a happy man. She stood, grabbing the tin cup as she did, and moved away. Orion pushed himself up on one elbow and silently cursed the now familiar weakness, determined to ignore it. He would watch Sarah until she returned to his side.

True to her word, Sarah was gone only a few minutes. Jubal had left his meager assortment of eating utensils arranged near the fire. Paying no attention to any of the nearby soldiers—including Adam and Lieutenant Fielding—she filled an enamel bowl with the savory-smelling broth and set it on a rock to cool while she hurried to the river and filled the tin cup. On the way back to Orion's side, she grabbed a roughly carved wooden spoon and the bowl, using a corner of the blanket around her shoulders to protect her fingers from the heated enamel. By the time Jubal and Private Wilson returned with the rest of the butchered antelope some twenty minutes later, Orion had emptied both the bowl and the cup and was obviously struggling to stay awake.

Sarah urged him to sleep, but he refused, insisting that he needed to speak to Jubal first. When the mountain man returned, Sarah dragged him to Orion's side. She did not hear all of their whispered conversation, but she heard her name mentioned twice and realized that Orion had been afraid to sleep without Jubal there to protect her. A knee-weakening tenderness washed over her. As badly injured as he was, his first thought was for her.

After that, she refused to leave his side, except for a brief foray into the stand of trees to see to her personal needs. Jubal brought her a chunk of the tender, roasted antelope haunch in the same bowl she had used to feed Orion, and had covered the meat with some of the broth. He also brought her a cup of fresh water, and his sole remaining buffalo robe.

"I can't nurse this invalid alone, so you roll up in this here robe and sleep next to him there," he said, his tone unusually loud and gruff. "I'll sleep on his other side. Between the two of us, we should be able to keep him alive 'til mornin'."

Puzzled at his manner, Sarah nodded her agreement, and only then realized that both Adam and Lieutenant Fielding had to have heard Jubal's brusque command. He was protecting her, as surely as Orion had, deliberately keeping her close. Her heart flooded with affection for the mountain man. When she finished her meal, she gave him the dishes and settled into the warmth of the buffalo robe, folding the blanket from her shoulders into a pillow. Her only concession for the night was to remove the pins from her hair. With a sigh of relief, she combed her fingers through the long strands, wondering if there was any decent way she could remove her corset. Deciding—regretfully—that there wasn't, she placed the hairpins under her makeshift pillow and nestled into the robe, determined to put both Adam and Fielding out of her mind. She stared up at the brilliant stars scattered across the black sky, found the constellation of Orion, so easily identified by his famous belt, and whispered a prayer for her earthly Orion's well-being. Just before she fell asleep, she remembered Orion's words about thanking the animals who died so that human life could be sustained, and she whispered another prayer of thanks to the spirit of the buffalo who had given its life so that she could be warmed on this cold autumn night.

Twice during the night, both times suddenly, Sarah woke from a deep, exhausted sleep. The fire had burned low, affording her little vision, but she could make out the rough outlines of the sleeping soldiers fanned out around the fire circle. Although Orion and Jubal Sage were much closer to her, they were farther from the fire, and both men were merely dark shapes in the night. The only way she could tell if Orion was still breathing was to place her hand on his chest to feel for his heartbeat, for the steady rise and fall of his chest. He did not awaken or move at her touch, but his warmth radiated through the blankets covering him, as did the beating of his heart.

The first time, his warmth comforted her, and she quickly fell back to sleep.

The second time, a nagging doubt formed. Was his warmth too warm? Was his heart beating just a little too fast? She placed the underside of her wrist on his forehead. He was indeed warm, but it did not seem to be the raging heat of a fever. That she remembered from nursing her mother. There was no mistaking a real fever. Again, she slept, but this time her rest was troubled.

She awakened early, just as the eastern sky was beginning to lighten. Jubal was already up and had the fire burning high. A few of the soldiers were stirring. Sarah turned to Orion and laid her hand upon his forehead; this time there was no doubt—he had a fever. He did not awaken at her touch. She scrambled out of the warmth of the buffalo robe and quickly twisted her hair into an untidy knot at the back of her head, securing it there with the hairpins. She threw the blanket upon which her head had rested around her shoulders and hurried to Jubal's side.

"He has a fever," she said in a low tone.

"I know." Jubal's voice was low, too, and somber. "I'm headin' out now to find a couple of travois poles. Should be ready to leave for the fort in an hour. You try to get some water into him, and maybe some of that broth."

She nodded her agreement and they went their separate ways. Adam did not speak to her, nor even come near her, and Sarah's heart ached at his cold treatment of her—but not enough to deter her from the path she had chosen for that day. Orion's well-being outweighed every other concern.

An hour later, just as the sun broke over the horizon, the small group set out for Fort St. Charles. Jubal had secured two long poles to the sides of his saddle, leaving them to drag on the ground behind his horse, and had lashed one of the buffalo robes to the poles, creating a bed of sorts. Orion lay on the bed, asleep again after rousing long enough to drink a little of the water and broth Sarah had pressed upon him. Jubal led his horse and the packhorse, while Sarah, once again wearing Jubal's hat and over Adam's protests, walked beside the travois so she could keep an eye on Orion. Dancer apparently had the same idea, for the wolf always stayed within a few feet of the travois. Except for a few comments shared among the enlisted men, the journey passed in silence.

Adam had been correct in his estimation that it would take all morning to reach the fort. When the detachment was about an hour away, Adam sent two soldiers on ahead to inform the colonel that they would soon arrive. Sarah asked that one of the men convey a message to Mrs. Rutledge, to explain the seriousness of Mr. Beaudine's condition and ask for her help in setting up a sick room as the fort did not yet have an infirmary. She offered her own room to be used for that purpose. The two soldiers left, and a little over an hour later, the detachment filed through the gate into the compound just as the bugler finished sounding mess call for the noon dinner. Dancer sat on top of a hill a short distance away, alert, his ears up, never taking his eyes from the fort.

Colonel Rutledge hurried from the headquarters building. "Thank God you found him," he said as he approached Sarah. "How is he?"

"Not well," she responded. "He's feverish, and hasn't awakened since we left the camp." Her shoulders slumped with weariness, and her feet ached from the hours spent walking on uneven terrain.

The colonel turned to Jubal. "Which tribe is responsible for this attack?" he demanded.

Jubal shrugged. "The arrows we pulled out of him had

Cheyenne markings, but it weren't no Cheyenne what did this."

"How can you be so certain, Sage?" Lieutenant Fielding glared at him. "We're right in the middle of their hunting grounds. Like all redskins, they're cowards, and they preyed upon a lone man. You noticed the detachment didn't have any trouble."

"Hunter Beaudine was raised with the Cheyenne," Jubal explained patiently, as if he were teaching a dull-witted child. "They don't attack their own kin. Someone wanted to make us think it was the Cheyenne. Hunter swears at least two of 'em were white men. Just can't figure out why they'd chose the Cheyenne, the one tribe no one would believe did it because of Hunter's connection to them. Someone made a stupid mistake."

"Gentlemen, can you please discuss this later?" Sarah begged. "We must tend to Mr. Beaudine now."

"Sorry, Miss Sarah," Jubal said apologetically. He eyed the colonel. "Where we gonna put him up?"

"In the headquarters office."

Sarah stared at him, appalled. "Colonel, Mr. Beaudine needs constant nursing for the next few days. His life is threatened from infection. Surely we can make a bed for him in your house, where Lucy and I can watch him around the clock. Did the soldier not tell you I'll give up my room?"

Colonel Rutledge shifted uncomfortably, not meeting her gaze. "That was kind of you, but not necessary. There is no heat in your room. The office has a big fireplace, and offers more privacy."

"With men trooping in and out all day?" Sarah frowned at him. "I don't mean to be argumentative, Colonel, but a man's life is in danger."

"Mrs. Rutledge has made all the arrangements, Sarah." The colonel took her elbow and led her towards the rough headquarters building. "I will use my parlor as an office for the next few days. No one will disturb you."

Suddenly Sarah understood. Harriet Rutledge had refused to allow Orion to stay in her house, even under such dire circumstances. Sarah's mouth tightened as anger flooded through her. The woman would launder her own linens if necessary to keep up appearances, but would not make room in her home for a seriously injured man. In that moment, a degree of Sarah's respect for Harriet Rutledge was irretrievably lost. "Very well, Colonel," Sarah ground out. "I'm certain Mr. Sage, Lucy, and I will manage just fine."

"Yes. Thank God you have some nursing experience, because none of my men do, and there's no telling when we'll get a surgeon posted here. We certainly won't get one in time to do Mr. Beaudine any good." The colonel escorted her into the headquarters office.

Despite her firm words, Sarah was taken aback at the minimal preparations Harriet had made. The table which had served as a desk was now pushed up against the far wall, and on it rested a single candlestick, a basin, a bucket of water, and a meager pile of clean rags. Two of the three original chairs had been placed next to the table—the third was nowhere to be seen—and a rude pallet of canvas stuffed with prairie grasses lay on the packed dirt floor in front of the fireplace. That was all. Not even a blanket had been left, let alone a pillow.

"Fine," she muttered.

"What did you say?" Colonel Rutledge asked.

"I said this is just fine," Sarah snapped sarcastically, glaring at the man.

He had the grace to look uncomfortable. "I know it isn't much, but there isn't much available."

"My cot, which I offered, is available, Colonel. My pillow is available, and surely, even in this wretched place, at least one blanket could have been found. The man is fighting for his life—he shouldn't have to sleep uncovered on the ground."

"I will let you make arrangements with my wife," the colonel said flatly.

Sarah got the message. Colonel Rutledge was not going to interfere with the decisions his wife had made regarding this matter. "Very well, Colonel. I will."

"Yes, well, I'll leave you to it, then," he said, not unkindly, and moved to the opened door.

Sarah marched behind him back outside. "We'll need some bedclothes, Mr. Sage," she called out as she continued on toward the colonel's house. "I shall return in only a minute."

She stomped up the porch steps and stormed into the house, praying she would meet Harriet so she could give the woman a piece of her mind, praying she would not, because she was so angry she felt she could not trust herself not to slap the woman. Harriet sat in a chair in the parlor, serenely rocking, stitching a narrow ruffle of lace to yet another doily. Sarah paused. Harriet did not so much as look up. Deciding that she did not have time for a battle now, Sarah darted into her bedroom to snatch the pillow off her bed, then hurried to the kitchen, where she found Lucy stirring a delicious-smelling something in a big crock.

"Lucy, do you know much about fevers and wounds?"

"I know some." Lucy did not look up from her chore. "That soldier said the Hunter is bad hurt."

"He is, and fever has set in. Mr. Sage and I will need your help caring for him."

"I'll do what I can, Miss Sarah," Lucy said, her voice barely above a whisper. Finally she turned her large brown eyes on Sarah. "But I have to be careful; the Mrs. Colonel don't want me over there."

"She has forbidden you to help us?"

Lucy held a finger to her lips. "Not in so many words. She loaded me with chores. I'll be up half the night as it is."

Sarah could not believe her ears. Her dislike of Harriet Rutledge was great—and growing—but she could not believe the woman capable of such cruelty. "Does she know how badly he's hurt?"

"Yes, miss."

"What did he do to her, to have earned such hatred?"

"I don't know, Miss Sarah." She looked pointedly at Jubal's hat, which had fallen low on Sarah's forehead.

"I am a sight, aren't I?"

Lucy merely nodded.

Sarah hurried back to her room, took her broad-brimmed hat off its nail, as well as her shawl, and grabbed her hair-brush from the narrow shelf that served as her dressing table. Then she made her way back to the kitchen, determined not to go near Harriet.

"I'll be at the headquarters building, Lucy, probably for the rest of the day. Has she forbidden you to cook for us?"

"Colonel Rutledge instructed that I cook for all of you."

"When shall I come to get something for us?"

"I'll bring it by in a bit."

"Thank you." Sarah went to the back door. She saw Adam's clothes hanging from the rope strung between the cabin and a nearby tree and remembered that she hadn't finished the laundry yesterday. Apparently Lucy had. "And thank you for finishing Adam's laundry," she said softly.

Lucy shrugged. "It wasn't nothing. You had to go with Mr. Sage."

"Thank you for understanding. No one else seems to."

"If you thank me one more time, I'm gonna spit," Lucy warned. "Go take care of that injured man. I'll handle things here."

Sarah had to stop herself from saying "thank you" again. "All right."

Harriet bellowed for Lucy from the parlor.

"I'll see you later," Sarah said quietly. She was halfway through the door when Lucy spoke again.

"Get you some willow from down by the river, if Mr. Sage

hasn't already done so. Boil the bark and make a tea. Have the Hunter sip on that—it helps bring down a fever."

Deeply touched, Sarah looked back over her shoulder and mouthed the words "thank you." Lucy rolled her expressive eyes and waved Sarah away. Harriet bellowed again, so Sarah took Lucy's unspoken advice and left, her hat, brush, shawl, and pillow clutched in her arms.

Ten

Later that afternoon, Sarah stood at the lone, small window in the headquarters office and stared out at the deserted compound, now obscured by a steady, wind-driven rain. The paned glass was old and wavy, distorting what little she could see. With a sigh, she turned back to the room, which seemed dim despite the light filtering through the window and the cheering fire in the old stone fireplace.

Orion rested on the pallet, made more comfortable with Jubal's buffalo robes. Another robe covered a few feet of the dirt floor beside the bed so Sarah could sit or kneel without soiling her skirts. Jubal had rejected her idea of bringing her cot from the Rutledge house, with the explanation that if Orion became delirious and began to thrash about, it would be better if he were on the floor rather than risk his falling from a bed. So far there was no sign of delirium, but Sarah was troubled by the fact that Orion did not awaken. His brow was covered with sweat, even though she had bathed his face with a wet cloth only minutes earlier. She returned to his side and settled down on the robe, then wrung water from the cloth that soaked in the basin near his head. With care, she patted his face and neck with the cloth, studying him as she did.

Even in his sick and injured state, Sarah found Orion Beaudine a beautiful man. His was a handsome face, with a broad forehead, a straight, aquiline nose, and a strong jaw.

His cheeks and chin were covered with a day's growth of dark beard, the contrast causing his skin to appear more pale than it actually was. Long eyelashes brushed the soft skin beneath his closed eyes, and his dark hair lay tousled around his head, spread out over the pillow—her pillow, she thought with guilty pleasure.

Her fingers lingered on his face before she moved the cloth to his neck, then she pulled the blankets down to wash his shoulders and the top of his chest. Both of his wounds, which she had checked earlier with Lucy's help, seemed to be healing; at least they didn't look any worse. Lucy did not think infection had set in. What was causing this infernal fever then? Following Lucy's advice, and with Jubal's blessing, she had prepared some willow bark tea and had managed to get Orion to drink most of a cup filled with the bitter brew, but, as far as she could tell, it had not yet offered him any relief. Orion still burned with fever, and worse, his long body had begun to shake with chills.

Sarah threw the cloth back into the bowl of water, wishing desperately for Jubal's presence. The mountain man had gone hunting, for both fresh game and medicinal herbs, and was not expected back until dark. If the storm kept up, he could well be forced to take shelter somewhere for the night, and not return until morning. Lucy had promised to bring supper, but that would not be for a few hours yet, and Sarah did not dare leave Orion alone even for the few minutes it would take to ask Lucy's advice. Somehow she had to get Orion warm again, which seemed ironic, considering that he was already burning up. She put more wood on the fire and covered him with the one blanket the colonel had sent over, but even that was not enough.

Orion moaned and tossed his head, then shifted to one side, as if he wanted to curl up. Fearful he would open his wounds, Sarah gently pushed him onto his back, and finally, in desperation, lay down next to him on top of the blankets.

With care, she put her arms around his shoulders and drew his head to her breast.

"Shh, shh. Orion, you must rest quietly," she whispered, pushing the sweat-dampened hair back from his brow. For several minutes she held him, murmuring soothing words, willing the warmth of her body into his. Gradually his breathing calmed, and he nestled his face against her breasts. Sarah gasped at the sudden, unfamiliar intimacy and almost pulled away from him, but since it seemed he had fallen into a more restful sleep, she lay still, content to stroke his arm and watch the firelight play on the rude walls and ceiling of the small room. The rain continued to drum upon the roof, and now the sound was comforting.

She was on the verge of dozing off herself when Orion spoke, his voice barely more than a raspy whisper.

"I was right."

A wild joy rushed through her at his odd words, not for the words themselves, but for the fact that he had spoken at all. She looked down at his face, saw that his eyes were opened, although only a fraction. "You're awake," she breathed happily.

"Not for long," he murmured. "But I was right about your breasts, Sarah Hancock."

Sarah froze, not sure what to say. Perhaps he was indeed delirious. "I beg your pardon?"

Orion's eyes drifted closed. "I suspected that if a man were lucky enough to rest his head against your soft breasts, he would be safe from the cares of the world. I was right." His last words ended on a sigh, and his even breathing told Sarah he had once again fallen asleep.

A flood of warmth that had nothing to do with the fire or the closeness of Orion's heated body filled Sarah. Never had anyone spoken such words to her. Deeply touched, she laid her cheek against the top of Orion's head and tightened her arms around him. "Heal, Orion Beaudine," she said softly.

"Heal." Her own eyes closed, and, moments later, she, too, slept.

"Miss Sarah!" Lucy's urgent whisper echoed in the small room. "For God's sake, you must wake up!"

When it appeared that Lucy was not going to cease shaking her shoulder, Sarah dragged her mind from the depths of sleep. "What's wrong?" she asked groggily.

"I find you all wrapped up with Hunter Beaudine and you ask me what's wrong?"

At that, Sarah awakened fully, surprised to find that she still held Orion in her arms, that his head still rested against her breasts, that his arm had somehow come from under the blankets to lay upon her waist. She blushed and fought the urge to jerk away from the injured man; she did not want to hurt him with any sudden movements, nor did she want to awaken him if it could be avoided.

"He was shaking with chills, Lucy. I didn't know how else to warm him." Even to her own ears, her tone sounded defensive.

"You're just lucky I'm the one who found you like that," Lucy retorted. She took Sarah's elbow. "Come on, now, get away from the man. You and the captain have enough troubles already; you don't need no one finding out about this."

Gently, Sarah eased herself from Orion's side, wondering at the sudden cold emptiness she felt. Surely it was only because the room had taken on a chill. Darkness had fallen, and the fire burned low.

As carefully as she had moved, though, Orion stirred. "Sarah." His voice was weak as his hand reached for her.

"I'm here." She caught his searching hand. "I'm here."

"And I'm here, too, Hunter Beaudine," Lucy added in a no-nonsense tone. "You rest easy, now, and behave yourself. Me and Miss Sarah, we're going to clean your wounds, and then you're going to eat some supper." She crouched down at his side, placing her hand on his forehead. "The fever still burns." A frown wrinkled her brow. "You'll have to drink more of that willow bark tea, and I think I'll ask *Señora* Gonzales if she has any cayenne."

Orion weakly grimaced.

"And I don't want to hear any sassing," Lucy warned. She straightened and bustled about the room, very businesslike. Soon the fire was built up again, the candle was lit, Orion's wounds were checked and covered with fresh bandages, his body washed free once more of the fever-induced sweat. Lucy and Sarah helped him to a semi-sitting position against the wall. The blankets fell to his stomach, and Sarah could see by the firelight that already a new coating of sweat had formed on his skin.

"It's a good sign that you're sweating, Mr. Beaudine," Lucy commented. "It helps cool you."

Orion merely grunted as he struggled to eat a piece of bread Lucy had given him.

"Do you not want the bread?" Sarah asked.

"I do, but my stomach doesn't seem to want it." Orion's hand dropped to the blanket. "I'm mostly tired."

"Try to eat a little of this stew before you sleep again," Lucy urged gently. "You don't have to eat much, but you should eat some. You need to keep your strength up." She knelt at his side and sat back on her heels, poised to serve him a spoonful of stew from the bowl she held.

"I don't need to be fed like a baby," Orion groused.

"No, but with your injured shoulder, it'll be easier." Lucy spoke calmly. "We all need help at some time in our lives, Mr. Beaudine, and you could use a little now. Let us help you."

Wearily, he nodded and leaned his head back against the wall. He accepted the stew Lucy offered with no further complaint. It broke Sarah's heart to see Orion so weakened, knowing how hard it was on him.

"Miss Sarah, since Mr. Sage isn't back yet, maybe you'd

be willing to go ask the colonel if he can come in a little while to help Mr. Beaudine see to his private needs."

Mildly embarrassed by Lucy's calm discussion about such personal things, Sarah looked down at her hands clasped in her lap. "Can you send him when you return to the house? I don't want to leave Mr. Beaudine."

Lucy fixed her with an uncompromising stare. "I know, but you need to for a while. I've left some warm water on the stove for you. You need to wash up and change your dress. And when you return, bring the pile of bedclothes I left on my cot. I stripped your bed and mine; we'll both sleep here tonight since our patient can't be left alone."

"Harriet agreed to allow you to stay here?" Sarah asked.

Lucy shrugged. "I didn't ask her, and I don't plan to. I'll go back and straighten up after supper, and I'll be there again before first light; she'll have no complaints, and if she does, I'll appeal to the colonel."

"He won't help you," Sarah said, her voice heavy with disgust. "For some reason, he won't stand against her in this."

"He will when I point out that Mr. Beaudine can't be left alone, and that it isn't proper that you stay with him by yourself."

"I'll be all right alone," Orion protested. "Don't make trouble for yourselves."

"There won't be any trouble, except for you if you don't eat more of this stew." Lucy offered him another mouthful, then turned to Sarah. "Go now, miss. You don't know how tired you are. You'll feel better after you freshen up. And I left your supper warming on the stove. It's the plate covered with a cloth. Just eat there in the kitchen."

Sarah gave in, knowing that it would be foolish to argue with Lucy. She nodded and stood up. "Is it still raining?"

"Only a little. Take my shawl."

"I have mine. Shall I bring anything else besides the bedclothes?"

"Maybe some of the colonel's brandy. A little of that will help the willow tea go down, and it might help Mr. Beaudine sleep easier."

"Waste of good brandy, to mix it with that vile tea," Orion protested.

Lucy merely rolled her eyes and held up another spoonful of stew.

Sarah wrapped her shawl around her shoulders and reached for the door latch. She glanced back at Orion one last time and was surprised to find him staring at her, his expression somehow one of longing. Her eyes met his intense and burning ones, and she felt the same flood of warmth she had felt when he had laid his head against her breast. Disconcerted, she let herself outside, grateful for the cooling effect of the evening wind. She stepped off the porch and turned her face to the heavens, allowing the light raindrops to wash her heated face. Lucy had been right; she needed to get away, for just a little while. Away from the mesmerizing and confusing presence of Orion Beaudine. But only for a little while. She hurried toward the Rutledge cabin.

Later, washed, fed, wearing a fresh cotton dress, Sarah did indeed feel better. She had chosen a dark green gown, as her black gowns were too formal for nursing duty, and, as was becoming common, had again forgone the hoops, feeling they would be ridiculous in the way while she watched over Orion. Her hair had received a thorough brushing and was now pulled back in a neat braid, as she would be lying down for the night before too long. She had also—daringly, she felt—taken off her corset. She had no wish to spend another night in that uncomfortable contraption. It now lay hidden in Lucy's folded bedclothes; she would find a way to put it on again in the morning.

When she had first arrived at the cabin, she had gone to the parlor, where the Rutledges and Adam sat, sipping their customary before-supper sherry. After a brief greeting to Harriet and Adam, she asked Colonel Rutledge to join her in the kitchen, where she had relayed Lucy's message to him, asked his permission to take some brandy with her when she left, and warned him that she would be washing up for the next few minutes and could he please ensure her privacy. He had kindly agreed to all three requests, and had left for the headquarters office a few minutes later, taking the brandy himself.

The colonel would return soon, and he, along with his unpleasant wife, would expect Lucy to serve supper. Knowing that Lucy would not leave Orion alone, Sarah grabbed her shawl and gathered up the pile of bedclothes.

"Sarah." Adam spoke from the other side of the curtained kitchen doorway. "May I come in?"

Sarah stiffened, then set the bundle of bedclothes back on Lucy's narrow cot in a recessed alcove. Resigned, she straightened and faced the door. "Yes, Adam."

He pushed the curtain aside and entered the kitchen. Sarah was struck anew by how handsome he looked in his captain's uniform, which of course he wore for supper. The light of Lucy's whale oil lamp brought out golden highlights in his blonde hair, and his blue eyes appeared very blue above his beard. His hard, almost cold expression was shadowed with a curious weariness.

"How are you?" he asked stiffly.

"I'm tired," she answered. "The last two days have been difficult."

"Yes, they have." He eyed her green dress, then her braid. "Will you be joining us for supper?"

As if Harriet would allow me at her table in such a casual state. "No. I've already eaten. Mr. Sage has not yet returned from his hunting expedition, and I am needed at the headquarters office so Lucy can get back here and serve your supper."

Now his gaze turned to Lucy's stripped cot and the pile of bedclothes. "Lucy is staying with him tonight?"

"Yes, as will I." Sarah lifted her chin and waited for Adam's reaction. It was swift in coming.

His head jerked up. "You're going to sleep over there with him?" he demanded.

"Adam, please. You saw him; you know Mr. Beaudine's wounds are serious. He needs constant care and cannot be left alone."

"Then let Lucy stay with him," Adam snapped. "Or one of the soldiers."

"Two people must stay, so they can take turns sleeping, and the colonel admitted that none of the soldiers have nursing experience. As you well know, I do. Both Lucy and I will stay, so there is no room for gossip." She looked at him. "We wouldn't have this problem if your aunt had been willing to let him stay here."

"Aunt Harriet has her reasons," Adam said defensively.

"I hope one day you will explain them to me. Perhaps I can be more forgiving of her lack of compassion if I can understand the reasons behind it." Sarah picked up the bundle from the bed, silently praying that her corset was securely hidden. "I must go. Your aunt will be expecting her supper, and I certainly don't want to keep her waiting." Try as she did, Sarah could not keep the note of sarcasm from her voice.

Adam seemed reluctant to see her leave. "There's trouble between us, Sarah. We have to talk about it sooner or later."

"I know. But you did not wish to speak of it last night, and I don't wish to this night. We are both weary. It will be better to speak in a few days, when we've both had a chance to get some sleep and to think things over." She moved toward the door, which at that moment opened to reveal Lucy.

"The colonel will stay with Mr. Beaudine until you return, Miss Sarah," Lucy said at Sarah's questioning look. "He wants me to get supper on the table."

"I'll go right now so the colonel can get back," Sarah said. She glanced at Adam. "Good evening, Adam."

He nodded stiffly in return. "Shall I escort you to headquarters?"

"That isn't necessary. It is probably better that you rejoin your aunt in the parlor."

Adam's lack of argument with Sarah's suggestion told her that he agreed with her. "Good night, then." He turned and left the room.

Sarah heaved a sigh of relief, then faced Lucy. "Did Mr. Beaudine eat?"

Lucy shrugged. "Enough, though I would have liked to see him eat more. You go now." She nodded toward the door. "I'll be over later."

After a moment of silence, Sarah said, "I know you don't want me to thank you, Lucy, but I do anyway. I don't know what I would have done without your help today, especially with Mr. Sage gone."

"You're welcome, Miss Sarah. Now go. The colonel must get back here if there is to be any peace in this house tonight."

Sarah needed no further encouragement. She hurried out the door and across the darkened compound, then knocked lightly on the headquarters door.

The colonel opened the door. "Hello, Sarah. Thank you for coming so quickly. I need to get back."

"I know." Sarah looked at Orion. He was lying down now, covered to his neck with the blankets. His eyes were open and he watched her intently. She crossed the room to deposit her bundle on the table, speaking over her shoulder to the colonel. "It won't do to upset Mrs. Rutledge."

"She is already upset."

With a sigh, Sarah turned to face the officer. "I know that, too, Colonel, although I don't understand why. She is not the one who lies on the floor, injured and ill. And surely it is not my absence from her home that causes her distress."

"I'm sorry, my dear, truly I am." A deep sadness ravaged the colonel's features, for only a moment, then he straightened his shoulders, his expression again schooled and professional. "I must go. Don't hesitate to send for me if any of you should need anything during the night. Sleep well, Mr. Beaudine. Good night, Sarah." Before she could respond, he was gone.

Sarah stared at the closed door, deeply troubled. Something was wrong, terribly wrong. Two men—Adam and Colonel Rutledge—both of whom she admired, whose opinions she greatly valued, defended Harriet Rutledge's strange hatred of Orion Beaudine, to the point that they allowed the woman to ignore accepted standards of basic human kindness and refuse a seriously wounded man a haven in her relatively comfortable home. Two men, both honorable and kind themselves, both intelligent and courageous, bowed to a bitter woman's petty cruelty.

Why?

What did they know that Sarah did not? Why would they not tell her? Why would Adam—her betrothed—not tell her?

"Sarah."

She turned to Orion. He was again braced against the wall, the blankets at his waist, his hand held up to her. His handsome face was pale, his brow covered with sweat and furrowed with pain. What effort had it taken him to pull himself up?

Sarah hurried to his side and fell to her knees, grasping his outstretched hand with both of hers. "You must lie still, Orion. You are very ill."

His fingers tightened on hers. "Don't worry so much."

Even those few words seemed to cost him some of his waning strength. Sarah's heart hammered with fear. "Please rest," she begged. "You need to heal. Sleep."

His green eyes seemed to glow in the muted light as he stared at her, his gaze capturing her, bewitching her. She could not look away, nor did she want to.

"Not now," he whispered. "I don't want to sleep when we are alone. Those times are too rare." Slowly he moved his injured arm across his body so that he could touch her braid with his free hand. "I love your hair down, even when it is confined in this accursed braid. Someday, Sarah, you will unbraid your beautiful hair for me."

"Orion." His name came out on a breath, which was all she could manage. She closed her eyes. His sensual words had started a flame in her, a flame she tried desperately—and unsuccessfully—to squelch. "You must not say such things. Please."

"I only speak the truth."

"I know." Oddly, she did know. Orion was sincere. For whatever reason, this man found her beautiful, and he told her so, with his words, with his incredible eyes.

"I want nothing but truth between us, Sarah. Always the truth, whatever it may be."

She opened her eyes and stared at him. His long hair tumbled about his shoulders, causing her fingers to itch with the desire to stroke those dark locks. "And if the truth causes pain?" she asked brokenly.

Orion was silent for a moment. "It still should be told. Whatever I say to you, ever, is spoken as truth."

"And I, you," she responded. "Now you must rest."

"That is the truth." He smiled at her, weakly, she thought. Slowly, his one hand retreated from her braid, but he did not pull back the hand she still held. With her help, he returned to a prone position, and his eyes drifted closed.

"Did you drink the willow bark tea?" she asked.

"Do you think Miss Lucy would have left had I not?" Orion retorted. He did not open his eyes.

Sarah smiled. "No."

For a minute the room was silent except for the hissing and crackling of the fire. Then he spoke, in a rough whisper.

"Don't leave me tonight, Sarah. I need you by my side."

"I won't leave you, Orion. Not tonight." She brought his

hand to her mouth and placed a kiss on his fingers. Another smile curved his lips, and Sarah was shaken with the fierce desire to kiss him there, too. Still holding his hand in her lap, she shifted her body until her back was braced by the rough log wall. Orion's even breathing told her that he slept.

Her head fell back against the wall, and she stared at the dancing patterns of firelight on the ceiling. What had happened to her in the last two days? What was there about Orion Beaudine that had driven her to risk—for his sake—not only the love of her fiancé, but a lifelong friendship? Last night in the wilderness, when Adam had warned Orion that he had been pushed as far as he would go, he was not only talking to Orion. Sarah saw that now. Adam's words were meant for her, as well. She was pushing him, too. Why? What was making her do so?

Sarah looked down at Orion, letting her gaze roam over his body, from his head down to his blanket-covered feet and back up again. The blankets still nestled around his waist, leaving his torso exposed, and the same friendly firelight that had danced on the ceiling now played off the soft hair covering his chest. She laid her hand over his heart, and was again filled with wonder at the power of his life.

Unable to take any more, Sarah pulled the blankets up to Orion's neck, covering the magnificent temptation he unknowingly offered. Again she leaned back against the wall, deep in thought, now stroking his hand.

She had never seen Adam's naked chest. If she had, would she have been as drawn to touch him as she had been Orion? Adam, too, was a handsome man, although his blonde good looks were a marked contrast to Orion's darker allure.

Orion shifted, as if he were trying to get comfortable. Sarah reluctantly released his hand and placed it under the blankets, startled when she accidentally touched the bare skin of his naked thigh. She mentally shook herself, then reached for the basin and the cooling cloth it held. As she gently wiped Orion's face, the eerie feeling that she was being watched came over her. She jerked her head around and caught the sight of a man's face framed in the small, paned window. The face then disappeared.

Sarah jumped to her feet and rushed to open the door. Lieutenant Fielding stood a short distance away, calmly smoking a cigar.

"Was that you peering in the window, Lieutenant?" she demanded.

Fielding slowly turned his head to look at her. "Such a caring nurse you are, Miss Hancock."

His voice dripped with sarcasm and sent a chill down Sarah's spine. How long had he been there? Had he seen her touch Orion's chest? She flushed with shame and fear, grateful for the darkness of the night. "Is there something you needed?" she asked with far more bravado than she felt. "You must know by now that Colonel Rutledge has temporarily moved his headquarters to his home."

"I know." Fielding dropped the cigar and ground it into the dirt. "And yes, Miss Hancock, I do need something, but not from Colonel Rutledge." His insolent gaze raked over her from head to toe with slow, insulting deliberation. "I can wait. All things come to he who waits." His thin lips twisted in a grin she could only describe as evil, then he walked away.

Sarah could not suppress a shiver. Feeling somehow unclean, she turned back into the sanctuary offered by the headquarters office—and Orion. She leaned against the closed door, tempted to bar it, afraid Lucy would think her foolish if she did. After hurrying to the table to blow out the candle, she tore the shawl from her shoulders and marched to the window. Utilizing a nail near the door and a crack in the wooden frame surrounding the window, Sarah was able to cover the glass.

With a sigh of relief, she returned to Orion's side and again settled herself on the floor next to him. As much as she longed to lay beside him and sleep, she would wait until

Lucy came back. Perhaps she would be able to convince Lucy that it would be wise for them to sleep next to Orion on opposite sides, as she and Jubal had done the previous night. And if so, she would be able to reach out in the night and again lay her hand on his chest, to reassure herself that he still lived, to take comfort from the strong, steady beating of his heart. For now, she indulged her earlier desire and lightly stroked his hair, content to watch him sleep, not caring if anyone saw her actions or not.

Eleven

It was close to midnight when Lucy returned to the headquarters office. Sarah had taken the liberty of making a bed of sorts on either side of Orion, and Lucy did not object to the arrangements. The two women settled down to sleep, and the night passed peacefully, although restlessly, and the rain began again.

Lucy was up before dawn. She helped Sarah change Orion's bandages, then slipped out the door, promising to bring breakfast in an hour or so. Orion's fever had not broken yet, which caused Sarah great worry. He would awaken periodically, but only for a few minutes before sleep claimed him again. The heat radiated from his body, even through the blankets, which were becoming damp with his sweat. She prayed for Jubal's return.

Colonel Rutledge brought the covered breakfast tray himself, and sent Sarah outside for a few minutes so that he could assist Orion with certain necessities. She stood on the porch with a blanket wrapped around her shoulders, watching with bleary eyes as the sleepy enlisted men hurried into formation for the reveille roll call. The rain had stopped again, but gray clouds hung in the sky, heavy with the threat to release more of their water. A light wind heightened the chill in the early morning air.

Colonel Rutledge joined her, pulling the door closed behind him. "His fever hasn't broken."

"No." Sarah turned to face him. "I wish Mr. Sage would return; I don't know what else to do."

"He was probably detained by the storm. I'm certain he'll be back today." The colonel adjusted his brimmed hat on his head. "The Hunter is a strong young man, Sarah. He'll pull through, especially with the care you and Lucy are giving him. Do you need anything?"

Sarah nodded. "Fresh blankets and sheets. His are sweat-soaked."

"I'll find some, and we'll get the others washed. I'll also have one of the men replenish your wood supply."

"Thank you, Colonel."

"And I thank you for taking on the role of nurse. I don't know what we would have done had you not been here."

Because your wife would not have tended him, even if he were dying, nor would she have allowed Lucy to, Sarah was tempted to say, but she kept the words inside. Instead, she shrugged. "If I were not here, Mr. Sage would not have left him to go hunting. He is a better nurse than I am."

The colonel smiled. "Well, all I can say to that is if I were a sick man, I'd much rather look upon you as my nurse than that querulous old mountain man."

Sarah nodded her thanks for the compliment, relieved that a semblance of peace remained between her and the colonel. She genuinely liked the man, and would have missed his friendship. It was perhaps best that they not speak of Harriet.

"It's time for inspection. I'll stop by later." The colonel stepped off the porch and strode toward the formation of soldiers, his body stiff with proud military bearing.

Sarah turned back into the office, determined that Orion would eat all of the bowl of oat porridge Lucy had sent for him.

She had to be satisfied with him eating only half. Even simple conversation seemed to exhaust him, and he soon fell into a deep sleep. Sarah decided it was a good time to wash up herself, and to put her accursed corset on. After assuring herself that Orion was truly asleep, she emptied the basin out the door, then poured some of the heated water from the cast-iron kettle into it. She undid the hooks down the front of her bodice and slipped out of the garment, laying it on the table next to the basin, then reached for a clean cloth.

Orion was not asleep.

He had shifted, trying to get comfortable, and had briefly opened his eyes to see Sarah unhooking her bodice. He could not have looked away had his life depended upon it. He watched as she wrung out the cloth in the steaming water, watched as she applied the cloth to her pale face, her lovely neck, her enticing upper chest, just to the top of her sleeveless chemise where the gentle swells of her breasts began. She wet the cloth again, wrung it again, and washed her slim, shapely arms. She lifted the thick braid and scrubbed the back of her neck, then set the cloth down and stretched her arms over her head, arching slightly backwards, causing the long braid to sway against her hips.

The movement pressed her breasts against the thin material of the white chemise, her hardened nipples thrusting upward like small, proud figureheads. Orion's mouth suddenly went dry. How he ached to caress those shapely mounds with his hands, to worship those glorious peaks with his lips and tongue. Someday he would, he silently vowed. Someday he would show her with his hands and mouth and body how he felt about her. Adam Rutledge did not know the treasure he had in Sarah, and the fool would eventually drive her away. When he did, Orion Beaudine would be waiting for her.

Orion ran his tongue over his dry lips, willing the suddenly most alive part of his body to settle down. He felt guilty about spying on Sarah and determined to close his eyes—in a moment. Slowly he allowed his gaze to wander over her, and that was when he saw the dark discolorations on the pale skin just above her elbow.

He jerked upright to a sitting position, causing the blankets to fall to his waist, ignoring the wave of dizziness that crashed over him. "How did you get those bruises?" he demanded.

Sarah gasped as she whirled to face him, grabbing her bodice and holding it protectively over her breasts. "I thought you were asleep," she said in a frantic whisper.

"Come here." Orion held his hand up to her. His eyes met hers, saw the fear and embarrassment there. "Please," he added in a softer tone. "Do not ever fear me, Sarah."

With a trembling hand, she reached for his outstretched one and allowed him to pull her down to her knees. He held her arm gently and examined the ugly bruises, recognizing the marks of a man's fingers for what they were. "Who did this?" he demanded, struggling to contain the fury that roared through him.

Sarah pulled her arm from his grasp and pushed it into the bodice sleeve. "It's not important. It won't happen again."

"Rutledge." He said the name as if it were an expletive.

"No!" she hissed. "Adam would never physically harm me." She pulled her braid forward over her shoulder, then fought to get her other arm into its sleeve. After tugging the bodice into place over her shoulders, she started on the row of hooks, beginning at her waist. One by one, the closing hooks hid her chemise, then her curves, then her skin from him.

Who? Who would want to hurt her?

He spoke the name as it came to mind. "Fielding."

Sarah bowed her head.

"Tell me what happened, Sarah."

After a long moment of silence, she sighed. "It was the day we found you, when Dancer came to get me. The soldiers were shooting at him, and when I tried to stop them, Lieutenant Fielding grabbed me and pulled me back. I don't think he did it on purpose."

Yes, he did. Orion laid his hand on her cheek. She raised her eyes to his.

"I will see that he never touches you again."

She shook her head. "There's no reason for you to get involved, Orion. Fielding is an arrogant donkey, nothing more. I intend to stay far away from him."

"Don't delude yourself. He's an evil man who takes delight in hurting other people. Just watch him with the troops; they fear and hate him. He has already been disciplined for brutality toward the enlisted men." His hand caressed the softness of her cheek, then fell away. He hated the weakness that consumed his body.

"He frightens me," she admitted. "I put my shawl over the window because I think he was looking in here last night."

Orion glanced at the covered window, his jaw tight. "I won't let him harm you," he promised.

The smile she gave him was gentle and somehow sad. "Thank you. Now you must rest."

He allowed her to guide him back to a prone position on the sheet-covered buffalo robe and sighed with contentment when she pulled the blankets up to his neck.

"Can I get you anything?" she asked.

"No. I'm quite comfortable." Actually, his wounds throbbed, his body was in the grip of a feverish inferno, and his head ached.

His heart ached.

"Then rest."

"You always say that."

She smiled again. "I do, don't I? It's only because you truly need the rest. I long for the day I see you again walking with Dancer, strong and healed, restored to your natural state."

"Will you walk with me then?" he asked, struggling to speak louder than a whisper.

"I will."

"Then I will rest." He closed his eyes. Her cool hand lay upon his brow for a moment, then was replaced with the cool cloth. The last thought Orion had before he fell asleep was that he had to warn Jubal to watch Fielding. The bastard would not hurt Sarah again.

Sarah stared down at Orion's pale face, her own face hot with embarrassment as she relived the last few minutes. He had seen her in her chemise. What a fool she had been to risk exposing herself. At least the soldiers had not come with fresh blankets and more wood.

Still, a curious excitement curled through her stomach at the thought of Orion's gaze on her when she was in such a state of undress. Had he enjoyed the picture she had unwittingly presented him?

Mortified, she turned away from him. Guilt pounded on her from all directions. How could she even think such a thing?

What about Adam?

With a groan of despair, Sarah got to her feet. She pulled her corset from under the blanket where she had hidden it the night before and wrapped it in another blanket. She would smuggle the blasted thing back to the Rutledge house and put it on there in safety and privacy. When she had straightened the small room, she again took up her post at Orion's side, bathing his face, neck, and shoulders with cool water.

He did not awaken again that morning. Sarah was disturbed to see him sometimes grimace with pain even as he slept. She alternately sat at his side and paced the room with anxious energy. When one of the soldiers brought fresh blankets and sheets, she enlisted his aid in changing the bedclothes both under and over Orion's heated body. Even then, Orion did not awaken more than to moan in pain. With each passing minute, the rock of worry in Sarah's stomach grew larger and heavier.

Shortly after noon, Sarah heard a commotion in the compound yard. Hopeful that Jubal Sage had returned at last, she hurried out to the porch. Jubal had indeed returned, and he was not alone. A detachment of soldiers accompanied him, along with a caravan of three wagons carrying several women, who were perched on top of the canvas-covered wagon loads.

Jubal broke away from the milling column, followed closely by two men, one an officer with a thick mustache and surprisingly long hair, the other a tall Indian dressed in buckskin whose black hair reached almost to his waist. The three men pulled their horses to a halt in front of her.

"Mr. Sage, how good to see you back," Sarah said fervently.

"Miss Sarah." Jubal dismounted, as did the other two men. "How is our patient?"

"His fever hasn't broken. I'm very worried." She glanced curiously at each of the other men. They somehow looked familiar, but Sarah was certain she had never met them. She would not have forgotten two such striking men.

Jubal joined her on the porch and patted her shoulder in an awkward attempt to comfort her. "He'll be all right, miss. The Hunter is too ornery to up and die on us. These men are his brothers. The one in the uniform is Captain Joseph Beaudine, and the other one is Gray Eagle. Brothers, this here is Miss Sarah Hancock, the one I told you about."

Orion's brothers. Sarah nodded at both men, now realizing that Joseph and Gray Eagle looked familiar because of their physical resemblance to Orion. They both were as handsome as their brother. Suddenly she regretted not pinning her braid up. What would they think of her, being introduced to strange men with her hair hanging down her back? She did not stop to wonder why the opinions of Orion's brothers mattered to her. "Your brother has told me about you, gentlemen." Surprised that she did not feel intimidated by the tall, fierce-looking warrior, she held her hand out to Gray Eagle. "I am pleased to meet you."

"The pleasure is mine," Gray Eagle responded.

Sarah did not know what she had expected, but she certainly had not expected Gray Eagle's English to be flawless and spoken with no hint of an accent other than a light southern one, as Orion had. But, she reminded herself, Orion had told her that their father had raised all of his children with equal education. She also saw that Gray Eagle had the same interesting color of eyes as Orion, while Joseph's were a warm brown. Gray Eagle released her hand and she held it out to Joseph.

"Captain."

Joseph took her hand in a friendly grip. "So you are Miss Sarah Hancock. Orion spoke highly of you when he was at Fort Laramie last week."

Joseph's equally accented voice was warm with . . . with what? Sarah wondered. Approval? Why would Joseph Beaudine approve of her? What had Orion told him about her? Curious though she was, now was not the time to ask questions.

"Surely you wish to see your brother, gentlemen. Let me show you and Mr. Sage in."

She turned and led the way into the office, which suddenly seemed very small and crowded. She hurried to Orion's side and sank to her knees, automatically reaching for the cloth that had slipped off his forehead. "He has a high fever that we've not been able to get down," she reported. "His wounds do not appear to be festering, but he is very weak and has little appetite. He has been sleeping almost continuously."

Joseph took his hat off and crouched down at Orion's other side. "Any sign of delirium?"

"No. When he does speak, he is coherent. But see? Even now, he does not awaken."

"Please set this on the table." Joseph handed her his hat.

She took the hat and set it up behind her on the table, then watched as Joseph pulled the blankets back to expose Orion's shoulders and chest. He lifted the shoulder bandage and peered under it.

"I brought some of the drawing poultice," Gray Eagle said quietly from his standing position at Orion's feet.

"Good. We'll need it. What have you been giving him, Miss Hancock?"

Although Joseph's tone was kind and calm, Sarah felt nervous and a little defensive. "Willow bark tea, some cayenne tea that Lucy got from the Mexican family on the other side of the river. As much water as he will drink. Stew, porridge. And a little brandy." She hesitated, then added, "We've kept him as clean and as comfortable as we could."

"You've done a wonderful job," Joseph said reassuringly. "Thank you."

Sarah's shoulders slumped with relief. "I just wish the fever would break," she murmured as she patted Orion's face with the cloth. At her touch, his eyes slowly opened. She smiled. "Orion, your brothers are here."

"My brothers?" he repeated in a hoarse voice.

"Your brothers, little brother," Joseph said cheerfully.

"Joe." Orion held his hand up, which Joseph grabbed. A weak smile curved Orion's lips. "Damn, it's good to see you again. Is Eagle here, too?"

"Right here, big brother." Gray Eagle hunkered down and grabbed Orion's blanket-covered foot to give it a shake. "What's this about you catching some arrows?"

"I got careless."

"You were ambushed," Sarah corrected.

Orion smiled at her—which had the unwelcome effect of speeding her heart rate—then returned his gaze to Gray Eagle. "What brings you here?"

"You. Thunder showed up at our camp on Elk Tooth Creek the day before yesterday, carrying bloodstains. Figured you'd gotten into some kind of trouble and was out looking for you when I ran into Joseph's column."

"I've been worried about Thunder," Orion admitted. His eyes closed. "Is he all right?"

"Fine. A bullet carved a furrow along his rump, but it's not serious."

Orion glanced up at Joseph. "What about you? You couldn't have been looking for me so soon. There's no way you could have known."

"Pure luck, Orion. Colonel Mackay has decided to keep Fort St. Charles open, for a while at least, and sent a detachment with supplies, more soldiers, laundresses, and a few family members. Winter is coming on, and this place isn't ready for it yet."

Sarah wrung the cloth out in the basin and reapplied it to Orion's forehead. One question was answered now. The fort would stay open. "What about a surgeon?" she asked.

"They've requested one, but he has to come from a post back East. He hasn't arrived at Fort Laramie yet."

"Has anyone seen Dancer?" Orion asked.

"We all have," Jubal answered. "He found me yesterday when I left and trailed along most of the time. He's out sittin' on the hill yonder. He won't go far with you in here."

"Just don't let those fool soldiers kill him."

"We won't," Jubal assured him.

"Jubal said something about the arrows being Cheyenne," Gray Eagle said.

"Wasn't the Cheyenne." Orion's voice had taken on a note of strength.

"We knew that," Joseph said. "Any idea who it was?"

"No, but I'd swear two of them were white men dressed like Indians. Someone's trying to make trouble."

"Do you think they deliberately let you live so you could tell the tale?" Gray Eagle asked.

"No. They were trying to kill me." Orion's voice had dropped to a whisper.

"Gentlemen, please, no more questions for now," Sarah begged. "He's exhausted."

"You're right, Miss Hancock," Joseph said. "You look tired yourself. Why don't you go get some rest and let us take over for a while?"

"No, I don't mind staying," Sarah protested.

"Come on, miss," Jubal said kindly, taking Sarah's elbow. "You're done in and don't even know it." He pulled her to her feet. "These boys have some doctorin' to do on their brother, and some of it might call for exposin' parts of the Hunter it ain't proper you should see."

Sarah blushed, wishing fervently that Jubal would not say such things in front of other people—especially in front of Orion's brothers. "Very well," she said. "I'm certain the brothers would like some time alone. But I'll be back later." She took her hat off the table, then realized her skirt was caught. When she turned, she was surprised to see Orion clutching her hem in his hand.

"Don't be gone long," he whispered.

Tenderness flooded through her. She crouched back down and laid her hand on his hot forehead. "I won't be," she promised. As she straightened, she caught Joseph and Gray Eagle sharing a curious glance, and suddenly she became nervous. It could not be denied that she and Orion felt affection for each other, but she had to remember that not everyone would be pleased to know that. She had to be more careful in the future, and at the first opportunity, she would warn Orion that he, too, should take care with expressing his feelings, even unintentionally.

After putting her hat on, she picked up the blanket-wrapped corset and the breakfast tray from the table. "Good day, gentlemen," she said briskly as Jubal led her to the door.

"Good day, Miss Hancock," Gray Eagle answered.

Jubal pulled the door closed behind them. "Let me take that there tray, Miss Sarah. Didn't you have a shawl or somethin'?"

"I hung it over the window last night," Sarah said as she handed him the tray.

"Too much light comin' in?"

When Sarah did not answer, the mountain man's eyes narrowed with suspicion. "Was someone lookin' in on you last night?"

"I saw a face at the window," she admitted as she stepped off the porch. "It startled me. When I came outside, the only person in view was Lieutenant Fielding. I think it was he who looked in, but I can't be certain."

"That sonovabitch," Jubal muttered. "Beg pardon, but I don't like that man. You steer clear of him."

"I try to, Mr. Sage."

Nothing more was said until Jubal guided her up the steps to the Rutledges' door and handed her the tray. "Get some rest, Miss Sarah," he urged, giving her shoulder a fatherly pat. "The Hunter's in good hands."

"I know. Thank you for your concern." Sarah was tempted to place an affectionate kiss on the man's weathered cheek, but she didn't, afraid it would embarrass him. "I'll go back later."

"See you then." Jubal turned and trotted back across the compound. Sarah watched until he disappeared inside the headquarters office before she turned to the door. She braced the tray on her hip and grasped the door latch, then paused. Suddenly, she felt every bit as tired as everyone told her she looked, and she prayed she did not have to face Harriet Rutledge. She didn't have the strength for it.

Luck was with her. There was no sign of Harriet. Sarah found Lucy in the kitchen.

"The Mrs. Colonel went to welcome Mrs. Major Dillard to the fort," Lucy said in answer to Sarah's question. "She was real excited, and I, for one, hope the Mrs. Colonel will be happier with another officer's wife around."

Sarah nodded in agreement. "Let's also hope Mrs. Major Dillard is a more respectable Army wife than I apparently will make. Mrs. Rutledge would be most displeased with another woman like me." She set the breakfast tray on the rough worktable, aware that Lucy's lack of comment indicated her agreement with Sarah's statement. Sarah took no offense. She had merely voiced the truth, and Lucy had silently agreed with it. "I'm certain Mrs. Rutledge will invite the Duncans to supper, Lucy. What can I do to help you?"

With her hands on her hips, Lucy critically surveyed Sarah. "You can march right into your room and get some rest, Miss Sarah. When you awaken, I'll heat you a bath, and help you wash your hair. Taking care of sick folks is wearing, and it has certainly taken its toll on you."

"So I've been told," Sarah said with a wry smile.

"Are you hungry?"

"No, but thank you. I'll see you in a few hours."

Lucy wiggled her fingers in a gesture of farewell and returned to her chores.

As tired as she was, Sarah wasn't sure she could sleep, but she still stretched out on her narrow, stripped bed. Her mind seemed to be running in circles, from Orion to Adam to Orion again. If she were honest with herself, Sarah had to admit that her feelings for Orion Beaudine were growing at an alarming rate, and she did not understand why. That she had feelings at all for him—other than friendship—was in some way a betrayal of Adam.

She was engaged to marry a man she cared for deeply, a decent man who would provide for her and their children, give them a good home, a good life. Adam was honest, hardworking, trustworthy, and handsome. He was everything any woman should want.

Why was she not satisfied with that?

Why had Orion Beaudine turned her head with his wild beauty, with his strength, with his quiet understanding of her? Why did she miss him even now, when she had been gone from his side for only a few minutes?

Because of Orion's injuries, because of his necessary nakedness and his temporary weakness, she knew his body far more intimately than she did Adam's. And thanks to her carelessness, Orion had seen her in an intimate state of undress. Adam never had. Was she merely experiencing the attraction of the forbidden? Was it compassion and sympathy for a seriously wounded man that was escalating her feelings for him?

Sarah groaned and covered her face with her hands. It was more than any of that. Her feelings for Orion Beaudine had flared out of control like a wild prairie fire.

How did he feel about her?

For the first time, Sarah considered the idea of breaking her engagement to Adam. The thought was terrifying, for both her sake and Adam's. Memories of their life together flashed before her eyes, the long years of comfortable friendship. Could she bear to hurt him like that? Could she hurt herself like that? Could she actually bring herself to break the promise she had made to her mother? What did she want from marriage that Adam did not yet—perhaps never could—offer?

Orion's words came back to haunt her. *You want passion.* How had he known that?

She wanted passion. Her mother had promised it would develop between her and Adam, in time. What if it never did?

She already had passion with Orion. A heady, frightening, exhilarating passion.

It was wrong.

Sarah rolled over to face the wall, confused, worried, scared. Her life was careening out of control, and she didn't know how to get that control back before someone, or several people, were hurt.

Several hours later, under a rapidly darkening sky, Sarah retraced her steps across the compound, bearing a heavily laden supper tray. Jubal met her halfway across the yard and took the tray from her.

"You look better, Miss Sarah," he said, apparently pleased.

"Thank you, Mr. Sage. I feel better." And she did. Much to her surprise, she had slept for almost two hours. The bath and hair washing had refreshed her, and now she was dressed in a black skirt and bodice, her clean, dry hair neatly arranged at the back of her head. "How is Mr. Beaudine? Has the fever broken?"

"Not yet, but we're workin' on that." He led the way up the step onto the porch outside the headquarters office and stopped in front of the closed door. "It's best you don't go no farther, Miss Sarah."

Sarah frowned. "Why not? I am very concerned about Mr. Beaudine. I wish to see him."

"Well, ma'am, it wouldn't be exactly proper. There's bare-chested men in there."

"For heaven's sake, Mr. Sage, I've seen Mr. Beaudine's bare chest for several days now. Please stand aside." Sarah brushed past him and knocked on the door. When a masculine voice called out to enter, Sarah lifted the latch and entered. She stopped short just inside the door.

The room was stifling and unbelievably hot, filled with sage-scented steam. A strange tent of blankets had been constructed before the fire. There was no sign of Orion, no sign of anyone.

"Could you please close the door?"

Sarah recognized Joseph Beaudine's voice, but she could not see him. Jubal nudged her farther into the room and entered himself, closing the door behind them. He crossed the room to set the tray on top of the tent, which Sarah now realized was supported by the table.

"Miss Hancock is here," Jubal said. "She brought supper."

Two figures materialized from behind the tent, backlit by the fire that roared in the fireplace. Sarah's mouth fell open to see both Joseph and Gray Eagle Beaudine standing there, naked to the waist.

"That's what I meant, Miss Sarah," Jubal said carefully.

"It weren't the Hunter I was concerned about, 'though he's naked as a jaybird under that there tent. He's hid, but I couldn't be sure these two would be. This ain't really the best time to come callin'."

"I can see that, Mr. Sage," Sarah said weakly. She spun around, determined to leave, but concern for Orion overrode all else, and she turned back. "Please tell me what you are doing to him."

"We are sweating the fever out of him, Miss Hancock." Gray Eagle's distinctive voice came to her through the mist of steam.

"It seems so warm and, uh, close in here." She wrung her hands.

Joseph spoke. "We wouldn't hurt our brother, miss."

Sarah brushed the perspiration off her brow with the back of one hand. "Of course you would not. I meant no offense. It's just that I tried so hard to keep him cool, and it's so . . . so . . ."

"Hot?" Jubal helpfully supplied. "That's the idea, Miss Sarah. It's an old Indian remedy."

"I see."

"Come back in the morning, Miss Hancock," Joseph suggested gently. "Orion will feel much better then."

"Either that or he'll be dead," Jubal added under his breath.

Sarah whirled around to face him. "You disagree with this treatment?"

Jubal shook his shaggy head. "No, ma'am. It's the best thing to do for him, and it usually works. Joseph is right; it will be better if you come back tomorrow. I'll come and fetch you myself. Come on, now. Let me take you on back to the Rutledges'. They have folks comin' for supper and all. It won't do for you to be late."

Joseph came around the makeshift tent, seemingly unconcerned about his bared chest. "I can see that you are concerned for my brother, Miss Hancock. Please be assured that we are, too. We'll take good care of him." He held out his hand to her.

Sarah grabbed his hand tightly with both of hers. "Thank you, Captain." She relaxed and released him. "I leave him in your capable hands. I will see you in the morning."

"Orion will be pleased to know you are coming," Joseph said kindly. "Good night, now."

"Good night, Captain." She glanced at Gray Eagle through the steam. "Good night, Mr. Beaudine."

Gray Eagle nodded at her. "Rest well, Miss Hancock."

"Come on, miss. We'd best take these here bedclothes and get." Jubal grabbed a pile of neatly folded blankets from the tabletop. "You and Miss Lucy'll be needin' these tonight." He took her elbow with his free hand and gently pushed her out the door, then closed it behind them. "You need to get back. They'll be a'waitin' supper on you." He escorted her off the porch.

"Supper seems unimportant when Mr. Beaudine is fighting for his life, Mr. Sage," Sarah said dispiritedly. "Besides, I am certain Mrs. Colonel Rutledge would rather I not appear at all."

"Then think of Captain Rutledge. He will want you there."

Sarah stopped and stared at him in the near-darkness. "Will he?"

Jubal's bushy eyebrows drew together in a troubled frown. "Has it gone that far then?"

"I don't know." Sarah's gaze dropped to the ground. "I don't know anything anymore." She looked back over her shoulder at the headquarters building. "I only know I am very worried about Orion, and even there, I am no longer needed."

"Joseph and Gray Eagle know what they're doin'. They'll keep the Hunter alive. He'll be there for you, if'n you decide he's what you want."

Sarah could only stare at him. How had the gruff old mountain man known of the turmoil in her heart?

"You best get back to the Rutledges' now." Jubal grabbed her hand and led her toward the cabin.

"I don't want to go," Sarah said softly.

"I know, but you have to." Jubal's fingers tightened on her hand. "There ain't no place else for you to go right now. Besides, you gotta face your life head-on, with your eyes open. Then you can't be blindsided. Face up to what you're facin' and make your choices with a clear mind and a strong heart. You got it in you, girl. You'll do just fine." He guided her up to the porch.

Sarah turned and faced him. "Thank you, Mr. Sage." She gave into her earlier impulse and kissed his cheek. "You are a wise and dear friend to me."

Jubal snatched his battered hat from his head. "Ah, shoot, Miss Sarah, you went and made me blush. I ain't blushed in . . . in, well, not for a long time." He smiled at her. "You just go in there and remember what I said." He handed her the pile of bedclothes.

"I will." Sarah moved to the door and paused with her hand on the latch. "This afternoon I promised Mr. Beaudine I wouldn't be gone long, and it appears I will be. Will you tell him I called on him?"

"Yes, ma'am. I'll tell him. He'll be pleased."

"Good night, Mr. Sage."

"Good night, miss."

She disappeared into the modest cabin. Jubal stepped back from the weak circle of light offered by the lamp hung on a nail near the door and twisted his hat in his hands. "It's gone that far, then," he muttered. "Damn." He clapped the hat on his head and strode off into the darkness.

Twelve

Somehow Sarah made it through supper, even though the strange depression maintained its grip upon her. She and Harriet were carefully polite to each other, Adam treated her with a courtesy that was lacking in warmth, Colonel Rutledge was kind. Sarah found it touching how obviously overjoyed Major Dillard was to have his beloved Penelope again at his side. Would Adam ever feel that way about her?

When the meal was finished, Sarah pleaded a headache and retired to her tiny room, grateful for the door that closed her off from the rest of the house. She made up her bed, slipped into her heavy flannel nightdress, braided her hair, and crawled between the chilled sheets. It felt strange to lay with no pillow under her head, but she took pleasure from knowing that Orion's head rested upon it. Praying for sleep, she closed her eyes. The sooner she slept, the sooner morning would come, the sooner she could see Orion. Her prayers were answered, for she quickly fell into the deep, dreamless sleep of exhaustion.

The next morning, she was helping Lucy prepare a breakfast tray for the Beaudine brothers when a knock sounded on the back door. Jubal Sage had come for her, just as he had promised, and a few minutes later they crossed the compound yard together, with Jubal carrying the heavy tray.

"How is Mr. Beaudine this morning?" Sarah asked.

"Just fine. The fever broke sometime after midnight. He's feelin' much better."

A flood of relief almost caused Sarah's knees to buckle. "The wounds are still free from infection?"

"Yup, sure are. Before long he'll be bouncin' off the walls with boredom. The hard part'll be keepin' him quiet so's everthin' can heal up."

"I'll help any way that I can. Perhaps I could read to him, or play cards." She fought to keep from breaking into a run, so anxious was she to see Orion.

Jubal eyed her, his bushy brows drawn together in worry. "You'd best be real careful, Miss Sarah," he said quietly. "You're promised to another man, and it don't take much to get gossip goin' in a place like this."

Sarah stopped abruptly and stared at the ground, guilt and fear swirling around in her stomach, making her sorry she had eaten. "I know."

"You need to talk to Captain Rutledge, girl, and soon."

Finally she raised her eyes to his. "I will today."

Jubal nodded with satisfaction. "Then let's get this here food to those brothers, else they'll be complainin'."

Sarah followed him onto the porch and through the door into the headquarters office. Just inside, she stopped and looked around in amazement.

No sign remained of the blanket tent. The table was back against the wall with a stack of neatly folded blankets resting on top, Orion's pallet was in its place, the air felt cool and comfortable. The only indication that Orion's brothers had filled the room with hot, suffocating steam the night before was the pleasant, lingering scent of sage and herbs. Gray Eagle was hunched over the fire, and there was no sign of Joseph.

Her gaze moved to the man on the pallet. Orion was sitting up, his back against the wall, the blankets rumpled at his waist, again exposing his chest. The beaded necklace again hung around his neck, and the bandage on his shoulder appeared very white against his skin. His long hair was brushed and laying around his shoulders, his face clean-shaven. And his green eyes, alight with pleasure, were on her. Sarah's breath caught in her throat.

"Good morning, Sarah."

The warm note of welcome in his voice invited her closer, and she answered its call. In an instant she was at his side, sinking to her knees, the silk of her black skirt rustling as it pooled around her legs. She placed a gentle hand on his forehead.

"How are you feeling?" Her voice was barely above a whisper.

"Better, especially now." His gaze burned into her.

"The fever's gone." She brushed aside strands of his hair as her hand trailed down his cheek to his shoulder, then to her own lap. How she longed to give her fingers the freedom to run through his hair! She was grateful that the presence of Jubal and Gray Eagle kept her from acting on her foolish impulse.

At that moment, Gray Eagle straightened from his position before the fire. "Good morning, Miss Hancock."

"Good morning, Mr. Beaudine."

"As you can see, we didn't kill him."

Sarah glanced up at him. Was he teasing her? It did seem that a smile lurked at the corners of his mouth. "He looks much better," she said shyly. "I meant no offense last night when I questioned what you were doing."

"None was taken. Our methods seemed strange, I know." He looked at Jubal. "Joseph had to go play soldier this morning. Will you help me load up on some firewood?"

"Sure thing. Then I thought I'd go check on that wolf." He glanced at Sarah before he headed out the door with Gray Eagle at his heels. The door closed, and she was alone with Orion. The only sound in the room was the crackling of the fire. Sarah suddenly felt very shy.

"I've missed you." Orion spoke quietly.

"And I, you," she admitted. "I didn't want to leave."

"I know."

She smiled at that. "Of course you did."

"Thank you for taking such good care of me."

Sarah shook her head. "Don't thank me, Orion." His Christian name now easily rolled off her tongue, at least when they were alone. "I was happy to be of help."

"You were more than just help. Jubal told me what you did that day, how you ordered the soldiers to stop shooting at Dancer, how you stood up to Fielding. Dancer came to you, something he has never done for any other woman, something he won't always do for me. You listened, you heard what he was trying to tell you. Against Captain Rutledge's direct order, you went with Jubal to look for me." Orion covered her hands with one of his. "You argued for my sick room, fought with the colonel, challenged his wife's refusal to let me in their home. Sarah, you defied your betrothed, the colonel and his formidable wife, Fielding, even the conventions of society, for me." He stared at her, his eyes burning. "Why?"

She looked down at her clasped hands, covered with one of his. "You were wounded and in danger," she finally said. "Simple human decency would dictate that you be cared for and nursed. I would have done the same for anyone."

"For anyone? Even Fielding?"

Startled, she looked at him. "I don't like the man, but he is a human being. If he were wounded or injured, yes, I would help him."

"With such devotion as you showered on me?"

Sarah felt ensnared by Orion's eyes. Her heart began to pound. "No."

"Then I am more than just another human being to you?"

She frowned, sensing where his questions were leading. "Of course you are. You are my friend."

Orion leaned his head back against the wall. "A friend."

He seemed disappointed by the word. "A close friend? A beloved friend? Or just a friend?"

Stricken, she cried, "What do you want of me?"

He stared at her, his expression suddenly sad and weary. "I want what's best for you, Sarah."

Her eyes filled with tears.

His hand came up to caress her cheek. "I've hurt you. Please forgive me."

She closed her eyes and leaned her cheek into his hand. "You haven't hurt me, Orion. I'm just so confused."

"I've complicated things, haven't I?"

"Yes."

His thumb lightly touched her lips. "It's wrong, I know, but I want to kiss you, Sarah Hancock."

At that, her eyes flew open.

He leaned forward. "God forgive me, I need to kiss you." His mouth was only inches from hers, his eyes scorched her. Her heart slammed against her ribs, and her breathing became shallow and quick. *Say something!* her conscience shouted. *Tell him no!* She remained quiet, knowing that with her silence she had answered the question in his eyes. His mouth descended upon hers, and the world stood still.

This kiss was different from the stunning one he had given her on the hill that day. Where that kiss had been breathtaking in its unexpectedness, in its intensity, this one was heartbreaking in its gentleness. His hand moved to the back of her neck, his lips tenderly—even reverently—moved over hers, somehow communicating deep longing and aching need. Her hands moved up to touch him, one stroking his arm, the other his ribs. His naked skin felt warm and so alive, so inviting. A sob caught in her throat as an agony of yearning washed over her.

His lips left her and he touched his forehead to hers. "Oh, Sarah," he murmured.

Sarah was incapable of speech.

They rested there, not speaking, their foreheads together, their hands moving slightly on each other.

"I'd better go," Sarah finally whispered. "Jubal and your brother will return at any moment." She pulled back from him, returning her hands to her lap, while he again leaned against the wall. "I am overjoyed that you are better, Orion," she said fervently. "I was so worried, and scared."

"I'll be fine, thanks in large part to you."

She shook her head. "Your brothers saved your life with their unusual remedy for fever."

"Which would not have done any good if I had not been found in time. Please accept my thanks. I'm grateful that I'm still here to look upon your lovely face."

Her eyes closed. "I accept your thanks, but please don't say those other things to me."

"I'm sorry." His voice was low and sincere.

"So am I," she whispered. Somewhat unsteadily, she got to her feet. "Lucy sent breakfast for all of you." She waved at the covered tray on the table. "Shall I set it down for you?"

"I'll wait until Gray Eagle and Jubal return."

Sarah backed toward the door, needing to leave, hating to leave. "I shall check on you later."

"I hope you do."

She turned away from him and grabbed the door latch.

His quiet voice reached her from across the room, as soft as a caress. "You have touched my heart, Sarah Hancock."

Her hand tightened on the latch, "As you have touched mine, Orion Beaudine," she responded without looking back at him. "Now I have to decide what to do about it." She wrenched the door open and stepped outside, pulling the door closed with more force than was necessary. Tears blinded her, and if Gray Eagle had not caught her shoulder, she would have crashed into him and the load of firewood he struggled to hold with one arm.

"Forgive me," she said automatically, and hurried away.

Two suddenly very concerned men watched her go.

* * *

"Adam."

Captain Rutledge stood on the banks of the river, watching as the enlisted men struggled with another load of freshly harvested logs from the distant forested hills. He turned when Sarah spoke.

"Sarah." His stance was stiff and formal. "Are you feeling better today than you were last night?"

She glanced away, looked up the river, and could not help wondering where Dancer was. "Not really. I doubt I shall truly feel better until we have resolved the problems between us."

When Adam did not respond, she looked at him. "As you said, we need to talk. Do you have time now?"

He stared at her for a moment, then turned away. "Lieutenant Fielding!" he barked.

From his position on the opposite bank, Fielding saluted. "Yes, sir!"

"Take command of the detail."

"Yes, sir!"

Adam turned back to Sarah and offered his arm. "Come. Let us walk."

She placed her hand on his arm. "Thank you."

In silence, he led her up the river, past the place where she had met Dancer the day the animal had come for her, even past the sun-drenched rock where she had spoken with Orion and where Dancer had allowed her to touch him for the first time. It all seemed so long ago now.

Finally, Adam stopped. Sarah took her hand from his arm, and for a time, neither of them spoke.

"Oh, Adam," she said sorrowfully. "What has happened to us that we can no longer speak in comfort and ease with each other?"

Adam clasped his hands behind his back and stared off into the distance. Sarah devoured him with her eyes, seeing his dear, handsome profile, his neatly trimmed beard, his proud military stance, his spotless uniform. She knew that if he faced her now, his blue eyes would be bleak with confusion and pain, just as she was certain hers were.

"I don't know, Sarah. Things are different now. We are different." He turned to her. "Do you regret coming out here?"

"No, I do not." Sarah looked around her. "I love this land."

"Do you love me?"

She met his gaze. "Yes, Adam," she said, with complete honesty. Relief flared in his eyes. "Do you love me?" she asked quietly.

His stern features softened. "I have loved you since we were children."

"Do you still wish to marry me?"

He frowned. "Of course. I have given my word. An Army officer doesn't break his word."

Sarah did not find his answer reassuring. "That is not a good enough reason. I will never be the kind of Army wife your aunt is. Are you willing to accept me as I am, with all of my faults and imperfections?"

Adam took off his hat and ran a hand through his hair. "Sarah, I have tried to make you understand that certain things are expected of an officer, of his wife, of his children. There are codes of behavior which must be followed, unspoken rules which must be adhered to, if I am to advance my career. We have been over all of this, many times. I don't expect you to be perfect, but I cannot excuse your disobedience of my direct orders." A note of anger crept into his voice. "Nor can I tolerate it. Surely you can understand how bad you have made me look in the eyes of others."

Sarah straightened and met his eyes. "I can understand that, and I deeply regret it. That is, I regret that you were made to look bad, but I do not regret my actions. A man's life was at stake." She paused, then spoke in a softer tone. "Why did you forbid me to follow the wolf?"

"Because it was . . . it was inappropriate. The search should have been left to the men."

"The men would have killed the wolf, and Mr. Beaudine would have died. Is that what you would have wished?"

"Of course not. Don't twist things."

"I'm not," she snapped. "Had the wolf been killed, I doubt we would have ever found Mr. Beaudine in time. He would have bled to death, or died of thirst and exposure. I knew what I was doing. I knew what Dancer was telling me as surely as if he had spoken aloud to me. You did not trust me."

"It had nothing to do with trust," he protested.

Sarah crossed her arms over her chest and arched an eyebrow. "Very well; then you did not believe me."

Adam shifted uncomfortably. "That's not exactly true. I think you were sincere."

"Then what was it? I insist you answer me, Adam. This is very serious."

He whirled on her, his eyes blazing. "Animals don't talk to people, Sarah, at least not to sane people. For God's sake, you made a fool of yourself, and of me, by obeying the imagined words of a goddamned wolf over the clearly spoken ones of your betrothed!"

Sarah flinched. Never before had Adam used foul language in her presence.

"I am to be your husband," he continued. "I must be able to depend upon your obedience."

"You think I am mad?" she asked quietly.

"No!" He shook his head, and his voice softened. "No, I don't. I think you are overwrought, and lonely. You still grieve the loss of your mother, and unfortunately, my aunt has not been able to ease that loss. My duties have caused me to neglect you, and thanks to the remoteness of this miserable post, there have been no other outlets for you. I hope that will change now that a few other women have arrived. And it will change for certain—I promise you—when I get transferred back East. All will be well then. You must believe me." His eyes entreated her, as did his outstretched hand.

"Oh, Adam." She put her hand in his. "I want you to be happy." She squeezed his fingers. "And I'm no longer certain you will be with me."

"Don't be silly." He pulled her closer. "Of course we shall be happy. We are the best of friends."

"That does not mean we shall make the best of mates." She resisted when he attempted to take her in his arms. "Please listen to me."

He set her back from him. "Are you having doubts about our marriage?" he demanded.

She met his gaze. "Yes, I am. I wonder how suited we really are to live as husband and wife."

His eyes narrowed with suspicion. "Have you been reading the works of that Catharine Beecher again? And those other women—Mott and Stanton? Is that what this is all about? Those idiotic demands for more personal freedom, for property rights and such? Is that why you refuse to obey me?"

"Don't patronize me," Sarah snapped. "This has nothing to do with those visionary women." Truly angry now, she poked his chest. "I will not obey anyone who commands that I betray my own instincts, my own judgement, my own knowledge of what is right and honorable. I am a woman grown, not a lackwit child. I am possessed of a certain degree of intelligence, and I am educated as well. I wish to be a helpmate and partner to my husband, not a mindless, simpering, *obedient* twit. If you wish to order your wife around, marry an enlisted man!"

Adam stared at her, incredulous. His lips quirked in a smile. The smile grew, until he chuckled, then shouted with laughter. "Sarah! My dear, spirited Sarah! I have been a lout, haven't I?"

Sarah was taken aback by his sudden change. "Well, yes, you have, frankly." She was even more astonished when her forthright words did not cause the smile to leave his face. "And I suppose I, too, have been somewhat rigid in my position," she admitted.

"There, you see?" Adam clapped his hat back on, then grabbed her hand. "We have been going about this whole marriage thing all wrong by prescribing to the dictates and expectations of society and my well-meaning but perhaps misguided aunt. Our friendship has always served us well; let's leave that as the basis of our marriage. I will no longer order you about, and you will no longer defy me in public. We'll put our best face forward, and pray to leave this god-forsaken frontier as soon as possible. I have no doubt that things will improve when we have once again reached civilization."

"You think this place is the culprit?" Sarah asked doubtfully.

"Yes, that and the lack of privacy. Think how well we always got along back home. We'll be fine once we are settled at a more civilized post, within our own house. You'll see, my dear." He again reached for her, and this time she did not resist him. "We'll make a fine life together." Adam's voice rang with conviction.

Sarah tightened her arms around his waist, taking comfort from his familiar presence. When he was close to her, and they were not arguing, Sarah felt that Adam was right, that all would be well. The passion between them had not grown as she had hoped, but Adam offered her steadiness and security; he wanted to share his life with her. Orion Beaudine had offered her passion, but he had not offered to make a life with her.

A sense of relief stole over Sarah as she made her choice, a choice she felt was logical and levelheaded, and in the best interests of all concerned. A choice that would allow her to keep her promise to her mother.

Yet, if it was such a good choice, why did her stomach feel sick? Why did she feel like a coward? Why did she feel that in renewing her commitment to marry Adam, she had betrayed her very soul?

Sarah decided that it was best to limit her visits with Orion, for all he did was confuse her. Whether by coincidence or design, Jubal Sage and the Beaudine brothers aided her in her desire to stay away. She was never again left alone with Orion, not even for a few minutes, and often when she called on him, she was informed that he was sleeping, that he was being bathed, that he was out for a short walk with one of his brothers, or that it simply wasn't a good time. After a few days, she stopped visiting him altogether.

Adam, true to his word, had relaxed his commanding attitude toward her and had even become more attentive. Sarah felt no need to argue with him over anything, and the problems between them seemed to fade away. It was as if their relationship had never been threatened. Even the situation with Harriet Rutledge eased, perhaps due in part to the presence of Penelope Dillard and her two small, unpleasant children. Harriet's attention had been diverted from Sarah, for now she had others to reform. Sarah was relieved that her life had settled into a peaceful existence again, but a gnawing dissatisfaction—which she tried desperately and unsuccessfully to ignore—ate at her heart. On the surface, all was well. Why could she not be satisfied with that?

Sarah learned through Jubal Sage that Orion healed rapidly once the fever was gone. He had moved out of the headquarters office and into Joseph's tent. Two weeks had passed since the ambush, and already he was up and walking about, at first with the aid of his brothers, then with a makeshift cane, and finally, under his own power. Sarah would watch him from across the parade ground, filled with a strange mixture of feelings—relief that he was healing and alive, intense longing to talk with him, fearful of talking with him, fearful that any day he would leave and she would never see

him again. She missed him, and prayed that in time that
feeling would go away.

With the help of the additional troops, work on the fort
progressed at an amazing speed. It seemed that in a matter
of just a few days, a snug log house had been erected for
Major Dillard and his family, another for Lieutenants Roe
and Fielding, the roof had finally been added to the barracks,
a dormitory for the laundresses had been constructed, as had
a large building that served as both meeting room and mess
hall, and the wooden stockade wall around the compound
had been completed. Plans had been drawn up to enlarge the
stables and, in anticipation of his marriage to Sarah, to enlarge Adam's small quarters as well, but those projects would
wait until spring. Now the enlisted men spent the majority
of their time putting in a supply of firewood to get them
through the coming winter, and catching up on the drilling
and marching exercises that had been neglected during the
construction of the fort.

Sarah spent a great deal of her time with Harriet and
Penelope, chatting, stitching, mending, watching the lively
children. After two weeks of such activity, she was ready to
go out of her mind with boredom.

Penelope Dillard was a sweetly vapid woman, plump, with
pale blonde hair and huge hazel eyes. She deferred to Harriet
in all things, but Sarah suspected the woman was not as
good-natured as she let on. There were lines of tension
around her mouth and eyes, a certain brittleness to her manner. She doted on her two spoiled children, allowing them
more freedom than Sarah felt was appropriate. Six-year-old
Neville was rude and on occasion downright obnoxious,
while three-year-old Clarissa was an angelic-looking child
with golden curls and a whiny, demanding nature that was
anything but angelic. A little time spent in the company of
the children was all Sarah could endure, and she found herself more and more often making excuses to avoid the Dil-
lards.

One afternoon, in desperation, Sarah excused herself from the noisy gathering in the parlor, explaining falsely that Adam had promised her a ride. As she hurried to change into her riding habit, she prayed that her little lie would go undetected, that Adam truly could break away for an hour or so. She fought down the memory of another day, and another ride, when she had worn this very outfit, when Orion had shown her the glory of the morning and the power of his kiss. With an annoyed shake of her head, Sarah left the room. It did no good to dwell on such things. If her marriage to Adam was to be successful, the memory of Orion Beaudine and the sweet temptation he had presented would have to be locked away in a secret part of her heart.

She had no luck in locating Adam. Finally, standing outside the stable, Sarah was ready to stamp her foot in frustration, for she knew none of the soldiers would saddle her mare unless she had an escort. Her shoulders slumped with dejection. She simply did not have it in her to return to the Rutledges' house right now.

"Looking for an escort, Miss Hancock?"

Sarah jumped at the sound of Lieutenant Fielding's arrogant, jeering voice. He was so close behind her that she could feel his breath on her neck. Why hadn't she heard him approach? She took a step away from him. "No, I am not, Lieutenant," she answered coolly.

Fielding continued as if she had not spoken. "Your fiancé is away for the afternoon, supervising a logging detail." He trailed a finger down her arm. "You'll ride with me."

"I will not." Sarah stepped away again, a hot anger beginning its pounding dance through her veins. "I told you I don't need an escort."

"You will ride with me," Fielding repeated forcefully. His hand darted out and grabbed her wrist.

Sarah twisted away from him just as a stern voice demanded, "What is going on here?"

Holding her aching wrist, Sarah turned with relief to face

Captain Joseph Beaudine, who looked tall and impressive in his captain's uniform. The furious expression in his brown eyes gave her cause to be grateful that his anger was not directed at her. "The lieutenant labors under the incorrect assumption that I am in need of a riding escort," she explained sharply. "He is most insistent that I accompany him."

Fielding snapped to attention. "Captain Rutledge has made it clear that he does not wish his lady to ride alone, sir."

"Miss Hancock was waiting for me, Lieutenant. Surely I qualify as a proper escort."

Sarah looked at Joseph, struggling to keep her surprise and gratitude from showing on her face.

"Yes, sir," Fielding answered, somewhat flustered. "The lady did not explain that to me. I was only trying to protect her."

Joseph's eyes narrowed, and his mouth tightened under his full mustache. "I know what you were trying to do, Lieutenant. As Miss Hancock obviously does not welcome your company, I hereby order you to keep your distance from her. Is that understood?"

The lieutenant's face flushed a bright red. "Yes, sir!"

Joseph leaned forward. "This goes beyond the Army, Fielding." His deep, accented voice took on a deadly tone. "If you disobey my order, if you so much as look wrong at Miss Hancock, you'll answer to me and my brothers. There won't be a rock you can crawl under to hide from us, especially Orion. He's called the Hunter for a good reason."

Fielding's face was now a pasty white, although his eyes fairly flashed with impotent rage. "Yes, sir," he spat. "May I go now, *sir?*"

"Get out of here."

Without another word and in direct breech of Army protocol, Fielding spun around and marched away.

Sarah heaved a sigh of relief. "Thank you, Captain. I try

to avoid the man, but he came out of nowhere. For a moment I feared he was prepared to drag me into the stable."

"I wouldn't put it past him." Joseph looked down at her. "May I escort you somewhere?"

"I was hoping Adam could take me for a ride, but apparently he is out with a detail."

"I would be happy to ride with you, Miss Hancock."

"Truly?" Sarah's heart leapt with joy. "You have the time?"

Joseph smiled. "I do." He held his arm out to her.

"Oh, thank you, Captain." Her voice dropped to a conspiratorial whisper. "I cannot bear the thought of spending another afternoon with Mrs. Major Dillard's little hellions."

Joseph laughed. "I understand perfectly. I was forced to spend three days with them on the trail from Fort Laramie. Come now; let's saddle your mare. And I think I'll take Thunder out. He could use a run, too." With that, he led her into the stable.

A half hour later, Sarah gave Star her head, allowing the mare to run, for evidently she had as much pent-up energy as Sarah. When she pulled Star to a halt near a stand of trees, she saw that Joseph Beaudine and Thunder had stayed right with her.

She leaned forward to pat Star's damp neck, feeling breathless herself. The exhilarating run, combined with the cool fall air, had cleared some of the cobwebs from her brain. She felt more alive, happier, than she had in days. "I hope you don't mind that I ran her," she said apologetically to Joseph. "I felt she needed it, just as I did."

Joseph looked at Sarah's flushed cheeks, at her sparkling blue eyes, at the wisps of dark hair that had escaped her hat, and he could see why Orion found her beautiful. "I'm sure the run was good for both of you," he answered approvingly. "You sit a horse well. Have you been riding long?"

"Only since I arrived in the West two months ago. Mr. Sage taught me to ride."

"I'm impressed, Miss Hancock."

Sarah smiled at him. "Thank you. Which way now?"

"Your choice."

She shaded her eyes with one gloved hand and studied the area for a moment, then pointed to a hill a short distance away. "There," she said softly. A strange, wistful look came over her face. "I'd like to go there."

"Very well. From here we'll keep the horses at a walk and let them cool down." Joseph led the way. They rode in silence for the fifteen minutes it took to reach their destination. He helped her down from the saddle, and she immediately walked to an outcropping of rock that offered a flat surface on which to sit as well as a breathtaking view of the land to the east. She gracefully sank down to a sitting position on the rock, her gray skirts covering her folded legs. Joseph came to sit beside her, and for several silent, companionable minutes, they soaked in the beauty of the place and the afternoon.

Suddenly Sarah turned to look behind her.

"What is it?" Joseph asked in a rough whisper, instantly on his guard. His eyes darted around the area as his hand moved to the pistol at his hip.

"It's Dancer," Sarah said happily.

Joseph stared at her in amazement, then searched the area again. He had seen nothing, still saw nothing. Then he did. Sure enough, Dancer materialized out of a thick stand of scrub oak about twenty feet uphill. As he watched, the wolf daintily picked his way through tall grass and sagebrush to Sarah's side and sat next to her, allowing her to put her arm around his neck.

"Hello, Dancer," she murmured as she scratched the animal's ears. "I've missed you."

She understands the Power of the Wolf.

Orion's words came back to Joseph as he watched Sarah and Dancer, and he knew his brother was right. She truly understood. He did not doubt that she also listened to the four winds and could hear Mother Earth, as Orion had said. As sure as he drew breath, Joseph knew in that instant that Sarah Hancock and his brother Orion belonged together, that they were meant for each other. Now he understood Orion's anguish over Sarah. It shook Joseph to realize he was looking at his new sister. The only problem was, she didn't know it yet. He could no longer be silent.

"My brother has powerful feelings for you."

Sarah slowly turned her head to look at him. The black gauze scarf that encircled the crown of her hat blew over her shoulder and floated on the cool breeze. "I know," she said quietly.

"You have powerful feelings for him as well, Sarah Hancock."

An incredible sadness came over her suddenly pale face, and her large blue eyes filled with tears. She turned away from him to look out over the vista to the east. "He brought me here once," she whispered. "He wanted to share the beauty of his world with me. Such a gift he gave me." Her voice caught. "I miss him."

"He misses you, too, but he will not intrude. It is you who must choose."

She stiffened. "I have made my choice, Captain Beaudine."

"Examine that choice carefully. You're not yet wed. You can change your mind."

She turned on him, her tear-filled eyes bright with despair. "I gave my *word*. There is another involved, a good, decent man who has cared for me all of my life. I have a responsibility to him, Captain."

"Your responsibility to yourself is greater."

Sarah turned away from him and buried her face in the thick ruff of fur at Dancer's neck.

Joseph sighed. "It's not right that I pressure you, ma'am. Forgive me." He paused. "Orion will be leaving."

At that, she looked back at him. "When?"

"Soon. Another small detachment is due to arrive tomorrow. Once they get settled, Colonel Rutledge wants to have a party of some kind, maybe a dance, to celebrate the completion of Fort St. Charles. Then some of us—myself, Orion, and Lieutenant Fielding, among others—are ordered back to Fort Laramie. I would guess that we'll leave within the week." Impulsively, Joseph put his hand on Sarah's forearm. "Search your heart, Miss Hancock. Before my brother leaves, tell him what you find there, for both your sakes."

Sarah nodded. "I will." She gave him a sad smile. "I should get back. Mrs. Rutledge will wonder where I am."

"She won't be pleased that you were with me," Joseph said as he stood up. He held a hand down to her.

"She doesn't like you either?" Sarah took his hand.

"No, but she tolerates me easier than she does my brothers. I guess my uniform gives me some respectability in her eyes." He pulled Sarah to her feet.

"I can only imagine her opinion of Gray Eagle." Sarah rolled her eyes. "Why does she hate your family so?"

"We don't know." He led her toward the horses, surprised that Dancer followed them.

Sarah stopped and bent down to pet the wolf. "I'm glad to have seen you," she whispered. Dancer whined and lived up to his name by dancing around her. She laughed in delight. "Oh, Dancer, Orion told me you could dance."

Joseph watched, again amazed. "Think on all I have said, Miss Hancock," he said quietly.

She straightened and looked at him, calm and resolute. "I will, Captain. Thank you for your concern."

There was nothing more he could say, nothing more he could do. Joseph helped her into the saddle, climbed onto Thunder's back, and led the way back to the fort.

Thirteen

Sarah fully intended to keep her word to Joseph, but an opportunity to speak with Orion did not present itself in the next few days. Just as Joseph had predicted, a detachment arrived the next day, consisting of sixteen cavalrymen, two more laundresses, and an officer by the name of Lieutenant Michael Gates, who not only was accompanied by his young bride Libby, but was also a good friend of Adam's from West Point. The new troops were to replace some of the enlisted men who had been at the fort since the summer, and those ordered to leave were overjoyed.

The fort was in a turmoil as the new arrivals sought to get settled, while those returning to Fort Laramie made their own preparations. Again a flock of white canvas tents sprang up on the grounds outside the walls of the fort. Adam, happy to be reunited with his old friend, magnanimously gave up his small cabin to the newlyweds. He moved into the cabin shared by Lieutenants Roe and Fielding, which made for crowded quarters, but Fielding would leave in a few days with the detachment bound for Fort Laramie.

Three days later, when everyone was relatively settled, Colonel Rutledge announced that a celebration would be held in two days' time. In a break with the age-old Army custom that forbade the mingling of officers and enlisted men at the same social gathering, he opened the festivities to all, claiming that the population of Fort St. Charles was simply too small to justify two separate events. Sarah could tell from Harriet's tight-lipped demeanor that the Mrs. Colonel did not agree with her husband's position, but there was nothing she could do except give in, albeit ungraciously.

Sarah faced the prospect of the party with mixed feelings. While she looked forward to getting dressed up, she also knew that the celebration heralded the imminent departure of the Beaudine brothers. In spite of her fierce determination to feel otherwise, the thought of Orion leaving broke her heart.

The night of the party, Lucy pulled Harriet's full-length standing mirror out into the parlor, since both Penelope Dillard and Libby Gates had accepted Harriet's invitation to dress at her house. Sarah now stared into that mirror, surveying the results of her efforts as dressmaker and Lucy's as hairdresser. It had been so long since she had dressed up—well over a year, since before her mother's death—that her reflected image was alien to her.

"You look lovely, Miss Sarah," Lucy said softly.

"Do I?" Sarah asked the question in all sincerity. She had made one of her mother's ball gowns over to fit her. The dress was of black silk, its full, flounced skirt worn over a modest set of hoops, the separate bodice hooked in back and pointed in a deep vee at her waist in front. The veed neckline rested off her shoulders, and short puffed sleeves reached to her elbows. Lucy had done her hair up in an intriguing arrangement of rolls and braids, leaving her neck bare save for the garnet necklace she wore and the long, matching earrings that hung from her earlobes. "The black is so . . . black. Isn't the overall effect rather stark?"

"Since your year of mourning for your mama isn't up yet, it's best to stay with black, miss, if you want to avoid the Mrs. Colonel's ire," Lucy said in a low tone. "You look very elegant, unlike others I could name." She inclined her head to the corner where Penelope preened in her elaborate gown and poor, young Libby looked decidedly self-conscious in the ill-fitting, tasteless creation Penelope had insisted she borrow. "The Mrs. Colonel will be pleased with you."

"You think so?" Sarah asked doubtfully.

"Yes, miss. You'll see. Now where's that fancy lace shawl of yours? The menfolk'll be here any minute."

"It's on my bed."

"I'll get it." Lucy hurried off.

"Won't you be relieved when your year is up, Miss Hancock?" Penelope drawled. "Black is such a dreary color. It makes one appear so washed out and colorless."

"One does the best one can," Sarah calmly replied, proud that she was able to resist the temptation to point out that if one wished to appear washed out and colorless, one need only have light-colored hair such as Penelope's and wear an all-white virginal gown like that Penelope wore. Not only was the style of the gown too young for the woman's age, but the combination of her plump figure and wide hoops brought to mind the image of a large snowball. Sarah covered her lips with her fingers to hide a smile. Harriet would be appalled when she at last came from her room. If nothing else, Harriet Rutledge had impeccable taste in matters of dress. Sarah doubted that the unsuitable gowns worn by her companions would ever be seen again at Fort St. Charles.

Lucy settled the shawl around Sarah's shoulders as Harriet came from her room, resplendent in a tasteful gown of aqua-colored silk decorated with scallops of lace and small bouquets of silk roses. When Harriet's gaze fell upon the two women in the corner, she reacted as Sarah had suspected she would.

"Lord have mercy!" she gasped, and hurried to the side table to pour herself a generous sherry. With her back to the others, she drained the glass and set it down, then straightened her shoulders.

"You look lovely, Harriet," Sarah said sincerely. "That color suits you."

Harriet turned around. "Thank you, Sarah. You look very

nice yourself, although your neckline is too low for a woman in mourning. However, it will do." She fixed her stern gaze on the two nervous women across the room. "On the other hand, much is to be desired with the two of you. Sadly, there is not enough time to remedy the situation. Our gentlemen will arrive at any moment. We shall simply have to make the best of it." She focused on Libby. "Where did you get that dress, child?"

"Mrs. Major Dillard loaned it to me," Libby squeaked. She darted a scowl at Penelope. "She insisted my gown was out of date."

"As if that one is not," Harriet said with a disdainful sniff. "And you, Mrs. Major Dillard. Your gown is more suited to a coming-out ball. Need I remind you that your debutante days are far behind you? Pinch your cheeks, for heaven's sake. You look like a ghost."

Penelope hurriedly obeyed, pinching herself hard enough to leave two brilliant red splotches on her cheeks.

Harriet drew herself up and stared at each woman in turn, Sarah included. "Fort St. Charles is here to stay for now, ladies. She is hardly the flagship of our country's military posts, but we shall behave as if she were. It is our duty to turn this wretched bit of dirt into an island of civilization in the wilderness. Among other things, our behavior and code of dress shall be above reproach, so that we may do our husbands, and our country, proud. Have I made myself clear?"

"Yes, ma'am," Libby breathed, a new light of adulation shining in her young eyes. "I do want Michael to be proud of me."

"And he shall be, when I am finished with you," Harriet assured her. She settled her cold gaze on Penelope. "Mrs. Major Dillard?"

"You have made yourself clear, Mrs. Colonel Rutledge." Although her tone was tinged with resentment, Penelope's expression was one of complacence.

Harriet arched an eyebrow, but said no more to the woman. She turned to Sarah. "Miss Hancock?"

Sarah met her gaze and spoke from her heart. "Your cause is a noble one, madam, and I applaud your endeavors."

Harriet blinked, clearly surprised. "Good," she finally said. She took a breath, and her voice regained its customary strength. "I believe I hear our gentlemen approaching, ladies. Let us put our best face forward, even under these unfortunate circumstances." It was as if a mask settled over her features, turning her into a woman with a pleasing countenance and a charming manner. "Lucy, please remove the standing mirror to my room."

"Yes, ma'am."

"I'll get the bedroom door for you," Sarah offered. When she and Lucy were alone in the bedroom, Sarah said, "You are coming to the party, aren't you? Colonel Rutledge invited everyone."

Lucy shrugged. "I have a nice dress. I thought I would."

"Good." Sarah wanted to ask if Lucy needed help dressing, but she sensed that would cross the invisible line Lucy had drawn between them. "I'll see you later, then." She moved to the door.

"You look beautiful tonight, Miss Sarah, no matter what anyone says," Lucy said softly. "The Hunter will be pleased."

Startled, Sarah paused and looked back over her shoulder. "I didn't dress for him."

"Well, if you dressed for the captain, chances are he won't even notice. But you mark my word. The Hunter will notice."

Without another word, Sarah hurried from the room, trying to beat down the rush of anticipation Lucy's last words had brought her. She had dressed for Adam. Surely he would notice.

He didn't, or if he did, he did not comment on it. He placed a perfunctory kiss on her cheek. "There you are, my dear."

"Adam." She smiled up at him. "How handsome you look tonight." She meant her words. With his wavy blond hair and neatly trimmed beard, wearing a full dress uniform that made his blue eyes appear even more blue, Adam Rutledge would turn any woman's head.

"Thank you, Sarah. Would you care for some sherry?"

"Are we not leaving for the hall right away?"

"No. We are to be fashionably late."

Sarah frowned. "But the colonel is hosting the party. Everyone will be waiting."

Adam shrugged. "We'll go over when he does. Have some sherry." He pressed a glass into her hand. "Excuse me for a moment. I want to speak to Michael."

Somehow feeling deserted, she watched as he crossed the small room. As if on cue, Libby left the two men and joined Sarah. Her face was flushed with excitement. "They all look so wonderful in their uniforms, don't they?"

"Yes, they do." Sarah took a sip of the sherry. The room was very crowded. In addition to the four men accompanying their women, the unattached Lieutenants Roe and Fielding had also come. Thankfully, Fielding had not so much as looked at her. Joseph Beaudine's words must have sunk in. Then she realized that Captain Beaudine was the only officer not present. Sarah wondered where he was.

"Wasn't Mrs. Colonel Rutledge stunning earlier?" Libby gushed. "I want to be just like her."

Sarah eyed the younger woman. "How old are you, Mrs. Lieutenant Gates, if you don't mind my asking?"

Libby looked down at her glass, suddenly self-conscious. "I'll be seventeen next month." She glanced at Sarah. "Is it so obvious?"

Sarah placed a comforting hand on the girl's arm. "Only in your innocent enthusiasm. I wish I had more of it. Your Michael is a lucky man."

Libby gaped at her. "You mean it, Miss Hancock?"

"Oh, yes. If you want to be an excellent Army wife, you could not have a better teacher than Mrs. Colonel Rutledge. She may seem gruff or impatient at times, but she knows of what she speaks and is fiercely devoted to her husband and his career. Follow her lead." Sarah lowered her voice. "However, be wary of Mrs. Major Dillard. She is not all she pretends to be."

"I learned that already." Libby squeezed Sarah's free hand. "Thank you, Miss Hancock. You'll make a perfect Army wife yourself." She left to join her husband.

A sadness washed over Sarah, for she doubted she would make a perfect Army wife, no matter how hard she tried. As she looked about the small, crowded room, Sarah felt strangely out of place. Perhaps it was the black gown that made her feel so separated from everyone; perhaps it was the fact that she was not yet an official "wife." For whatever reason, she was suddenly very anxious to leave the stuffy room and join the rest of the post at the meeting hall. And, she assured herself, Orion Beaudine had nothing to do with her increasing sense of impatience.

Orion stood near a side wall of the meeting room with his brothers, waiting, as everyone else was, for the arrival of the colonel and his wife, and the rest of the officers and their ladies. He was annoyed at their tardiness. Until they arrived, the festivities could not begin, and he could not see Sarah.

The room was crowded with an interesting variety of people. The three Mexican families who lived across the river kept to themselves at one table, troopers in dress uniform milled about, speaking in low voices, and the laundresses congregated in a corner, laughing and talking together. The women were wise to rest while they could, Orion thought, for once the small band started up, they would not have a chance to catch their breath for the rest of the evening. There were five laundresses, three Mexican women, three officers' wives, Sarah, and Lucy, if she came, to dance with close to sixty men. Some of the men would eventually tie scarves around one arm, indicating that they were "female" dance partners, but it would prove to be a tiring night for the women just the same. Orion's gaze again returned to the door. *Sarah.* He longed to see her.

The last few weeks had been an agony of waiting, and she had never come. When Joseph told him of the ride with Sarah and her declaration that she had made her choice, it had taken both of his brothers to physically keep him from storming up to Colonel Rutledge's house and demanding that Sarah see him. Only Joseph's assurance that he had begged Sarah to reconsider, and her promise that she would, kept Orion from following through on his original impulse over the next few days. Joseph had urged him to give Sarah time. He had, and still she had not come.

Surely she would come tonight. If she didn't, he vowed that he would go find her. He had no intention of leaving in the morning without seeing her one more time.

Orion was dragged from his anxious thoughts by the approach of Jubal Sage.

Jubal drained the tin cup he held, smacking his lips in satisfaction. "I'm headin' to the barrel of whiskey out back," he announced. "Any of you boys want some?"

Orion glanced at his brothers, both of whom shook their heads. "Not now, Jubal, but thanks," he said. "You'd better watch it. You've already had three doses of that stuff."

"Four," Jubal cheerfully corrected. "And I aim to have many more. When I pass out, I want one of you to make sure no one steals nothin' off me, and that I'm covered with a blanket or somethin'. I don't want to freeze to death tonight."

"Maybe you should change out of your fancy duds, Jubal, if you intend to be lying on the floor before long," Joseph suggested.

Jubal scowled and scratched at the perfectly tied neckcloth he wore, which looked out of place with his buckskins. "I only put this blasted thing on for the ladies. If'n the rest of 'em don't get here soon, I'm gonna take it off."

"I wish you'd take off some of that hair tonic you plastered all over yourself," Gray Eagle complained. "I can smell you coming at thirty paces."

"And it's a right pretty smell, ain't it?" Jubal demanded. He ran a hand over his long, neatly combed gray hair, then over his beard. "You're just jealous, Eagle, 'cause I'm gonna be fightin' off all them women tonight. I offered to share my tonic with you, but none of you took me up on my generous offer. Now you'll have to stand aside and watch while I dazzle all the ladies."

Joseph hooted with laughter. "We'll be sure to take notes, Jubal."

"Y'all could use some lessons," Jubal retorted over his shoulder as he made his way to the back door. "Your pa, rest his soul, never did teach you boys much about women. That's why none of you are married yet. You listen to old Jubal now." He disappeared out the door.

The brothers laughed again, then turned toward the front door as a silence fell over the room and the center of the floor cleared. At last the officers had arrived.

Colonel Rutledge entered first, with his wife at his side, followed closely by Major and Mrs. Dillard, and Lieutenant and Mrs. Gates. Roe and Fielding came next, and finally, Captain Rutledge and Sarah.

Sarah.

She was dressed all in black, and the effect was stunning. Her perfectly tailored dress exposed her lovely shoulders, enticed her breasts to swell intriguingly above the low neckline, flattered her narrow waist, and belled gracefully down to the floor. Her hair was pulled up, revealing her neck, which Orion suddenly and desperately wanted to kiss. And her lovely face, pale in contrast to her dark hair and gown except for her large eyes, was serene. She glanced about the room, and when her gaze fell on him, she stared at him, then smiled shyly just before she looked away. Orion slowly let out his breath.

"She's a striking woman, big brother," Gray Eagle commented.

"That she is," Joseph added. He looked at Orion and frowned. "Are you all right?"

"I'm fine," Orion lied. "My shoulder's a little stiff, but that's all." His shoulder was indeed stiff, but he was far from fine. He had not seen Sarah, except at a distance, for two weeks now, and the sight of her tonight had affected him like a blow to the stomach.

She simply did not belong with the officer at her side.

Sarah Hancock belonged with him.

Orion ached to take her in his arms, to hold her, to dance with her, to kiss her, to take her away from this crowded room to some dark, secluded spot and make sweet love to her, to show her that she truly did belong with him.

"I think he needs some of Jubal's libation," Gray Eagle said to Joseph, as if Orion were not standing between them.

Joseph nodded in agreement. "I think you're right, little brother," he said, and it was clear to Orion that neither brother was speaking in jest.

Nothing more was said then, though, for Colonel Rutledge had finally reached the hastily constructed bandstand, on which the seven enlisted men who made up the small but enthusiastic band waited. After a thankfully short speech welcoming everyone, and extolling the admittedly dubious attributes of Fort St. Charles, the colonel ordered the band to strike up the music. As was customary, the officers and their ladies danced the first dance alone, and Orion was both grateful and surprised that Sarah and Captain Rutledge did not join them.

Then he remembered she was still in mourning, and realized why she was dressed in black. His feelings were mixed, because, while he did not relish the idea of being forced to watch Sarah dance with her betrothed, he had also hoped she would dance with him.

The first dance ended, and Colonel Rutledge granted permission for all to dance. Cheers erupted, women squealed as they were grabbed as partners, and the room suddenly became an impassable melee. Sarah disappeared from Orion's view.

Sarah sat on a chair next to the wall, fanning herself. Adam had left her so that he could fulfill his duty of dancing with the other officers' wives. Although she couldn't see him in the crush of revelers, Sarah knew that he led his aunt around the floor with careful, plodding steps, listening intently while she spoke in his ear about who-knew-what. Even while dancing, Harriet could not relax her vigil. The woman was probably telling him of another of her—Sarah's—unintentional transgressions.

With a sigh, Sarah turned her attention to the exuberant dancers, but she didn't really see them, for now she allowed herself to dwell on the sight that had greeted her when she entered the hall.

Orion.

Just as she would never forget the first time she saw him, coming to her across the meadow, never would she forget the sight of him standing there tonight with his brothers. What a picture they had made, those three tall, handsome men; Joseph in his dress uniform, his brown eyes crinkled with laughter, his lips curved in a smile under his full mustache; Gray Eagle, dressed in a black suit, complete with a perfectly fitted frock coat and elaborately arranged neckcloth, his interesting eyes watchful and alert, his hair hanging past the middle of his back, pulled away from the sides of his face into two narrow braids, one of which was decorated with a lone eagle feather; and Orion, in dark trousers and frock coat, a white shirt, and a black cravat, his long hair flowing around his shoulders, his green eyes burning with that familiar intensity when he looked at her.

Sarah had fought the urge to leave Adam's side and hurry across the room to join the Beaudine brothers, to bask in the warm acceptance and friendship she sensed they all offered her. She had the strange feeling that they would have formed a protective circle around her. But instead of going to them, she had looked away, before Orion could read the longing that she feared showed in her eyes.

She sighed and looked about the room. As much as she loved to dance, she was grateful that her well-known mourning period kept the men from asking her. Adam was a poor dancer, and besides, he would not have broken with tradition and asked her, but once she had seen Orion, he became the only person with whom she wished to dance.

Sarah closed her eyes in anguish. What was she to do about the maddening man? He only had to look at her, and all her forbidden longings—longings she had tried so desperately to suppress—came rushing back with new vengeance. Sarah felt that if she did not soon speak to Orion, touch him, surely she would die. Was this what passion did to a person? Did it bring this exquisite agony, and the hope, perhaps the promise, of equally exquisite ecstasy? So far, all she had known was the agony. Perhaps she did not want it after all.

"Are you all right, ma'am?"

At the sound of a soft female voice, Sarah's eyes flew open. She saw an unfamiliar woman leaning over her, watching her with wide, concerned brown eyes. "Ma'am?" the woman repeated.

"I'm fine, thank you," Sarah responded. "It was kind of you to ask."

The woman straightened, and Sarah saw that she was slender, perhaps thirty years old, dressed in a neat, modest, blue gown, with golden hair arranged in a simple style.

"I know you're in mourning, and I know what that is like." A look of deep, haunted grief flashed across the woman's thin face and was gone. "I just wanted to be sure you were all right. Good evening, ma'am." She turned to leave.

"Wait, please," Sarah said. "Please sit with me." She waved a hand at the empty chair next to her.

Obviously startled, the woman hesitated before she spoke. "You want me to sit with you?"

Sarah assumed the woman was one of the laundresses and wondered if the same unspoken rules to which Lucy adhered applied to this woman as well. "Yes, if you wish to, that is."

"Ma'am, I'm Theodora Byrd." She spoke as if her name would mean something to Sarah. It didn't.

"And I am Miss Sarah Hancock." Sarah held out her hand. "I'm pleased to meet you, Miss Byrd. Or is it Mrs.?"

Theodora glanced nervously about, then took Sarah's hand. "It's Mrs., but I'm widowed."

Sarah tightened her grip on Theodora's fingers before she released her. "I'm so sorry for your loss, Mrs. Byrd. Please join me."

"Are you sure, Miss Hancock?"

"Please."

Theodora sank into the chair. "Thank you." Looking like a nervous chicken in a fox den, she wrung her hands in her lap and finally blurted out, "Don't you know who I am?"

"I assume you are one of the laundresses. Am I correct?"

"Yes, ma'am. But there's more to it than that." Theodora straightened, and a curious, resolute strength settled over her. She stared ahead, away from Sarah. "After my husband's death, for a time I was forced to earn my living in a less than respectable manner. Most folks here know that, which is why I was so surprised you invited me to sit with you." She jumped up from the chair. "I'll go now. It was nice to meet you, ma'am."

Sarah's heart twisted, and impulsively, she also stood, clasping her hands together so that she did not reach out to the defensive woman next to her. "Please, Mrs. Byrd, don't go. I would like you to sit with me for a while, if that would suit you. I would enjoy the company."

Theodora continued to stare straight ahead, now blinking rapidly. "It would suit me just fine, Miss Hancock."

Both women settled back into their chairs and spent the

next few minutes sharing cautious pleasantries with each other. Sarah was acutely aware of the curious glances and outright stares directed toward her. At one point, she caught Harriet Rutledge's ominous, critical eye on her, and raised her chin a notch higher. Regardless of what the others thought, Sarah was drawn to Theodora's gentle kindness, as well as her unflinching honesty. It took a great deal of courage to admit that one had an unsavory past.

"Will you just look at this?" Jubal Sage's jovial voice jolted both Sarah and Theodora out of their conversation. He executed a rather courtly bow, and Sarah was struck almost forcibly with the powerful scent of a robust hair tonic.

Jubal continued. "I swear I have never seen a lovelier sight than you two ladies." He ran a hand over his slicked-down hair and honored them with a slightly inebriated smile. "I'm just a-dyin' to dance, and the choice would be awful if one of you wasn't in mournin'." He reached down and drew both women to their feet. "But it wouldn't be right to leave Miss Sarah sittin' here all alone, so you two come along with me."

"Mr. Sage," Sarah said affectionately as she took Jubal's arm. "Have you been drinking?"

"Yup," Jubal said proudly.

Sarah peered around him. "Mrs. Byrd, are you acquainted with Mr. Sage?"

Theodora nodded, her lips curved in a small smile. "I had the pleasure of meeting Mr. Sage at Fort Laramie a few months ago."

"Come on now. There's some folks I want you to say howdy to, then me and Mrs. Byrd'll dance." Jubal steered both women along, guiding them with surprising skill across the crowded room, considering his impaired state. He came to an abrupt halt near the back door. "Ladies, I present to you the Ugly Brothers." He waved a hand to indicate the Beaudines, all of whom eyed Jubal with cocked eyebrows and lenient expressions on their handsome faces.

Even though Orion's smoldering gaze threatened to take

her breath away, Sarah could not stifle a laugh. "The Ugly Brothers?" she repeated incredulously. "Mr. Sage, how much have you had to drink?"

"Too much," Theodora murmured.

"Boys, this here is Mrs. Theodora Byrd, my new dancin' partner, and I believe you are acquainted with Miss Hancock." Jubal rocked proudly on the balls of his feet, as if he were introducing President Taylor himself. "Mrs. Byrd, this is Gray Eagle, Joseph, and Orion Beaudine. Y'all say your howdies fast, cause I'm takin' Mrs. Byrd away."

True to his word, after hasty greetings from all parties, Jubal pulled Theodora into the crowd of rowdy dancers and they were soon lost from sight.

"You look lovely this evening, Miss Hancock," said Gray Eagle.

"You do indeed," Joseph chimed in.

"Thank you, gentlemen." Sarah felt the heat of an annoying blush color her cheeks. "All three of you also look very nice, contrary to Mr. Sage's name for you." She refused to look at Orion's face, for she was afraid of what she would see in his eyes, and even more afraid of what he might see in hers.

"That was a term of endearment," Gray Eagle explained.

"Oh, I know. I'm certain he is very fond of all of you." *As I am,* she added silently as she fanned her face. Did she only imagine that the glance Joseph and Gray Eagle shared was wrought with unspoken communication?

"It's getting stuffy in here," Joseph commented. "Would you like to get some air, Miss Hancock?"

"Yes, I would, Captain. Thank you." With a quick glance at Orion's impassive face, Sarah took Joseph's offered arm, and he led her to the back door. She was acutely disappointed that Gray Eagle and Orion did not follow them.

The relief she felt when she stepped out into the cool night was immediate; she had not realized how uncomfortably warm it had become inside the crowded meeting hall.

Thanks to lighted lanterns hung outside the door and on nearby trees, Sarah could see that others had left the celebration. Two enlisted men were stumbling in the direction of the barracks, a few more were standing near the corner of the building smoking, and several were congregated around a large wooden barrel set up on a table a short distance away.

Joseph led her in the direction of the deserted parade ground. "Are you warm enough with only that shawl?" he asked.

"Yes, thank you. And thank you for bringing me outside, Captain. The cool air is welcome."

"It's obvious that you and my brother have not spoken."

Sarah blinked in surprise at Joseph's abrupt change of subject. "There has been no opportunity."

"We are leaving at dawn."

"I know." The very thought distressed her. "I shall miss all of you."

Joseph stopped and faced her, taking her hands in his. "I'll send him out to you, if you wish."

The nearly full moon had risen over the tops of the trees, and in its light, Sarah could see Joseph's long, uncovered hair touching the captain's bars on his shoulders, could see the concern and kindness in his expression. A rush of affection filled her, and complete trust. "I would like that, Captain," she admitted. "You don't know how much."

"I have an idea, little sister. Wait here." Joseph released her hands and turned away.

Sarah stared after him. *Little sister.* Why had he called her that? And why had she liked it so much?

Joseph had not gone far when he stopped. Sarah looked beyond him and saw that Gray Eagle and Orion were coming from the direction of the meeting hall.

Her heart started pounding.

The three brothers conversed quietly for a minute, the muted sounds of their masculine voices reaching her across the parade ground. Joseph glanced back over his shoulder at her, his handsome face creased in an encouraging smile, then he and Gray Eagle disappeared between two buildings.

Across the distance that separated them, Sarah could feel the heat of Orion's gaze, the power of his longing, for her feelings matched his. For a long moment, they stared at each other.

Then, just as when he had crossed the meadow that first day, he came to her.

Fourteen

With his long, powerful stride, it seemed to Sarah that Orion covered the distance between them in an instant. He stopped before her, an arm's reach away, and stared at her. The same moonlight that had revealed Joseph's expressions to her offered the same service to Orion, and the look on his face took Sarah's breath away. Without saying a word, he conveyed to her tenderness, longing, and a touch of frustration. A breeze lifted a few strands of his hair from his shoulder, and the silence grew long. When he finally spoke, his words surprised her.

"Would you like to dance with me?"

She nodded shyly. "Very much, but I fear it would spark a scandal, and I have no wish to go back inside."

"I had no intention of going back inside." He held his hand out to her. "We can hear the music well enough to make do right here."

Sarah glanced around. In the distance she could see a few people near the buildings, but no one appeared to be watching the almost deserted parade ground. How many times in her life would she have the opportunity to dance in the moonlight with Orion Beaudine? She placed her hand in his and smiled up at him.

He put his hand on her waist and drew her closer, but not so close that their bodies touched. She put her free hand on his shoulder and he began to move slowly in time to the faint music, in the steps she recognized as a waltz.

Where had a frontiersman learned to waltz?

Sarah gave herself up to the delight of the dance, to the excitement of being in Orion's arms. How she had missed him! He led her around the uneven ground with care, keeping a firm hold on her waist, more than once steadying her when her foot caught on a clump of grass or in an indentation in the earth. The music came to an end, and riotous applause and cheering resounded from the meeting hall, and still Orion led her on, as if he heard a ghostly or angelic orchestra of his own. Sarah was content to follow him, for she knew this was a magical time, one that would all too soon be over.

It was. Orion stopped suddenly and pulled her into his arms, holding her tightly. "Sarah," he whispered against her hair. "Oh, Sarah."

Instinctively, her arms encircled his waist, and she clung to him. His heart pounded against her, his hair brushed her cheek, his clean, sage scent enveloped her. A well of longing opened in her heart, calling to her, beckoning her. She knew that if she gave in, all would be lost. She would give Orion Beaudine anything he wanted.

With a sob, she pushed back from him. "I can't!" she cried softly.

"You can't what?" Orion asked, his voice hoarse. His hands, warm and strong, still rested on her bare shoulders.

"I can't give you what you want from me, Orion. I want to, but I can't. I won't. I made my choice long ago, before I ever came West, and you won't change my mind. I owe Adam that much." Orion dropped his arms to his sides, and Sarah suddenly felt cold and terribly alone.

"Do you think he wants your life if it doesn't include your heart?" There was a dispirited stillness to his voice.

Sarah turned her head away from him. "We are lifelong friends, and I love him."

"Of course you do. There has never been any doubt of

that. You love him like a friend, perhaps even like a brother. But you don't love him like a lover, and he doesn't feel that way about you, either. His lack of interest in you as a woman is clear evidence of that."

Her head snapped around and she glared at him. "How dare you? You are out of line, Mr. Beaudine."

"Oh, Sarah." Orion reached for her hand, and his hold on her tightened when she tried to pull away. He came closer. Too close. Sarah had a difficult time breathing when Orion's free hand came up to so lightly touch her hair, her cheek, her neck.

"Did he tell you how beautiful you are tonight, how that gown suits you, how lovely your shoulders are?" As if to emphasize his point, his fingers trailed along the top of one of her shoulders and back to her neck. His voice dropped to a whisper. "Did he tell you that if he didn't kiss your neck he would go out of his mind?" His warm lips brushed the side of her neck.

Sarah could not suppress a shiver of delight, and she closed her eyes.

His mouth moved on her again. "He didn't tell you any of those things, did he? He used your mourning period as an excuse to leave you sitting alone most of the evening, didn't he?"

She bit her lip to keep from answering him, for the truth shamed her.

"He didn't tell you how beautiful you are because those thoughts never came to him. He didn't notice."

Sarah's eyes flew open and she stepped back, humiliated. "You're right," she snapped. "He didn't notice. Does that please you? Adam is driven by his ambition, fascinated by his work, determined to have a successful career, and he is willing to share that with me. I am to be his helpmate and his friend. We have our plans made."

"But you want passion in your life as well." Orion grabbed her upper arms in a firm grip, and his own voice took on a note of passion. "From the first time I saw you, I sensed it in you. You feel everything deeply, and with passion. You have passion for life itself, for this land, for your beliefs and convictions. Someday you will feel it for one very lucky man. But you don't feel it for Adam Rutledge, nor does he feel it for you. In fact, your very aliveness frightens him, because he can't control you."

Her gut knotted with the terrible fear that Orion was right. Sarah tried to twist away. His hold tightened, but he did not hurt her.

"I won't let you go, not yet," he said. "You must hear me out. I care too much about you to stand by and watch you give yourself to a man who does not understand you, who may not even deserve you. If you marry Rutledge, he will break your spirit. Not out of cruelty, as some men would, but out of what he will view as necessity. I beg you, sweet woman, think on what I have said." Orion pulled her against his body and held her tightly with one powerful arm around her waist and one hand cradling the back of her head.

Sarah resisted his hold for only a moment, then she relaxed against him. She could hear the sincerity in Orion's voice. He did care for her, and deeply.

"Perhaps I'm not what you need, Sarah," he whispered. "But Rutledge definitely is not. Don't let your history with and affection for the man and the fact that you are alone in the world dictate your decision to marry him." He stroked her back. "I know I have no right to say these things to you. But I see your spirit as I see Dancer's spirit, and I know it must be free. It won't be if you marry him."

She pulled back from him. "Even if what you say is true, and I'm not certain that it is, I have given my pledge. There is nothing more to be said about it." The bleak look in Orion's eyes broke her heart. "I need to go home now," she said, even though it struck her that she did not consider the Rutledge cabin her home.

"I will escort you."

"That isn't necessary."

"Please allow me to." Orion took her elbow in a gentle grip, and they walked in silence.

Sarah fought to keep her composure. She had been so desperate to see Orion, to talk to him, to touch him, and now that she had, her shy joy had been turned to a pain the like of which she had never known. It felt as if her heart were literally being ripped in two.

The lantern that Harriet insisted be lit each night was in its customary place on a nail next to the front door, giving off a feeble light. Orion guided her up the steps to the porch and released her.

"Good night, Sarah, and goodbye. I'll be leaving for Fort Laramie in the morning with the detachment."

"I know. Captain Beaudine told me. Are you healed enough to ride such a long distance?"

Orion nodded. "I will miss you."

Sarah looked down at her clasped hands. "It would be easier if you wouldn't say such things, but the truth is, I will miss you, too." She raised her head to look at his face, his dear, handsome face, and the ache in her heart renewed itself. "I will miss you terribly."

His jaw clenched as he stared down at her. Sarah's breath caught as the agonized look of intense longing in his eyes impaled her with such force that she stepped back.

Orion stepped closer.

Again, Sarah stepped back, then could go no farther, for the rough wood of the door brushed her shoulders and pushed her hoop skirts out in front of her like a last bastion of defense.

He pressed against her skirts, the determined look on his face telling her that he had made some kind of a decision. He braced his hands on the door, one just above each of her shoulders.

"You will not forget me, Sarah Hancock."

"No," Sarah breathed. "Never."

His head lowered and his lips brushed hers. A bolt of lightning shot through Sarah's abdomen and her breath quickened. She clutched at the material of his shirt where it covered his chest. Orion shifted one hand to turn the wick on the lantern so low that the flame was extinguished, leaving them enveloped in an intimate darkness. That hand returned to caress her neck as his mouth once more captured hers.

Sarah sagged against him, no longer able to fight the rising tide of desire that roared through her. She opened her mouth to his gentle, inquisitive tongue and surrendered.

With a low moan, Orion took what she offered. He couldn't get enough of her sweet mouth, of her sweet scent, of her innocent passion. He pulled her as close as he could, crushing her hoops between them, pressing his hips toward hers, his hands on the soft bare skin of her upper back, then on her shoulders, then on her neck, then tangled in her thick hair.

Her hands traveled over him, over his ribs and his back and his shoulders. She nibbled lightly on his lower lip with her teeth, then followed timidly with the tip of her tongue, delighting in the gasp that came from him. He tore his mouth from hers and held her face between his hands. Enough moonlight filled the porch to allow her to see that he was staring at her. After a long, breathless moment, he lowered his mouth again. His kisses trailed from her mouth across her cheek to her ear, and the feel of his soft breath and teasing tongue on that sensitive flesh brought a whimper from her throat. Then his hand covered her left breast, and Sarah thought she would faint from the pleasurable shock.

"Orion." She whispered his name and leaned into his hand, allowed him to caress her, his thumb brushing the taut tip of her nipple as it strained against its prison of silk.

He gently pressed her breast upward, causing more of that soft mound to swell out of her bodice, then lowered his head and covered her exposed flesh with maddening kisses.

Sarah rested her head back against the door and fought

with the need to reach behind her, to unhook her bodice in order to give his wonderful mouth access to her aching nipple. Never had she known such wild, consuming desire. The force of it frightened her. Instead of unhooking her bodice, she at last gave her fingers the freedom to stroke Orion's long, silky hair, and she pressed his head to her breast.

This time was completely different from the last time his face had been at her breast, when he was ill and seeking a port in an emotional storm. This was not peaceful at all, not for her, and she knew not for him.

At last Orion pulled his face from her skin. He grabbed one of her hands and placed it inside his open coat, over his thundering heart. "Do you feel that?" He moved her hand over his chest and stomach. "Feel me, Sarah. I am alive, in the same sense you are." He took her hand to his waist, then to his hips, then back around to his firm buttock. His hand pressed against hers, pressed his hips closer to hers.

She couldn't believe what he was doing, couldn't believe how wonderful his warm, powerful body felt, couldn't have told him to stop. Her other hand moved behind him as well, and she pulled him closer of her own accord.

"You have not felt this before," he said, his voice hoarse.

"No," she whispered.

"I don't just mean a man's body, Sarah. You have not felt this passion before, the fire in your blood, the ache in your gut." His hand again caressed her breast, briefly, then was gone. "Would you now choose to live without that?"

His words sobered her. Suddenly ashamed of how far she had allowed things to go, Sarah pushed against his chest. "No, not if I were free. I would take everything you are offering me, and gladly. But I'm not free."

"You want that passion in your life," he insisted.

"Not this way!" she cried. "Not if it brings this pain! I can't bear this agonized confusion and insatiable longing. Go now, I beg you. Leave me to the life I have chosen."

"You are not such a coward." He said the words confidently.

"Perhaps I am," Sarah snapped. "But I certainly am not an idiot, Orion Beaudine. There are reasons behind my choices, well-pondered, valid reasons."

"Reasons that justify compromising the rest of your life?" he demanded, his anger and tension building. "Are the reasons that good?"

"I don't know any longer!" She clutched the sleeves of his coat. "At one time they were. Please try to understand." She stared up into his eyes. "Adam and I have a twenty year history together, one that goes much deeper and is far more complicated than you, or perhaps anyone else, can comprehend. To you, the answer to my dilemma may seem simple. Trust me enough to know that the answer is not simple to me. I need time."

The anger and frustration seemed to flow out of him. His features softened, and he reached out to touch her cheek. "I can understand that. I will leave now, but promise me one thing, Sarah Hancock."

Her heart lurched at the expression of tenderness on his face. "What is it?" she whispered.

"Promise me you won't marry him before I return."

"We had not planned to marry before spring."

"Thank God for mourning periods," Orion muttered.

"It wasn't only that," Sarah insisted. "I didn't want to hurry things. Even my mother, bless her, urged me to take a year in order to be certain that marriage to Adam was right for me, although she was so sure it would be that she begged for my promise to wed him."

Orion hesitated before he spoke. "You promised your mother?"

"On her deathbed, so she could die in peace. She was terribly worried about what would happen to me." Her voice dropped to a whisper. "She was so certain Adam and I would be happy together."

"And you weren't certain?"

"Not at first. Then I was. And now . . ." Her voice trailed off.

"And now?" Orion prodded.

"Now I'm not certain of anything anymore."

Orion frowned. "Sarah, don't let a sincere but unrealistic promise given to your mother ruin your life. I know she had your best interests at heart, but she could not have foreseen how both you and Rutledge would change. She could not have foreseen my coming into your life. I never met her, but I can't believe she would want you to be unhappy."

"No, she would not."

"Then I beg you, don't follow through with your marriage plans only because of a promise made to your dying mother." Orion's hands tightened on her shoulders. "And if you decide to end your engagement, don't do it because of me. End it because you and Rutledge aren't suited, because you know in your heart that it isn't right. For your sake, that must be the only reason. Otherwise you may regret it, or perhaps you will never be able to forgive yourself."

Trembling, Sarah met his intense gaze. "All I can promise for now is that I will not wed anyone before you return."

"That will do, for now."

A sudden fear grabbed her heart. This was the end of October; spring was several months away. "Will you be back before spring?"

"Oh, yes. I could not stay away from you for so long." He pushed a strand of hair behind her ear. "I have ruined the lovely arrangement of your hair."

"It's all right," Sarah said tiredly. "I'm going straight to bed."

"Someday I will be going to bed with you." Orion brushed her lips with his as he made the vow, then he stepped back.

Sarah stared at him, her heart pounding as the image of him lying beside her, both of them naked, flashed in her mind. She forced the shocking, intriguing image away.

"Good night, sweet Sarah. I will torment you no more." He grabbed her hand and kissed the palm, warmly and wetly, then released her and stepped off the porch. He strode away without another word.

"Yes, you will, Orion Beaudine," she whispered after his departing form. "You will torment me forever."

Orion decided that he needed time to allow his body, and his mind, to cool before he joined his brothers again. He left the confines of the fort, calling a greeting to the unlucky men who had drawn guard duty, and crossed the low wooden bridge to climb a hill a short distance away. He welcomed the physical strain of the climb and pushed himself to hurry. Near the top of the hill, he settled down on a patch of dried grass. Snatches of sound reached him, telling him the celebration below continued, but things were beginning to quiet down. Even the rowdiest of soldiers remembered that dawn came early, and celebrating too long only made it that much more difficult to get up. The fort and the group of tents that were clustered near the main gate would soon settle into silence.

A crisp breeze roamed over him, lifting strands of his hair from his shoulders, bringing the cooling relief he had sought. Orion let his eyes wander over the moonlit view of the fort and the prairies beyond, fingering Sarah's black lace shawl as he did. He had found it when he retraced his steps across the parade ground and wondered if she even knew she had lost it. He pressed the fragile garment to his nose and breathed in the delicate scent of lavender. Her scent.

A pang of aching loneliness ripped through him, and his loins tightened again. How he wanted her, in all the ways a man wanted a woman—as a friend, as a partner, as a lover, as the mother of his children. He knew now that he loved her, deeply and completely.

A rustle in the nearby brush drew Orion from his thoughts

and made him realize he had left the fort without his rifle. The only weapon he had with him was the knife he habitually carried in his boot as a precaution. Cursing himself for a distracted, lovesick fool, he pulled the knife from its hiding place and waited, listening, watching. A form materialized from behind a clump of scrub oak.

"Dancer." He breathed the wolf's name on a sigh of relief.

Dancer padded to his side and sat down. Remembering Sarah's display of affection for Dancer, Orion imitated her and impulsively put his arm around the animal's neck in a self-conscious hug. He half-expected Dancer to pull away, but the wolf didn't. Dancer lapped his face with a wet tongue, then sniffed at the shawl.

"Yes, that's hers, boy," Orion said. Dancer whimpered as he laid down, and rested his head on his paws.

Orion slipped the knife back into his boot, grateful for Dancer's company. He realized that he had missed the wolf over the last few weeks, when he had been laid up in the fort. It would be good to be on the trail again tomorrow, to get back into the wilderness he so loved. He would give Thunder his head, let the big stallion carry him across the prairie so that the wind could clear his brain and cleanse his body. His only regret was that Sarah would not be with him, riding behind him, with her legs spread and nestled next to his, her arms around his waist, holding him tightly, her breasts pressed into his back.

With a groan of frustration, Orion rose to his feet, then reached down to pat Dancer's head. "See you in the morning, boy."

The wolf whined what Orion knew was a wolf-type fare-well. When he reached the bottom of the hill and looked back, he saw Dancer standing now, outlined against the sky. The wolf raised his head and howled at the moon, then disappeared from sight.

Orion made his way to Joseph's lit tent and ducked under the flap. Loud snores assailed him from a pile of buffalo robes in a far corner, and he knew Jubal had found a safe place to sleep off his overindulgence of whiskey. Both Joseph and Gray Eagle were also there, in various stages of undress. They watched him intently.

"Hello, brother," Gray Eagle finally said.

"Hello." Orion set the shawl on the foot of his pallet and loosened his cravat.

"How did things go?" Joseph prompted.

Orion shrugged as he jerked the neckcloth clear. "I did the best I could. It's up to her now, just like it always was."

Joseph eyed the piece of lace on Orion's blanket. "She gave you a memento to take with you?"

"No. She dropped it on the parade ground. I'll give it back to her tomorrow."

"If you see her tomorrow."

Orion sighed wearily. "If I see her tomorrow," he repeated. There was no guarantee Sarah would come to see them off, not after the way he had pushed and tormented her tonight. He shrugged out of his frock coat.

"We could always disguise ourselves as Indians and carry her away," Gray Eagle suggested as he stripped off his white shirt.

"You *are* an Indian," Orion retorted affectionately, "and Joe and I might as well be." He smiled at his two concerned brothers. "I've done everything I know to do. We'll save the kidnapping for a last resort, but I swear I'll seriously consider it if Sarah tries to go ahead with this ridiculous marriage."

"Just let us know," Joseph said as he laid down on his cot. "Like I told Eagle, she's our little sister. We won't let her hurt herself."

Orion stared at him. "You feel she is your sister?"

"I know she is. I saw her with Dancer. She is your woman, Orion. And I think she knows it, too, deep down. Miss Sarah Hancock is no fool."

"Then why is she fighting me?" Orion demanded. "Why does she insist that she will marry Rutledge?"

Joseph leaned up on one elbow. "Because her feelings of loyalty and love run deep. Her hesitation is commendable, if you look at it rationally. She doesn't give her word lightly. Remember that she has known and cared for Rutledge most of her life; she has no wish to hurt him. Give her time."

Orion pulled his shirt off, wincing when he twisted his still-healing shoulder. "She has time now. I won't be around to distract her." He fixed his brother with a troubled gaze. "You don't think my leaving is a mistake, do you?"

"No. I think it's best for now."

"So do I," Gray Eagle added.

"What if she still decides to marry Rutledge?" Orion dropped down onto his pallet and pulled off a boot.

"Then we'll carry her off," Gray Eagle assured him with a wide grin.

"Get some rest, Orion," Joseph advised. "That is, if you can sleep over Jubal's caterwauling. Tomorrow will be a long day." He laid back down and pulled the blanket up over his naked shoulder. "All will be well."

"I hope so," Orion muttered as he pulled his other boot off.

"Sleep well, brother," Gray Eagle said. He blew out the lantern and the tent was plunged into darkness.

Orion slipped out of his trousers, grabbed Sarah's shawl, and crawled under his blanket. He held the scented shawl to his chest and stared up at the white roof of the tent, trying to ignore Jubal's snores.

The idea of kidnapping Sarah was so appealing that it disturbed him, for such an extreme measure went against everything he believed in. No one had the right to force anyone else to do anything. Sarah was a woman grown, intelligent, educated, capable, loving. She had the right to make her own decisions regarding her life. And if he felt that some of those decisions were mistakes, that was just too bad.

Still, he thought as sleep began to overtake him, the idea

of stealing her away, lifting her onto Thunder's back, taking her so far into the wilderness that no one could ever find them, was enough to promise him sweet dreams indeed.

Fifteen

"Miss Sarah, are you still awake?" Lucy's soft voice reached across Sarah's small room, pulling her back from the edges of a restless, troubled sleep.

"Yes, Lucy." Sarah sat up, blinking her aching, tear-swollen eyes against the light of the candle Lucy carried. "Is something wrong?"

Lucy crept into the room and closed the door behind her, then set the candle on the shelf under Sarah's hand mirror. "The colonel and his wife, they'll be here soon, and I wanted to check on you before they arrive. The Mrs. Colonel is real upset that you disappeared from the party without saying anything to anyone, even though Captain Beaudine explained to her that you weren't feeling well when he escorted you out the back door."

Sarah silently blessed Joseph for his quick thinking. Now she was very grateful that Orion and Gray Eagle had not left with them, for there would have been no explaining why she would have left with all three brothers. "The room had become very stuffy," she said carefully. "I needed some air."

Lucy nodded wisely. "And you sure got it, waltzing around the parade ground. But the man you were dancing with wasn't wearing no uniform."

After only a moment's hesitation, Sarah said, "No, he wasn't." She met Lucy's gaze straight on. "Would you like to sit down?" She waved in the direction of the chair that rested near the door.

"Only for a minute. We don't have much time." Lucy grabbed the chair and yanked it forward, then plopped into it. Sarah realized for the first time that Lucy was wearing hoops, and a very nice rose-colored gown decorated with lace and piping. Matching silk roses peeked from her neatly styled black hair. It was the first time Sarah had seen Lucy without a scarf covering her hair.

"Lucy, you look beautiful," Sarah blurted out. "I'm glad you went to the party."

Surprise flashed in Lucy's expressive dark eyes before she waved Sarah's comment away. "Thank you, but there's no time for chitchat. We have to get our stories straight."

Sarah stared at her. "What do you mean?"

"Captain Beaudine told the Mrs. Colonel that he escorted you home because you had the headache. Even though the Mrs. Colonel didn't pay her much mind, that nice Mrs. Byrd backed the captain up, saying you had told her your head was hurting something fierce. You and I both know you don't have no headache, but I don't think anyone else does, except the Beaudine brothers and Mrs. Byrd, and they won't tell anyone any different. We just have to pray no one else saw you and the Hunter dancing on the parade ground."

The knot in Sarah's stomach tightened to the point that she felt she could not breathe. "Why are you helping me?" she whispered.

Lucy met her gaze. "Because you are a good and kind-hearted woman, Miss Sarah, and you're caught in a terrible dilemma of the heart. You need time to make up your mind, and if I can help you buy a little time, I will." She stood up and put the chair back in its place, suddenly very business-like. "I'll bring a compress for your head, and when the Mrs. Colonel insists upon seeing you, as she most assuredly will, you will be out of your mind with pain. Is that clear?"

Sarah managed a small, grateful smile. "Yes."

"It won't be that far of a stretch, to tell the truth." Lucy squinted at her in the dim light. "Your eyes look awful. Pretend it's from the headache rather than from crying. And just to warn you, I think Captain Rutledge is coming to check on you, too." She slipped out the door.

Suddenly overcome with a debilitating weariness, Sarah fell back on her pillow. As if dealing with the anguish Orion had left her with wasn't enough, now she also had to face the Rutledges. She covered her heated eyes with her surprisingly cold hands, thankful that she had no tears left to cry.

"I don't care if she *is* sleeping!" Harriet Rutledge's angry voice sounded from the parlor. "She owes us an explanation, especially poor Adam here. He has been worried sick about her."

Yet he didn't come to look for me, did he? Sarah silently demanded of Harriet. She was very grateful for the comforting lavender- and mint-scented compress Lucy had placed over her eyes.

Harriet's tirade continued. "And why was the porch lantern out? You know I insist it be checked and lit every night."

Sarah's gut twisted with guilt as she heard Lucy's quiet voice offer an explanation she couldn't make out.

"But there *is* oil in it," Harriet insisted. "The wick is turned too low."

Then Adam's voice came to her, again with words she could not discern, but obviously he was attempting to calm his aunt.

"Very well," Harriet snapped. "Let us see her then. She can offer her own explanation, whatever it may be."

Sarah steeled herself for the coming confrontation. A moment later her door opened.

"Sarah, we have come to speak with you."

Harriet's voice grated on Sarah's nerves, threatening a real headache for the false one she was about to plead. Following Lucy's advice, she did not lift the compress from her eyes, nor did she sit up. "My head aches, Harriet," she said quietly. "There is nothing wrong with my hearing." She heard Harriet's barely stifled gasp of outrage.

Someone took her hand, and she realized it was Adam when he spoke in a low, soothing tone. "Aunt Harriet is worried about you, Sarah. We all are. You disappeared without saying a word."

"I apologize, Adam. The room had become unbearably warm, and Captain Beaudine offered to escort me outside for some air. I did not know when we left that I would not return, or I most certainly would have told you." *That much is true,* Sarah thought.

"Of course you would have." Adam patted her hand.

"If you weren't feeling well, you should have told Adam. It was his place to escort you home, not that Captain Beaudine's." The sneer in Harriet's voice made clear her disapproval of Joseph Beaudine.

Something in Sarah snapped. She lifted one side of the compress and glared past Adam at Harriet. "Adam was busy with his friends, and I had not seen him for some time. Captain Beaudine was kind to offer his assistance, as would any gentleman. If you so disapprove of the man, perhaps you should be thankful that it wasn't one of his brothers who made the offer to escort me outside. Both were there, and either would have been willing."

Harriet stared at Sarah, her eyes wide with horror. "You would not have allowed that long-haired scout or that . . . that *Indian* to escort you."

"Yes, I would have. They are both gentlemen, much more so than at least one Army lieutenant I can name."

After waving her hands in an angry gesture of dismissal, Harriet turned to the door. "I can see there is no talking to you when you are in such a state, Sarah. Good night, Adam."

"Good night, Aunt. Please tell the colonel I'll be out in a minute."

"Very well." Harriet disappeared from view, and Sarah

heaved a sigh of relief as she released the compress so that it once again covered both of her eyes.

"If you had let me know you weren't feeling well, I would have brought you home myself," Adam said. "I hope you don't feel that I neglected you."

Of course you did! Sarah's tired mind screamed the words, but all she said was, "No, Adam. I know my mourning period is a tedious thing to put up with. We couldn't dance, and I certainly didn't expect you to stick by my side all evening. You have your duties."

Adam patted her hand. "I knew you would understand."

Sarah was grateful for the compress covering her eyes, for she did not think she could bear to look at Adam, so great was the rush of guilt she felt. She had not missed Adam's company. He *had* neglected her, as he often did, but that did not excuse what she had done. How she had betrayed him! She had allowed another man to kiss her, to caress and fondle her. Not only had she allowed it, she had longed for Orion's touch, had enjoyed the feel of his mouth and his hands on her. Her mind and her body had responded to Orion in a way they had never responded to Adam. A low, despairing moan escaped her lips.

"My dear, I'm keeping you awake when you most need to rest. My uncle has invited me to join him for a brandy, so I'll be in the parlor for a while longer if you should need me." Adam released her hand, and she felt the tickle of his beard when he brushed a kiss on her cheek. "You'll feel better in the morning. We'll talk more then. Sleep well."

"Good night," Sarah said softly. A moment later, the distinctive smell of an extinguished candlewick reached her nose, and she heard the door close.

Sarah jerked the compress from her face and stared up at the dark ceiling as a new wave of anguish came over her. What on earth was she going to do?

* * *

She resolved that she would not go to see the detachment off in the morning, telling herself it would be better not to see Orion again so soon after what had happened between them. But when reveille sounded in the cold light of dawn, Sarah knew she could not stay away. There was no telling how long it would be before Orion returned to Fort St. Charles. She had to see him one last time.

Sarah splashed her face and swollen eyes with the cold water in her wash pitcher, then dressed hurriedly in her dark green gown, and pinned her hair up. She was not surprised to find Lucy already up when she went into the kitchen. The comforting smell of freshly ground coffee permeated the air.

"Thank you for your help last night," Sarah said quietly.

Lucy stood at the worktable, slicing thick slabs of salt pork for the cast-iron frying pan. She shrugged. "It's all right. Like I said, you need time."

"I heard Mrs. Rutledge chastise you about the porch lantern being out, and I apologize for that. I forgot all about it." Sarah poured steaming coffee into an enamel mug.

"How did that happen?" Lucy asked. "I know I lit it."

"You did. Mr. Beaudine turned it out." A blush heated Sarah's cheeks.

Lucy turned her knowing, expressive eyes on Sarah, but made no comment.

Sarah's blush deepened. Desperate to change the subject, she asked, "Do you know when the detachment is leaving for Fort Laramie?"

"The colonel said right after breakfast."

Sarah tied an apron around her waist and without another word, set to work laying dishes and silverware out on the dining room table.

Although she would have much preferred eating with Lucy in the kitchen, a short time later she joined Harriet and Colonel Rutledge for an uncomfortably quiet meal. No mention was made of the night before except for Colonel Rutledge's comment that he hoped Sarah was feeling better, and she assured him that she was.

As she and Lucy were clearing the table when the meal was finished, Harriet came in from the parlor, where she had just seen the colonel off to his daily duties.

"Sarah, both my husband and my nephew have requested that no further mention be made of your behavior last night. They feel the incident was nothing more than a lack of judgement on your part, due to your aching head."

Sarah gritted her teeth but made no comment as she continued to gather the soiled dishes. Lucy discreetly retreated behind the curtain to the kitchen.

Harriet continued. "I will abide by their wishes after I have said my piece."

With resignation, Sarah set the dishes down and looked at her. "What is it?"

"Perhaps there was no more to it than a lack of judgement, but in my opinion you exhibited exceedingly bad manners in leaving a gathering without notifying your betrothed and thanking your hosts."

"You are right, Harriet. I apologize. Normally, I would never do such a thing, but as I explained last night, I didn't know when I left that I would not return."

"You are taking this better than I expected, which pleases me." There was a slight note of approval in Harriet's tone. "Perhaps there is hope that you will make a proper Army wife after all."

Sarah looked down at her clasped hands, determined that Harriet would not goad her into another argument.

"As I have told you many times," Harriet continued, "we as wives must remember that our actions can and do affect our husbands and their careers, both positively and negatively. This brings up the issue of your keeping company, however briefly, with those Beaudine brothers and that disreputable Jubal Sage, to say nothing of the disgraceful Mrs. Byrd."

Anger boiled up in Sarah, and her resolve to avoid an argument disappeared. "Please stop right there. I have warned you that I will tolerate no ill talk regarding my friends."

Harriet crossed her arms over her chest. "Your lack of discernment in choosing your 'friends' not only demonstrates your poor taste, Sarah, but, worst of all, it reflects badly on Adam. The Beaudines and that mountain man have lived with the savages—one *is* a savage himself, for God's sake—and Mrs. Byrd is a harlot. Remember the saying that a man is judged by the companions he keeps. You must consider what others think of you."

Sarah planted her hands on her waist. "This may come as a shock to you, but, with the exception of very few people, I don't care what others think of me, and that includes you. If that means I will make a terrible Army wife, so be it. But the decision to marry me was Adam's. So far he has not changed his mind."

"He is blinded by his love for you," Harriet snapped. "He does not know you as I do."

At that, Sarah laughed, harshly. "Adam, blinded by love? On the contrary, our lifelong friendship has given him the freedom of taking me for granted, as his inattention to me should have made very clear to you long before now. And for what it's worth, he knows me far better than you ever will."

"If he goes through with this marriage, you will destroy his career!"

"If you truly believe that, perhaps you should warn him away from me." Sarah retrieved the stack of plates she had set down earlier.

"It is my duty as a loving aunt," Harriet warned.

"Then do so, Harriet, with my blessing. I certainly would not want you to neglect your duty." She moved toward the kitchen.

"He'll send you packing."

Sarah paused and looked back over her shoulder at the furious, self-righteous woman. "Perhaps he will," she said sadly. "But if he does, it won't be because of anything you told him."

A look of confusion passed over Harriet's face, and she was apparently surprised into silence, for she said no more.

Sarah continued on into the kitchen and set the dishes next to the washbasin. She turned and met Lucy's sympathetic gaze. Afraid Harriet would overhear, she kept her voice low. "The funny thing is, Harriet's right. I don't have what it takes to make a good Army wife."

"You have plenty of everything you need, Miss Sarah," Lucy answered just as quietly. "The problem isn't the Army; it's the man you're thinking of marrying. If you felt about Captain Rutledge the way the Mrs. Colonel feels about the colonel, you would be the best Army wife the world has ever seen."

"What do you mean?"

"Think if Hunter Beaudine were an Army officer, and you were promised to *him*. You don't think you'd feel differently about some of this stuff the Mrs. Colonel is trying to pound into you?"

Sarah shifted uncomfortably and frowned. "Are you telling me I don't love Adam enough to try?"

"It isn't a matter of 'enough.' I'm saying you don't love him in the right way. And maybe you don't love the Hunter in that way, either, but that man has touched your heart somehow. I can tell by how you look at him." In a rare gesture of emotion, Lucy grabbed Sarah's hand. "Think carefully before you tie that knot, Miss Sarah. Marriage is for life, and that's a long time to be unhappy if you make the wrong choice."

"Why can so many people see what I apparently can't? Am I such a fool?"

"You're no fool," Lucy said firmly. "I think you see it plain as day, deep down. But it's hard for you to really face up to it because you're all tangled up with the past, with that promise to your mama, with what the captain has always meant to you. You don't want to hurt him. And maybe you're just a little bit scared. You know what to expect from life with the captain, but a man like the Hunter is a different story. He's wild and free, and while that's exciting, it can be scary, too." Her fingers tightened on Sarah's, then she released her. "If you're going to see that wild, free man off, you'd best get. The detachment will be pulling out soon."

Sarah nodded. "I need to say goodbye to him."

"Yes, you do." Lucy set some soiled plates in the washbasin and reached for the steaming kettle of water on the stove. "You'll be just fine, Miss Sarah Hancock. You'll work through this, and whatever decision you make, you'll be fine, 'cause you won't be going into anything with your eyes closed. You got a good head on your shoulders." She poured hot water over the dishes.

"I hope you're right, Lucy."

"I am."

Sarah couldn't help being reminded of Orion always telling her he knew things, and a smile curved her lips for the first time that day. She impulsively said, "Why don't you come with me? Seeing a detachment leave is kind of like watching a parade."

Lucy looked at her. "Maybe I will. These here dishes can wait a bit." She untied the apron at her waist. "You get your hat, and I'll tell the Mrs. Colonel we'll be back in a while."

With a nod, Sarah left the room.

As the two women hurried across the parade ground a few minutes later, Sarah was grateful that Lucy had urged her to go. It was not yet nine o'clock, but the men leaving for Fort Laramie had already gathered outside the gates of Fort St. Charles. Although they and their horses now milled about in seeming confusion, it was apparent they would soon mount up. Sarah frantically searched the crowd for a sign of the Beaudine brothers.

"Can you believe that whole tent city is gone?" Lucy marveled.

"It is amazing how fast they move sometimes," Sarah said distractedly. "There's Mr. Sage." She hurried to Jubal's side, with Lucy following close behind her. "Good morning, Mr. Sage," she said breathlessly.

Jubal winced as if he were in pain. "There's no reason to shout, girl."

Sarah frowned in bewilderment. "Did I shout? Forgive me; I didn't mean to." She peered more closely at the man, saw that his eyes were bloodshot and squinted, as if the morning light hurt him. Then she remembered his unusual joviality of the night before. "Mr. Sage, did you drink too much last night?" she asked kindly.

"Sure did, and 'though I'm payin' for it now, I had a damn good time. Uh, beg pardon for my swearin', ladies. Miss Lucy, it's nice to see you. Thanks for dancin' with me last night. I'm real sorry about stompin' your foot. I hope Captain Beaudine made a better dance partner."

Lucy smiled at him. "Don't worry about my foot, Mr. Sage. And the captain was a fine dance partner, although he didn't exhibit quite the, uh, energy, that you did."

Jubal rocked proudly on his heels. "I told them young fools they couldn't keep up with me."

"No one could," Lucy said with a laugh. She looked closely at him. "If you boil some cayenne in hot water and drink the tea, you'll feel better."

"Thanks, ma'am, but I'd miss the misery. That's what keeps me from doin' this too often." He focused on Sarah. "Your eyes don't look too good, neither, Miss Sarah. No offense, but did you drink too much, too?"

"Of course not," Sarah protested, suddenly self-conscious. Did her eyes really look that bad? "I only had one glass of sherry, and it was a small one at that."

"Well, I'da been surprised if you'da been swillin' like me." A concerned expression came over Jubal's weathered, bearded face.

Desperate to keep the shrewd mountain man from asking any more questions, Sarah blurted out, "Have you seen the Beaudine brothers, Mr. Sage? I want to wish them Godspeed and farewell."

An understanding light came into Jubal's bleary eyes. "Yep, I know right where they are. You two ladies come with me." He took Lucy's arm, then Sarah's, and led them through the mass of men and animals.

Their way was suddenly blocked by Lieutenant Fielding. He looked at Sarah with a malevolence that chilled her blood.

"I'm leaving for Fort Laramie, Miss Hancock, but we will meet again."

There was no mistaking the threat in his seemingly innocent words. Before Sarah could react, Fielding was gone, swallowed up by the crowd.

"I'm glad he's leaving," Lucy declared. "There's something about that man I just don't like."

"He's evil," Sarah whispered, remembering Orion's words to her the night Fielding had spied on them through the window.

"He's a man to stay shy of, that's for certain," Jubal said as he led them on their way.

Then Sarah saw Joseph and Gray Eagle. Orion was nowhere around.

"These ladies wanted to wish you Godspeed," Jubal announced. "You know, say goodbye to you."

Joseph turned with a smile that matched the one on Gray Eagle's face. "Good morning, ladies," he said. "It was sure nice of you to come and see us off."

Sarah was struck again by the handsomeness of the brothers. She realized with a pang that she would genuinely miss them—not as much as she would miss Orion, but she would miss them all the same. Especially Joseph. There seemed to be a bond between her and the captain. He stepped toward her now, and held out his hand.

"I'm glad to have met you, Miss Hancock. You are everything my brother told me, and more."

Sarah took his hand and smiled up at him, hoping that the shadow caused by the brim of her hat would help camouflage her eyes, for Joseph was very observant. "Thank you, Captain. I, too, am glad we met."

A look of concern crossed Joseph's face as he covered their joined hands with his other one. "Are you well?" he asked in a low tone.

"No, but I will be."

"I'm certain of that. You are a wise and strong-hearted woman. You'll make the right decision."

"I hope so, Captain."

"I know you will."

Sarah smiled at that. "You and Orion share many traits."

Joseph cocked an eyebrow in mock doubt. "Is that good?"

"Yes."

"Good." Joseph brought Sarah's hand to his mouth and kissed it lightly. "I like you, Sarah Hancock."

An unfamiliar warmth flooded Sarah. Not since her mother's death had she felt so *accepted.* "I like you, too, Captain Beaudine. Farewell and Godspeed."

"We will meet again. Until then, be well and happy."

"I'll try." Sarah fought the urge to embrace Joseph, for she had the strange sense that she was saying goodbye to a brother.

Joseph released her hand, and she turned to Gray Eagle. He was again dressed in buckskin, and his long hair moved in the wind, causing his signature lone eagle feather to flutter as if it were alive. Sarah held out her hand to him. "I'm glad to have met you as well, Mr. Beaudine. I hope someday we have the chance to become better acquainted."

As Joseph had, Gray Eagle took her hand in both of his. "We will; I am certain of it."

Sarah smiled up at him. "There is no shortage of confidence in your family."

"No, there is not." Gray Eagle smiled at her.

"Farewell and Godspeed, Mr. Beaudine."

"You be well, also." He gently touched her cheek.

His kindness touched her heart. "I will."

Gray Eagle released her hand. "Orion went to get his horse. He will be here any moment. I know he wants to see you."

Sarah nodded and stood back as Lucy and Jubal joined Gray Eagle and Joseph in animated conversation. She gathered her strength for the coming meeting with Orion, for she knew a part of her was going to want him to pull her up behind him, as he had done that day so long ago, and take her with him, wherever he went.

He came then, riding tall in the saddle, carefully guiding Thunder through the crowd. Like Gray Eagle, he wore leggings and a buckskin tunic. A broad-brimmed hat covered his head, and the long beaded necklace hung around his neck. His intense eyes held her in their familiar spell as he closed the distance between them. He drew Thunder to a halt at her side.

"I hoped you would come," he said without preamble.

"I considered staying away."

"I know."

"Will you stop saying that?" Sarah cried.

Instantly concerned, Orion leaned down out of the saddle and touched her chin, drawing her face up. "Oh, Sarah," he said sorrowfully. "I want to bring you joy, not torment and sadness. I'm not worth crying over." His thumb brushed her cheek, and he pulled his hand away.

Sarah met his gaze. "Yes, you are, Orion Beaudine."

Some emotion Sarah could not name flashed in his eyes before he reached toward his saddlebag. "I found your shawl on the parade ground last night."

"I didn't even notice it was gone." She nervously glanced

about, wondering how she could have been so careless as to lose her mother's shawl. Thank God Orion had been the one to find it. "It could be awkward to explain how you came to have it."

His hand stilled in the saddlebag. "That's true. I could keep it for a while."

"That might be best."

Orion nodded and closed the leather flap. "I'll keep it until we meet again." A look of satisfaction came over his face. "I will treasure it, Sarah."

Her heart lurched at his words.

He removed his hat long enough to ease the necklace over his head, then leaned down to her again, holding out the beads. "I want you to have this as a memento of me."

As if I need a memento to remind me of you, Sarah thought. Knowing it was inappropriate that she accept his gift, not caring that it was, she closed her fingers around the necklace and drew it to her breast. "And I will treasure this."

"Good."

She smiled up at him. "At least you didn't say 'I know.' "

Over the noise of the group, Joseph's voice rang out, calling the command to mount up. He swung up into his saddle and guided his horse to Orion's side, where he touched the brim of his hat and nodded down at Sarah. "Farewell, Miss Hancock, until we meet again."

A lump formed in Sarah's throat. "Goodbye, Captain."

Joseph smiled at her and rode off to the head of the rapidly forming column.

Now also mounted on his horse, Gray Eagle came alongside her and leaned down out of the saddle. "Trust your heart, little sister," he said quietly as he passed.

Not certain she had heard him correctly, Sarah stared after him. Gray Eagle flashed a smile at her, which told her she had indeed heard him correctly. The lump in her throat grew.

"Remember all that I said last night," Orion said softly.

Sarah looked up at him, and a poignant current seemed

to charge between them when their eyes met. She clutched the necklace tightly. "How can I forget? I am besieged on all sides—by Adam, Harriet, your brothers, Lucy, Jubal, you, even my own body. My conscience is at war with my heart." She managed a little smile. "Go with God, Orion Beaudine, but, for my sake, go, just for a while. And then come back safe."

"I will, Sarah Hancock. Remember your promise to me."

She nodded. "I will be unwed when you return."

"And I won't be gone too long." He touched his fingers to his lips, then to hers, then took up the reins and nudged Thunder into a slow walk.

Sarah stared after him, deeply moved by the symbolic kiss he had given her. "Watch after Dancer," she called to him.

He looked back over his shoulder. "We'll both come back." His eyes seemed to burn as he looked at her for a long moment before he turned around and urged Thunder to a trot.

Joseph gave the command to move out, and the column started forward. Jubal and Lucy came to stand on either side of Sarah, and in silence they watched the men leave.

"You aren't going with them, Mr. Sage?" Sarah asked.

"Nope, not now. I got a trip of my own to make. I'll be headin' out tomorrow or the next day."

A crushing loneliness assailed Sarah. Orion was gone, and, right or wrong, a part of her heart had gone with him. His brothers were gone, and soon Jubal would be gone as well.

She had asked for time, and now she had it.

Sarah clutched the beaded necklace as if it were a lifeline, and headed back to the privacy of her bedroom.

Sixteen

For the next several days, Sarah saw little of Adam. With the leaving of the twenty-odd men who had gone with the Beaudines to Fort Laramie, the continuing preparations for the coming winter kept all of the remaining soldiers busy from dawn until dusk, and often into the night. Officers were no exception. The women were occupied with their own seasonal pursuits.

Jubal postponed his departure for a few days, for which Sarah was grateful, although she did not see much of him, either. He had become good friends with Theodora Byrd, and he spent most of each day at her small cabin near the river, working to make it safe and comfortable. Theodora had decided against living in the dormitory with the four other laundresses, and had claimed a deserted cabin on the other side of the bridge not far from the fort.

One day Sarah took lunch down to the cabin for both Jubal and Theodora. When she asked Theodora about her decision to live alone, Theodora only said that she preferred the solitude, but Lucy later told Sarah that the other laundresses had ostracized Theodora. She couldn't understand why, Lucy had said with a derisive sniff, since at least two of the women had been caught in compromising situations with enlisted men as recently as the previous week.

Sarah tried not to dwell on thoughts of Orion, but it was difficult to keep him out of her mind. She kept remembering everything her friends had said to her—Joseph, Gray Eagle, Jubal, Lucy, even Orion himself. In the end, she decided that Lucy was right, that Orion was right. Her love for Adam was genuine, but it went no further than the love for a dear friend, for a sibling. She suspected that Adam's feelings for her were the same.

One night about a week after Orion's departure, Sarah brushed out her hair as she prepared for bed. Adam had joined them for supper that night, and it had been good to see him. Her heart had swelled with affection for him as she studied his handsome features in the candlelight. She had hoped he would stay for a while, sit with her in the parlor or take her on a walk, but he had claimed that pressing work awaited him in his quarters, and after giving her a quick kiss, he had gone, leaving her feeling anxious and frustrated. She had immediately retired to her room.

Sarah had taken off her long-sleeved bodice, but nothing else. Her chemise and corset did little to keep her upper body warm in the chilled room. Now, as she pulled the brush through her long hair, she thought of Orion, remembering his promise to someday take her hair down for his own pleasure, remembering his kisses, remembering the feel of his hands on her body. Sarah sank down onto the bed with a moan that was close to a sob. Her hair fell around her like a curtain, caressing the skin of her arms and upper back with its warm softness.

Orion wanted her. He found her attractive and desirable, and had shown her with his words, with his mouth, with his hands.

Adam treated her with kind affection, always polite, if sometimes distracted. Rarely did he compliment her, but he was gracious and well mannered. However, he had never even hinted that he thought of her as a desirable woman, had never looked at her in a way that indicated he wanted her. What thoughts did Adam have on sharing the marriage bed with her?

Sarah threw her head back and trailed a cold hand down her throat, down her chest, down to the valley between her breasts. Unbidden, the memory of Orion's hand on her breast burst forth, and a surge of longing jolted through her. Her nipples tightened just at the thought of him touching her there again, touching her in other intimate places. She forcibly replaced Orion with Adam in her mind, and found that the thought of her lifelong friend touching her so intimately made her feel uncomfortable and strange. It was difficult to imagine Adam in a state of passion over her, for she had never seen him like that save for the passion and fascination he sometimes displayed toward his work.

But Orion was right—she wanted passion in her life. He had given her a taste of the passion shared by a man and a woman. Was there any hope such a passion could develop between her and Adam, as her mother had promised it would? So far there was no sign of it. Did she still want it to develop?

"I need to find out," Sarah whispered to the empty room. "Now. I can't bear this confusion and indecision any longer."

She jumped up from the bed and grabbed her bodice from the nail where it hung. She slipped it on and fought with the row of hooks. The memory of her impassioned embrace with Orion reminded her that the hoops she wore could get in the way, so she lifted her overskirt and untied the strings of that cumbersome undergarment. She pushed away the thought of Orion; tonight, she had to discover what was left of her relationship with Adam.

Should she leave her hair down? Sarah decided that might shock Adam too much, so she pulled the long locks back and tied them in a ribbon at her neck. Then she grabbed her shawl and rushed out the door before she could change her mind.

The late October night was cold, and the shawl did little to protect her. Sarah hurried across the compound to the small cabin Adam shared with Lieutenant Roe. She hesitated before she knocked. How could she and Adam talk privately with the lieutenant there? It was too cold to take a walk together. Where could they go to be alone?

"I don't care if we have to go to the stables," Sarah muttered. She rapped on the rough wooden door.

"Come in," Adam called.

Sarah took a deep breath and opened the door. She slipped inside and leaned back against the wood, looking around the single room. There was no sign of Lieutenant Roe. She sighed with relief.

"Sarah." Obviously surprised, Adam stood up from the desk at which he had been working, closing the top buttons of his uniform coat. Concern and a shade of irritation shadowed his face. "Is something wrong?"

"I think so, yes. We need to find out what it is."

Bewilderment creased his brow. "I don't understand."

Sarah stepped closer to him. "I'm sorry for interrupting your work, but we need to talk, Adam, and it seems you are always working. I will have to interrupt you sooner or later, and I can't wait any longer."

Adam frowned. "This sounds important."

"It is. At least it is to me. Where is Lieutenant Roe?"

"He was invited to supper at Major Dillard's this evening. He hasn't returned yet, and may not for some time. They like to play chess, and their games often go late." Adam pulled a chair next to his. "Come and sit down."

Suddenly very nervous, Sarah crossed the room, but she did not sit. She stopped before Adam and looked up into his familiar blue eyes. "I want you to kiss me," she said quietly.

"What?"

Sarah took a step closer and placed a hand on Adam's chest. "I want you to kiss me."

"Sarah, I don't have time now for flirtatious games."

"This is no game. I am very serious." Sarah pressed her body to his and put an arm around his waist.

Adam stared down at her, his eyes clouded with confusion.

"Please," she whispered. "Before my heart breaks."

He lowered his head and kissed her briefly as his arms went around her. "What is wrong, my dear? I've never seen you like this."

"I want you to really kiss me, Adam." Sarah placed a light kiss at the corner of his mouth. "Kiss me like a man kisses his wife, his lover." She then covered his mouth with hers and pushed the tip of her tongue against his lips.

She knew Adam was astonished by her behavior because of his lack of immediate response. Finally he tightened his arms around her and returned her kiss. Sarah melted into him, opened her mouth for him, and waited for the same bolt of lightning to strike her stomach that had struck the night Orion kissed her.

There was no bolt.

There was nothing, except a very evident sense of reluctance in Adam's touch. Then he set her back from him.

"What is this all about, Sarah?"

Filled with disappointment at her own lack of response, Sarah pulled her tied hair forward over her shoulder. "We are to be wed." She waved a trembling hand at the cot in one corner of the room. "Someday we will share a bed, and I need to know that you will want me in yours."

"Don't be silly. Of course I will."

"You have never shown it, Adam." Sarah looked directly into his eyes as she pulled the ribbon from her hair. Then she shook her head and sent the long locks swirling about her shoulders. "Show me now."

Even in the uncertain light of the whale oil lamp, Sarah could see that Adam paled. His hands clenched, as did his jaw.

"What do you want of me?" he asked in a strangled whisper.

"I want you to want me." Sarah fought past a rush of embarrassment. "I want you to desire me."

Something akin to horror flashed in Adam's eyes, and his

voice took on an angry tone. "You want me to seduce you? Now, before we are married? You think me that dishonorable?"

A crushing sadness overwhelmed her. "You are incapable of being dishonorable; never would I think such a thing. And no, I don't want you to seduce me, for the very term indicates a reluctance on my part. I am perfectly content to wait until we are wed before we consummate our marriage. It's just that I don't understand why there seems to be no desire on your part *now*. I keep expecting you to want to kiss me, to touch me. And you don't, Adam. You don't."

"Where has this come from?" he demanded. His eyes narrowed in suspicion. "Is this a result of your ill-advised friendship with that Byrd woman?"

Sarah stiffened as an answering anger began to grow in her. "For the sake of our marriage, if there is to be one, and for the sake of our friendship, I suggest you start paying more heed to my words and less to those of your embittered, self-righteous aunt." She placed her hands on her hips. "My thoughts are my own, and you insult me by suggesting that I am so easily led by the influence of others. If that were true, your aunt would have made me into a model Army wife by now, and, as she gladly will verify, I am far from that." Her tone softened. "Can't you see that I am speaking from my heart?"

As if nothing else she said had reached his ears, Adam incredulously repeated, " 'For the sake of our marriage, if there is to be one?' Are you thinking of calling off our engagement?"

"Yes, and I will, if you cannot bring yourself to desire me as a woman, as a lover."

"Stop it!" Adam shouted. "Stop that disgusting talk at once. What has gotten into you? A lady would never speak of such things."

"Perhaps not, but a *woman* will," Sarah shot back. "There is a difference. 'Ladies' suffer in silence, never expressing their wishes, and over the years, the resentment builds, like it has in your aunt. Hatred is not a far step from resentment. Is that what you wish me to become? Or would you rather have a content and fulfilled partner, one who is satisfied with the choices she has made?"

"You will be satisfied if I grovel at your feet, and tell you how beautiful you are, maybe paw at your breasts?" Adam grabbed her arm. "I can play that game." He kissed her, violently, his mouth bruising hers. One hand closed on her breast in a tight, painful grip. "Is that what you want, Sarah? Does that make you feel desirable? Are you happy now?"

Shocked at the cruel anger in his voice, Sarah twisted away from him. She stared at him, breathless and furious, and then her hand cracked across his cheek. Adam's eyes widened in shock, and he touched his reddened face.

Her voice shook when she spoke. "If you had touched me thus in love, rather than in anger, yes, I would have been happy. Your actions just now were dishonorable."

"I thought that was what you wanted!"

"I want honest passion!" She shouted the words. "I want my husband to want me!"

Adam ran his hands through his hair. "That will come, in time." Not even he sounded as if he believed his own words.

Sarah retrieved the ribbon from the floor. "My mother said the same thing, but I don't think it will." Her voice was dead, flat. She felt that her heart was breaking. "There should be some kind of natural spark between us, and there isn't. Such a thing can't be forced. We are fighting nature, Adam. This marriage was not meant to be."

He gaped at her. "You are ending our engagement?"

"Yes." Sarah moved toward the door.

"You can't!" He paced a few steps. "Where will you go? What will you do? How will you support yourself?"

"I don't know yet. But I'll think of something."

"Sarah, don't do this."

She turned with her hand on the door latch to find him

reaching toward her, a beseeching look on his face. The ache
in her heart became a violently physical thing, cutting off
her breath and threatening her consciousness. She fought off
the wave of nauseating dizziness. "I am so sorry," she whispered. "I should have listened to my heart long ago, before
I ever came out here. I made a terrible mistake, and have
grievously hurt both of us as a result. Please forgive me."
She jerked the door open, then stumbled outside. She had
taken no more than a few steps when Adam's cry rang out.
   "Sarah!"
Steeling herself, Sarah hastened in the direction of the
Rutledge cabin. It struck her, very forcibly, that, as always,
Adam did not come after her.

After a long and sleepless night, marked by a few bouts
of quiet crying, Sarah sat up in bed and held her aching head
in her hands.
   It was over.
   The grief struck her anew. It was truly over. She had ended
her betrothal to Adam, and she knew, deep in her heart, that
she would not change her mind. As difficult as the decision
had been to reach, as painful as the aftermath now was, she
had made the right decision, for both her, and, even if he
could not see it now, for Adam.
   "Forgive me, Mama," she whispered to the empty room.
"I couldn't do as you asked."
   Orion had been right when he had warned her that if she
chose to break her engagement, it was important that she do
it for her own sake, and not because of another man. Even
then, he had been concerned about her well-being more than
his own desires. Orion had been the catalyst; her powerful
and undeniable attraction to him had forced her to face the
truth about her feelings for Adam, about their relationship.
Under any circumstances, she would not have let things go
as far as a marriage ceremony. The reluctance she had felt

from the very beginning had only grown, and sooner or later, things would have come to a head. Orion had merely ensured that it happened sooner.

Now what?

As much as she had hated to see Orion leave, she was glad he was gone for a while, even now. She needed time to herself, to grieve for her lost relationship with Adam, to sort out her feelings about Orion, about life in general. She needed peace.

And she wouldn't get it in this house. Sarah shuddered to think what Harriet Rutledge's response would be to the broken engagement. That the woman would be overjoyed, Sarah had no doubt. That she would throw Sarah out of the house was a very real possibility. Even if Harriet did not insist that Sarah leave, it would be intolerable for her to stay.

What were her options?

She had no family, few friends, very little money, and was stranded in the middle of the Western wilderness. The Beaudines were gone, as was Jubal Sage.

She was alone.

Sarah jumped out of bed and paced the cold floor of her tiny room in the predawn darkness, fighting a terrifying sense of panic.

There was no one to turn to but herself.

Trust yourself.

Make your choices with a clear mind and a strong heart.

You are a wise and strong-hearted woman.

Trust your heart.

You will be fine.

The words came to her out of the darkness. She heard them—Orion, Jubal, Joseph, Gray Eagle, Lucy—as surely as if they were standing with her now.

They were right.

Sarah reached for her skirt and pulled it on over her night dress.

She would be fine.

* * *

Twenty minutes later, Sarah stood outside Theodora Byrd's small cabin, shivering in the cold, slowly lightening sky. She forced herself to refrain from knocking until she saw a dim light fight its way through a crack in the small, shuttered window near the door. Then she could wait no longer. She rapped on the rough wooden door with a numb fist.

There was no answer.

Sarah knocked again. "Mrs. Byrd, it's Sarah Hancock," she said quietly.

She heard the sound of a bar being removed, and a moment later, the door opened a crack, revealing the gleaming barrel of a rifle.

"Miss Hancock? Are you alone?"

"Yes." Sarah wrapped her shawl more tightly around her. "Forgive me for intruding upon you at such an early hour, but I must speak to you at once."

Theodora opened the door, lowering the rifle as she did. She pulled a shawl up over the shoulder of her nightdress. "Is something wrong?"

"Yes. Something is terribly wrong."

"Please come in." Theodora reached for Sarah's hand. "I have tea water on. Nothing seems so bad after a cup of good strong tea."

Sarah managed a weak smile. "That is encouraging." She allowed Theodora to pull her into the cabin, and was comforted by the sound of the bar dropping back into place. Theodora guided her to one of two rough benches that sat on either side of a battered but serviceable table.

"Sit here," Theodora invited. "The tea will be ready in a minute."

Sarah obeyed, sinking down onto the bench. She was silent for a moment, watching the other woman move about the small space, selecting two enamel cups and a beautiful, strangely out-of-place china teapot from a shelf.

"May I ask you something?" Sarah said.

"Of course." Theodora set the cups and the pot on the table.

"The night of the celebration, why did you tell Mrs. Rutledge that I had complained to you of a headache?"

Theodora shrugged. "I saw you leave with Captain Beaudine. After a few minutes, his brothers left also. Later, the Captain and his Indian brother returned, but you and the Hunter did not." She glanced at Sarah with an understanding smile. "There was no need for Mrs. Rutledge to know that. Mr. Sage and I were with the brothers when Captain Rutledge and his aunt came to ask about you. Captain Beaudine explained that he had escorted you home because you were suffering from the headache, and I saw no harm in adding a little more weight to his story."

"I appreciate that, but I must ask why you were willing to perjure yourself. You hardly knew me."

The smile fled Theodora's thin face. "Because you were kind to me, even knowing my reputation. The Mrs. Colonel, besides being a most unpleasant woman, is a judgmental snob. It was clear that she was very angry with you, and I wanted to defuse some of her anger. Did my ploy work?"

"It helped, for a time. But I fear the troubles between Mrs. Rutledge and me are irreparable." Sarah looked down at her tightly clasped hands. "As are the troubles between Captain Rutledge and me."

Theodora came to the table bearing a tin of tea and a steaming cast-iron kettle. "Oh, Miss Hancock, I'm sorry." She sank down on the opposite bench. "Is there anything I can do to help?"

"Perhaps." Sarah looked Theodora in the eye. "Would you like a boarder?"

Later that morning, just before the noon meal, Sarah asked Colonel and Mrs. Rutledge to join her in the parlor.

"This had better be important," Harriet warned as she settled into her rocking chair.

Colonel Rutledge looked closely at Sarah, who stood in the middle of the room. His brow furrowed in concern. "I'm certain this is important. Go ahead, my dear."

Suddenly unsure how to begin, Sarah stared down at her clasped hands.

"Sarah, luncheon is waiting, and the colonel must soon get back to his duties."

"Harriet, please be quiet." The colonel fixed his wife with a no-nonsense look.

Harriet's eyes widened in astonishment and her mouth opened slightly, as if she were about to say something, but she only sagged against the back of the chair, apparently deeply wounded.

Colonel Rutledge returned his attention to Sarah. "What is it, Sarah?"

She met his kind gaze and spoke clearly. "My engagement to Adam is ended. I have made plans, and I wanted to share them with you."

The colonel stared at her in shock.

"He broke it off." There was a distinct note of triumph in Harriet's statement. She now sat up straight in her chair.

"If that is the tale you wish to tell," Sarah responded.

"Sarah, please sit down." Colonel Rutledge guided her to the camelbacked settee. He shot another warning glance at his wife, then sat next to Sarah. "What happened?" he asked.

"I am reluctant to discuss the very personal reasons that led to this decision." Sarah twisted her hands. "Perhaps Adam will wish to take you more deeply into his confidence, but for now, suffice it to say that we have realized that we simply will not suit in terms of marriage. It is my fondest wish that our long friendship will survive this change in our plans."

"Thank God Adam listened to me," Harriet said fervently.

"Harriet, that is enough!" the colonel barked. "Can't you see the pain Sarah is in?"

"Of course she is, now that Adam has thrown her over." Harriet rose from her chair and turned on Sarah. "What did you expect, after the way you have behaved? I tried to warn you, but you wouldn't listen to me. Adam is no fool. You deserved this!"

"Harriet!" the colonel roared.

Sarah put a hand on the colonel's arm. "It's all right, Colonel. Like the problems between Adam and me, this has been building for a long time." She stood up and met Harriet's furious gaze. "I ended it, Harriet, not Adam. Our engagement was wrong from the start, but not for the reasons you think. And the real reasons are none of your business."

"I don't believe you ended it, not for one minute," Harriet snarled. "You are a penniless orphan, with no family, no livelihood, and no prospects. Adam is a kind, handsome, decent man, with a brilliant future ahead of him. Do you expect me to believe you would throw away a man like that?"

"I don't care what you believe, nor do I care what stories you choose to tell. Ask Adam. Or will you think he is lying also, when he backs up my story?"

An expression of doubt flashed across Harriet's face. "Adam is not a liar."

"No, he isn't. As you said, he is a fine man, one most women would be proud to claim as husband. Sadly, my only feelings for him are those of deep, abiding friendship. But I'll not waste my breath trying to convince you of my honesty."

Colonel Rutledge spoke. "Sarah, is there no hope of salvaging this?"

"No."

Harriet crossed her arms over her chest. "Then you'd better make plans, and quickly, young woman, for you'll not continue to live here under our roof."

Colonel Rutledge advanced on his wife with a raised forefinger. "I'm warning you for the last time to be quiet."

"I'll not obey you in this, Edward." Harriet met her husband's astonished gaze unflinchingly. "This woman has already harmed Adam's career, and I'll not allow her to do the same to yours. She will be gone from here by day's end. Let her go live with that damned wolf she loves so dearly."

Sarah felt sorry for Colonel Rutledge, for it seemed he could not find his tongue. And for good reason, Sarah thought. If she had not heard it and seen it herself, she never would have believed that Harriet would swear, that she would be—*could* be—so insubordinate to her beloved husband. But even in that moment, Sarah could see that Harriet really believed her own words.

"Please, both of you, listen to me," Sarah pleaded. "I don't want to cause problems between you. I will be gone within the hour. That is why I asked you to meet with me now."

The colonel turned to her. "Where will you go? How will you live?"

"Mrs. Byrd has invited me to share her quarters, and I will work with her as a laundress."

Both of the Rutledges gaped at her.

"You intend to stay with that harlot?" Harriet gasped.

"Mrs. Byrd is a kindhearted, courageous woman, for whom I have nothing but the highest admiration." Sarah held up a warning finger when Harriet opened her mouth to speak. "I will tolerate no further slander of her, Harriet."

"You will not order me about in my house!"

"But I will." Colonel Rutledge took his wife's arm. "I'm going to insist that you rest for a while." He spoke kindly but firmly, and just as firmly led the astonished Harriet into their bedroom. The sound of his soothing voice was joined a moment later by the sound of quiet sobs.

Sarah sighed. Things were not going as smoothly as she had hoped.

The colonel closed the bedroom door and came to her side.

"I apologize for upsetting her, Colonel," Sarah said. "I didn't mean to. Harriet and I seem to rub each other the wrong way."

"It's not your fault. I know Harriet has been very hard on you." He passed a hand over his eyes in a gesture of weariness. "I just hope you can understand that there are reasons for some of her rigid beliefs—painful reasons—and perhaps you can find it in your heart to forgive her."

"There is nothing to forgive, although sometimes I wish I knew what her reasons are." She held up a hand when it appeared the colonel was about to speak. "No. No one has felt it necessary to explain it to me before now, and now it no longer matters. I suspect Harriet would prefer that I not be told."

"She would." Colonel Rutledge looked at her. "Are you absolutely certain there is no hope for you and Adam?"

Sarah nodded sadly. "Absolutely."

"Although I can see you are determined, it will not keep me from hoping for a reconciliation. For now, what can I do to help you?"

"Nothing, really. I am packed and ready to leave. *Señor* Gonzales is coming at noon to take my trunks to Mrs. Byrd's cabin, and I will trouble you no longer."

Colonel Rutledge took her hand, and to Sarah it seemed that he had aged ten years in the last half hour. "What are your long-term plans? What will you do for money? I know you have no family to turn to, and I'm very concerned about you."

Sarah patted his hand. "I'll be fine. I have some skill as a dressmaker, and I can launder uniforms. I also have a little money left from my mother. For now, I am content to stay here."

"You have no wish to return to the East?"

"No. I love this country, and for the first time in my life,

I am free to go where I choose, with no need to answer to anyone for my choices." Sarah smiled at him. "It is quite a heady feeling."

The colonel frowned. "I don't mean to embarrass you, but I can help with additional funds if that is the problem."

"Truly, Colonel, it's not, at least not now. If you wish, you may check on Mrs. Byrd and me periodically, to make certain we have enough firewood. I've heard the winters here can be brutal."

"You may rest assured that fuel will not be a problem," Colonel Rutledge promised.

Sarah's thanks were interrupted by a knocking at the door. The colonel left her side to answer it, and a moment later he showed Adam into the room. It appeared he had not slept much more than she had.

"I'll leave you two to talk," the colonel said. "Please excuse me." He disappeared into the dining room.

Sarah's stomach twisted in a knot. "Hello, Adam."

"Sarah." Adam nodded at her, seemingly reluctant to meet her gaze. "I didn't come earlier because I wanted to give you time to reconsider your decision to end our engagement."

"There is nothing to reconsider," Sarah said gently. "I do not regret my decision. I only wish I had been possessed of the courage to end it sooner. Perhaps it would not have caused us both so much pain if I had."

Adam slapped his hat against his leg. "I don't understand!"

"I know, and I'm sorry for that." Sarah placed a hand on his arm. The wool of his uniform coat felt rough to her fingers. "Someday, when you meet a woman who makes you feel that you can't wait to kiss her, to take her hair down, to take her to bed, then you will understand, and you will thank me."

"I don't want another woman," Adam growled.

"Then I don't know what to tell you, Adam, because it is clear that you don't want me, either."

Whatever Adam was about to say was cut short by another knock at the door.

Hoping it was Pablo Gonzales, Sarah opened the door and was relieved to see that it was indeed her friend. "Come in, *Señor* Gonzales. Thank you for your help. My trunks are in the room off the dining room." She pointed him in the direction of her bedroom.

"You're leaving?" Adam demanded.

"I must, for all our sakes. Not only would it be intolerable for me to stay under these circumstances, but your aunt has made it very clear that I am no longer welcome in her home."

"Where will you go?"

"For now, I am going to stay with Mrs. Byrd and earn my living as a laundress."

Pablo tracked back through the room with a trunk balanced on his shoulders.

"You are refusing my offer of marriage to live with a—" Adam paused at the warning look Sarah threw him, then cautiously continued. "With a woman of questionable reputation, and to wash other people's filthy clothes? You insult me."

"I'm sorry you feel that way, for that is not my intention."

Once more, Pablo walked through the parlor and disappeared into her bedroom.

Adam tried again. "Sarah, you must come to your senses."

She eyed him thoughtfully. "That is exactly what I have done. Please, Adam. This is difficult for both of us, and prolonging it won't make things easier."

"I promised to look after you, and I intend to keep my word," Adam warned. "I'll call on you."

"I would rather you didn't." Sarah moved out of Pablo's way as he carried the second trunk outside. "I feel very strongly that it will be best if we don't see one another for a while."

Adam merely glared at her.

"Please excuse me for a moment." Sarah went through the dining room and pulled aside the curtain covering the doorway into the kitchen. Colonel Rutledge held a loaded tray in his hands, and Lucy set a napkin on it as she looked up.

"I'm leaving now," Sarah said. "Thank you both for your many kindnesses to me over the last few months."

"I'll check on you soon, Sarah," the colonel said. "Farewell, my dear."

"Thank you, sir."

"If you'll excuse me, I'll take this tray to my wife."

Sarah nodded and stepped out of his way. When he passed her, Sarah looked back in on Lucy. "Thank you for helping me pack this morning." As she expected, Lucy waved her thanks away.

"I warned you about overdoing the thanks."

"So you did." Sarah hesitated, then blurted out, "I will miss you."

Lucy shook her head, her features set. "Not that much, you won't, because I'm down at the river fairly often. I might look in on you, might ask you for a cup of tea or something."

Sarah repressed the urge to hug the woman. "I would like that very much. I'll see you soon, then."

"Yes, you will." Then Lucy looked up. "You're a brave woman, Miss Sarah. You'll do fine."

"I'm terrified, Lucy."

"Sure you are, but you'll be fine. Go on now, or you'll still be here at suppertime."

Sarah smiled as she lifted her hand in a gesture of farewell, then dropped the curtain back into place. She ducked into her barren room to retrieve her hat from the stripped cot and returned to the parlor, tying the hat ribbon under her chin as she went. Adam still waited there, standing stiff and sullen in his spotless uniform.

"You're really going to do this," he snapped.

"I must. Please forgive me for hurting you. God knows I never wanted to do that." She moved to the opened door, then paused one last time. "Like I said, someday you'll be grateful."

"You're making a terrible mistake, Sarah."

"I don't think so. Farewell, Adam." She stepped out onto the porch.

"Time will prove me right!" Adam shouted.

"We shall see," Sarah whispered to herself.

Pablo led the mule-drawn cart in the direction of the main gates. Sarah took a deep breath, straightened her hat, and followed him.

Seventeen

"Lord have mercy!" Sarah exclaimed. She stepped back from the huge, steaming washtub in the yard and patted her face with the hem of her apron. "I feel that I can't breathe after a while."

Theodora looked up from her rinse tub with an understanding smile. "I know. But there are some benefits to that steam. I think it helps the complexion, and I swear it helps the lungs, too. I haven't had a cough for well over a year now."

Sarah looked ruefully at her chapped and reddened hands. "This work may be good for the lungs and the complexion, but it sure is hard on other things." Her back ached miserably, as it did almost all the time now.

"That's true," Theodora said.

Sarah reached for the wooden paddle she used to move the clothes around in the washtub. After soaking them for another half hour, she would begin the laborious process of scrubbing each article of clothing on the washboard. Then she would turn the clothes over to Theodora to be rinsed, wrung, and hung to dry. Tomorrow they would iron the clean garments, and the next day the routine would start again, with Theodora washing and Sarah rinsing and wringing. Sundays were their only days off, and that day they often spent making improvements on their home and the yard surrounding it. She and Theodora had become fast friends, and they worked efficiently together.

As she stirred the clothes, Sarah reflected upon how her life had changed in the two weeks since she had moved into Theodora's snug cabin. Whereas before she had often found the days dragging by slowly, now time flew by, occupied as she was with hard work. She and Theodora had turned the little cabin into a decent home, for all it had a packed dirt floor and the stone fireplace was the only source of heat.

Adam had honored her request that he not call upon her, so she had not seen him, nor had she seen Harriet. Colonel Rutledge came by every few days and was always cordial, and Lucy had visited several times. Both Sarah and Theodora looked forward to Lucy's visits, and a new closeness was developing between the three women. Since Lucy insisted upon calling Theodora "Mrs. Byrd," and again refused Sarah's request that she drop the "Miss," both Sarah and Theodora now called her "Miss Lucy," and would not be swayed from doing so despite Lucy's protests. After all, Sarah had pointed out, they were all truly equal now—three women working to support themselves.

And never in her life had Sarah worked so hard. Her arms, shoulders, and back still ached almost constantly, although the pain was not nearly as bad as it had been the first few days. Theodora had promised the aching would ease as Sarah grew stronger, and that had proven true. She had indeed grown stronger, and her body had changed in subtle ways. Her bodices and the waistbands of her skirts fit looser now, and in the evenings, when she washed while wearing only her chemise, Sarah could see a new and shapely definition to the muscles in her upper arms. She could live with aching muscles, for they were proof that she was earning her living, but Sarah hated the condition of her hands and made a point of applying an oatmeal paste to them each night before she fell into an exhausted sleep.

She thought often of Orion and his brothers, but there had

been no word from any of them. She wondered if the news had reached Fort Laramie that she and Adam were no longer betrothed. She had toyed with the idea of sending Orion a message with the next dispatch, but did not want to seem forward. He had not made her any promises, other than that he would return before too long. He had spoken to her of passion, had shown her that he desired her, but he had never mentioned love. He cared for her, she knew, and he wanted her as his lover, but did he want her as his wife? He had never said so, and Sarah could not count on him to make that kind of commitment, nor was it fair that she demand it of him. She had to make plans for her own life, independent of Orion Beaudine and Adam Rutledge, or any other man, for that matter.

And one thing was certain, Sarah thought as she grabbed the washboard and bent over the tub. She did not intend to work the rest of her life as a laundress.

"Sarah."

The tone of warning in Theodora's voice caused Sarah to raise her head and look at her friend. Theodora nodded in the direction of the bridge.

Sarah's heart sank at the sight of the approaching uniformed man. Now the sound of Adam's boots on the wooden bridge reached her ears. As much as she didn't want to see him, she also was not prepared to resort to rudeness and so resisted the urge to dart into the cabin and bar the door. Instead, she straightened and dried her hands on her apron, her face schooled into a calm expression that belied her true feelings. She briefly touched Orion's necklace, which she now wore every day. The feel of the beads gave her comfort and a strange infusion of emotional strength.

Adam nodded at Theodora in passing and came to stand on the other side of Sarah's steaming tub.

"Hello, Sarah."

"Adam."

"I came to see how you are faring."

"Quite well, thank you. How are you?"

"Fine."

The single word hung between them, sharp and heavy.

With his hands clasped behind his back, Adam looked around the neat yard, examined the face of the small cabin, grimaced at the sight of men's long underwear waving from a rope in the cool autumn breeze. His piercing and disapproving gaze returned to her. "I don't believe you are doing well at all."

Sarah sighed. "Then believe what you will. I won't argue with you. If there is nothing more, I'll bid you good day. As you can see, we have work to do." She waved in the direction of a pile of soiled uniforms on the ground not far from her feet.

Moving so quickly that Sarah was startled, Adam came around the washtub and grabbed her hand. He stared at the red, cracked skin, then raised his angry gaze to her face. "You call this doing well?" he demanded, his voice practically a snarl. "My God, Sarah, look at yourself! Look at where you live. Look at what you have become."

"I have become a laundress," Sarah snapped as she jerked her hand from his. "I work hard at an honorable profession, and I am paid for my labors; there is no shame in that. My home is modest, but neat and clean. I have clothes on my back, food on the table, and a few good friends. I need nothing more."

"You deserve more than this," Adam insisted, waving his hand in disgust.

"Says who?" Sarah planted her aching hands on her hips. "You, Adam? You no longer have a say in my life." The flash of pain in Adam's eyes gave her pause, and she forcibly clamped down on her rising anger. She spoke again in a softer voice. "I don't mean to be unkind. I told you it would be best if we didn't see each other for a while, and I think that is still true. Perhaps you should go."

Adam stared at her. Even through his beard, she could see

his jaw clenching. "I can't believe you gave up a life with me for this. Was it really that bad?"

"It wasn't bad as much as it simply wasn't right, not for either of us. It's better this way. You must believe that."

"Is this truly better for you? I don't understand, Sarah. Please help me understand."

Sarah briefly closed her eyes against the pain and sorrow that rushed through her, then faced her old friend. "I don't think I can help you understand," she said gently. "And yes, this truly is better for me. Can't you see? My life with you would have included your aunt, who despises me, and the Army, which insists upon a regimented way of life that I am unsuited for. In the end, you would have seen our differences as my shortcomings, as your aunt does. And perhaps she is right that I could have harmed your career. You would have resented me, perhaps even grown to hate me."

"How can you think I would ever hate you?"

"It might have happened. Or perhaps I would have grown to resent you, for expecting me to sacrifice my very soul."

Adam stiffened. "Don't be melodramatic. I've never asked such a thing from you, nor would I."

"No, you didn't ask it, but I believe you expected it."

"Why? How?" Adam took his hat off and ran a hand through his hair. "I deserve an answer, Sarah. What did I do?"

Reluctantly, sadly, Sarah said, "You told me, many times, that appearances were more important than my feelings." She stopped, twisting her hands in frustration. "Adam, the reasons don't matter anymore now that we've gone our separate ways. We'll only hurt each other further by discussing this."

A strange expression crossed Adam's face as his gaze fell to her breasts. "What is this?" He reached toward the beads, but Sarah grasped the necklace protectively and stepped back.

"Obviously, it is a necklace."

"And a cheap one at that, like the Indians make. Why are you wearing such a ghastly thing? Where did you get it?"

"A friend gave it to me, not that it's any of your business."

He stared at her, and understanding dawned in his blue eyes. "You accepted a gift from a man? There is another man?"

"I accepted a gift from a friend who happens to be a man, yes." Sarah crossed her arms over her chest. "But I did not end our engagement because of another man, if that's what you think. Don't try to place the blame for the serious problems between us on someone else."

Adam appeared stunned. "I can't believe you would accept the attentions of another man."

Sarah did not respond.

He grabbed her wrist. "Did you lay with him?"

"No!" Sarah twisted away from his hold. "But I wanted to. God help me, I wanted to. And that frightened me to my very soul, because it went against everything I believe in, everything I believe about myself. I tried to warn you. I begged you to listen to me, I even begged you to want me."

Now it was Adam who did not respond.

"A marriage between us would have been disastrous," Sarah said quietly. "Surely you can see that now."

"Who is he?"

"Is that all you can think of?" Sarah cried. "Have you heard anything else I've said?"

"Who's your lover, Sarah?"

"He's not my lover! He's not even here!"

Adam's eyebrows drew together. "Fielding?"

"Oh, for God's sake. Adam, just go. There is nothing to be gained from prolonging this conversation."

"Beaudine."

Sarah merely stared at him.

"I thought you didn't like the Army," Adam jeered.

He suspected Joseph! Sooner or later, Adam would learn the truth. It would be better if he learned it from her, and now, when Orion was away. "Captain Beaudine is my friend, but he did not give me the necklace. His brother Orion did."

Adam gaped at her. "You accepted a gift from that long-haired, Indian-loving scout?"

Sarah sighed and shook her head. Even now, after all she had said to him, all she had told him, Adam didn't understand. He blamed Orion for the problems between them, and based his judgement of the man on his connection to the Cheyenne and the length of his hair. Adam would be shocked if he knew how she fantasized about running her fingers through Orion Beaudine's long, beautiful hair. But there was no point in getting into any of that. "He is my friend," was all she said.

After a long, tense moment, Adam crammed his hat back on his head. "I don't know you at all, Sarah Hancock."

Sarah calmly met his offended, bewildered gaze. "No, you don't."

Without another word, he turned with stiff military precision and marched away. Her heart heavy with sorrow, Sarah watched him go. Theodora came to her side and placed a comforting hand on her shoulder.

"Why do I feel so bad?" Sarah asked her. "I'm the one who ended it."

"Because you still care about him, even if you don't love him."

"I wish he could understand that my decision is best for both of us."

"Someday he will. Give him time." Theodora patted her shoulder. "Would you like some tea?"

Sarah managed a smile. A cup of strong tea was Theodora's answer to every ailment, including those of the heart. "Not yet. I want to get this tub of wash done, and the rest in soaking."

"Just don't work out your frustration by wearing holes in those uniforms on that washboard."

Now Sarah genuinely smiled. "I won't." She gave Theodora a quick hug. "Thank you."

Clearly surprised, Theodora awkwardly patted her shoulder. "It's all right." She smiled herself, shyly, then returned to the rinse tub.

As she attacked one of the soaking uniform coats with the washboard, Sarah realized that she was very blessed in her new friends. Jubal Sage, the Beaudine brothers, Lucy, and now Theodora—they understood her and accepted her, even if Adam, her long-time and once dearest friend, no longer did.

A few days later, as Sarah and Theodora labored over the ironing tables they had set up in the yard, Lieutenant Callahan Roe approached.

"Good afternoon, ladies," he said as he removed his hat.

Sarah straightened and brushed a hand across her forehead, wondering what the reason could be for Roe's visit. "Hello, Lieutenant," she said. "Was there a problem with your laundry?"

"Oh, no, ma'am. The two of you do a much better job than those gals at the fort. I've been bragging about you, so don't be surprised if you get more work."

"Well, thank you, Lieutenant," Theodora said. "That's real nice of you."

"Ah, it's nothing, ma'am."

The young man looked at Theodora with a strange expression on his face, and Sarah realized with a start that it was one of longing. Roe's professional, polite attitude had never indicated that he harbored special feelings. She glanced at Theodora and wondered if her friend was aware of the lieutenant's interest.

When the lieutenant didn't say anything further, Sarah finally asked, "What can we do for you, sir?"

A dull blush colored Roe's face as he tore his gaze from

Theodora and turned to Sarah. "I have a message for you, Miss Hancock." He patted his chest, searching. "Here it is."

Sarah's stomach knotted. She had no wish to hear from Adam, and she could not imagine that anyone else would send a messenger. Aside from Lucy and Colonel Rutledge, neither she nor Theodora had any friends at the fort, and either Lucy or the colonel would come themselves with a message rather than send the lieutenant.

Roe triumphantly retrieved a paper from within his coat. "Here you go, ma'am. This came in this morning with the dispatch from Fort Laramie." He held the folded paper out to her.

Sarah stared at the small white object; her stomach knotted even tighter and her heart started pounding. *Orion.* Had he written to her? How she had longed for some word of him, some word from him. How she longed for *him.* But why would he write to her? Why did he not come himself? Had he changed his mind about coming back?

"Miss Hancock? Don't you want the letter?"

Sarah blinked and forced her eyes to focus on the lieutenant. "Of course. Thank you very much, Lieutenant." She took the paper and shoved it into her apron pocket.

Roe frowned at her. "Aren't you going to read it, ma'am?" he blurted out, then he caught himself. "I'm sorry, ma'am, that's none of my business. It's just that getting a letter is so rare and special, and most folks would . . . want . . . to . . ." His voice trailed off.

"I want to savor it for a while, then read it later," Sarah explained lamely.

"Yes, ma'am. If you want to send a reply, the courier will be heading back to Fort Laramie in the morning."

"Thank you, Lieutenant."

A silence fell over the group for a moment, then the lieutenant said, "Well, I'd better get back." He seemed reluctant to leave, and stood there, twisting his hat in his hands.

Sarah mentally shook herself. "Lieutenant, I fear receiving the letter has addled my wits, and I hope you will forgive my bad manners. Would you care for some refreshment? We can offer some cool water, or a cup of tea." She glanced at Theodora, hoping that the impromptu invitation did not upset her friend.

Theodora did not seem upset when she seconded the invitation. "I could make coffee, if that is what you would prefer."

Roe looked from one woman to the other, obviously wanting to stay. "But I'm interrupting your work."

"I think we're overdue for a break, don't you agree, Sarah?" Theodora asked.

"Yes, we are. I'd welcome a break."

"In that case, ladies, I'd be honored to visit for a few minutes."

Theodora smiled. "Coffee, water, or tea?"

"Your choice, ma'am."

"Very well. I'll make a pot of tea then. The water is already hot, so it will take only a few minutes to steep." Theodora moved in the direction of the cabin.

"Let me make it," Sarah suggested. "I'll take the opportunity to read my letter."

Lieutenant Roe flashed her a grateful smile, and Sarah went into the cabin.

After measuring the tea leaves into Theodora's lovely china teapot and adding the hot water from the kettle on the hearth, Sarah sat down on a bench in front of the table. She pulled the letter from her apron pocket with a trembling hand. Her name was written on the front of the folded paper in black ink, in a bold and curiously graceful hand. When she turned the letter to glance at the back, she saw a wax seal with an elaborate B in the center. It had come from one of the Beaudine brothers, no doubt. Her heart raced with anticipation as she carefully lifted the seal and smoothed the letter on the table, shifting her body out of the shaft of light that came from the open door. She began to read.

Friday, 2 November, 1849

My dear Sarah,

I had hoped to be on my way to Fort St. Charles, and you, by now, but unforseen circumstances have arisen. I have been dispatched to Fort Kearny as a courier, and will be many days in the traveling, perhaps as long as three weeks. By the time you read this, I will have departed. Rest assured that I will return to your side as quickly as I can.

Remember your promise to me; I expect to find you a maiden still upon my arrival at your door. I shall count the hours until I can again look upon, and touch, your beauty.

Ever yours,
Orion Beaudine

Although she was alone in the cabin, Sarah blushed deeply as the paper fell from her fingers. Orion's subtly passionate words sent thrills of excitement racing around in her stomach, and she closed her eyes against the wave of longing that engulfed her. He could easily be gone for another month, and that seemed like an eternity. How could she bear to wait that long?

Sarah had just received her first love letter, and in it, Orion had practically promised that he would touch her again, and she knew it would not be the touch of a friend, especially when he learned of her broken engagement. The thought increased the racing feeling in her stomach and caused her to lick suddenly dry lips.

How should she respond to his letter?

She snatched the paper up and read it again, with a soft, secret smile on her face.

"Sarah?"

Sarah jumped at the sound of Theodora's voice.

"Is the tea ready?" Theodora stepped into the cabin and out of the light from the door so that she could see Sarah's face. "Is everything all right? The letter wasn't bad news, was it?"

Sarah's face heated again. "No, not bad news. I'm sorry about the tea. I'm sure it's ready now." She shoved the letter in her pocket as she stood up. "The lieutenant must think me rude."

Theodora smiled. "He's far too polite for such a thought to even cross his mind." She peered at Sarah curiously. "That must be some letter."

"It's a nice letter," Sarah admitted.

"We'll talk more later. You are going to join us, aren't you?"

"I'd rather stay in here, if you don't mind. I'm not very good company right now."

Theodora sobered. "I hope you're not playing match-maker, Sarah."

"No, honestly, I'm not." Sarah looked at her friend. "Would you rather I came out?"

"I would," Theodora admitted. "The lieutenant is a very nice man, but I don't want to give him false encouragement."

"Then I'll come, on the condition that you don't expect me to be witty and clever."

"Agreed."

"You take the pot, and I'll get the cups."

Later that evening, Theodora sat on her bed, brushing her long blonde hair, while Sarah sat at the table, laboring over a response to Orion's letter. Even though he would not receive it until he returned from Fort Kearny, she wanted to send it with the courier leaving in the morning, as there was no way to know when the next dispatches to Fort Laramie would be sent. For the third time, she crumpled a piece of precious paper, and with a groan of frustration, set the pen down next to the bottle of ink.

"Do you want to talk about what is troubling you?" Theodora asked gently.

Sarah rubbed her tired eyes. "I'm trying to respond to the letter I received today, and I'm not sure how to. I've never received a love letter before."

"I *knew* the letter was from a man!" Theodora said triumphantly.

"I'm sure it was quite obvious, judging from my addled behavior today." Disconcerted, Sarah looked at her friend. "I have no experience with such things."

Theodora's brow knitted in puzzlement. "Captain Rutledge never sent you letters?"

"Not like this one. That's one of the reasons we are no longer betrothed."

"I see. Well, I need a little information before I can advise you. What did Mr. Beaudine say?"

Sarah stared at her. "How did you know it was from him?"

"Remember? I was aware that you and he never returned to the celebration that night. Besides, I saw how you looked at him. It was easy to see that you have special feelings for him."

"I was that obvious?"

"Oh, he was, too, Sarah. He feels the same way about you." Theodora resumed her brushing. "What did he say?"

"He said that he has to go to Fort Kearny with dispatches and will be gone for several weeks, and that he will return to me as soon as he can."

Theodora raised an eyebrow. "That's all?"

Sarah blushed. "There is more, but it's rather personal."

"And that's the part you're not sure how to respond to."

"Yes."

Theodora thought for a minute before she spoke. "If he kept his letter short, I'd do the same. And you've probably already come up with some of this stuff, but I think I'd express my hope that his journey is safe, that I will look forward to seeing him again, and then I would close with something about how I feel in my heart. That part you can make as personal as you are comfortable with, but I would always be honest with him."

Sarah smiled nostalgically at that. "We promised each other long ago that we would always be honest, even if it caused pain." She reached again for the pen. "Thank you, Theodora. I think I know what I'll say now."

The room settled into a silence broken only by the crackling of the fire and the scratching sound the nib of Sarah's pen made as it moved across the paper.

> Tuesday evening, Nov. 6th, 1849
>
> My dear Orion,
>
> I was pleased to receive your correspondence today, but am concerned about the dangers you surely will face on your journey. This shall not reach you before your departure for the East; therefore, I can only hope and pray for your safe return to Fort Laramie so that you may read this note.
>
> There is no question I shall be unwed upon your return to Fort St. Charles, not only because I promised you so, but also because I have broken my engagement to Captain Rutledge. It is you who have not kept your promise to me, in that you will be away for far too long. You shall have amends to make, sir.
>
> Pray be safe, dearest. I could not bear it were something to happen to you.
>
> Yours truly,
> Miss Sarah Hancock

"That will have to do," Sarah muttered. She folded the paper and neatly addressed it to Mr. Orion Beaudine, Fort Laramie, then turned it over and affixed some sealing wax. Her own seal was a simple imprint of a rose. "There," Sarah said with satisfaction. "I don't know if this qualifies as a love letter, but Orion should be pleased with it."

A wistful look came over Theodora's face. "My husband used to write me the loveliest letters."

Sympathy for her friend filled Sarah's heart to the point of an ache. "Tell me about him," she invited.

"Nolan?" Theodora smiled. "Oh, I suppose to other people he didn't seem too special, but he was to me. He was a decent man, hardworking yet gentle. And so good to me. No one in my life has ever treated me with such kindness. We loved each other deeply." Tears formed in her eyes.

Sarah scooted off the bench and crossed the room to sit at Theodora's side. She placed an arm around her friend's shoulders. "I didn't mean to make you sad by asking about him," she said sorrowfully. "Please forgive me."

"No, I like to talk about him every now and then. If I concentrate on the good times, then maybe the memories of the bad times will fade." Theodora brushed the back of her hand across her eyes. "He was a cobbler, and had a dream of starting his own business in Oregon. So we headed west in the spring of '46, but he fell ill with cholera a few weeks out of Independence and died within two days. I became ill, too, and lost the child I was carrying. I have often wished that I had died with them. Part of me still longs to be buried out on the plains with my husband and child, so that we can all be together."

"Oh, Theo, I'm so sorry." Tears formed in Sarah's eyes, too. "Life is so cruel sometimes."

After a pause, Theodora glanced at her. "I know you wonder how I fell into that other line of work."

"That is none of my business, and it isn't important, anyway," Sarah said firmly.

"Actually, I want you to know. Sometimes it helps to talk about terrible things, and Mr. Sage is the only other person who knows what happened." Theodora moved a little distance from Sarah and both women turned so they were facing each other on the narrow bed. "After Nolan died, the captain of the wagon train would not allow me to go any farther unless I married one of the bachelors at once. He said there was a rule against single women traveling alone, that a single woman caused problems among the men, like a bitch in heat does with a pack of dogs."

Sarah gasped. "He said that?"

"Those were his exact words. When I refused—not only was I devastated with grief, but the choice of men left much to be desired—he threw me off the train. He confiscated my wagon and oxen in payment for the money he gave two trappers to return me to the East, since we were too far out from Independence for anyone from the train to take me back and be able to catch up with the train." Theodora's voice took on a curious flat tone. "Along the way, one of the men insisted that since I had no family to turn to, and no money, I would need a way to make a living. He raped me, Sarah, claiming that my only choice was to be a whore, and that I might as well get used to it."

"Theo, no!" Sarah's eyes were wide with horror.

"He paid me every time he did it, and made his friend pay me, too. Said if they paid for it, it wasn't rape."

Sarah felt sick to her stomach. A picture of Harriet Rutledge's self-righteous face flashed in her mind; what would the woman say if she knew Theodora's story?

Theodora continued in that same wooden tone. "They took me to Omaha, and the trapper found me a place to live and even sent his friends to me, so for a while I really did work as a whore. He was right; I got used to it, mostly because I just didn't care if I lived or died." Her voice took on a thoughtful note. "You know, I think that man really believed he was helping me. He was kind to me in a way, sort of watched out for me."

Sarah kept her own decidedly unkind thoughts about the trapper to herself. That any man could do such a thing to any woman was heinous; that the trapper did it to a woman recovering from a near-fatal illness, grief-stricken with the loss of her husband and unborn child, probably not even physically healed from the miscarriage, was downright evil. A flash of fury roared through Sarah, making her wish for the opportunity to meet that trapper someday, when she had a rifle or a knife in her hands.

"But then you got out," Sarah stated as calmly as she could. "You survived, Theo."

Theodora nodded. "I saved every penny I could, intending to leave as soon as possible. Then one night I had a bad customer. He beat me horribly, in addition to . . . to everything else. That was it. When I recovered, I took my little stash and went south to Independence, determined to get to Oregon one way or the other. I had to make Nolan's dream come true for at least one of us. But they still had the rule about single women traveling on the trains. Said there was no sense in my going, since a single woman couldn't own land in Oregon anyway. So I hired on with the Army as a laundress. I keep volunteering to go with the companies sent West, and someday I'll get all the way to Oregon."

Sarah looked at her friend in admiration. "I am certain you will. But surely you don't intend to set up a business as a cobbler."

"No. That was Nolan's talent. If I have to, I'll continue to take in laundry. I'll make do."

"There's one thing I don't understand." Sarah chewed thoughtfully on her lip. "Your life in that other job was over when you went to work for the Army. How did people find out?"

A look of hatred flashed across Theodora's face and was gone. Her features looked as if they were set in stone. "Pure bad luck. At Fort Kearny last summer, one of the officers recognized me from before, and wanted me to resume my old occupation. When I refused, he tried to force me, but I escaped and reported his behavior to his commanding officer. He was disciplined, and in retaliation, he tried to have me fired, but was only successful in ruining my reputation."

"An *officer* did that?" Sarah demanded. "The despicable snake. His actions go against all military and moral codes."

"You know him," Theodora said softly. "And you would be wise to stay far away from him if you ever meet him again."

Sarah stared at her. "Who was it?"

"The same man who beat me so badly that last time in Omaha. Lieutenant Roger Fielding."

Later that night, Sarah stared up into the darkness from her bed on the opposite side of the room and considered how very lucky she was. Like Theodora, she was a woman alone in the world, and had been through some difficult, painful times, but Sarah felt that her life had been charmed compared to that of her friend. And yet Theodora maintained a cheerful if guarded disposition, went about her work without complaint, and did not bemoan or dwell upon the misfortunes that had befallen her. She held fast to her dream of getting to Oregon, and was determined to let nothing sway her from the march toward that goal.

What goals do you have, Sarah Hancock? The voice came out of her head, demanding an answer.

Sarah pondered the question, fingering the beaded necklace she now held in one hand. What indeed were her goals? For now, she was determined to earn her living as a laundress and seamstress. When she had enough money saved to be able to move, then she would examine her choices and decide where to live. In a larger town or city, she would be able to teach again, if there was any demand in the West for teachers of French and polite dancing. For Sarah had decided that she wanted to stay in the West. She loved the spirit of this raw, new land, perhaps because it matched her own spirit in some ways.

And what of Orion?

Sarah felt under her pillow for his letter, a smile touching her lips when she found it. Before she could make any long-term plans, she had to see him again, had to know what he wanted of her, if anything, had to decide if she was willing to give him what he wanted. And what did she want of him?

Images of him filled her mind—Orion striding across the meadow toward her, with Dancer at his side, Orion lying naked under the blankets, his beautiful body in the first stages of healing, Orion coming to her in the moonlight, dancing with her, kissing her, touching her, forcing her to face her heart.

She loved him.

And Sarah knew in that moment that she would gladly give Orion Beaudine whatever he asked of her.

Eighteen

The month of November passed, slowly, to Sarah's way of thinking. The weather turned colder, and the first snow fell around the middle of the month. Sarah was now grateful for the warmth of the steam and the hot water and the fires around which she and Theodora always worked. They still set up their washtubs outside, and would continue to do so whenever the weather allowed. The days warmed again, slightly, and the snow melted, adding mud to the myriad other substances that needed to be removed from the clothes the soldiers brought them for cleaning.

She and Theodora were kept busy, for their customer base had grown in direct proportion to their growing reputations as excellent laundresses. Lucy visited almost every day, and Colonel Rutledge sent enlisted men with carts of cut firewood every few days. The deer Jubal Sage had left for Theodora was gone, but the two women managed well on stores they purchased from the post sutler.

There was no further word from Orion, although Joseph Beaudine sent a letter with one of the couriers, expressing his concern for Sarah's well-being after hearing of her broken engagement. She had written back to him, a warm, friendly, and heartfelt letter, assuring him that she was doing well, but that she missed all of the Beaudine brothers, and Mr. Sage as well. There had been no word from Jubal.

One morning in early December, Lucy and another woman

crossed the bridge and came into the yard where Sarah and Theodora were setting up their washtubs. Sarah was surprised to recognize Libby Gates as Lucy's companion.

"Good morning," she called out, her breath forming a white cloud.

" 'Mornin', ladies," Lucy answered. "Sure hope you have some tea water on."

"That we do, Miss Lucy," Theodora said with a welcoming smile.

"Mrs. Byrd, this here is Mrs. Lieutenant Gates; Mrs. Gates, this is Mrs. Byrd."

Theodora and Libby nodded greetings to each other.

"Mrs. Gates, how nice to see you again," Sarah said warmly. "How have you been?"

"Well, Miss Hancock. And you?"

Libby spoke with stiff reservation, which saddened Sarah, because she genuinely liked the young woman. She could only wonder at the stories Harriet must have told.

"I've been well, too, thank you. Won't you both come in where it's warmer?" She waved Lucy and Libby into the cabin, and she and Theodora followed.

When their guests were seated on one side of the table and the tea leaves were steeping in the prized china pot, Sarah looked pointedly at Libby.

"Somehow I doubt this is a purely social visit, Mrs. Gates. Is there something Mrs. Byrd or I can do for you?"

"Oh, I hope so," Libby blurted out. "I'm just sick about this." She pulled a white cloth from a burlap bag she carried. "This table linen was given to us by my husband's grandmother on our wedding day." Tears formed in Libby's eyes. "I treasure it, and now I have ruined it! I don't know how to tell my husband."

Sarah took the cloth and unfolded it. "Let us see what we have here," she said thoughtfully. An ink spot about the size of a large orange showed itself almost directly in the center of the cloth. Theodora peered over Sarah's shoulder.

"I know I should have pushed the linen back on the table before I set the ink bottle down, but I intended to leave it there only for a moment while I retrieved my writing paper. Then I felt a little dizzy, and I knocked the bottle. The lid was not on tight, and you can see what happened." With wide, despairing eyes, Libby looked from Sarah to Theodora. "Miss Lucy said that you might be able to help and suggested I accompany her this morning. Oh, please tell me there is something you can do!"

"You haven't tried to clean it yourself?" Theodora asked.

"No, ma'am."

"Good. Then the stain has not been set." Theodora looked at Sarah. "If the sutler has any lemons left from that last shipment, we'll get one and soak the spot with the juice several times, letting it dry between each soaking. Then, if we apply some soap and some vinegar, I think it will come out."

Hope shined in Libby's eyes. "Oh, ma'am, really?"

"We'll try. It's the best thing I know to do." She examined the cloth near one lace-edged border. "And here's a scorch mark."

Libby looked down at her hands, shamefaced. "Yes, ma'am. I did that, too."

Sarah examined the mark. "If you don't mind the cloth being shortened just a little, I can remove the lace, cut away the scorched part, and reattach the lace. I have experience as a dressmaker, and can make this look as good as new."

"I never thought of that," Libby breathed. "Oh, yes, please do, Miss Hancock."

"We should be able to have it for you by tomorrow, I would guess." Sarah looked up at Theodora, who nodded in agreement.

"Oh, thank you," Libby said fervently. "I don't know what I would have done."

Theodora poured the tea then, and the three older women spent the next twenty minutes in casual, friendly chatter.

Libby remained very quiet, but the stiff look left her young face, and she seemed to relax.

Suddenly, a male voice called out from outside. "Miss Sarah Hancock!"

Sarah exchanged startled glances with Lucy and Theodora as she rose from the bench. She opened the door cautiously and was thrilled to see Gray Eagle in the yard, astride a magnificent horse, dressed in beautifully beaded buckskins. His long hair moved in the chilling breeze, as did his eagle feather.

"Mr. Beaudine!" she cried. She hurried outside. "How good to see you!"

"Likewise, Miss Hancock." His eyes fell on the beaded necklace Sarah wore and a look of approval flashed across his handsome face. "Good morning, ladies."

Sarah glanced over her shoulder and saw her three friends crowded in the doorway. Libby's eyes were huge with fear.

"Good morning, Mr. Beaudine," Theodora called. "Would you care for some tea?"

"Thank you, but no, Mrs. Byrd. I must be on my way. I ran into Jubal a few days ago, and he mentioned that you and Miss Hancock were living alone. Thought you might be able to use this deer I brought down early this morning." He patted the carcass that Sarah now saw draped across his horse's rump.

Deeply moved by Gray Eagle's thoughtfulness, Sarah looked up at him. "Thank you."

"My pleasure." He lifted one long leg over the saddle horn and slipped to the ground. Sarah was struck again by how tall he was, and by his uncanny resemblance to Orion. A wave of longing rose up in her, so powerful that it took her breath away.

Gray Eagle looked at her curiously. "Are you well, miss?"

Sarah nodded with a rueful grin. "It's just that you look so like your brother," she admitted.

"And you miss him."

"I do. Very much."

"He feels the same. The Hunter will be back for you."

A surge of warmth swirled around Sarah's heart. "I know," she said. It made her smile to repeat Orion's often-said words. "How is Mr. Sage? We have missed him, too."

"He is well. He is courting a woman in a camp not far from mine." Gray Eagle untied the deer carcass from its position behind his saddle.

"Mr. Sage is courting?" Sarah stared at Gray Eagle, wondering if he was teasing her.

"Yes. It seems he has taken a fancy to a Cheyenne woman named Sweet Water." Gray Eagle shook his head in amusement. "I guess you're never too old for love." He heaved the deer over his shoulder. "Where would you like this hung?"

Sarah saw that the animal was already gutted and cleaned. "Over here, on the side of the cabin. Mr. Sage built a smokehouse of sorts, actually a lean-to, next to the fireplace." She led the way around the cabin and unlatched the door to the tall, narrow space, then stood back and watched as Gray Eagle hooked the animal's tied back legs over the big iron hook that protruded from the ceiling. He pulled a wicked-looking knife from his belt and swiftly skinned the unfortunate deer.

"Rub the carcass down with salt at once," Gray Eagle instructed as he worked. "Let it hang for a few days, then get one of the men to butcher it further for you." He rolled the skin and handed it to her.

Sarah glanced down at the skin and whispered her thanks to the animal's spirit. Gray Eagle made a few quick slashes with the knife and pulled away two large chunks of meat, then returned his knife to its sheath.

"These are haunch steaks," he said. "They will make a good supper tonight, and there should be enough for a stew, also. It depends on how hungry you are."

"Thank you," Sarah said again.

Holding the steaks, Gray Eagle backed out of the lean-to,

and Sarah latched the door, then led the way into the cabin. Libby moved away, obviously still very much afraid.

Immediately defensive of Gray Eagle, Sarah fixed Libby with a stern gaze. "Mrs. Gates, I would like to introduce you to Mr. Beaudine. Mr. Beaudine, this is Mrs. Gates. Her husband is a lieutenant in the Army."

"Ma'am." Gray Eagle nodded politely to Libby, then laid the venison steaks in a pie tin Theodora held out to him. She set the tin on a shelf and pointed Gray Eagle in the direction of the washbasin.

"But he's an . . . an *Indian!*" Libby squeaked, her hand at her throat.

"I know that," Sarah snapped. "He is also my friend, and I would appreciate it if you would treat him accordingly."

Libby's face flamed. "My apologies," she murmured. She sank down on the bench and stared at the tabletop.

Gray Eagle dried his hands on the cloth Theodora handed him, then accepted the rolled deer skin from Sarah and followed her back outside.

"I'm sorry," she said in a low tone.

"It happens all the time. Don't worry about it." He tied the skin behind his saddle.

"Well, I don't like it," Sarah muttered. She placed her hand on his arm. "Thank you for your kindness, Mr. Beaudine. Both Theodora and I are grateful for the gift."

"It was the least I could do, little sister." Gray Eagle smiled at her, patted her hand, then vaulted onto his horse's back in one fluid motion.

Sarah looked up at him. "Why do you call me that?"

"Because you are my sister. I feel it here." Gray Eagle laid a fist over his heart, then gathered the reins. "You will see the Hunter soon. Until then, fare you well, Sarah Hancock." He touched his heels to the horse's flanks and trotted away, the hoofbeats on the wooden bridge sounding loud in the crisp air.

Sarah watched him until he was gone from sight. Affection

for Gray Eagle filled her heart, and made her long even more for Orion. At last, she turned back into the cabin.

Libby was still seated at the table. "Please forgive my rudeness, Miss Hancock," she hastened to say. "I have never met an Indian before, and all I have heard of them are terrible things. Mrs. Colonel Rutledge says they are all murdering heathens, and should be exterminated."

"Mrs. Colonel Rutledge is wrong," Sarah said firmly, trying not to take her anger toward Harriet out on Libby. "While some Indians may be murderers, so are many white men. As far as Mr. Beaudine is concerned, he is as proud of his Cheyenne heritage as he is of his white heritage, and honors both of his parents. He is an educated gentleman, and, as I said earlier, a good friend of mine."

"Yes, ma'am. I shall strive to be more charitable." Libby pushed herself up from the table. "I need to get back home. Chores are waiting." She took a step toward the door, then paused and closed her eyes.

"Are you all right?" Lucy asked, taking Libby's arm.

"Just a little dizzy. I'll be fine in a minute."

Sarah frowned. "You said you got dizzy when you knocked the ink bottle. You're sure you're not ill?"

Libby smiled at her, shyly, yet with a touch of pride. A delicate blush rosied her pale cheeks. "Not ill, as such. I think I'm expecting a little one, because my monthly time hasn't come for a while now." One hand covered her stomach.

Lucy, Theodora, and Sarah all broke into wide grins.

"Congratulations!" Sarah cried.

"Land sakes, Mrs. Gates," Lucy scolded. "Why didn't you tell me? I can make you some ginger tea that will help with that dizziness, and your stomach, too, if it bothers you in the mornings."

"It does," Libby admitted.

"Let's get on our way, then." Lucy hustled her toward the door. "I'll see you home, then come by later with some tea.

Thank you, Miss Hancock, and thank you, too, Mrs. Byrd, for welcoming us into your home. This was a real nice visit."

Libby stopped at the door and turned to Sarah and Theodora. "Neither of you ladies are anything like Mrs. Colonel Rutledge said you were," she blurted out. "You have been very kind to me, and I thank you for your hospitality."

With a parting smile, she allowed Lucy to pull her outside. Sarah stepped to the door and watched the two women cross the yard. She waved when they reached the other side of the bridge and looked back. They waved back and continued on their way, soon disappearing between the open gates to the fort.

So Libby was going to have a baby. How lucky she was! Sarah placed one hand over her own flat stomach and clutched the beaded necklace with the other. Would Orion's child someday grow inside her, the seed planted by its father in the ultimate act of love? Just the thought sent deep, primeval tremors of desire throughout Sarah's body. What greater gift could Orion give her? What greater gift could she give him, than to accept and nurture his seed, and bring forth into the world his son or daughter?

A new wave of loneliness washed over her. "Hurry back, my beloved," Sarah whispered into the cold air. "Hurry back."

Two nights later, Sarah was awakened from a sound sleep by a pounding on the cabin door. Loud male voices sounded from outside, demanding that their owners be let in.

With trembling hands, Sarah reached for the matches and candle that rested on the shelf near her head.

"Theodora!" she whispered loudly.

"I'm awake," Theodora answered.

The candle jumped to life when Sarah touched the match to the wick. She saw that Theodora was out of bed, wearing nothing over her nightdress, and standing barefoot with her rifle aimed at the door.

"Who is it?" Sarah asked, suddenly very fearful. She had never seen such a look on her friend's face, a look of cold anger and stark determination.

"I don't know, but whoever it is means trouble, Sarah. Arm yourself. We may be fighting for our virtue, if not our lives, within the next few minutes."

Her mouth suddenly dry, her heart hammering, Sarah jumped out of bed and hurried across the dirt floor to the fireplace. There she took up the heavy iron poker.

"Whoever you are, go away!" Theodora shouted.

"Not yet, sweet thing!" a man shouted back. "We brung you gals some presents—big, hard presents! Open this here door so's we can give 'em to ya!" A chorus of rough laughter followed, and more pounding on the door.

Sarah looked at the stout bar across the door and blessed Jubal for his thoughtfulness. Would that bar hold, though, if those men outside decided to ram the door? She started to drag the sturdy table across the floor, and for the first time was thankful that there was only one small, high window in the cabin, and that it was shuttered with wood rather than made of glass.

"Go away!" Theodora commanded again. She laid her rifle on the table and helped Sarah shove the heavy piece of furniture up against the door.

"Not 'til we get what we come for!" A note of anger had crept into the man's voice. "There's four of us, and two of you. We're willin' to take turns, and we already drawed straws. Treat us right, and maybe we'll pay ya extra."

Sarah tried to ignore the shudder of revulsion that rippled through her. "Who are these men?" she asked in a low tone. "I can't believe the soldiers would be doing this."

"They're not soldiers," Theodora said grimly. "I recognize the leader's voice, and he's bad news. His name is Bartholomew Cutler; I had the misfortune of meeting him at Fort

Laramie. He's a trapper who's real upset about the decline of the beaver trade, and he's mean and ugly to boot."

"Open this door!" The furious shout seemed to echo in the room. The door shook with the force of something—or someone—slamming against it.

Sarah grabbed the poker and stood ready.

"No! Get away from the door or I'll start shooting!" Theodora warned. "The gunshots will bring the soldiers!" She pulled back the hammer, then raised the rifle to her shoulder and took aim at the door.

The door was slammed again. "You bitches! You'll pay for this!"

"Seems like a strange hour to be picking up your laundry, gentlemen." A new, strong voice sounded over all the others.

"Orion!" Sarah breathed. "Theodora, it's Orion!"

Theodora lowered the rifle. "I hope he's not alone, Sarah," she said soberly. "Cutler is vicious."

A different kind of fear raced through Sarah's body now. If Orion was alone, he was outnumbered. The pounding on the door ceased, so she had no trouble hearing the heated discussion outside.

"You have to wait your turn, Beaudine," the first voice snarled. "We was here first."

"I don't think you have any laundry to pick up, Cutler." Orion sounded almost relaxed. "If you do, come back in the morning. For now, I suggest you do as the ladies asked and leave."

"Don't be orderin' us around, Hunter Beaudine."

Sarah could stand it no longer. Soundlessly, she eased the bar from the window and opened the shutter enough to peer outside. One of the men near the door carried a torch, so she could see the group of four men. Theodora was right; they were not soldiers, but long-haired men dressed in filthy buckskins. She could smell the rank scent of body odor from where she stood. Behind the four men, Orion sat atop Thunder, his rifle cradled in one arm, his other hand resting on the hilt of the knife at his waist. Most of his face was hidden by the shadow of his hat brim, but she could see his tense jaw and pursed lips. She knew him well enough to know that he was furious, and she almost pitied the four men.

Almost, but not quite. She felt a sense of grim satisfaction when Orion shifted his rifle so that the barrel pointed directly at the man who appeared to be the leader.

"You will leave now, all of you."

"You fool enough to take us all on?" The man Sarah assumed was Cutler brandished a large knife. "One against four?"

"Wait just a minute, Cutler," the man holding the torch protested. "You said we was gonna get us some tail; you din't say nothing about tanglin' with Hunter Beaudine." He started backing away. "If'n we cain't have these whores tonight, that's all right. I just want to stay alive so's I can poke my stick somewheres else the next time."

"Shut up, Foster," Cutler snarled. "And stay where you are, or I'll kill you myself. This man is tryin' to cut in line, is all. He wants both of 'em at the same time."

Sarah watched with horrified eyes as the other two men faced Orion, one with a knife, one with a rifle.

"That ain't right, him cuttin' in," one of them muttered.

"Even if he is Hunter Beaudine," the other added.

Orion pulled the hammer back on his own rifle and aimed it at Cutler. "Let me explain something, gentlemen."

Sarah moved from the window and began pulling at the table, now desperate to get it away from the door. "Orion needs help," she whispered frantically to Theodora. Theodora nodded and assisted with the table.

Outside, Orion's voice continued, sounding calm and clear in the night. "If Cutler so much as breathes wrong, my itchy finger is going to pull this trigger. You may get me after that, but Cutler won't be around to see it, because I'll blow a hole in him you'll be able to see through. Then there's the matter of my wolf. You may have heard something in the brush."

In the silence that followed, Sarah could hear the distinct sound of growling. She could also imagine the wary looks those four men would direct toward the darkness. With a final heave, she shoved the table out of the way.

Orion continued. "If anything gets started here, at least one of you will become unpleasantly acquainted with Dancer. And just so you get it straight, the two women in that cabin are not whores, and I'll kill any man who says they are. They are decent ladies who wash other folks' clothes to make a living." He paused. "All of you could do with some laundering."

Sarah quietly lifted the bar from its slots and pulled the door open barely an inch. Theodora eased the tip of the rifle barrel through the crack. Sarah grabbed her poker, and the two women waited, breathless and tense.

"We was told they were whores, and would welcome our money," one of the obviously disappointed men said.

"Cutler knows they aren't whores, don't you, Bartholomew?" Orion's voice had taken on a dangerous tone. "You intended to force them."

"Fielding told me you was sweet on one of 'em," Cutler snapped. "That would have made it that much better. I would've enjoyed samplin' her."

Sarah's hands tightened on the poker until she couldn't feel her fingers. That man Cutler wanted to hurt Orion, and had been prepared to use her to do it. She was tempted to charge out the door and brain the bastard herself.

"Do you want to die tonight, Cutler? If so, I'd be happy to oblige you."

The deadly tone of Orion's voice made Sarah shiver. Either Bartholomew Cutler was a fool, or he was so twisted by hate that he couldn't think straight.

"You brung us to the Hunter's woman?" one of the men asked disbelievingly. "If we had hurt her, the Hunter and his brothers would have been on us like flies on dung, and we'da never shook 'em off. Was you tryin' to get us all killed, Cutler?"

"Gawddamn," another muttered. "Hunter Beaudine's woman."

"It's sure lucky you come along when you did, Mr. Beaudine," the man called Foster said in an unsteady voice. "Nothin' happened, so now you don't hafta kill us. Your brothers don't hafta come after us, neither."

"Mrs. Byrd. Miss Hancock," Orion called. "Would you open the door, please?"

Self-conscious about appearing in her nightdress, with her hair down in a braid, Sarah grabbed the blankets off her bed and handed one to Theodora before she obeyed Orion's request. Somewhat covered, she and Theodora stepped into the doorway, their weapons still at the ready.

Orion removed his hat and spoke in a softened voice. "Are you both all right?"

"Yes," Sarah answered.

"These men owe you an apology." He nudged Thunder forward, then knocked Foster's hat off with the barrel of his rifle. "You're in the presence of ladies," Orion said. "Mind your manners."

Two other men snatched their hats off, but Cutler remained defiant.

"Take your hat off, Cutler, or I'll shoot it off. And you know I can." Orion took aim with the rifle. "Of course, I might accidentally crease your scalp . . . or clip your ear . . . or kill you."

Cutler did not move, except to tighten his grip on the knife he still held in one hand.

With a muttered curse, one man marched over and jerked Cutler's hat off, thrusting it at his chest. "Take yore gawddamn hat off and apologize to the ladies. And put that knife away. We was wrong here, and I don't wanna die for it."

Cutler glared at him, but he returned the knife to its sheath at his waist.

The man turned to Sarah and Theodora. "My name's Will Mayhew, ladies, and I'm powerful sorry for this mess. Cutler here lied to the rest of us, and with all the drinkin' we did earlier, well, I just hope you'll accept my apology for disturbin' you." He looked over his shoulder at Orion. "I got no quarrel with you, Hunter Beaudine, and I don't want one. If you're satisfied with my words, I'd like to go now."

Orion nodded.

Mayhew strode off. Foster and the other man offered hasty apologies, and Orion, after instructing Foster to give Sarah the torch, sent them away with a jerk of his head. When Cutler moved to follow them, Orion spoke.

"Not you, Cutler. Not yet. You'll apologize to the ladies before you go anywhere, and then I'll give you a message for Fielding."

"I ain't gonna apologize to no gawddamn laundry maids," Cutler snarled. "And you ain't gonna make me."

From where she stood, Sarah saw Cutler lower his hat toward his waist so that Orion could not see that his other hand moved toward his knife handle. Without thinking, she thrust the torch into Theodora's hand, then lunged forward with the poker and jabbed Cutler, keeping the weapon pressed into the man's back. "Don't touch the knife, Mr. Cutler, or this laundry maid will skewer you." She increased the pressure she was exerting on the poker and struggled to keep from gagging at the man's stench, sickened by the thought of him touching her, forcing himself on her.

Cutler held his arms out to the sides, his hat crushed in one meaty hand.

"Sorry," he muttered hatefully.

"What?" Orion held a hand to one ear. "I couldn't hear you."

"I said I'm sorry, gawddamn it!" Cutler shouted.

"Don't curse in front of the ladies," Orion said coldly. "And give this message to Fielding the next time you see that cowardly weasel. My brother Joseph has already warned him about coming anywhere near Miss Hancock. The same warning now also applies to you, and our protection extends to Mrs. Byrd. If either of you so much as whispers a wrong word about either of these two ladies, you will deal with me and my brothers, and I guarantee you won't like it. Have I made myself clear?"

Cutler only glared at him.

Sarah jabbed harder with the poker. "He asked you a question," she hissed.

"Yes!" Cutler shouted.

"Get out of here," Orion ordered.

Cutler lowered his arms and stepped away from Sarah's poker. He glanced over his shoulder at her, sending her a malevolent look that chilled her blood. Then he turned and walked toward the bridge. He paused when he came alongside Thunder, and glared up at Orion.

"This ain't over, Beaudine, not between you and me, not between me and your woman. You both'll pay for this night."

Later Sarah tried to remember exactly what happened next, but Orion moved so fast that she would never be entirely sure. One moment he was astride Thunder with his rifle in hand, the next the rifle was in its beaded leather case and Orion sailed out of the saddle. Cutler had no time to react. Orion knocked him to the ground and straddled his stomach, the blade of his knife at Cutler's throat.

"You have nothing to settle with my woman, Cutler. She's never done anything to you. So help me, I'll kill you if you ever come near her again." Orion's voice was cold with deadly intent. "I'll ask you again: is that clear?"

When Cutler didn't answer, Orion grabbed the front of his stained shirt, pulled him up off the ground, then slammed his head back down. "Is that clear?"

"Yes," Cutler spat.

"Good. And any time you want to settle things with me, you just ask. How about right now?"

With his long dark hair and his buckskin clothes, Orion

looked as much like an Indian warrior as Gray Eagle did. Sarah thought that the worried look on Cutler's bearded face was well justified. Again, the man said nothing.

"I didn't think so," Orion said, his voice heavy with disgust. "You'll take on two women when you have three men backing you up, but one on one with a man isn't much to your liking, is it?" He rose to his feet. "Get out of here."

Cutler pulled back on his elbows until he was away from Orion's legs, then lumbered to his feet. Without another word, he lurched toward the bridge and disappeared into the darkness.

Sarah felt faint with relief. She stared across the yard at Orion. In the flickering light of the torch Theodora still held, she took in the glad sight of her beloved's face. The familiar, intense look in his eyes wreaked havoc with her ability to breathe normally, and she dropped the poker. Orion shoved the knife into its sheath and once again strode toward her.

With a glad cry, Sarah hurled herself into his outstretched arms.

Nineteen

"My sweet, brave woman," Orion murmured against Sarah's lavender-scented hair. He held her tightly to him, relishing the feel of her slender body against his, of her breasts pressed to his chest. "When I saw those men battering your door, I . . ." His voice trailed off. He didn't want to admit that, for the first time in his life, he'd almost shot a man in the back. When he recognized Bartholomew Cutler, Orion had gone as far as to take aim at the big trapper's back. Only the strong sense of honor instilled in him by his father had stayed his trigger finger. "I was crazed with rage," he finished lamely.

"It's all right now," Sarah said soothingly. "I am so happy to see you, Orion." She stood on tiptoe and placed a gentle kiss on his mouth.

With a deep groan, Orion pulled her even closer, and there was nothing gentle in his return kiss. All of the months of pent-up longing and frustration and fear of losing her poured out of him as he moved his mouth over hers, pressing for entry at her sweet lips. It was the first time he could kiss her without guilt, and he took full advantage of it.

She met him with equal measure. Her arms held him tightly, her mouth was as hungry as his. Her lips parted under his onslaught while his hands pressed her hips to his growing hardness, and he plundered her mouth until she whimpered. Finally he pulled his mouth away. "Sarah," he whispered.

"Orion, you must let me breathe," she gasped.

His hand climbed from her hips to her neck, where he felt her pulse pounding. "Forgive me, my love. It's just that it's been so long. And now you are free." Suddenly, he frowned and set her back from him, his hands on her shoulders. "You are free, aren't you?"

"Yes. Well, not entirely." She looked up into his eyes. "I'm not free of you."

"Do you want to be?"

Sarah placed a gentle hand on his cheek. "No."

Orion captured her hand and turned his head so that he could place a kiss in her palm.

"All right, Mr. Beaudine," Theodora called. "You've kept Miss Hancock out in the cold long enough, with her barefoot and wearing only her nightdress. Bring her inside at once." The torch light disappeared as Theodora went into the cabin.

Orion looked down at Sarah's feet, but could see nothing in the dark. "Barefoot," he muttered, annoyed with himself that he hadn't noticed. Sarah had to be freezing. Without another word, he picked her up and carried her toward the cabin. Her arms went around his neck, and she sighed contentedly.

"What about Thunder?" she murmured. "And Dancer? And don't forget the fire poker."

"In a minute," Orion growled. He carried her over the threshold into a modest but surprisingly comfortable-looking cabin. A welcoming fire was gaining strength in the stone fireplace, and Theodora had just set a match to a candle on the mantel. Another candle burned on a shelf near a narrow bed along one wall. Skirting the table that stood in a strange position not far from the door, Orion crossed the room and set Sarah down in a sitting position on the edge of the bed. He dropped to his knees in front of her and took her feet in his hands. He was struck by how small and dainty her feet looked next to his hands, and he was very concerned by how cold her skin was.

"Your feet are frozen, Sarah. Why didn't you put something on?"

"There wasn't time," Sarah said. She pushed a lock of his hair behind his ear, her hand lingering on him. "We had no warning; Theodora and I were both asleep, and all of a sudden they were here, pounding on the door. We were afraid they would break in, so we pushed the table against the door and armed ourselves. I barely had time to get us blankets when you asked us to open the door."

That explained the odd position of the table. "I hope you don't have frostbite," Orion said worriedly.

"No, no, it's not that bad." She smiled at him. "Really. Everything happened so fast. I wasn't outside that long."

She had been outside long enough that severe shivers shook her body. Orion pressed the bottoms of her feet to the tops of his buckskin-clad thighs and rubbed her chilled skin. Then his gaze fell on the hand that rested in her lap. The skin was red and chapped, even split in places. He grabbed her hand and held it in the candlelight for further examination, appalled at what he saw. Sarah pulled away from his grasp. Slowly, Orion raised his gaze. Her hands were now tightly clasped in her lap. He noted that her thick braid lay forward over one shoulder, resting on her breast, appearing very dark against her white nightdress. His gaze continued upward. A blush colored her cheeks, and wisps of dark hair framed her face. Her blue eyes were downcast.

"What have you done to yourself?" he whispered.

"Mr. Beaudine, would you mind retrieving the poker from the yard?" Theodora asked. "I'll tend the fire and make some coffee or tea for you."

Frowning, Orion stood up. "Of course, Mrs. Byrd. I'll be right back." With a last troubled glance at Sarah, he turned to Theodora, who held the still-lighted torch out to him. He took it and left the cabin.

His relief and joy at seeing Sarah were slowly being replaced with a smoldering anger. How had she gotten herself into such straits? Why was she living in such primitive—and dangerous—conditions? Had Rutledge thrown her out, cut her off with no means of support? Orion's fist tightened on the torch. Adam Rutledge would answer to him if that proved to be the case. The captain had brought her out here in order to marry her; since the betrothal had been broken—for whatever reason—at the very least, Rutledge should have taken the responsibility to get Sarah safely back home, especially since she had no family to turn to.

"Some friend he is, Sarah," Orion muttered as he grabbed up the fire poker. If Sarah had indeed been forced to work in order to earn her keep, why weren't she and Mrs. Byrd living in the dormitory with the other laundresses, within the confines and safety of the fort?

Sarah had been right in her letter to him—that treasured letter—when she wrote that he had been gone too long. He had been. Now he wanted some answers, and he wanted them fast.

Sarah pulled a pair of thick wool socks over her cold feet, then shoved her arms into the sleeves of a dark green wrapper, and tied the belt. She tossed her braid back over her shoulder and smoothed the blankets on the bed. Was it only her imagination, or had Orion seemed upset when he returned with the poker, expressed a preference for tea over coffee, and announced that he would be back after he had stabled his horse? He had positioned the heavy table where Theodora had indicated, then had left, with a firm admonition to bar the door and with no more than a glance at Sarah. What had happened to anger him?

Sarah straightened the benches on either side of the table and smoothed the tablecloth. "Did Mr. Beaudine seem upset just now?" she asked Theodora. Her friend had also covered her nightdress with a robe and was now seated on her own bed, slipping her feet into fur-lined moccasins.

Theodora considered Sarah's question. "No, I don't think so," she finally said. "I think he was in a hurry to get his horse put up. If he is angry, I'm sure it's those men he's angry with. You haven't done anything." She fixed Sarah with an affectionate smile. "In my opinion, he was very pleased to see you. So pleased, in fact, that I fear he'd still be kissing you outside had I not called him in."

A light blush heated Sarah's cheeks. "It is good to see him," she admitted. "I have longed for this reunion."

"I don't know either man very well, Sarah," Theodora said as she stood up. "But I think Mr. Beaudine is much better suited to you than Captain Rutledge was. The captain is a polite man, and an excellent officer, I'm sure, but he is lacking a certain warmth, a certain . . ."

"Passion?" Sarah softly supplied.

"Yes, that's it." Theodora took her teapot down from the shelf. "When Mr. Beaudine looks at you, there is no doubt you are very special to him. On the other hand, Captain Rutledge, the few times I have seen him with you, always seemed rather distracted, and he certainly never looked at you the way Mr. Beaudine does." She frowned into the tea tin. "We're getting low on tea. I hope the soldiers' payroll comes soon, so they can pay us."

"Perhaps Mr. Beaudine brought it," Sarah said. She set out three cups, then began to pace the large woven straw mat that covered the center of the packed dirt floor. The fire had warmed the room somewhat, and the chill was finally beginning to leave Sarah's body.

Suddenly she remembered Dancer. Impulsively, Sarah raised the bar and stepped outside. It was very dark, and quiet. Aside from the sound of the nearby river and the wind in the leafless trees, all was still.

"Dancer," she softly called. Her breath puffed white in the frosty air.

Theodora came to peer over her shoulder. "Who is Dancer?"

"Orion's wolf." His first name slipped out without Sarah's notice.

"A wolf?" Theodora repeated uncertainly.

Sarah nodded eagerly. "He's very wary of most people and around settlements, so I don't know if he'll come this close to the cabin." She hesitated a moment, then called out again. "Dancer."

She heard a rustling in the juniper bushes near the side of the cabin, and a moment later made out a shadowy form. "Dancer." Sarah took a few steps and crouched down, holding out her hand. The wolf stepped daintily into the circle of pale light coming from the opened door and licked Sarah's outstretched hand.

"I don't believe my eyes," Theodora whispered in awe.

"I told you he was magnificent," Sarah said proudly. She scratched the wolf's ears, then looped her arms around his neck for a quick hug. "I've missed you, Dancer, just as I have missed your master."

"I'm not his master."

Sarah started and looked around. Orion's voice had come from the darkness; evidently, his moccasin-clad feet made no noise on the wooden bridge.

"No one is," Orion continued. There was definitely a sharpness to his tone. "Dancer and I are best described as friends." He came into the light, and Sarah saw that in addition to his long rifle, he carried a bedroll and his saddlebags. "I told you to bar the door. I expected you to leave it barred until my return."

Puzzled by his obvious anger, Sarah straightened. "Those men are gone, Mr. Beaudine, and I doubt they will trouble us again. Besides," she motioned toward the wolf, "Dancer is here. He wouldn't let anything happen to us." Dancer nuzzled her outstretched hand.

"I agree that three of those men won't bother you again." Orion dropped the bedroll and saddlebags by the door as he took her elbow and guided her inside the cabin. "But don't

underestimate Bartholomew Cutler, Sarah. He is a killer."
Orion closed the door and barred it, then leaned his rifle
against the wall.

Sarah fought down a rising tide of irritation. "We appreciate your concern, and shall take great care," she said cautiously. In addition to being annoyed, Sarah was also
confused. Her long-awaited reunion with Orion was not going as she had envisioned it would.

"The tea is ready," Theodora said cheerfully. "I'm certain
we'll all feel better after we have some. Won't you sit down,
Mr. Beaudine?"

Orion took a place next to Sarah on one of the benches
as Theodora, who sat opposite them, poured fragrant tea into
the three cups.

After a moment, Theodora broke the awkward silence.
"Tell us about your journey to Fort Kearny, Mr. Beaudine.
I trust all went well."

"Except for a snowstorm on the way out, the trip was
uneventful. Joseph sends his regards to both of you."

"Gray Eagle brought us a deer a few days ago," Sarah
said quietly. "It was good to see him, although he only stayed
for a few minutes."

"His thoughtfulness was touching," Theodora added. "We
had run out of meat."

"And he said Mr. Sage is courting a Cheyenne woman
named Sweet Water," Sarah said, becoming more animated.
"Do you think she will accept his suit?" She finally dared
to reach for her cup, careful to keep her hand in the shadows
as much as she could. Orion had not been pleased when he
saw her hands; she had not imagined that.

Orion smiled, evidently relaxing a little as well. "Oh, yes.
Jubal is considered a great warrior by the Cheyenne. He is
also respected as a wise man. Sweet Water will be pleased
to have him." He hesitated. "I'm glad to hear he plans to
marry again. I wasn't sure he'd ever get over his first wife's
death."

"I didn't know he was married before," Sarah said.

"It was a long time ago. He was married to an Arapaho woman for several years. They even had a couple of children. Then, at the time of the last great rendezvous, back in '34, one of the traders brought smallpox with him." Orion shook his head. "Jubal had had it as a boy, so he was immune. But his wife and kids never had a chance. The Indians have no resistance to many of the white man's diseases. My father thought the grief was going to drive Jubal insane. That's when they became such close friends. My pa had already buried two wives; he knew what it was like."

"Burying a spouse is one of the worst experiences a person can have," Theodora said quietly. "But I think burying a child is even worse. Somehow it's against nature, having to bury your young ones. They're supposed to bury you."

Sarah remained quiet. She had buried her parents, and each experience had been terribly painful. But the thought of burying Orion . . . she closed her eyes. He wasn't even her spouse, and yet she couldn't imagine how she would ever get through such an ordeal.

"Well," Theodora said. The lightness of her tone seemed forced. "We certainly let this conversation take a morbid turn. Let's all hope that Mr. Sage and his new bride enjoy a long and happy life together." She held up her cup.

"Here, here," Orion added, knocking his cup gently against Theodora's, then Sarah's. They all drank.

Theodora spoke again. "It's late, and I, for one, am exhausted; I'm going to bed." She stood up. "Mr. Beaudine, would you like more tea?"

"No, thank you. No doubt it's been a long day for all of us. We all should get some sleep." Orion pushed his end of the bench back and stood up.

Sarah also rose. "Where will you sleep?" she asked shyly.

"Right outside your door," Orion said firmly. "No one will disturb you again tonight."

"It's much too cold for you to sleep outside," Sarah protested.

"It certainly is, Mr. Beaudine," Theodora added. "We won't hear of it. If you insist on watching over us tonight, you will sleep in here. I'm sorry we can't offer you more than the floor, but it will at least be warmer in here."

Orion appeared to be about to protest.

Theodora fixed him with a stern look. "Please don't tell me you're worried about my reputation." Her lips curved in a smile. "And if you're worried about Sarah's reputation, hers isn't much better than mine right now. She and I will act as chaperone for each other. You'll either sleep in here, or you'll go back to the fort."

"Yes, ma'am," Orion said meekly.

Sarah looked at him. His lips were twitching at the corners, as if he were fighting a smile of his own.

Theodora gathered the empty cups. "I never did thank you for coming to our aid tonight, Mr. Beaudine. I appreciate your help."

Any trace of a smile fled Orion's face. "I'm glad I was here, Mrs. Byrd. I don't want to think of what might have happened."

"Mr. Sage's reinforced door and the bar he made for it would have held," Theodora said calmly. "I would have fired a few shots through the door, which I was ready to do when you appeared. The sound would have brought the soldiers from the fort, and the incident would have ended. Chances are Sarah and I would have endured nothing more than a good fright."

"Maybe, maybe not. Like I said earlier, don't make the mistake of underestimating Cutler."

Theodora's mouth tightened, as if even the mention of the man's name was distasteful. "I don't." She set the cups in the washbasin and went to her bed. "I'll keep my eyes closed so you two can have at least some privacy, and I promise I'll fall asleep as fast as I can. Good night." She slipped out of her wrapper and took off her moccasins, then crawled under her blankets.

"Good night," Sarah said.

"Good night, Mrs. Byrd." Orion took the bar from the door and brought his things inside, then secured the door again. The small cabin seemed much smaller with him in it.

Sarah suddenly felt very shy, and couldn't understand why. She had waited for this moment, longed for the time when she and Orion would be together again without the spectre of Adam hanging over them. And now that they were together again, everything seemed strange and uncomfortable. Not knowing what else to do, she retreated to her bed and sat primly on the edge, watching as Orion spread his blankets near the fireplace. He seemed content to work in silence, so she did not speak either.

After a few minutes, he turned and looked at her. Because his back was to the fireplace and the meager light from Sarah's candle did not reach across the room, she could not see the expression in his eyes, but she could feel the heat of those eyes as surely as if he had touched her. He stepped around the table and stopped about five feet from her bed.

Now Sarah could see his expression.

Once again, the familiar tendrils of excitement began their dance in her stomach. "Orion," she whispered.

He held his arms out to her, and Sarah needed no further invitation. She rose and walked into his embrace, her arms closing around him as she leaned her head against his shoulder and closed her eyes. His buckskin shirt smelled of smoke and sage, and of Orion. She loved the feel of his strong body pressed against her, loved the way his hand stroked her hair, toying with her braid.

They stood that way for a long time, just holding each other. Finally, Orion kissed the top of her head, and she looked up at him. His mouth met hers in a sweet, reverent kiss, and when she nibbled on his lips, asking for more, he smiled and shook his head.

"If we start that again, I'll carry you to that narrow bed and claim you tonight. And as much as I want you, this isn't the time or the place. I want us to be alone, to have the freedom to explore each other completely, to make as much noise as we want to."

"Noise?"

"Oh, yes," Orion whispered against her ear. "I want to hear you cry out your pleasure, to beg me for more, to tell me that you love me."

Sarah didn't know whether it was started by Orion's warm breath caressing her ear, or his powerful hands cupping her bottom and holding her against him, or his unbelievably exciting and sexual words, but a fire of desire roared to life in her belly and threatened to consume her. Her nipples tightened, her breath quickened, and she felt a strange, aching need in that mysterious place between her legs. She instinctively rotated her hips against him, causing him to draw in a startled breath of his own.

"Sarah!" His whisper sounded almost strangled. "Oh, God, woman." He moved away from her, just a little, and now cupped her face in his hands. His eyes searched hers, seemed to touch her very soul with their fire. "I have dreamed of loving you, Sarah Hancock. Now I know it is a dream that will come true."

She laid one hand over his heart, reveling in its strong, steady beat, knowing that it represented the rhythm of life. "It has been my dream, too, Orion."

They shared a tender kiss before Orion guided her to her bed. From behind, he reached around her and untied the belt of her wrapper, then opened the garment, revealing her nightdress. He placed one hand flat against her lower stomach for just a moment, then slowly moved both hands upward. Sarah's head fell back against his shoulder; her eyes closed; her lips parted; her arms hung limply at her sides. His hands moved up over her breasts in a slow caress, his thumbs pausing to rub her taut nipples while he kissed her neck. Then his hands continued up to her shoulders, and he slipped the wrapper off her. He scooped her up in his arms and set her on the bed.

Her eyes drifted open. "You heartless man," she whispered longingly. "You started a fire you won't put out now." Her lower lip protruded in a small pout.

Orion leaned down and nibbled on her lip. "Not tonight, sweet woman. And if it's any comfort to you, you're not the only one on fire." He took her hand and brushed it against his hardness.

Sarah gasped. She longed to more fully explore that fascinating part of him, but Orion moved her hand away and brought it to his mouth.

"Tomorrow we'll talk, Sarah." He ran gentle fingers over her injured skin. "I want to know all that has happened since I left. I am concerned about you."

"I'm fine, except for this problem with my hands."

"We'll talk tomorrow," he firmly repeated. He crouched down and pulled the socks from her feet. "You also have a problem with cold feet," he commented. "We'll get you a pair of fur-lined slippers like Mrs. Byrd has." He kissed the top of each foot, causing a whole new set of thrilling sensations to further jumble Sarah's already addled senses. "Do you have a warmed brick?"

"Yes," Sarah murmured.

"Good." Orion slipped the socks back on her feet before he swung her legs up and under the blankets. "Good night, sweetheart."

Sarah clung to him for a minute, then lay back on her pillow. "Good night, Orion." All of the feelings in her heart poured out in her voice.

After lightly touching her cheek, Orion blew out the candle and moved away. She watched him bank the coals in the fireplace, sending the room into a strange, shadowy darkness. He laid down on his rough bed, and the outline of his body blended with the darkness in the room. As she closed her eyes, a deep sense of peace stole over Sarah, easing the fires of desire.

Orion was back.

Twenty

"So he threw you out?" Orion's angry voice reverberated through the cabin.

"No! Harriet did," Sarah snapped. "And even if she hadn't, I would have left anyway. Can't you see that I had to?"

In frustration, Orion raked a hand through his hair. After their sweet, intoxicating time together last night, he had hoped this discussion with Sarah—which he had insisted upon having—would go smoothly. It hadn't. He was thankful for Theodora's tactful announcement that she had to visit the sutler's store after breakfast, thereby giving him and Sarah some real privacy for the first time since his return. But their pleasant small talk and tempting kisses had given way to an escalating argument. Why couldn't Sarah understand his position?

Orion tried again, deliberately calming his voice. "Given the history of your relationship with Mrs. Rutledge, I can understand why it would have been extremely uncomfortable to stay with the colonel and his wife. I just feel that, in light of your circumstances, Captain Rutledge should have taken better care of you. You claim he is such a *good* friend to you. If he is, how could he let his injured pride get in the way of doing what was best for you?"

"It was not his place to decide what was best for me," Sarah argued. "I insisted that he stay away, and he has honored my request. Adam has no obligation to me, Orion. I am perfectly capable of taking care of myself."

"He brought you out here, knowing you have no family, nothing to return to," Orion said stubbornly. "He should have continued to see to your well-being when the engagement was ended."

"I wouldn't let him." Sarah spoke the words slowly and distinctly.

"He should have insisted."

Sarah stared at him. "You think he should have taken me into the cramped quarters he shares with Lieutenant Roe? Is that where you would have wanted to find me? I suppose I could have made my new home in the barracks. Or in the mess hall, perhaps?" She planted her hands on her hips. "Be reasonable, Orion. There was nothing Adam could have done for me, no place for him to put me, and under the circumstances, I did not feel it was fair to expect him to. I left him, remember?"

Orion's jaw tightened. "He could have seen you safely to Fort Laramie."

"You think he should have taken me to *you?*" Sarah was incredulous. "I would not have insulted him like that. Adam had no idea of my feelings for you until recently. Besides, you had made me no promises except that you would return. Do you think I am the kind of a woman who would just appear on a man's doorstep uninvited and saddle him with my presence and my problems? I have my pride, too, you know."

"I know," Orion said tiredly. "But you put yourself in danger, and I can't bear the thought of anything happening to you." He looked at her, begging her with his eyes to understand. She was on the opposite side of the table from him, standing proud and stiff, two spots of color on her cheeks as much an indication of her anger as her flashing blue eyes. His heart grabbed. God, she was magnificent!

"I have not been in danger." Her words were firm, but her

expression softened. "I think Theodora was right about last night—the incident would not have gone much further. Everyone else treats us with grudging politeness or ignores us altogether, with the exception of a few friends. And thanks to the help of Mr. Sage and your brother, we have managed quite well."

Orion came around the table to grab Sarah's hands. His thumbs stroked her rough, red skin. "I want more for you than this."

Sarah jerked her hands away from him and backed up. "Someday I'll have more, but right now this is all I have, and it suits me fine." She stared up at him. "I followed your advice," she said heatedly. "I ended my engagement to Adam because I believed it was best for both him and me. We would have been miserable married to each other, and I finally found the courage to face that fact. No matter how I am living now, I don't regret my decision. Understand this, Orion Beaudine: I did not leave Adam for you."

"I know what I told you," Orion said angrily. Then he paused. Was there more behind her words than he understood? His heart started hammering. "Are you telling me that you don't want me?"

"No!" she cried. "I do want you. But I won't allow you to dictate my life. I'll not allow anyone that liberty again. To appease my mother, and Adam, and his mother, I agreed to marry him, against my better judgement. I buried my own spirit trying to become all that Harriet Rutledge and Adam expected of me as an Army wife. Then I met you." Her voice softened. "You understood me. You accepted me the way I was, and didn't demand anything of me save that I be true to myself. You offered me the purest form of friendship, Orion. What has happened to change that?"

"Nothing has changed that."

"Something has changed," she insisted. "I thought you would be pleased with what I have done. I took my life in my own hands—chapped and injured though they be—and

I survived, beholden to no man. I'm proud of what I have accomplished; I thought you'd be proud, too."

He reached for her, placing his hands on her shoulders. She stiffened at his touch, but did not pull away.

"Dear woman, I am proud of you."

Sarah raised her chin. "You're not showing it."

"No, I suppose I'm not," Orion admitted. "It's just that I keep thinking of all that could have happened to you, and I wasn't here to protect you."

"But nothing happened, and it wasn't your place to protect me," Sarah said firmly.

"Nothing happened because you were lucky, and it *is* a man's place to protect his woman."

"When you left, I was Adam's woman, remember?"

There was a brittle, sarcastic edge to Sarah's voice. Orion did not answer her. She continued.

"Then I threw off his yoke, and for a time, assumed I was free. Am I now your woman? Have you staked your claim on me, like I'm some stray cow, or do I have a say in the matter?"

"You have a say," Orion ground out between gritted teeth. "I'll not force any woman to accept me."

"You don't need force." Sarah's voice was barely above a whisper. "I would follow you anywhere, if you would only ask."

Orion looked into her wide, beautiful eyes, which were shimmering with unshed tears. His stomach grabbed at the love he saw there.

Sarah shrugged away from his hands. "But you must ask," she said. "You will not order me about, nor will you criticize my choices and decisions, for I won't tolerate it. And now I think it best that you leave for a while. I have work to do."

"I'm only trying to protect you, to watch out for you."

"You are treating me like a child, Orion Beaudine. I don't need Adam Rutledge, or you, or any man, to ensure that I have a safe and happy life. These past several weeks have proven to me that I can depend upon myself, and if necessary, I'll continue to do so for the rest of my life. I'd much rather be lonely than unhappy." Sarah went to the door and opened it, standing there with her hand on the latch.

"Fine," he muttered. He grabbed his hat off the table and marched out the door. "I'll be back later," he warned. "As long as I'm at Fort St. Charles, I'm staying here at night, even if I have to sleep outside."

"Suit yourself," Sarah said coolly. "I can't stop you."

"No, you can't."

He was almost across the yard when Sarah spoke again. "We'll have supper for you, if you'd like to join us."

A satisfied smile threatened to curve Orion's lips, but he steeled his expression before he turned around. "I would like that, Miss Hancock."

She nodded, then closed the door.

Orion crammed his hat on his head and strode across the bridge. "Hellfire," he swore under his breath. "Women."

If Miss Sarah Hancock thought she could scare him away with her declaration of independence, she was greatly mistaken. She *was* his woman; they *belonged* together, for crissakes! She would come to realize that if he had to shake her.

Or kiss her.

Or make love to her.

Knowing Sarah, he'd probably have to do all three.

Now Orion allowed himself to smile. He would do all three.

Sarah sank down on the bench, shaking with anger and aching with hurt. The arrogant man! Who did he think he was, marching back into her life and criticizing her? Adam had basically ignored her, and now Orion was taking too much interest. Sarah found neither approach appealing. Surely there had to be some kind of middle ground.

She propped her elbows on the table and buried her face

in her hands, ignoring the scrape of her roughened palms against the softness of her cheeks.

How had things with Orion gone so wrong so quickly?

Her hopes and expectations had been so high. During the long weeks of separation, when she was finally free to think of Orion as often as she wanted to, with no reason to feel guilty, he had taken on a dreamlike quality. She had held that idealistic image of him to her heart as surely as she held the beaded necklace he had given her. Perhaps that was the problem. She had savored the memory of every meeting with him, every tender word he had spoken to her, every tantalizing touch. Had she carried it so far in her mind that the real man could never hope to live up to her dream?

Had he done the same to her, putting her up on some kind of pedestal where there was no room for chapped hands and independent thought?

"Oh, God," she whispered brokenly. "What have we done to each other?"

Sarah did not see Orion again until that evening. He brought several sage grouse with him and spent some time in the yard cleaning the birds and chatting with Theodora, who was finishing the last of the day's ironing while Sarah made supper. Dancer laid close by, near the juniper bushes, his head resting on his paws, his golden gaze drawn to the birds near Orion's feet.

The sun had gone down behind the foothills to the west, and Sarah knew it was already too cold to work outside comfortably. She went to the door, wrapping her shawl more tightly around her shoulders.

"Why don't you both come in now?" she called. "Supper is about ready." A big cast-iron pot full of savory venison stew bubbled merrily on the hearth. The table was set and a steaming pot of tea made; all that remained was to slice the loaf of fresh bread that waited on the work shelf.

"We'll be right in," Theodora answered. Her breath made a cloud in front of her mouth.

As Sarah watched, Orion tossed Dancer one of the cleaned birds, which the wolf happily caught. "Are you certain he won't come in out of the cold?" she called out.

"He won't come," Orion assured her. "He doesn't need to. Nature equipped him with all he needs to survive in this country, as long as he can avoid man." He stood up and carried the string of cleaned carcasses to the river, where he rinsed them in the clear, cold water.

Sarah ventured outside to help Theodora gather up the finished laundry. With the coming of the cold weather, the chore of doing laundry had become more difficult, due to the discomfort of working in the cold and the fact that the clothes took much longer to dry. The only consolation was that the soldiers didn't seem to dirty their clothes quite as quickly, so there wasn't as much to do, but that also had the effect of cutting down on their income. Sarah had taken up some of the slack with her mending and alteration skills, but still, the winter promised to be a lean one.

The two women hurried inside with the neatly folded stacks of uniforms and placed them on the shelves behind the door, while Orion stored the grouse in the makeshift smokehouse.

Supper was a quiet affair, for both Orion and Sarah were cautious with each other, and Theodora, who glanced curiously from one to the other, did not understand what was going on.

"That was a fine meal, Sarah," Orion said as he placed his napkin next to his empty bowl.

Sarah nodded her thanks, toying with the remains of her own stew. She didn't have much of an appetite.

"I'm going to the stables for a while; I want to give Thunder a good brushing tonight. Then I'll set up my bedroll outside and turn in early. Last night was a short night for all of us."

"You're not sleeping outside, Mr. Beaudine," Theodora said firmly. "We've already had this discussion once, and I don't wish to have it again. I don't know what has caused this chill between you two, and it's none of my business. But no matter what the problem is, I can't believe Sarah would want you to sleep outside in such cold."

"No, I don't," Sarah said honestly. "I don't want Dancer sleeping outside, either."

"I'm glad I merit as much of your concern as the wolf does," Orion said.

Not certain if he was teasing or not, Sarah answered a little sharply. "You know you do, Mr. Beaudine. You infuriate me sometimes, but I do care about you."

"My heart is greatly lightened, Sarah." Orion grabbed her hand and kissed it, then shrugged into a buffalo hide coat. "I'll be back soon, and, bowing to your wishes, ladies, I shall make my bed on your hearth. Bar the door after I leave."

Sarah rolled her eyes. "Yes, sir!"

Orion winked at her and was gone.

After a moment of silence, Theodora asked, "Do you want to talk about it?"

"Oh, I don't know." Sarah gave up on her supper and stood. "He's just so . . . so *bossy* sometimes." She set her bowl outside for Dancer and closed the door, then placed the bar in its brackets. "He was actually angry last night with *us*, Theo, for placing ourselves in what he feels is a dangerous situation. I could not convince him that we have managed quite well so far."

"His concern is for you, Sarah. The man loves you."

"He cares about you, too. You heard him warn those men away from you. He meant what he said. If anyone bothers you again, the Beaudine brothers will make them regret it. And if Orion does love me, which he has not yet told me, he has a strange way of showing it. All he has done so far is claim that I am his woman and criticize what I do!" Sarah set Orion's bowl in the washbasin with more force than was necessary.

Theodora stood up. "He's a proud man, and a strong-willed one. And you have your pride, too."

"I told him that," Sarah interjected.

"It's going to take some time for you two to work things out," Theodora said soothingly. "This is the first time you've been together when both of you are free. Now the dream you share about a life together has a real chance of coming true. But now also, you have to face the truth about each other; you must really get to know each other. There's bound to be conflict, and that can make for some tough times."

Sarah frowned in confusion and weariness. "I thought love was supposed to be easy."

"No, Sarah." Theodora smiled, a gentle smile. "It's not easy. You and Mr. Beaudine are two very different people, coming from very different backgrounds, both with very set opinions and beliefs, both very strong, both willing to fight for those beliefs, even with each other. What both of you have to decide is whether the love you share is worth it. You both must be willing to compromise, and you must have a deep, basic love and passion for each other that will carry you through the tough times."

"I *think* we have that." Sarah sank down on the bench, deep in thought. "The Rutledges have it. That explains the success of their marriage. They are devoted to each other."

Theodora sat down next to her. "Nolan and I had it, too," she said sadly. "I love him still, and that's why I think this ache in my heart will never completely go away."

"Oh, Theo." Sarah put her arm around her friend, and the two women rested there, gazing at the fire.

"Don't let him get away, Sarah," Theodora finally said. "You and Mr. Beaudine have something special. Find the courage to accept the gift you've been given. Fight for him if you have to, even if it's him you have to fight. It will be worth it."

"I think you're right," Sarah said softly. "I think you're right."

Later, when Orion returned to the cabin, he gathered an armload of firewood before he knocked on the door. "It had better be barred," he muttered. To his relief, it was, for he could hear the sounds of the bar being moved. Sarah opened the door and stepped back out of his way.

"Do we need more wood?" she asked, eyeing the load in his arms.

"A storm is coming." He entered the room and saw in a glance that the supper dishes were cleaned and put away, the fire roared cheerfully, Theodora sat up in her bed reading by candlelight with a thick shawl wrapped around her shoulders, and Sarah had obviously been at the table, working on some mending. The pleasing scent of soap and herbs permeated the room. The scene was warmly domestic and very welcoming, and Orion was seized by the wish that he had just come into his own home, that Sarah had been waiting for him, and that Theodora, bless her heart, either lived somewhere else or had her own room. *And the bed,* Orion silently added as his gaze fell on Sarah's narrow, neatly made bed. *We need a bigger bed.* He passed Sarah and deposited the wood in the corner by the fireplace. "We may have snow by morning," he said, keeping his voice carefully neutral. "I want to get plenty of wood inside, where it will stay dry."

"Thank you, Mr. Beaudine. That's a good idea," Theodora said from her bed.

Sarah picked up a bowl from the ground near the door before she closed it. "Evidently Dancer likes my cooking, too," she commented as she set the bowl in the washbasin. "That bowl is so clean I don't have to wash it."

Orion stared at her. Was she teasing him? What had happened to lighten her mood while he was gone? "Dancer always was good at washing dishes," he said calmly.

A smile lit up Sarah's face as surely as the morning sun lit up the sky. Totally captivated, Orion could not look away. Her dark hair, pulled back into a loose chignon from which engaging tendrils had escaped, framed her face, offering a lovely contrast to her pale skin, and her blue eyes sparkled in the candlelight as if they had been kissed by the stars. If Theodora had not been there, he would have reached out to touch Sarah, to try to draw some of her mystical light into him.

She looked at him for a moment, obviously puzzled. "Mr. Beaudine? Are you all right?" She touched her cheek, then her lips. "Do I have something on my face?"

Orion blinked. "Uh, no. You look fine. In fact, you look beautiful. Forgive me for staring."

A delicate blush colored her cheeks, and she looked down, suddenly shy. "Thank you for the compliment."

"I'll, uh, get some more wood." Orion moved toward the door.

"I can help," Sarah offered.

"So can I," Theodora added. "Won't take me but a minute to put on my wrapper and slippers."

"No, you two stay in here where it's warm. I'll bring a bit more in, then cover part of the pile outside with an old buffalo hide I brought just for that purpose." He went out the door.

"A bit more" wood turned out to be a large stack that filled the corner of the room and spilled under the work shelf.

"I think this might be a real blizzard coming," Orion explained at Sarah's questioning look. "If it is, it could last for days, and we might well be trapped here for the duration. It's better to be safe than sorry." When he went to the door for one last trip, Sarah followed him.

"Could you give me just a few minutes to change my clothes?" she asked.

He nodded. "I'll check on Dancer, although I'm sure he knows something's blowing in, too."

"I wish he felt comfortable coming inside," Sarah said worriedly.

"We'll invite him if it gets real bad," Orion assured her. "He'll sometimes come into my tent or tipi when it's just me there, and he seems real friendly with you, so he might surprise us. But don't worry; I won't let anything happen to him. I'll rig up some kind of shelter for him." He smiled at her and left.

When Orion came back in about fifteen minutes later, the light in the cabin had dimmed. He saw that Theodora had extinguished her candle and was now hidden under her blankets. Only the top of her nightcap-covered head showed on her pillow. The other candle, still lit, remained in the center of the table, but there was no sign of Sarah's mending. She sat on the bench facing away from the table, her white nightdress peeking out where her wrapper had pulled apart below her knees, her feet covered with socks. Her hair was in its customary nighttime braid, again draped forward over her shoulder and breast, the end tied with the piece of buckskin fringe he had given her so long ago. She looked up at him, her eyes wide and clear.

"Dancer is fine," he said in a whisper, not wanting to disturb Theodora.

Sarah nodded with satisfaction. She glanced back over her shoulder at Theodora, then patted the bench next to her in invitation. Orion shrugged out of his heavy coat and hung it on a hook near the door, next to Sarah's cape, and joined her on the bench. She took his hand and held it in both of hers.

"I've done a lot of thinking today," she said in a low, quiet tone.

Orion swallowed, suddenly nervous. Sarah seemed very calm and determined. Had he pushed her too far this morning? She had already left one unhappy and restrictive relationship. Did she fear that a relationship with him would become unhappy as well? He tightened his fingers on hers and prepared himself for the worst, even though he knew that he would not gracefully accept an end to their relationship before it even got started. He would fight for her.

"Before, when I was engaged to Adam, there was a bittersweet quality to our feelings—yours and mine—for each other, because we felt we could not fully act upon those feelings." Sarah searched his eyes with hers, as if she was begging him to understand. "Things are different now. Now we can really be together, in every way, if we decide that is what we want. Now we have a decision to make."

"Is that what you want, Sarah? To be with me in every way?" Orion held his breath while waiting for her answer.

"Yes, it is, if that's what you want, which I think it is since you have claimed me as your woman."

With a relieved smile, Orion reached for her, but Sarah stopped him with a small hand braced against his chest. Her expression became very serious. "Do you also intend to claim me as your bride, Orion Beaudine?"

In a flash, Orion was on one knee in front of her, his hands clasping hers, looking up into her eyes. "I do intend that, Sarah Hancock." At her small frown, he hastily added, "If you are willing, that is," although he had no intention of giving her such a choice. She *would* marry him, if he had to kidnap her, carry her off, and get her with child. His belief that they belonged together was so strong that he was willing to do anything to convince her of the same truth.

"Probably I am willing," she said.

Probably? Orion stared at her, searching for some sign that she was teasing him. He found none. When he opened his mouth to speak, she pulled a hand from his grasp and laid a finger on his lips to silence him.

"You're not the only one who gets to stake claims, Orion. I insist that our relationship be an equal one, so I claim you also, as my man."

Orion caught her hand at his mouth and kissed it. "Do you also intend to claim me as your husband?" he asked, almost bursting with confidence and pride.

"Probably."

There was that hated word again. Orion frowned.

Sarah continued. "It depends on how well you court me."

"Court you? Sarah, I've asked you to marry me."

"I don't think we're in a position yet to make such a decision. We have lovely dreams and ideals about each other, but how well do we really know each other?"

"I know all I need to know about you," Orion said stubbornly. All of a sudden, he felt foolish on his knee. He dropped her hands as he straightened, then returned to the bench.

"Please try to understand, Orion," she pleaded. She took his hand again and held it to her breast. "I think I know all I need to know of you as well. I admire and respect you; I find you beautiful; I want you; I love you. But I thought I knew Adam, too, and yet even a lifetime of knowing him wasn't enough. I want to be certain that you and I will suit each other for marriage. I intend to marry only once, and I want to do it right. Does that make sense?"

He sighed. "Yes. It makes sense." He smiled and moved his hand on her breast in a gentle caress. "So you want to be courted, Miss Hancock?"

She gasped and pulled his hand away, clinging to his fingers. "Yes." She looked down at her lap. "I've never been courted," she admitted. "I'd like to be, just once."

Orion found her vulnerability deeply touching, and he couldn't help but think that Adam Rutledge was a complete clod. "Then you shall be courted, Miss Hancock. I must admit that I've never courted a woman before, but I'll do my best. Maybe Jubal can give me some pointers."

Sarah looked up at him with shining eyes, and Orion prayed that as long as he lived, he would never do anything to make that love light in her eyes go away. For the first time, he wondered if he truly deserved her, and the doubt shook him.

"Just don't get carried away with the hair tonic," she said softly.

Orion stifled a laugh. "I won't," he promised. Then he held his breath as she stroked his hair with one hand.

"I have always loved your hair," she whispered. "Don't ever cut it short." She pressed a lock to her mouth and kissed it.

Orion closed his eyes and shuddered, struck by a wave of love and desire so strong that he felt he couldn't bear it. He bolted to his feet and pulled her up with him. He took her sweet face between his hands and kissed her, deeply and passionately. When he released her mouth, she seemed breathless and dazed.

"There's just one thing, Sarah Hancock," he whispered. His hands dropped from her face to her shoulders, then briefly to her breasts before they settled on her waist and he pulled her close. Very close.

"What is it?" she gasped.

Orion felt that their forced whispering to avoid disturbing Theodora added an erotic element to the conversation. He placed his mouth close to her ear. "I won't give you a lifetime to get to know me, like Rutledge did. You have one month. By the new year, I will expect an answer to my proposal."

"One month?" she repeated.

"One month. I will not make love to you until you agree to be my wife, and I can't wait longer than one month for that sweet experience." Orion lowered one of his hands to caress her bottom and suddenly wasn't sure he could wait even that long. Maybe he should have said two weeks. No, from the look in her eyes, he should have said one week. *One day.* He groaned and held her tightly. "You'd best get to bed now, woman, before I forget all my good intentions."

"All right." She stood on tiptoe and pressed a quick kiss to his lips before backing away. As she crossed the floor to her bed, she slipped out of her wrapper, then hurried under her blankets. "Good night," she whispered.

"Good night, Sarah." Orion blew out the candle. He moved to the shelf where he had stored his blankets that morning, retrieved them, and made up his bed by the light of the dying fire. The wind had come up and now howled around the little cabin. Orion dropped down to his makeshift bed and sat cross-legged, staring into the struggling flames, clutching the lavender-scented lace shawl he had pulled from his saddlebag—the shawl he had not yet returned to Sarah.

Suddenly, Orion Beaudine was very afraid.

Everything he had ever dreamed of for his life was wrapped up in the spirited, dark-haired woman who lay across the room from him. It was fine to think that he would go as far as to carry her off if in the end she rejected his suit. But now he wondered if he would really do that. Wouldn't such an act be an insult to Sarah? Didn't she have the right to choose her own life? He would simply have to make certain that she chose him.

Orion whispered a prayer to the spirit gods of his Cheyenne brother and, leaving nothing to chance, another to the Christian God of his mother, that he would prove to be worthy of Miss Sarah Hancock.

Twenty-one

Orion had correctly predicted the weather. When the occupants of the small cabin awoke the next day, a major storm had blanketed the entire region in heavy snow. The wind howled with relentless fury, blowing fine white powder in under the door, around the window, and through every previously hidden crack in the chinked log walls, including one over Sarah's bed. She had awakened to discover a small snowdrift across one part of her blanket. No wonder she had been cold all night. Her body was stiff and aching from hours of being curled up in a tight little ball.

Although Orion kept the fire high, by noon the chill was still not gone from the room, and he said that it wouldn't be until the weather itself warmed up. Sarah pulled on an extra pair of socks and wore her winter boots, as well as an extra petticoat, and kept her thick, serviceable shawl wrapped around her shoulders.

There wasn't much they could do to occupy themselves other than talk or read, and even reading presented something of a challenge, as firelight was all they had to read by. Their supply of candles was low, and they decided to hoard the remaining ones because there was no way to know how long the storm would last.

Orion would not allow the women outside even to see to their personal needs, explaining that it was frighteningly easy to get lost in a blinding snowstorm only a few feet away from the house. Periodically throughout the day he would step outside, presumably to see to his own needs while giving Sarah and Theodora an opportunity to use the chamber pot with some degree of privacy. Upon returning from one of his excursions, Orion brought with him several of the sage grouse.

"How is Dancer?" Sarah asked as she seasoned the grouse with salt and dried sage.

"He's curled up in the little den I made for him near the woodpile, with his tail over his nose. He's fine." Orion deftly impaled the birds on a spit as Sarah finished with each one.

"He wouldn't come in?" She gave him a few cleaned wild onions to put on the spit as well.

"Not yet. I'll try again when it gets dark." Orion looked at her with an understanding smile. "Don't worry about him so." A day's growth of beard darkened his cheeks and chin, making his eyes appear to be even more green.

Sarah longed to reach out and lay her hand against his cheek, to feel the fascinating roughness of his beard, to have him turn his head and kiss her palm, as he had done before. She wished for a chance to be alone with him, then felt guilty. This was Theodora's home first; she and Orion were the guests here.

Although Theodora was warm and generous toward both Sarah and Orion, her very presence lent caution to the topics they discussed. Every time they touched accidentally, it was as if a lightning bolt passed between them, so heightened was their awareness of each other. At least Sarah felt it; she suspected Orion did, too, simply from the way he looked at her. It was frustrating to be so physically close to him in such close quarters and to be unable to talk to him freely, to be unable to touch him, to stroke his long hair, to kiss him. For she certainly had all those impulses. In Theodora's presence, Sarah did not even feel it was appropriate to call Orion by his first name, although he did not seem to have any reservations about addressing her by her first name, as he did now.

"Sarah, do you play chess?" he asked.

"I used to, long ago, when my father was alive," she answered. "But I'm not sure I remember how."

"I do," Theodora chimed in. "Nolan and I used to play often."

"Do you have a set?" Orion asked.

"No. Our chess set was taken when the wagon captain appropriated our wagon and team after Nolan died. He probably would have let me have it, but I was too sick to even think clearly at the time." She shrugged. "I'm lucky I managed to save the teapot and a few other things that had belonged to his mother."

"I have a set, but it's rather primitive." Orion pulled a rolled and tied piece of hide about a foot and a half long from his pack. He loosened the tie and spread the hide out on the table. A leather pouch was revealed, along with a checkerboard pattern dyed onto the scraped hide. Orion opened the pouch and dumped the contents on the makeshift board. An interesting array of carved wooden figures lay before them. "My father made this set the first summer he spent with the Cheyenne," he explained.

Sarah picked up one of the figures and examined it curiously. "There are few markings on this one," she commented.

Orion squinted at it in the dim light. "That's a pawn. The others are a little more elaborate, just enough to tell them apart." He shifted his gaze to Theodora. "Would you like to play, Mrs. Byrd?"

Theodora smiled. "Yes, very much. But since we are now sharing a house, you must call me Theodora."

"Very well, Theodora. Please call me either Orion or Hunter, whichever you prefer. I answer to both." Orion stood and lifted the corners of the hide chessboard, then carried everything to the floor in front of the fireplace. For the next

two hours, the three people sat on the floor in front of the
warm and comforting fire, their attention riveted on the
game. Periodically, Sarah would turn the spit on which the
grouse and onions slowly cooked, filling the cabin with a
wonderful aroma. Although a fierce storm roared around
them, she felt safe and protected in the sanctuary offered by
the stout little cabin. For a while, the worries and dangers
of the outside world faded away. Her man and her dear friend
were with her, they had shelter, fuel, and food. If only Dancer
would come in from the storm, she would be perfectly content.

The afternoon passed quickly and pleasantly. Again and
again, Sarah caught herself staring at Orion's hands as he
moved the chess pieces around the board. His long fingers
were well shaped and graceful, the nails clean and neatly
trimmed. She remembered the feel of those strong hands on
her face, and neck, and shoulders. She remembered the sight
of his hand against the bodice of her gown, covering her
breast, and fantasized about his same hand in that same place
without the barrier of cloth between her flesh and his. Her
eyes closed as the seductive picture came to life in her mind,
then she caught herself and forced her eyes open. Although
she was seated close to the fire, Sarah knew it was a blush
that heated her cheeks and not the warmth of the friendly
flames.

Orion Beaudine had ensnared her in an erotic web of desire
without saying a word, without touching her, without even
looking at her, for his mind was focused on the chess game
that seemed destined to end in a draw. Sarah found the extent
of his power over her a little frightening.

A short time later, the chess game did indeed end in a
draw, and Sarah announced that the grouse were cooked.
Supper was a lighthearted affair, shared in the warm light of
one precious candle, and all found the simple, sturdy fare of
roasted grouse, onions, and bread surprisingly delicious.
When the meal was finished, Orion took two of the roasted

birds out to Dancer while Sarah and Theodora cleaned up, then the three again met at the table with a fresh pot of tea. Orion scooted close to Sarah on the bench they shared and draped an arm around her shoulders. Surprised that he would act so forward in front of Theodora, Sarah raised questioning eyes to his face. He smiled down at her with a warmth that took her breath away, then he looked across the table at the obviously amused Theodora and spoke.

"Just so you know, Theodora, I'm now officially courting Miss Hancock, so I must beg your indulgence. These are close quarters, not giving any of us much privacy, and I may be tempted at times to do foolish things in front of you, like kiss her." He planted a noisy kiss on Sarah's cheek to emphasize his point. "And if you hear us talking real low, it's not because we're talking about you, and it doesn't mean you aren't welcome to join in the conversation; it's just that courting couples like to talk privately sometimes." Any note of teasing left his voice. "I hope you understand."

"Of course I do." Theodora bestowed a happy smile on both of them. "I only regret that the storm prevents me from giving you some privacy."

"Please don't, Theo," Sarah begged. "This is your home. We've waited this long. Another day or two isn't going to matter."

"Speak for yourself, woman," Orion growled in her ear as he tightened his hold on her.

Shivers of delight raced down Sarah's body as his warm breath tantalized her sensitive skin, but she still slapped his thigh under the table in warning. "Behave yourself," she whispered. She did not want her relationship with Orion to be a constant painful reminder to Theodora of what she had lost when her husband had died.

"Oh, Sarah." Theodora winked at her and stood up. "You're going to have your hands full with that man."

"That is my intention," Orion said. The smile on his face turned positively lecherous, and Sarah blushed.

As discomfited as she was with Orion's blatant flirting, his words and the possessive touch of his arm around her shoulders made her feel warm inside. Warm and protected. And wanted. She nestled closer to him and let her hand remain where it rested on his thigh.

Theodora set her teacup in the washbasin, then rubbed her hands over her shawl-covered arms. "It's early yet, but I think I'm going to get into bed. Maybe I can get warm there."

Orion cleared his throat. "I have something to say on that subject."

Both Sarah and Theodora looked at him.

"I think we should make a common bed for all of us on the floor in front of the fire," he said. "That may sound shocking, but I'm very serious. That poor old fireplace simply can't heat this cabin, and Sarah's bed especially will be freezing. If we combine all our blankets and robes, we'll all be more comfortable."

"Makes sense to me," Theodora said.

"Me, too," Sarah added. She could see the logic in Orion's plan, for her bed had indeed been chilled all night, but the logic was not the only appeal of the plan. The thought of sleeping next to Orion filled her with a warmth that had nothing to do with the prospect of extra blankets.

That decided, the three went to work making their bed. Orion moved the benches and table back, turning the table on its side at the end of the "bed," to block drafts, he explained. Sarah and Theodora created a large, comfortable-looking sleeping area, utilizing all of their combined bedclothes.

"I'll sleep in the middle," Orion said. "Leave most of your clothes on; you'll stay warmer. Only take off things like boots and corsets." He moved to the door. "I'll be back in a few minutes." A swirl of snow charged into the room on the coattails of a blast of freezing air, then the door closed and he was gone.

Sarah looked at Theodora. "Are you certain these arrangements are all right with you, Theo?"

Theodora nodded vigorously. "I'm certain. We should have done this last night. I don't know about you, but I was miserable. I swear, my jaws hurt this morning because my teeth chattered all night."

"I was uncomfortable, too," Sarah admitted. "It was so cold that the little snowdrift on my bed didn't melt."

"We should mark some of those cracks in the wall and see about getting them plugged," Theodora said as she pulled the pins from her hair. "It's going to be a long winter, and we may not always have your man to snuggle up with. Or I may not," she corrected herself. An expression of sadness flashed across her face. She looked at Sarah. "Sooner or later, you and he will set up housekeeping on your own, and I sure will miss you."

"I'll miss you, too, when the time comes," Sarah said, pulling her own hairpins free. "But I don't know where Orion plans to live. If he's going to be gone for days or weeks at a time on his scouting missions, maybe we should just enlarge this cabin for all three of us." She thoughtfully pulled her brush through her hair. "I suppose he and I should discuss that sometime."

"I suppose you should," Theodora said, her tone affectionately scolding. She plaited her blonde hair into a long braid and tied the end. "You two really haven't had time to do much more than fall in love. First Captain Rutledge was in the picture, and you couldn't even consider a future together. Now that you can, this storm and my presence are in the way."

Stricken, Sarah hurried to her friend's side and gave her a quick hug. "Theo, you aren't in the way. Please don't even think such a thing. I'm glad you're here. If he and I had been snowbound together, alone, I know what would have happened." A blush heated Sarah's cheeks, but she forced herself to continue. "And it would have been too soon. Orion and I need time to sort through our feelings, to be certain that what we feel for each other is not merely the passion of forbidden love."

Theodora stared at her. "Surely you don't think that's all it is."

"No, I don't. And neither does he."

"Well, neither do I."

"Still, a little time will be good for us." Sarah worked her hair into a braid.

Theodora sat on a bench and took off her boots. "I didn't put on a corset this morning, so I reckon I'm ready for bed. I'll get the warming rocks wrapped."

Since Sarah had foregone her corset that morning as well, she, too, was ready for bed. She helped Theodora wrap three stones and placed them at even intervals at the foot of the big sleeping area. Theodora crawled under the blankets on the far side and nestled down until only her eyes and the top of her head showed. "I'm warmer already," she declared.

With a smile at her friend, Sarah sat down on the blankets to wait for Orion. It seemed he had been gone for a long time. A few minutes later, she started to get worried. After all his warnings to them, had he gotten lost in the storm himself? Just when she was about to go to the door in order to call him, he came in. Surprisingly, he did not close the door right away, but seemed to be waiting for something. Sarah pulled her shawl more tightly around her shoulders and shivered, now sorry that she hadn't gotten under the blankets as Theodora had done. She frowned at his back, then a moment later her eyes widened when she saw a furry head appear in the opening.

"Come on, boy," Orion said soothingly.

Dancer. Sarah held her breath, not wanting to move even enough to breathe, fearful she might startle the wary animal. Dancer raised his head and sniffed, then ventured farther into the room. After another cautious pause, he moved forward far enough to allow Orion to close the door. Sarah glanced at Theodora and saw that her friend's exposed eyes were as large as saucers. She mouthed the words, *It's all right,* then placed a finger on her own lips. Theodora nodded and remained quiet.

Sarah held her hand out to the wolf. Dancer took a few more slow steps and stretched his neck until his cold, wet nose touched her hand.

"Hello, sweetie," she whispered. "I'm glad you came in from the storm." The wolf pushed his nose against her hand in the silent, age-old request that she pet him, and Sarah happily complied. As she scratched Dancer's snow-dampened ears, she looked up at Orion. "Will he stay through the night?"

Orion shrugged out of his coat. "I think so. If he wants to leave, he'll let me know." He hung his coat on the hook, then grabbed a drying towel from next to the washbasin and rubbed it over Dancer's snow-covered back. The wolf wiggled with pleasure.

Theodora cleared her throat. "I don't have anything to worry about, do I?" she asked in a hoarse whisper.

"No." Orion smiled down at her. "He won't venture far from the door." He turned to the fire and added more wood. "We have plenty of wood, so I'll try to keep the fire going all night. I think we'll all be much more comfortable tonight." He brushed off the snow that clung to his buckskin pants, then gracefully dropped to a sitting position on the floor. He pulled his boots off and set them next to the fireplace before he smiled at Sarah. "You have a friend for life," he said softly, nodding at Dancer.

Sarah looked at the wolf, who had laid down next to her. "I love him," she said simply. "I can't explain it, but there is something about his spirit that calls to mine. He is a wise and noble soul." The words just popped out, and, suddenly feeling foolish, she shrugged and raised her gaze to Orion. "I guess that sounds strange, doesn't it?"

"Not to me."

It seemed to Sarah that the warm flames of the fire had

leapt into Orion's eyes, so intense and scorching was the look he gave her. She saw respect there, and love, and desire. Heat flashed through her stomach again, and for one guilty moment she silently took back her assurances to Theodora and wished that she and Orion were alone in the room. The image of lying naked with him under the inviting pile of blankets tormented her. She forced herself to again focus on Dancer, smoothing the silver fur between his ears. "I think I'll try to get some sleep, too," she said.

"Good night," Theodora mumbled sleepily.

"Good night," Orion responded. He slid under the blankets, then held them up for Sarah.

Without a word, she crawled under them, and held her breath when Orion reached over her to tuck the blankets around her side. She turned to face him as he laid down on his back. The firelight glinted off his dark hair, and she smoothed a strand away from the side of his face. She loved the beard-roughened feel of his cheek and silently told him so with a caress.

He caught her hand and pressed a kiss to her palm, sending another quiver of desire through her.

"Sleep well, my love," he whispered. His warm breath caressed her palm before he kissed her again, then he moved her hand under the blankets and placed it over his heart.

Sarah snuggled closer to him, resting her forehead next to his shoulder, and lay still, contented with the steady beat of his heart against her hand, with the rhythmic rise and fall of his chest. A few minutes later, she became aware of another comforting warmth, this one at her back, and she realized that Dancer had moved closer to her. Nestled between the wolf and the man, she felt safe and blessed, and within minutes was peacefully asleep.

The storm raged for another day. Dancer went outside periodically, sometimes staying out for an hour or longer, but scratched at the door when he wanted back in, as if he had lived there all of his life. Theodora was as captivated by the wolf as Sarah was, and was thrilled when Dancer allowed her to touch him. The day passed in easy camaraderie, with games of chess and meals of simple but hearty food. Sarah had an opportunity to whisper to Orion her concerns about upsetting Theodora if they got too cozy in front of her, and he agreed to be very discreet.

Consequently, they rarely touched each other, and then only by accident or in passing, and they spoke in friendly, neutral tones on friendly, neutral topics. To Sarah, though, the feelings that were communicated between them when they looked at each other heated the room far more than the valiant fire did. It had only been two days, but suddenly she could not wait for the infernal storm to pass. She wanted—needed—to be alone with her man.

Orion had many of the same feelings. He appreciated Sarah's sensitivity about the pain their obvious affection might cause Theodora, and as difficult as it was, he tried to treat both women equally. But after all the months of wanting Sarah, of longing for her when she had belonged to someone else, the frustration of not being able to express his feelings for her now that she was free almost drove him crazy. He wanted to hold her, to touch her, to tell her the loving, private things a man told his woman, to pull her down onto the big bed and slowly remove every article of clothing between them, to pull every pin from her sweetly scented hair and spread the long locks out over the pillows. He wanted to join his body with hers, bury himself deep within her, touch her soul with his. Again he whispered prayers to the gods, this time that the storm spend itself and allow the sun to shine once more.

On the morning of the third day, his prayers were answered. They awakened to an eerie silence, and Sarah finally realized that the wind no longer wailed and screamed. She scrambled out of the warm cocoon of her bed and stepped over Dancer to cautiously open the door. The still air wrapped icy fingers around her, and she saw that a waist-high snow-drift blocked the exit, but the sky was clear and the sun would soon appear over the eastern horizon. She looked around in wonder, searching for some recognizable landmark. Although she could see the fort on the other side of the river, the river itself had disappeared under a white blanket, and even the bridge was almost obliterated by piles of drifted snow. Unless the weather warmed and helped melt the snow, it would take days to dig out.

"Lord have mercy," she muttered as she pushed the door closed and replaced the bar. She dove back under the blankets and snuggled against Orion's warmth.

He put an arm around her and kissed her forehead. "The storm has ended."

"Yes. But the whole world is buried under several feet of snow. It will take some hard work just to get to the bridge. And the bridge itself is entombed, and the river has disappeared."

"Colonel Rutledge will put the enlisted men to work. By this afternoon, things will look a lot different. We'd best get to work ourselves." Orion threw back the blankets, uncovering both himself and Sarah, and jumped to his feet.

Sarah shivered and scooted back under the blankets.

Theodora stirred, then poked her nose out. "What is it?" she asked sleepily.

"The storm has moved on," Orion answered. After adding more wood to the fire, he pulled his boots on, then took his coat from its hook. "I'll see what I can accomplish with the shovel. I'll at least be able to trample down a path to the bridge."

"We'll straighten up in here and get breakfast on," Sarah said. "I'll call you when it's ready."

"Sounds good." Orion covered his hands with a pair of beautifully beaded fur-lined leather gloves, then opened the door. "Well, Dancer, let's push through this snow."

The wolf followed him outside and Orion pulled the door closed.

Sarah rolled over on her stomach and rested her chin on her flat hands as she stared at the hungry flames in the fireplace.

The storm had moved on, taking with it the isolated, secure little world she, Orion, Theodora, and Dancer had built together in the tiny cabin. Adversity made strange bedfellows, literally.

Her life was about to change again. Now Orion would begin his courting in earnest. Would he continue to stay in the small cabin, in order to offer her and Theodora protection? Would he even be here for the next month, or would he be sent back to Fort Laramie? If so, would he want her to go with him?

What of Theodora? She couldn't be left completely alone, not with men like Bartholomew Cutler around.

And what of Dancer? Would the wolf return to his wary, solitary ways now that there was no pressing reason for him to be in the cabin? Sarah hated the thought; she wanted Dancer to live with her always, as a pet dog would, but even as she thought the words, she knew that wouldn't be fair to Dancer. The wolf was a child of the forests and the mountains, and he deserved the freedom to roam where his spirit led him. Orion had always respected that freedom; she must, also.

And finally, what of the future? Where did Orion intend to make their home? Would he continue to work as a scout? Would he expect her to continue her work as a laundress? She would, if necessary, and happily, but she wanted to know.

There were so many questions, and so few answers.

She and Orion had just been reunited, then everything between them had been pushed to the back burner because of the storm and the lack of privacy—the questions, the answers, the decisions that faced them. Life-changing decisions. Now all would be brought to the fore again.

"What are you thinking about?" Theodora asked softly. "You look so serious, and almost sad."

Sarah faced her friend—her dear friend—and slightly shook her head. "No, I'm not sad. But the storm has ended, Theo. The cocoon it wove around us with its shrieking wind and barriers of snow will be dissolved. Life will return to normal; there will be clothes to wash, some people to greet and others to avoid, problems to face and solve, just as there were before, and yet I have this powerful feeling that nothing will ever be the same."

Theodora laid a comforting hand on Sarah's bent elbow. "No, it won't be. The Hunter is back, and he has claimed you. You are preparing for a new journey now."

"Yes," Sarah whispered. She looked back at the fire. "A new journey." With Orion Beaudine at her side.

Twenty-two

"They are closing the fort?"

Orion almost smiled at the incredulous look on Sarah's face. He was familiar with the sometimes nonsensical workings of the United States government; apparently she was not. "That's the message Jubal brought. We've been ordered to pack up as quickly as possible, and get to Fort Laramie with as much as we can safely carry. Later, when the weather permits, a detachment will be sent to retrieve what we can't take now."

Three days had passed since the end of the storm; the weather had turned unseasonably warm, which was not unheard of in that part of the country, and much of the snow had disappeared. The disappearance of the snow had caused the reappearance of both Laramie rivers, and both were flowing high and fast. Jubal had arrived that morning, bearing dispatches from Fort Laramie and a new wife.

Sarah brushed a strand of hair away from her forehead with the back of one hand. The steam from the tub of heated water over which she labored had turned her cheeks a pleasing shade of pink and caused wisps of fine hair to curl around her face in a most becoming way. Orion fought the urge to grab her and kiss her right there, in the yard, in full view of Theodora and the small detail of soldiers working on the nearby bridge.

"All this work for all these months," she said disbelievingly, waving a hand in the direction of the fort. "And they are just going to abandon it?"

Orion shrugged. "It's happened before, and it will happen again. Sarah, you must understand that the men in Washington who make these decisions have no idea of what it is really like out here. None of them have been here. They base their decisions on their own personal whims, on the political climate of the day, and on the opinions of the officers sent here—most of whom also have no clear understanding of the reality of life in the West. Fort St. Charles never should have been developed in the first place. It's too far south of the Oregon trail, and too far north of the Overland trail. And I can tell you now that the trail to the north is the one that will be used. The army needs to focus on Fort Laramie, and build other forts farther west, along the Oregon trail."

A frown wrinkled Sarah's brow in a way that Orion found absurdly endearing. "Why did it take them so long to figure that out?" she demanded. "Why didn't they ask you? Or Mr. Sage? I'm certain he agrees with you. Orion, this is such a waste, of money, of time, of labor." She waved at the stockaded walls of the fort and her voice softened. "Of trees."

"I know." Orion moved to stand behind her, placing his hands on her shoulders. The soft scent of lavender teased his senses. "It *is* a waste. Unfortunately, when people find a land of plenty, many tend to become wasteful."

Sarah leaned back against him and heaved a troubled sigh. "Are the Indians wasteful?"

"No. They use every bit of everything, and give thanks to their gods and the spirits for the ability to do so. But they have their own problems." Orion dropped his hands from her shoulders to her waist and pulled her close, not caring who saw them.

"Like what?"

Orion sighed himself. "Like waging war on each other, as they have done for centuries, long before the white man's shadow darkened their shores. Even now, when facing their greatest enemy, they cannot unite for their common good."

"Their greatest enemy?" Sarah repeated softly.

"Us, Sarah." His hold on her tightened. "The white man. Like the wolf, the Indians must face the white man, and, unlike the wolf, the Indians underestimate the danger. My brother Joseph is convinced that one day the whites will rule this land, that the Indians will disappear. I pray he is wrong, but I fear he may be right. He says there are simply too many whites, that they will one day slow down on their mad rush to the west coast, and they will look around and see what we see, what you see: a land of beauty; a land of plenty. And they will want it." He felt Sarah shiver, and held her even tighter.

"Joseph is right," she whispered. She turned in his arms to face him, her own arms going around his waist, clasping him with desperate strength. "A simple study of history will prove that since the day he set foot on the shores of this continent, the white man has inexorably marched farther and farther west, like a swarm of locusts, devouring everything in his path." Sarah looked up at him with tortured eyes. "Yet I have felt it myself—the need to come west, to start anew, to leave the past behind." Her head fell forward on his shoulder. "God forgive me, I have felt it, too. I answered its call. And now that I am here, I want to stay."

"I know, sweet woman." Orion held her close, placed his hand at the back of her head. He was astonished at her insight, yet knew he should not be. She was, after all, Sarah. His heart swelled with love for her. "I heard the call, too, as did my father. But some of us are different, Sarah. My father, my brothers and sisters, Jubal Sage, you, and others. We want to stay, but we have no desire to destroy what we have found here. We don't feel the need to make this land over into what we left. We accept it, and its people, its wildlife, its trees and plants and rivers, as they are, as we found them.

Like the Indian, we take what we need to live, giving thanks for the bounty of the land, and we let the rest live in peace."

"There are not enough of us," Sarah said. The sadness in her voice broke Orion's heart.

"No, my love, there are not."

The evacuation of Fort St. Charles proceeded at a surprisingly productive rate. Sarah determined that while the decisions made by the federal government in Washington sometimes did not make sense, the men who were entrusted to carry out those decisions were a dedicated, hard-working, relatively efficient group of men. In three days, all was ready.

The sutler, Miles Breen, and his Indian wife would remain behind, their business once more becoming a simple trading post rather than a bustling military mercantile. The three Mexican families also had no intention of leaving, although Sarah suspected they would move from their humble cabins along the river into some of the larger buildings within the stockade. The Rutledge home, modest though it was, was considered luxurious by frontier standards, and would not be vacant for long.

Now, wearing her riding boots and her warm, hooded cape, Sarah stood inside the little cabin she had shared with Theodora and, for the last several days, Orion. Overcome by a sense of nostalgia, she looked around the tiny, empty room. All had been packed; the trunks belonging to her and Theodora had been loaded on one of the freight wagons, and Theodora had offered the table and the benches, as well as the two large washtubs outside, to one of the Mexican families. Nothing remained in the cabin except for the two braced shelves that had served as beds, the work shelf under the window, and the laundry shelves behind the door. The stone fireplace, so long a source of warmth, comfort, and cheer, was now cold and silent, almost forlorn.

She had been happy here.

Within the walls of the primitive cabin, she had found herself again. For two months she had shared the close, sometimes uncomfortable quarters with Theodora, worked harder than she had ever worked in her life, and planned her future. She had been truly free.

Then Orion had returned, making the sanctuary of the cabin that much more precious with his beloved presence. And now it was ended.

It seemed to Sarah that since her mother's death almost a year earlier, her life had evolved into a series of endings: the loss of her mother; the leaving of her life in the East; the end of her engagement to Adam; the leaving of the Rutledge home and the Army way of life; and now, the leaving of this small cabin and all it had come to represent to her.

"Sarah?" Theodora's voice reached her from the open door.

With a smile, Sarah turned, holding out her gloved hands. Theodora stepped inside and took Sarah's hands.

"Orion has our horses saddled; he's bringing them now." Theodora looked at her curiously. "Are you all right?"

"Yes. I'm just feeling a little pensive. I'm so thankful to you for allowing me to live here with you, to work with you. I don't know what I would have done otherwise."

Theodora's hands tightened on hers. "Oh, Sarah, it is I who should be thanking you. Your friendship brought joy back into my life. You are my dearest friend."

"And you are mine." The sound of approaching horses reached Sarah's ears. "It's time to go." She gave Theodora a quick hug, then, after a last look around the room, followed her friend outside.

Orion held the reins of three horses in his gloved hands. "The column has been given the order to move out," he reported.

Sarah shaded her eyes and looked to the north. Sure enough, the advance riders were moving, the flags of the United States and of the company fluttering in the mid-morning breeze. A wagon which, due to the three opened parasols Sarah saw, obviously carried the officers' wives and the two excited Dillard children followed, then one with the other laundresses. Twin lines of mounted cavalrymen came next, and four heavily laden wagons brought up the rear, followed by the herd of approximately fifteen horses, guarded and guided by six more soldiers on horseback themselves.

"Surely they did not fit everything into those four wagons," Sarah commented as Orion helped Theodora up into her saddle.

"No. The mess hall is almost filled with furniture and supplies, including Mrs. Rutledge's precious dining room set and that cast-iron stove she insists on hauling all over the country. She wasn't happy about leaving them, although the building has been well barricaded and the colonel has paid the sutler handsomely to watch over things. She'll be reunited with her belongings soon enough, if she has to hire it transported herself." He cupped his hands for Sarah, and when she placed her foot there, he boosted her up into the saddle.

Sarah arranged her skirts and cape around her legs as Orion adjusted the stirrup lengths. "Won't the Army come and get the things left behind?"

"Eventually." Orion rested his hand on her thigh, sending a shiver through her body that had nothing to do with the chill in the December air. "But probably not soon enough to suit Mrs. Rutledge. She comes from a wealthy family, and has the means to arrange transport for her things."

"That explains how she manages to keep such a luxurious house, and pay for Lucy's services," Sarah commented.

Orion climbed into his own saddle. "That's right."

"I never could have competed with that, even if I had wanted to," Sarah said softly. "I never would have pleased her. No one could."

"Oh, I think the right woman might, one who is meek and submissive. I think Harriet would be very generous with her nephew's wife if she approved of the match." Orion leaned out of the saddle to take Sarah's hand. "I'm glad she didn't approve of your match with Captain Rutledge." He winked at her. "For all her faults, the Mrs. Colonel is a smart woman. She knew you and the captain would never suit."

Sarah cocked an eyebrow. "If she is so smart, does she think you and I suit?"

"Most definitely." Orion straightened in the saddle. "She considers both of us to be reprobates, and beneath contempt. I'm certain she thinks ours is a match made in heaven."

Sarah laughed, then her smile softened. "Ours *is* a match made in heaven."

"I know." The fire in his eyes warmed her.

"Don't you two start," Theodora affectionately warned. "We have to catch up to the column, and it looks like Mr. Sage and his new wife are waiting for us."

Orion sighed. "You're right, of course, Theodora. Let's go." He turned Thunder's head and led the two women across the wooden bridge for the last time. Jubal Sage and his stocky wife, Sweet Water, waited in front of the opened main gates to the eerily silent fort.

"Good morning, Mr. and Mrs. Sage," Orion called out jovially. "Are you joining us on the journey to Fort Laramie?"

"For a bit," Jubal answered. "We'll go as far as Elk Tooth Creek, then we're turning southeast. I want to hook up with Gray Eagle's band, maybe spend the winter with them."

Orion nodded. "I've been thinking of doing the same. But first I have some courting and marrying to do." He looked at Sarah with such obvious love in his eyes that she blushed.

"So I heer'd," Jubal said approvingly. "It's about time, if you ask me."

"It's about time we caught up with the column," Sarah said tartly. She touched her heels to Star's sides and led the way at a canter, leaving no more time for teasing or talking.

Eventually Orion and Jubal guided the three women to a position near the wagons at the head of the column, where

Orion instructed them to keep their mounts at a walk and ride a little off to the side of the column so they wouldn't have to breathe what little dust was being sent up from the mostly frozen earth. He and Jubal then went on ahead to confer with Colonel Rutledge. Sarah saw the piercing look Adam threw Orion, saw the tightening of his mouth. Surely he knew Orion had been staying at the cabin with her and Theodora. Did he also know that she and Orion now had an understanding? If Adam did know, Sarah doubted he would be happy about it.

Lucy and Libby Gates both waved as Sarah and Theodora fell into place alongside their wagon, but Harriet Rutledge and Penelope Dillard gave them no more than a disdainful glance, probably as much for the fact that they were riding astride as for their reputations. Sarah shrugged and turned in her saddle, motioning for Sweet Water to join them. The stalwart Cheyenne woman did not speak English, but she was friendly to Sarah and Theodora, and was obviously very devoted to Mr. Sage. Sarah had liked her instantly. Sweet Water smiled broadly and urged her horse next to Sarah's, and the three women rode in companionable silence.

Both Orion and Jubal Sage left the column at a gallop, Orion riding north along the river, Jubal to the east. Sarah watched the two men go, knowing that the colonel had sent them out to scout, trying not to let the sudden, nagging knot of worry in her stomach grow any bigger. If she wanted a life with Orion Beaudine, she was going to have to get used to his potentially dangerous scouting excursions. Forcing the memory of Orion's arrow-pierced shoulder and leg from her mind, she whispered a prayer for the safe return of both men, and tried to focus her attention on the cold beauty of the day.

Patches of snow still remained in places the sun could not reach, along the north side of rock formations and among stands of trees. Although Sarah knew the river was close, the icy waters were not visible from where she rode, nor could the tumbling waters be heard over the noises of approximately fifty people and twice that many animals, including horses and mules. The endless prairie stretched out to the east, its tall, winter-dead grasses waving in the constant wind, while the western horizon was one long, continuous chain of snow-capped mountains, some near, some far, all marching north and south as far as she could see.

She breathed deeply of the cool air, loving the clean, sharp scent, loving the painfully blue sky, loving the wild and beautiful land that rested beneath it. Orion was much like the land, Sarah decided—wild and beautiful, powerful, strong, deserving of respect. Any man who took Orion—or the land—too lightly did so at his own peril. Just like Orion, the beauty now spread before her could turn dangerous and deadly at a moment's notice, catching the foolish or the unprepared by surprise, perhaps even leading them to their doom.

Sarah was not foolish, nor was she unprepared. She had come to the West with her eyes opened, had seen and accepted the land for what it was, and had grown to love it. Just the same, she saw Orion for who and what he was, had accepted him as such, and had grown to love him. He belonged out here, and she belonged with him.

Much to Sarah's frustration—and Orion's, she was sure—there had been little time or opportunity for real courting since the end of the storm. A great deal of work had been necessary to dig out from under the heavy blanket of snow and to replenish stores and firewood in anticipation of the next storm, whenever it might come, and then came the rush of preparations to evacuate the fort. They had been able to steal moments here and there, to take short walks in the brisk air, to have quiet discussions while Sarah ironed and Orion cleaned firearms and leather halters, or dressed the game he brought in, to sit before the fire in the evening, nestled together, talking in low tones of their plans for the future. But the combination of Theodora's kind, tactful, yet constant presence, the smallness of the cabin, and the uncooperative weather had made the idea of any real privacy merely an aching dream, and Sarah was beginning to doubt the wisdom of asking for a courting period.

Long ago, Orion had started a fire in her, perhaps on the first day she had met him. When the sun had given his wet body a fiery glow that day, her internal fire had begun as a glowing ember; it now raged out of control. Every time she saw him, her heart was appeased, but her body was only tormented more. She longed to be alone with him, to be free to kiss him, to hold him, to peel those buckskins off his body and touch him wherever she pleased. Absentmindedly, Sarah moved her hand under her cape and clutched the beaded necklace she wore. One day—soon—she wanted to present herself to Orion wearing nothing more than his necklace.

"Sarah?"

Sarah started and looked around.

"Are you all right?" Theodora asked, her concern apparent in her eyes. "You're acting dazed, or ill."

"No, I'm fine. What makes you think I'm not?"

"You looked a little strange, and I asked you a question, and you didn't respond, like you didn't hear me." She nudged her horse nearer to Sarah's.

"I'm sorry, Theo. My mind was a million miles away, and I truly didn't hear you."

Theodora snorted. "A million miles, indeed. I think it's more like your mind is only a mile or so away, wherever your Hunter is."

Sarah smiled. "You know me too well. What was your question?"

"I was wondering if you know where the Hunter and Mr. Sage went."

"Orion didn't say anything to me before he went on ahead to talk to the colonel, but I assume they are scouting the area."

"Does the colonel expect trouble?"

"Not that I know of." The hood of her cape kept her warm,

but did little to soften the glare of the day, so Sarah shaded her eyes against the bright noon sun as she surveyed the distance. There was no sign of either scout. "Orion can make it to Fort Laramie in two days, but he said this trip will take us twice as long because of the wagons. Since he headed north along the river, he may be scouting a campsite for tonight, one with enough fuel to support such a large party. And Mr. Sage may be scouting for game, or, as a precaution, for trouble." She looked at her friend. "Are you worried?"

"No, just curious."

Sweet Water said something in her unfamiliar language and pointed to the northeast. Where a moment ago there had been no sign of life, Sarah now saw a lone rider coming over the crest of a small hill. Even at a distance, she could tell it was Orion, and she fought the urge to kick her mount to a gallop and ride out to meet him.

In a matter of minutes, he joined the caravan, stopping to speak first with Colonel Rutledge before he rode to her side.

She offered him the welcome of a warm smile, determined to hide the relief she felt. The Hunter was at home in the wilderness, she knew, but even he had not been able to avoid ambush. Because she feared he would think her foolish or weak, she did not want him to know how she worried about him when he was out in the wilderness alone.

"Did you miss me?" he asked teasingly.

Sarah resisted the impulse to smile even wider and nod like a lovestruck fool. Instead, she managed an exasperated sniff and said, "Hardly. Theo and I have enjoyed a most delightful conversation. I didn't even think of you." She knew by the sparkle in Orion's eyes that he didn't believe her, and Theodora's dramatic rolling of her eyes didn't help, either.

"You're a terrible liar, Sarah Hancock," Orion retorted merrily. He guided Thunder into place next to Star.

"I am, aren't I?" Sarah caught Adam's disapproving eye and looked away, focusing on the man beside her. "Of course

I missed you, you conceited oaf. Where did the colonel send you?"

"To scout a campsite for tonight."

"Did you find one?"

"Yes. I had a place in mind, but wasn't sure of the wood supply, so I wanted to check it. We'll soon be stopping for the midday meal, and we'll probably rest the horses and the ladies for an hour or so, then it will take maybe another three hours to get to the site."

"You went that far and back in just a few hours?" Theodora asked. "Your poor horse!"

"He's fine." Orion slapped Thunder's neck affectionately. "He needed the run, and besides, he can go much faster than this column, and over a shorter trail that's too rough for the wagons to follow."

At that moment, Colonel Rutledge gave the command to halt. Sarah accepted Orion's assistance in stepping down from the saddle and was astonished to find that her legs were numb. She staggered against him.

"Oh," she gasped. "I must be more chilled than I realized."

Orion steadied her with firm hands at her waist. "More likely you aren't used to being in the saddle for so long. You might be pretty sore by the time this journey is finished."

"Or calloused," Sarah muttered. Suddenly, the insides of her thighs announced how unhappy they were, as did her ankles. Either the cold had numbed her legs, or she had been too absorbed in her sensual daydreams of Orion to notice the growing discomfort of her body. "Why do my ankles hurt?" she asked in disbelief.

"Because they've been twisted a little in order to get your feet in the stirrups. It's probably been some time since you went riding, and now you've been in the saddle for hours. You'll feel better after you walk around a bit." He looked at Theodora, who had accepted Lieutenant Roe's help in dismounting. "How do you feel?" he called to her.

Theodora grimaced, keeping a firm hold on Roe's arm. "Just like Sarah does."

Sweet Water slipped off her horse and began to gather firewood, apparently not affected at all.

"Maybe you ladies should ride in the wagon with the other women this afternoon," Lieutenant Roe helpfully suggested.

Sarah glanced over her shoulder to where the three officers' wives and the two complaining children stood, waiting impatiently for a flustered enlisted man to start a fire. Harriet Rutledge met her gaze with narrowed, hardened eyes, and deliberately turned away as another soldier brought chairs from one of the freight wagons.

"I don't think so, Lieutenant," Sarah said, unable to avoid wincing as even more feeling returned to her legs. "I'll be much more comfortable on my horse."

"Me, too," Theodora added through gritted teeth, her usually calm face now a mask of determined cheerfulness.

"If you say so," Roe said doubtfully.

"Lieutenant Roe!" Adam's terse voice reached them from where he stood at Harriet's side. "Come here!"

"Yes, sir!" Roe's pleasant face flushed red with obvious embarrassment while his jaw clenched in annoyance and perhaps even anger. "Forgive me, Mrs. Byrd," he said stiffly. "Duty calls."

"There's nothing to forgive, Lieutenant," Theodora assured him, her face soft with understanding. "Go, before he yells again."

"Yes, ma'am." The lieutenant hurried away.

A minute later, after speaking to Adam, Roe was unhitching the team from Harriet's wagon. Sarah knew that Adam's order was humiliating for an officer, and one no doubt meant to punish Lieutenant Roe for his violation of Harriet's unspoken rules of conduct concerning her and Theodora. Or perhaps the rules had been spoken, and Roe had defied them.

"The witch," Sarah muttered in disgust.

"I agree," Orion added, his voice tight with anger. "She just won't let it go."

A pained look crossed Theodora's face. "It's my fault," she said dejectedly.

"No more than it is mine, or Sarah's," Orion said firmly. He held out an arm to her. "We are all on Mrs. Rutledge's list of outcasts, just as my brothers are, and Jubal, and no doubt Sweet Water, too."

"Simply because she's an Indian?" Theodora asked as she took his arm.

Orion nodded. "Actually, I'm proud to be on the list. I'm in good company." He smiled at each woman in turn. "Now let's take a little walk and get you two delicate creatures to feeling better." He led them away from the column and the distressing emotions some of the people in it evoked.

"I feel better already," Theodora declared softly. "Thank you, Hunter Beaudine. You are a true gentleman."

"My sainted pa would be proud to hear you say that. He wouldn't believe it, but he'd be proud."

Theodora laughed, as did Sarah. Feeling warm with love, she looked up at Orion, drinking in the sight of his handsome face as he chatted with Theodora. Sarah suspected that Jedediah Beaudine would have no trouble believing that Orion was a gentleman, because he no doubt had raised him to be one, as he had all his sons. She regretted that she would never have the opportunity to meet the famous frontiersman, for she knew she would have liked him a great deal—perhaps even loved him as a second father.

Orion's prediction that a short walk would loosen stiff muscles and ease some of the discomfort Sarah and Theodora suffered was proven true. By the time the trio returned to their horses, Sweet Water had a cheery fire going, as well as a pot of coffee. In fact, several fires dotted the area, offering a small amount of smoky warmth to the people gathered around them.

"What about the horses?" Sarah asked Orion as she nuzzled the velvety nose of her mare.

"They'll graze on what they can find while we're stopped here, and when we start again, I'll lead the column to the river so the horses and mules can be watered." He loosened Thunder's cinch.

"Are you going to remove the saddles and give them a rest?"

"No. They're sweaty, and they'll get too chilled. I'll loosen the cinches for now, and we'll rub them down good when we stop for the night." He moved to Theodora's horse. "They'll get a ration of oats then, too. This is actually luxurious conditions for the horses, compared to most marches."

The sound of a horse approaching at a gallop reached Sarah's ears and she turned, as did Orion. She was relieved to see that Jubal Sage had safely returned. To her surprise, he did not report to Colonel Rutledge first, but instead rode directly to Orion's side.

Jubal said something in a language that Sweet Water apparently understood, for she smiled and nodded at him. Then he slipped off his horse. "Miss Sarah, Mrs. Byrd. Howdy, Hunter. What'd you find up north?"

"Nothing unexpected. There's enough wood at the whitewater stretch of the river to sustain the column for tonight, so I suggested to the colonel we stop there. We haven't made good time today, but I guess there's no real hurry."

"There'd better not be, with this bunch." Jubal lifted a bushy, disgusted eyebrow in the direction of the overloaded freight wagons. "Let's hope another blizzard don't blow up before we get them silly gals and whiny kids to Fort Laramie." He now indicated the group gathered around Harriet, where Lucy was serving a hot meal to the wives and children while everyone else, including Colonel Rutledge, made do with bread and cold meat. "I don't reckon the Mrs. Colonel would like the weather gettin' in her way. Might cause her some discomfort, and we cain't have that."

"No, we can't," Orion agreed, obviously struggling to conceal a smile, just as Sarah was. "What did you find to the east?"

"A small herd of buffalo, some Cheyenne sign—a hunting party. And the frozen body of Enos Foster about two miles out."

Orion frowned. "The blizzard got him? I always figured Foster had more brains than that."

"Yeah," Jubal drawled, leaning on his rifle. "The blizzard got him, after someone shot him in the back and scalped him."

Foster. Sarah covered her mouth with one hand in an instinctive gesture of horror. Like a bad dream, she once again saw in her mind the four disreputable buckskin-clad men outside Theodora's cabin the night Orion returned to Fort St. Charles. Foster had been the one with the torch, the one who seemed almost pathetic.

The one Bartholomew Cutler had threatened to kill.

Sarah forced her hand away from her mouth and glanced at Theodora. Her white-faced friend was obviously as horrified as she was.

"Indians?" Orion asked.

"Don't think so, the scalpin' aside. Warn't no arrow that made that big hole in him. 'Course, Indians can have rifles, too, but I just don't think it was them."

Deep in thought, Orion rubbed his chin. "I still think white men were in the party that attacked me."

"That bunch what attacked you was up to somethin' we don't understand yet. This was murder, pure and simple." Jubal's voice was tight and angry. "Foster got on my nerves at times—hell, most of the time—but it ain't right he was killed like that, just shot down like he was a rabid dog or somethin'."

"No, it isn't right," Orion agreed soberly. He glanced at Sarah. "We're upsetting the women, Jubal. We'd better let them rest while we go talk to Colonel Rutledge."

Jubal snatched his battered hat from his head. "Sorry, ladies. I forget myself sometimes. You didn't need to hear that miserable story."

"It's all right, Mr. Sage," Sarah responded. "Mrs. Byrd and I were acquainted with Mr. Foster, briefly. The circumstances under which we met him were unfortunate, but he didn't seem to be a bad man. I'm saddened to hear of his death."

"You knew Foster?" Jubal asked, clearly puzzled.

"That's another miserable story," Orion said firmly, taking Jubal's arm. "I'll tell you later. Right now, you need to report to Colonel Rutledge." He led Jubal away, his voice trailing back over his shoulder. "You broke rules by coming to me first instead of him."

"What rules?" Jubal demanded. "I ain't employed by the Army, not like you are."

"Just rules," Orion replied. "You'll be lucky if you aren't unhitching teams and hauling water by nightfall, as punishment."

Jubal's reply to that was very ungentlemanly, and they moved out of hearing range.

Sarah watched the two men go, torn between amusement at their friendly bantering and lingering horror at the fate of poor Foster.

"Cutler told Foster he'd kill him for backing away from the Hunter that night," Theodora said quietly.

"I remember," Sarah responded.

"Remember that he threatened you, too, Sarah, just as he threatened your man." Theodora put an arm around Sarah's shoulders. "Never forget. Always be on your guard when he is near."

"Mr. Foster was shot in the back," Sarah said bitterly. "Do you think he knew Cutler was near?"

"Probably not," Theodora admitted.

"Then how will we know? Even Orion was ambushed, Theo. Even the great Hunter was ambushed, and nearly killed." She turned despairing eyes on her friend. "Cutler's stench will give him away if he gets close enough, but he doesn't have to get close if he has a rifle or a bow and knows how to use them. We are at his mercy, and I think it's safe to say that he has none."

"We'll just be careful," Theodora said stubbornly. "And don't underestimate the power of the Beaudine name. The reactions of the three other men that night were not unusual for those faced with the threat of Beaudine vengeance. Cutler is evil, but he's not stupid. If he hurts one Beaudine, he knows he'll answer to the rest of the clan. He's a bully, and at heart, bullies are cowards."

"That's true." Sarah heaved a sigh of relief, intent upon forcing the knot of fear in her stomach to relax. Still, her eyes searched out Orion's tall figure among the group of officers gathered around Jubal Sage, and she whispered a prayer for his continued safety. And added one for her own. In order for their dreams of a life together to come true, they both had to live.

Twenty-three

The rest of the afternoon passed uneventfully. Shortly before dusk, Colonel Rutledge called a halt for the day at the site chosen by Orion. The order to dismount was given, as well as the command to "water at will," and the organized column broke into a somewhat organized melee. From her travels across the prairies to Fort Laramie the previous summer, Sarah knew that the first priority of every soldier was his horse, and only after the needs of the animals had been met would the men see to the building of fires, the pitching of tents, and the forming of water brigades. The presence of women and children did not alter the routine.

The animals were taken care of, and soon the area was dotted with camp fires, a few tents glistened white in the deepening dusk, and the appetizing aroma of roasting meat and frying pan bread wafted through the air.

By silent mutual consent, Sarah, Theodora, and Orion shared a fire with Jubal and Sweet Water. The women saw to the fire and supper preparations while the men looked after the horses. By the time Orion and Jubal returned from picketing the animals, a venison roast—the last of Gray Eagle's gift—was sizzling on Jubal's metal grate alongside several wild onions. Sweet Water had prepared another pot of coffee, and Theodora's heavy cast-iron teakettle steamed merrily, waiting for the tea leaves she would soon add.

"I'd like to get settled somewhere so that I can start a

garden when spring comes," Sarah said from her kneeling position near the fire. Her legs felt like quivering masses of jelly, and she couldn't trust them to hold her up as she turned the heavy roast. "I crave fresh vegetables."

"I know." Theodora looked up from the pot she was stirring. "Dried corn just doesn't taste the same as fresh, no matter how much water you add or how long you cook it."

"Supper smells good, ladies," Jubal declared as the men rejoined the group. He made his way to Sweet Water's side and kissed her cheek. In return, his wife handed him a cup of steaming coffee and waved him away, but Sarah could tell that Sweet Water was pleased, just as she herself was pleased when Orion greeted her with a warm smile.

"Major Dillard's silly wife was complainin' about how far we are from the river," Jubal commented, hunkering down next to the fire. A mischievous gust of wind blew a cloud of smoke in his face, which he barely seemed to notice. "She couldn't understand why we didn't make camp on the bank, so we wouldn't have to go so far for water."

Sarah looked at him. "Why didn't we camp on the bank? I don't mind that we didn't, but I'm sure there's a good reason."

"The noise of the water," Orion answered. He accepted the cup of coffee Sweet Water offered him and murmured his thanks in Cheyenne. "If you're too close to the river, especially near white water, like here, you can't hear if something or someone were to approach."

"Not that we could hear anything anyway over the clamor this bunch makes," Jubal said disgustedly. "Especially them kids. One or the other is always whinin' about somethin'. All they need is a firm voice and a little paddle on the hind end—would straighten 'em right out."

Sarah smiled, forced to agree with Jubal. But she couldn't imagine Penelope Dillard taking a firm hand with her spoiled children, and Major Dillard deferred to his wife in all matters of child rearing. She suspected that little Neville and the angelic-looking Clarissa would whine all the way to adulthood, and maybe beyond.

Although she craved fresh vegetables, Sarah found the simple supper delicious. She still had not become accustomed to the monotony of meals offered by life with the Army, but every now and then, even the most mundane of foodstuffs tasted like a feast. Tonight was such a night. When the companionable meal was finished, she and the other women made short work of cleaning and organizing the modest campsite while Orion and Jubal collected a sizable pile of firewood. As the night promised to be a mild one, the group had decided against pitching a tent, agreeing with Jubal that the fire would offer more warmth.

"Have you seen Dancer?" Sarah asked when Orion returned with an armload of branches.

"Not yet, but he'll show. As slow as we moved today, I'm certain he had no trouble keeping up." He dropped the branches on the growing pile of firewood.

"I saved some supper for him."

Orion smiled at her. "He'll appreciate it." His smile took on a sultry look. "I know it's almost dark and it's getting cold, but I want to walk out with you."

Sarah crossed her arms over her chest, trying to camouflage her pleasure. "Because it will be good for my legs?"

His voice dropped to a sensual growl. "Because I can't wait much longer to kiss you, woman."

Giving up any attempt to tease him, Sarah whispered, "I feel the same way. We'd better go right now, or I'll throw propriety to the wind and kiss you myself right here." She was thrilled to see fire leap in Orion's eyes at her words, and raised her voice. "Of course I'll help you gather firewood, Orion."

"Gather firewood, indeed," Theodora retorted with a disbelieving sniff. "Go on, you lovebirds. Take some time alone."

Orion needed no further invitation. He grabbed Sarah's

hand and led her toward the river. Because their little campsite was on the perimeter of the general camp area, in only a few moments they were out of sight of everyone. Orion turned abruptly and pulled Sarah into his arms. Her hood had fallen back, and he buried his face in her fragrant hair.

"I'm crazy with wanting you, Sarah Hancock," he whispered. He slipped one hand inside her cape and ran it over her back, then down to her bottom and pulled her closer yet. "I love you so." He rained light kisses on her forehead and cheeks before claiming her mouth. With a moan of welcome, she parted her lips and leaned into him.

His blood pounded as he lost himself in the sweetness of her mouth. After a few minutes of frenzied kissing, they were both breathless. Sarah leaned back in his arms, peering up at him in the near total darkness.

"I have wanted to do that all day long," she said huskily. "Truthfully, I dreamed all day of doing much more than that." As if to demonstrate her point, Sarah opened the clasps down the front of his buffalo robe coat, threw her cape back over her shoulders, and plastered her body against his.

Orion groaned and held her close. "So have I, sweet woman."

"I've been thinking," Sarah said, her voice muffled against his chest. "Maybe my idea of a courting period wasn't such a good one, Orion. The circumstances and the weather have made it impossible, and I don't see much chance of things changing in the near future. Maybe we should just get married as soon as we reach Fort Laramie."

If possible, Orion's heart beat even faster. "You deserve to be courted, Sarah. I want to do that for you. A woman should have some romance in her life."

"You give me that. This little walk is romantic." She raised her head far enough to plant a kiss on his jaw.

"This little walk is freezing," Orion corrected as he rubbed her back. "We can't stay out here much longer."

"We could pitch our own tent," Sarah suggested. "That would be romantic." She wiggled her hips against his.

Orion clenched his jaw and closed his eyes, fighting the enticing image of sharing a tent with Sarah alone. "That would be scandalous."

"We're already scandalous."

"I know." Orion held her close and rested his cheek against her head, gratified when she clung to him. "We'll wait until we get to Fort Laramie," he finally said. "We'll plan our wedding then, even if it takes place the next day. I want honor for us, Sarah, and privacy, and some degree of comfort. When I truly make you my wife, I want it to be beautiful for you. Joseph will give us the use of his quarters, at least for a while, if that's what we want, or we can set out for Gray Eagle's camp and spend the rest of the winter with the Cheyenne, in our own tipi."

"All right." There was a catch in her voice, as if she were crying.

"Sarah?" Concerned, Orion leaned his head back and put a finger under her chin. Sure enough, he saw the shimmer of tears in her eyes, and his heart slammed against his ribs. "What's wrong? Did I hurt your feelings somehow? Would you rather do something else? Sweetheart, please don't cry."

"Nothing is wrong, Orion." She smiled up at him, her eyes shining in the dim light. "In fact, everything is perfect. Never have I felt so loved." She pressed a tender kiss on his lips. "Never have I loved so deeply."

Orion wasn't sure why her obvious joy had led to tears, but he accepted her words as the truth he knew them to be. For a long time, they stood together in the cold darkness, sharing the warmth of his coat and her cape—and each other—contented to be silent. They stood there long enough for the nearly full moon to begin its ascent in the eastern sky, sending a pale light out over the land.

Suddenly Sarah stiffened and turned her head.

"What is it?" Orion demanded, his hand instantly on his knife handle.

"Dancer," Sarah whispered joyfully. She turned away from him, and, a moment later, Orion saw Dancer pick his way over the rocky shore of the riverbank.

Amazed at her uncanny knowledge, Orion asked, "How do you know when he is here?"

"I feel him." Sarah crouched down at the animal's side and put an arm around his furry neck. "I don't know how else to explain it. I get a sense of his presence."

A strong shiver worked its way through Orion's body. "That is very powerful medicine, Sarah Hancock. No doubt the Wolf is your spirit animal."

She looked up at him, puzzled. "Powerful medicine? My spirit animal? What are you talking about?"

As Orion watched, Dancer licked Sarah's cheek, eliciting a giggle from her. *Powerful medicine, indeed.* But how to explain the religious philosophy of the Cheyenne—something it had taken him most of a lifetime to learn and understand—to her before they both froze to death on the bank of the rushing river?

"The term 'powerful medicine' is difficult to explain briefly, but it usually refers to something that is mystical or potent. And as for spirit animals, the Cheyenne believe that each person adopts what they call a spirit animal, based on an animal species whose positive characteristics resemble that person, or appeal to that person." He crouched down beside her. "The Hawk, the Bear, the Elk, the Badger, the Wolf, even the Mouse; all are spirit animals. Sometimes a Cheyenne learns of his spirit animal in a dream, or in an incident involving an animal; sometimes a person has a special communication with an animal, like you do with Dancer. Sometimes it's no more than a fascination with or an understanding of a certain species. Then that person claims that animal as his spirit animal."

"Then what?" Sarah asked, clearly puzzled.

Orion shrugged. "Then nothing. You might ask your spirit animal to guide you, to give you its strength, or to protect you. You might dream of your spirit animal or see one in the flesh and interpret the dream or the animal's presence as a sign of some kind. It is entirely up to each person."

Sarah frowned. "So you pray to your spirit animal, like many people do to God?"

"I guess you could call it prayer. It's a very individual thing, Sarah. There are no set rules, no liturgy to follow."

She eyed him curiously. "What is your spirit animal?"

"Like you, the Wolf. Joseph's is the Horse, Gray Eagle's is, perhaps obviously, the Eagle."

"How did you all learn that?"

"I found my spirit animal through Dancer, like you did, except that I don't have the level of intuitive communication with him that you do." He spoke with no trace of envy, for he felt none. Rather, he was in awe of Sarah's gift with the wolf, for he knew how rare such a connection was. "Joseph has always had a way with horses, and Gray Eagle saw an eagle in a dream. Actually, it was more than a dream; it was a vision." He shifted uncomfortably, wondering if she would ridicule what he said. When he dared to glance at her face, he found not ridicule, but honest interest.

"If it weren't so cold," Sarah said through chattering teeth, "I'd ask you questions all night. I want to learn more about the Cheyenne, Orion." She planted a kiss on Dancer's forehead. "But Dancer wants his supper, and I need the fire. My legs are stiffening up, and the rest of me is freezing."

Orion straightened, then grabbed Sarah's elbows and helped her up. "I've kept you out here too long."

"You kept me out here just the right amount of time," she responded. "And now it is time to return." She took a few steps. "Tipis are warm, aren't they?"

"In an established camp, they are quite comfortable." He felt her falter and, without a word, swept her up in his arms. She did not protest, but instead wrapped her arms around his neck. He continued. "You probably know that the Chey-enne are a nomadic people, as are most of the Plains tribes. If the band is going to be at a site for a while, such as through the winter, the women have time to make the tipis very com-fortable, with sleeping shelves cut into the earth, and furs and robes everywhere. With the fire in the center, they stay warm."

"I wish we were going to one now," Sarah said sleepily.

"I wish we were, too," Orion muttered. "One of our own." He glanced back over his shoulder to ensure that Dancer was following, which he was. "We might let you share our tipi," he said to the wolf. "If you mind your manners."

Sarah giggled. "He is one of the best behaved beings I have ever met. He is certainly better behaved than the Dillard children are."

"You can say that again."

Reveille sounded early the next morning, bringing Sarah out of a deep, restful sleep in her nest made of a thick buffalo robe. Dancer was curled up in a ball next to her, his tail over his nose, while Orion's now empty blankets lay on her other side. Assuming he had gone to see to the horses, she stretched, then pulled her arms back under the robe, startled to see frost on the ground. Her breath made a white cloud in front of her face.

"Only two more nights outside," she promised herself in a whisper. "Then you'll be at Fort Laramie." Steeling herself, she scrambled out of her warm bed, noting with a smile that Dancer remained curled up on his blanket, and hurried to the fire Orion had already built up. Shivers wracked her body as she slipped her feet into her fire-warmed boots. She tried unsuccessfully to brush the wrinkles from the skirt she had slept in, then smoothed her equally untidy hair. She would be a sight by the time they reached Fort Laramie.

Theodora was stirring in her bed on the other side of Orion's blankets, and Jubal and Sweet Water were still wrapped up in their robes some distance away. Sarah had never known Jubal to be abed when the sky was growing light in the east. It probably had something to do with having a woman in his bed, she mused with an understanding smile. Perhaps she and Orion would also be reluctant to leave their bed, once they were sanctioned by marriage to share one. She snatched up the empty coffeepot and headed toward the river.

The closer she got to the river, the more the sounds of the stirring camp faded. She could understand what Orion meant about not being able to hear anything if one was too near the water. The usually docile river was at this point a wild stretch of rapids, roiling and swirling over rocks and long-dead tree trunks as it rushed northeast to join the North Platte. Eventually its clear waters would be swallowed by the muddy Platte, then the Missouri, the Mississippi, and finally the Gulf of Mexico. Sarah took up a stick and threw it in the water, wondering if the foot-long piece of wood would travel all the way to the warm waters of the Gulf.

The water along the bank was covered with a thin layer of ice, so Sarah carefully made her way to where a large rock jutted out into the faster moving water. As she crouched down and rinsed the coffeepot in the icy waters, she let her gaze wander over the land to the north. Somewhere up there was a site Jubal had told her about called Warm Springs, where the water came out of the earth as warm as bathwater. She wanted to see that, wanted to ease her body into the soothing warmth of the mineral springs. Jubal had said it wasn't far from the Platte, although it was a good distance west of Fort Laramie. Perhaps one day Orion would take her. The image of sharing a steaming bath with him teased her mind, and Sarah wondered where such thoughts came from. She had never envisioned such things with Adam.

But then Adam had never made her feel as loved as Orion had last night, with his simple declaration of how he wanted things to be when they reached Fort Laramie. Adam had never asked her what she wanted from life, or where she wanted to live. He had never resisted the most powerful of temptations because of love and honor, had never assured her that he wanted their first physical joining to be pleasurable for her, to be comfortable and warm. Of course, as far as Sarah knew, Adam had never experienced the temptations both she and Orion had, so perhaps there had been nothing for him to resist.

"Which was exactly the problem," Sarah muttered. "One of many," she corrected herself as she filled the pot one last time. She gathered the folds of her skirt and her cape in preparation of standing up when her gaze fell on something caught on a fallen tree a short distance downstream. Sarah squinted in the dim, early morning light, trying to make out what it was. Her eyes widened in horror to see an arrow protruding from the brown object, which she now realized was big enough to be an animal.

Or a man.

Sarah stumbled to her feet, spilling a good deal of water from the pot. *Orion.* She hadn't actually seen him with the horses; she had only assumed that was where he was.

"Oh, God," she whispered. Flinging the pot aside, Sarah clutched her skirts in a death grip and ran in the direction of the fallen tree. As she drew nearer, she could see that it was indeed a man she had found, that he wore buckskins and that he was motionless and face down in the water. She almost sobbed with relief when she realized the poor man's long hair was too light-colored to be Orion's.

Was the man still alive?

If he was, he wouldn't be for long. She couldn't go for help until she knew for sure. Certain the water was deep enough to fill her boots if she left them on, Sarah used the tree trunk for support and pulled her boots off before she hiked her skirts and stepped into the freezing water. When the water reached her knees, she was close enough to touch him.

"Sir?" she called out. One touch of his very white, very cold, very hard hand was all Sarah needed to know that the man was beyond human help. She struggled back out of the water, trembling with cold and horror. As if in a dream, she took up her boots and retraced her steps to the camp in soaking, stockinged feet.

Jubal stood near the fire with Orion, who had his back to her. Sweet Water was cutting thick slices of bacon into a cast-iron frying pan, while Theodora folded blankets and buffalo robes. Dancer was nowhere to be seen. It was Jubal who saw her first. His smile of welcome turned to a look of grave concern when her boots fell from her numbed fingers.

"Miss Sarah?"

Orion's head snapped around, and he was at her side in an instant. Without a word, he picked her up and carried her to the robe Theodora hurriedly spread near the fire. He carefully set her down in a sitting position, but when he started to move away, she clung to him. Theodora fell to her knees and pulled Sarah's wet stockings off before enfolding her legs in the robe. She rubbed Sarah's feet and ankles through the robe, her brown eyes dark with worry.

"What happened?" Orion asked in a gentle tone, as if he were speaking to a skittish mare.

"There's a dead man in the river," Sarah said woodenly. "For a moment, I thought it was you."

Orion exchanged a glance with Jubal, but his expression did not change. "Where, honey?"

"By the trees; his shirt caught on a dead tree, one that's laying in the water." Sarah clutched at Orion's coat. "There's an arrow in his back." Her voice fell to a whisper. "I thought it was you," she repeated.

"I'm fine, Sarah." Orion held her close, stroking her hair.

She rested against his warmth, against his strength, and watched as Jubal spoke to his wife, then trotted toward the river, obviously following Sarah's wet footprints. He disappeared around the stand of cottonwoods.

"I should go help Jubal, honey," Orion said. "Will you be all right if I leave?"

Sarah nodded. Of course he had to help Jubal. She knew that, but still she felt both an aching loss and an unreasonable fear when Orion stood up. Theodora moved into place beside her and put an arm around her shoulders.

"I'll watch her, Hunter," Theodora said. "Go. We'll be fine."

"Hurry back," Sarah whispered.

"I will." Orion ran toward the river and was gone from sight.

Sweet Water set the frying pan aside and joined Sarah and Theodora on the robe. She awkwardly patted Sarah's shoulder, her large, brown-black eyes wide with sympathy. Deeply touched, Sarah grabbed the woman's hand and held on.

The three women waited, their gaze drawn to the trees and the river beyond.

"I'll be damned." Jubal settled on his haunches and stared at the dead man laid out in front of him. "Linus Harley. I ain't seen him in years. Thought he'd settled back East somewheres."

"This is a Cheyenne arrow," Orion commented, examining the feathers at the end of the arrow he had broken off at the point of entry into the unfortunate Linus Harley's back. "How long do you reckon he's been dead?"

"Hard to say, with him bein' all froze up, like Foster was. Maybe a day, maybe two." He squinted at Orion. "You think the Cheyenne did it? He ain't scalped."

"They could have. Maybe he wasn't dead when he went in the water." Orion gazed off into the distance, looking at nothing, seeing nothing. "This is the same kind of arrow you dug out of me, Jubal. Maybe old Linus met up with the same bunch I did."

Jubal stroked his beard. "And maybe he was part of that bunch, and they had a fallin' out. As I recall, Linus was real flexible with his code of honor. He was a likeable enough fella, but I never did trust him."

"Well, there are no answers here. We could try to back-track upstream, try to find where he went in the water, but I think it's more important that we get these people to Fort Laramie." Orion slapped the broken arrow against his thigh. "Something's going on out there, Jubal. Something bad." His gaze again traveled the area, more carefully this time. He didn't expect to notice anything unusual, and he didn't. "I don't like it."

"I don't, neither." Jubal straightened. "We'd best get back to the women, explain that Linus wasn't part of our group, then one of us better go talk to the colonel."

Orion nodded his agreement, and the two men returned to the camp. The three women made a curious picture, sitting side by side near the fire, with Sarah in the middle. As he drew closer, Orion saw that Theodora's arm still encircled Sarah's shoulders, and that Sarah was holding Sweet Water's hand. Love for Sarah welled up in him, so strong that he wondered if he could speak. He cleared his throat.

"We found him, Sarah," he said gently. "It may comfort you to know that he wasn't part of this company."

Sarah nodded. "I'm glad for that. He appeared to be a frontiersman. Do you know who he was?"

"Yes, ma'am," Jubal answered. "He's an old trapper by name of Linus Harley. He's been gone from the frontier for a while; I ain't seen him in years."

Theodora stared up at Jubal, her face sheet white. "Did you say Linus Harley?" she asked.

"Yes, ma'am, Mrs. Byrd." Jubal glanced at Orion, then back at Theodora. "Does that name mean somethin' to you?"

She did not answer until she had stood up. "I want to see him," she said firmly, her hands clasped in front of her.

Sarah looked up at her. "Theo, what is it?"

"I want to see him," Theodora insisted. "I *need* to see him."

Orion's gaze traveled from Theodora to Sarah. She met his gaze, and was clearly as baffled as he was. She shrugged and nodded.

"I'll take you," Orion said. He held out a hand to Theodora, and she grabbed it, holding onto him tightly. He guided her over the uneven ground to where Linus Harley's frozen body lay. She dropped his hand and approached the body, staring down at it. Orion stepped back, giving her some room.

He turned at the sound of approaching footsteps, and was surprised to see Sarah coming, accompanied by Jubal. She had thrust her bare feet into her dry boots, and now came forward to stand at his side.

"Theo might need me," she said quietly.

Orion looked down at her, his heart swelling with pride. Sarah had not yet recovered from her own ordeal, and here she was, ready to face the horror again, for her friend. He reached for her hand and held it.

After several minutes of not moving, of not speaking as she stared down at the body, Theodora brushed a hand across her cheek. Sarah pulled away from Orion and went to her friend's side. For a long moment, she just stood there. Finally, she spoke.

"Who was he to you, Theo?"

After another long moment, Theodora spoke. "He was the man the wagon master hired to take me back to Independence."

Theodora's remark obviously meant something to Sarah, for she sucked in her breath and closed her eyes, even as she reached out to touch her friend's arm. Orion glanced at Jubal, who had come to stand beside him. Judging from the mountain man's clenched jaw, Theodora's words meant something to him, also.

"How different my life might have been," Theodora said sadly, "if this man had been possessed of any degree of honor, or human kindness."

Sarah put her arm around Theodora's waist.

Theodora leaned into her. "I'm ready to go now," she said wearily. Sarah turned her around and led her away, staring with great sadness into Orion's eyes as she passed.

When the women had passed from earshot, Orion faced Jubal. "What was that all about?"

"Have you ever wondered how a good, decent woman like Mrs. Byrd could have worked as a whore?" Jubal asked, his voice tight with suppressed rage.

Taken aback, Orion answered, "Well, I wondered, I guess, but I figured it was none of my business."

"A few years back, her husband died of the cholera on a wagon train headed for Oregon, and Mrs. Byrd nearly died her own self, and lost a baby. That bastard," Jubal pointed a finger at the body on the river bank, "was hired to take her safely back to Independence. Instead, he raped her for days, sold her to his friends, and set her up as a whore."

Orion stared at his friend, filled with a curious mixture of horror and rage. If Harley weren't already dead, he would have killed him on the spot. He suspected Jubal felt the same way.

"She never told me who it was," Jubal said, " 'cause she knew I'd track down the bastard and kill him. Now he's dead, and she wouldn't even spit on his body, that's how decent she is." He looked at Orion, his eyes flashing fury. "Well, I ain't that decent." He turned back to the body. "May you rot in hell, Linus Harley, for the wrong you done that good woman, and all the other wrongs you did in your miserable life. I wish I could kill you all over again, just on principle. One death ain't enough for the likes of you." He spit contemptuously, hitting his mark, then spun around to leave. "I'll have no part of buryin' the son of a bitch," he warned as he passed Orion. "Leave him to the buzzards, I say." He stormed off.

Orion understood exactly how Jubal felt. He watched until the angry mountain man disappeared around the stand of cottonwoods, then looked up the river, in the direction from which Harley's body had come. There were answers up there, he was sure of it. The nagging warning bells that had started tinkling in his head when Jubal told him about Enos Foster's death were now loudly clanging. Enos Foster, Linus Harley, and Bartholomew Cutler were connected somehow; he was sure of it. The attack against him no doubt was tied into it, too, and perhaps even the incident at Theodora's cabin that night. But how?

The sound of excited voices reached his ears. Jubal had probably reported to Colonel Rutledge, and in a moment, soldiers would be swarming all over the place. As much as he wanted to scout upriver, Orion felt a stronger urge to get Sarah and Theodora to the safety of Fort Laramie. He and Jubal would come back later, with the hope that all the sign hadn't been destroyed by the elements.

For now, he would put the column on alert and try to keep everyone alive.

Twenty-four

News of Sarah's grisly discovery traveled fast among the members of the column, and the effect was immediate and sobering. It seemed to take only minutes for tents to be struck, fires to be doused, mules harnessed and horses saddled, and the group was ready to move out. Soldiers and civilians alike were suddenly very anxious to reach the safety of Fort Laramie, and Orion mentioned to Sarah that it might not take four full days to make the journey now. Indeed, he and Jubal had to warn the lead riders not to travel too fast for the sake of the animals.

After a brief stop at noon to rest the horses and mules—during which no fires were built, so all ate a cold meal—the column continued on its relentless march to the northeast until dusk had almost turned to darkness. A hasty camp was set up, with the fires kept low and a double guard mounted.

Sarah stirred a pot of the ever-present reconstituted corn, while Sweet Water kept an eye on the roasting carcasses of three lean jackrabbits and Theodora mixed up a batch of pan bread.

"I'll feel better when the men return," Theodora said as she scraped the mass of dough into a large cast-iron skillet.

"So will I." Sarah straightened and looked out into the blackness surrounding the camp. Her stomach felt sick from worry. Orion and Jubal had left over an hour earlier to scout the area. There was no real cause for concern yet, but Sarah would not relax until the two men returned. Even then, the night would no doubt prove to be a long one. Sarah had never seen Orion so serious and somber, and Jubal's mood was the same. If the two scouts were concerned, there was something to be concerned about.

Her suddenly tingling senses told Sarah that the rustling in a stand of nearby juniper bushes was Dancer. She softly called his name. The rustling ceased, but the wolf did not appear. Sarah was not surprised. As a precaution, the encampment tonight was much more tightly knit than it had been the night before, and Sarah knew the close proximity of so many people made the wolf reluctant to come closer. Later she and Orion would take some of the rabbit out to Dancer. If Orion got back. She pulled the cape more securely around her and again searched the darkness, praying for the moon to rise quickly, praying for Orion and Jubal's return.

A half hour later, the men led their weary mounts into camp. Not caring who saw her, Sarah ran into Orion's arms and held him close.

"Thank God," she whispered.

Orion put an arm around her shoulders and kissed the top of her head. "I'm fine, sweetheart."

She looked up at him in the flickering firelight. "Did you find anything?"

"No, and I don't know if that's good or bad. I just can't shake this feeling of impending trouble. It's like the calm before a storm. All seems well, but you know something's on its way." He tightened his arm around her for a moment, then released her. "There's no sense worrying about it now, though. It sure smells like you ladies did a good job with supper. I'm starved."

"Everything's ready," Sarah assured him. "You can eat right away."

Orion shook his head. "Not until we see to the horses. We'll be along in a few minutes." He placed a light kiss on her lips, then led Thunder away.

Supper was a quiet affair. Not even Jubal could complain of the noise that night, for it seemed the entire encampment was subdued and nervous. Sarah had little appetite, and finally gave up when she realized she was merely rearranging the position of her food on the enameled plate. Dancer would be well pleased with his supper tonight, she thought.

Later, when they sat around the low flames drinking tea, a man appeared at the edge of the faint circle of firelight.

"Permission to approach the fire."

Sarah recognized Lieutenant Roe's voice.

"Come on ahead," Jubal invited. He squinted up at Roe. "We ain't Army folks, Lieutenant. No need for such formality." He waved at a clear space of buffalo robe next to Sarah, who happily scooted closer to Orion. "Make yourself to home. Mrs. Byrd will pour you some tea, if you like."

"Thank you. I would enjoy that." Callahan Roe dropped to a sitting position at the indicated spot. He nodded his greetings to those around the fire, including Sweet Water. "Good evening. Thought I'd come and see how the ladies were feeling after their second full day on horseback."

"We're making it," Theodora said as she handed him a steaming cup. "I can offer some sugar for the tea, but no milk."

"This will be just fine, ma'am. Thank you." He reached inside his double-breasted Army-issue wool coat and pulled out a pint flask. "I have a little brandy I'd be honored to share, if the ladies don't object."

Even in the flickering firelight, Sarah could see Jubal's eyes shine with anticipation. "Shoot, the ladies might actually like a dollop in their tea on a cold night like this," he said. "Mrs. Byrd and Miss Hancock, I mean. My wife don't drink spirits at all."

Sarah noticed the pride in Jubal's voice when he said the words "my wife," and she smiled. "I wouldn't mind a little," she admitted.

"Neither would I," Theodora added. "It was kind of you to think of us, Lieutenant."

"Ah, it's nothing, ma'am." He handed the flask to Sarah. "I'm glad for the company."

Theodora watched him. "Are you sure your visit won't bring more trouble down on you?"

"I don't care if it does." Callahan wrapped both hands around his cup. "Captain Rutledge and the Mrs. Colonel have no right to tell me who I can speak to. There's no shame in unharnessing mules, and I won't mind doing it again if that's what happens." He shrugged. "I always liked mules."

Jubal laughed out loud. "Me, too. A lot better'n I like a lot of people. A man always knows where he stands with a mule." He accepted the flask from Theodora and poured a small amount of brandy in his cup, then returned the flask to Roe.

Callahan added some brandy to his own cup before he set the flask down. He raised his cup. "Here's to a safe journey to Fort Laramie for all of us."

"Here, here," Orion said.

"You got that right," Jubal muttered. He said something in Cheyenne to Sweet Water, and she raised her cup along with everyone else.

They all drank, and Sarah could not help noticing that Theodora's gaze did not move from Callahan Roe's earnest, attractive face. He looked at Theodora and smiled, which caused her to look away, but not before the corners of her mouth curved upward. Sarah smiled into her own cup. Perhaps Theo would look upon Lieutenant Roe more favorably now. He certainly was going out of his way to pay courteous attention to her, and he risked punishment by doing so.

The men discussed the route they would follow tomorrow and the locations for possible ambush. Sarah refused to allow herself to become distressed and instead focused on the warmth of Orion's body next to hers, the comforting feel of his arm around her shoulders, the feel of his thigh under her hand. Tomorrow would come as surely as the sun would rise, and what would happen would happen. Worrying about it tonight would only ruin tonight. As long as Orion was next to her, she was content.

Callahan Roe left about a half hour later, and everyone turned in for a long, cold, uneasy night.

The bugler had no reason to sound reveille in the morning, for the entire encampment was already awake when the first light of dawn touched the eastern skies. Sarah, Theodora, and Sweet Water cleaned the breakfast dishes and folded blankets and buffalo robes while the men saddled the horses. Sarah did not relish the idea of another long day in the saddle, and her legs and bottom didn't look forward to it, either, but she felt the same sense of anxiety and urgency everyone else did. She would be overjoyed to see the rough buildings of Fort Laramie, as much for the safety offered by the fort as for the prospect of her marriage. As she struggled with a large, heavy buffalo robe, her gaze fell on Orion. He was saddling Thunder, and the thought of that beautiful man becoming her husband sent a thrill of such magnitude through Sarah's body that she was left trembling.

"Sarah, would you like some help with that robe?" Theodora asked.

Sarah blinked and pulled her mind away from her beloved. "Ah, yes, please. I seem to be making a real mess of it."

"This robe *is* heavy," Theodora replied, and took up one end. "And especially difficult to fold when your mind is elsewhere."

There was no mistaking the teasing note in Theodora's voice. "You know me too well, Theo," Sarah said with a sigh. "Just don't tell Orion how often you catch me daydreaming about him. I don't want him getting overconfident."

Theodora shrugged. "It's too late. The Beaudines were *born* confident, every one of them. And that man is very confident that you are his. You couldn't get rid of him if you tried."

"I'll never try," Sarah assured her. The two women came close together in a final folding of the robe. "And what of Lieutenant Callahan Roe?" Sarah asked in a quiet voice.

"What of him?" Theodora added the robe to a pile of folded blankets.

"He likes you, Theo. Surely you can see that."

"I can see it." A curious flatness crept into Theodora's tone. "I wish he didn't."

"But why? He seems like a very nice man, kind and honorable." Sarah watched her friend carefully. "Is it that you feel nothing more than friendship for him?"

Theodora clasped her hands together and paused before she raised tortured eyes to Sarah. "It's my past. It's always there, Sarah, like a spectre in the night. No man will be able to overlook that."

"Don't you think he already knows?" Sarah asked gently. "The rumors about you are widespread, dear friend. I think he knows, and just like your past doesn't bother me, or Mr. Sage, or Orion, it doesn't bother him. He is interested in you as you are now, not in what happened long before he ever met you."

"Do you really think so?"

"Absolutely. He is willing to risk the wrath of Harriet Rutledge for you. He must genuinely care." Sarah put her hand on Theodora's arm. "Who knows what the future will bring? Let things be for a while. See what happens."

"His association with me could harm his career," Theodora protested.

How Sarah hated those words! "I know. Harriet often told me I would ruin Adam's career."

Theodora's eyes widened in disbelief. "That's ridiculous. You?"

"She thought so. Unfortunately, there is some truth to her words; an officer's wife *can* help or hurt her husband's career.

But there are many Army posts, Theo, most of them far away from Harriet Rutledge and her circle of influence, and for all you know, Lieutenant Roe may one day wish to resign his commission."

"Why would an officer want to resign his commission?"

Sarah shrugged. "Many reasons: no room for advancement, a change of personal goals, an opportunity offered elsewhere, perhaps even differing philosophies. Orion told me his brother Joseph is considering leaving the Army because he doesn't agree with the military and political policies toward the Indian nations."

A small degree of hope flared in Theodora's eyes.

"If you like him, don't shut the lieutenant out," Sarah urged. "Accept his offer of friendship and see what happens. Perhaps you will find that you and he make better friends than lovers. And perhaps you will find that love grows between you, a love that might show you that you can be happy again." Her fingers tightened on Theodora's arm. "You deserve to be happy, Theo."

Tears formed in Theodora's eyes. "I don't dare hope," she whispered.

Sarah put her arms around her friend. "It's difficult, I know. If you can't hope right now, at least don't give up. Take things as they come."

Theodora nodded against Sarah's shoulder. "I will." She tightened her arms around Sarah for a moment, then stepped back. "We'd best get ready to go; we certainly don't want Mr. Sage scolding us for lollygagging."

"As if he'd ever scold us." Sarah smiled at her friend and was rewarded with a return smile. "I'll take these blankets to Orion." She grabbed an armload of the folded coverings and took them to Orion's side.

"What was that all about?" he asked as he tied several of the blankets to the back of Sarah's saddle.

"Just woman talk," Sarah answered.

"About men, no doubt."

"No doubt." She stood on tiptoe to plant a kiss on his whisker-covered cheek. "I'll tell you no more, so don't try to get it out of me."

At that, Orion turned and took her in his arms.

"I have my ways," he whispered against her ear, his tone low and sultry. "I can make you tell me anything." One of his hands slipped inside Sarah's cape and boldly closed over the mound of her breast.

Sarah gasped and closed her eyes against the rush of excitement and pleasure that his gentle caress brought forth. Her own arms snaked inside his coat and closed around his waist. "I believe you, sir. But I am a strong-willed woman; I may need a great deal of persuasion."

Orion groaned. "You torment me, woman. You know well this isn't the time or place for gentle persuasion."

"You started it," Sarah responded tartly, pinching his rear.

"And one day soon I'll finish it," Orion growled. He nipped her ear with his teeth, sending another wave of delight through her.

"I am going to hold you to that, Orion Beaudine." Sarah pinched him again, then reluctantly left the warmth of his embrace to help the other women.

Once again, Orion had made her ache with unfulfilled desire, but at least he had given her something to remember and fantasize about during the long, uncomfortable ride ahead. The day promised to be a cold one, and a blanket of tension and worry hung over them all, but Sarah still felt the warm, soothing light of the love she shared with Orion. That love would see them through whatever the day—and life— had to offer.

The attack came late that afternoon, just as the sun began its final descent toward the mountains in the west.

One moment the column marched across an open stretch of prairie land in watchful silence, the next moment the air was filled with bloodcurdling war cries, the whining of bullets, and the strange whooshing sound of arrows in flight. Riders in buckskin and war paint rode down on them seemingly from all directions.

Her heart pounding and her mouth dry with fear, Sarah struggled to control her terrified mount. Before her horrified eyes, arrows struck the side of Harriet's wagon, sending the occupants into a litany of screams.

"Get down!" the driver shouted. "Get down!"

The women did as they were told. Sarah wildly searched the area for Orion. A moment earlier he had been talking to Colonel Rutledge; now the colonel was galloping back toward the wagons and Orion was nowhere to be seen.

Jubal Sage raced by her, shouting that the column follow him. The colonel reiterated the command. The usually recalcitrant mules needed little urging to run, and a second later the entire column fled after Jubal. Lieutenant Roe waved Sarah, Theodora, and Sweet Water closer to the hurrying wagons and rode on their exposed flank, his pistol drawn. Sarah glanced over her shoulder and saw that Adam had dropped back and was commanding the cavalrymen. Following Adam's orders, the two lines of mounted soldiers split and separated, some falling back to help with the herd of horses and to flank the slower-moving supply wagons, the others riding ahead to protect the wagons carrying the women and children. She noticed two horses running next to Harriet's wagon, their saddles ominously empty. Neither horse was Thunder, but fear and grief tore at her anyway.

A short distance ahead, Jubal waved an arm in a circular motion, indicating that the wagons be drawn into a semicircle in front of a large outcropping of rock. The drivers, aided by riders alongside the teams, obeyed his commands. The open wagons carrying the women and children slowed to a stop first. Sarah, Theodora, and Sweet Water followed them.

"Get out of the wagons!" Jubal shouted. "All of you, get down! Roe, get them women and kids into the rocks!"

Callahan Roe pulled Theodora from her saddle as Sarah jumped down from hers. Sweet Water was already hurrying toward the rocks. The wagon drivers helped the three officers' wives, the two children, Lucy, and the four laundresses down from their wagons and sent them scurrying after Sweet Water. The capable Cheyenne woman clambered up into the rocks, stopping here and there to point at a protected spot, and soon the two crying children and all the women were concealed, except for Sarah and Theodora. Callahan hurried them toward the rocks.

"Where is Orion?" Sarah cried.

"I don't know, ma'am, but knowing the Hunter, he's fine. You get yourself under cover so he doesn't have to worry about you on top of everything else." He urged her and Theodora to safety behind a large rock.

Sarah stared up at him, astonished at the level of fierce and mature determination on Callahan's young face.

"I want all of you ladies to stay down," Callahan called out in a firm voice. "And try to keep those children quiet."

"What can we do to help, Lieutenant?" Theodora asked.

Callahan looked at her. "You can pray, Mrs. Byrd. I don't know yet how serious our situation is and how many we're up against, but I'm sure any degree of divine assistance would be helpful and welcome." He hurried off, directing a few of the cavalrymen into positions among the rocks, ordering others to calm the horses. Three of the supply wagons lumbered into position behind the first two wagons, and the fourth was held back until the herd of horses was guided into the makeshift corral formed by the wagons and the rocks. Sarah was relieved to see that Adam was among the soldiers, as was Colonel Rutledge.

The day fell suddenly and eerily silent.

Sarah leaned against the sun-warmed rock and prayed as she had never prayed before. *Orion.*

The sound of a galloping horse reached her ears, and she looked around the rock to see Thunder bearing down on them, with Orion and a soldier on his back. She felt dizzy with relief as Orion guided the horse into the half-circle formed by the wagons, and it took every bit of self-control she had not to leave the protection of her rock and run to him. But Lieutenant Roe was right; Orion didn't need to be worried about her on top of everything else.

The soldier with Orion was obviously injured. Soldiers helped him down, and Orion jumped to the ground as Colonel Rutledge and Adam approached him.

"Two more soldiers are back there, but they're dead, Colonel," Orion reported. "One was Private Wilson, and I didn't know the other one."

"Who else is missing?" the colonel barked.

As the men took a quick roll call, Sarah leaned her head against the rock, numb with shock and grief. Private Wilson was the nice young man who had escorted her to Dancer's side the day the soldiers shot at the wolf, who had gone with Jubal to retrieve supper the night they had found Orion injured. She pictured the soldier in her mind, with his red hair and friendly manner. He was much too young to die. She said a quick prayer for the peace of his soul, and for that of the other soldier.

"Why did the shooting stop?" Major Dillard asked.

"They're regrouping," Orion explained. He looked up at the rock formation. "We need to get some men up there to watch the back side of the hill."

"The women and children are hidden in the rocks," Lieutenant Roe said.

"Good."

"Let's have a report on casualties," Colonel Rutledge called out.

"I'm hit, but it's not serious," one enlisted man said.

"Me, too," another added.

"My horse caught a bullet, and I think he's in trouble."

"We lost a few of the horses from the herd in the run, maybe three, maybe four."

Jubal looked up from where he was examining the wounded soldier Orion had brought in. "This one's in trouble, too. We gotta get the arrow outta his back and stop this bleedin' or we'll lose him."

Colonel Rutledge faced Orion. "Will they attack again?"

"Yes, sir."

"Who are they? How many are there? What are they after?"

"They're dressed like Indians, but I think there are white men among them. I would guess there are thirty, maybe thirty-five altogether. They're after either horses and booty or scalps and women."

"We outnumber them, and probably have more ammunition, but I don't want to have a battle with women and children present." Colonel Rutledge turned to the horse handlers. "Release all the extra horses. See if that satisfies them."

The colonel's order was obeyed. The horses were sent from the dubious protection of the enclosure at a run.

"Someone's coming!" one of the soldiers hidden among the rocks shouted from his vantage point. "Looks like Indians to me!"

With a great deal of whooping and hollering, three riders raced up and drove the freed horses off. The Dillard children began to cry again. Sarah heard Penelope and Harriet soothe the children. An uneasy silence fell over the group, broken only by the restless movements of the remaining horses.

"We'll wait awhile," the colonel announced. "See to the wounded and check on the women and children."

Sarah turned to Theodora. "They'll need help with the wounded."

Theodora nodded. "Let's go."

The two women carefully climbed down from the rocks, while Major Dillard and two enlisted men climbed up to check on the others. Lucy joined Sarah and Theodora as they approached Jubal Sage, who crouched over the wounded soldier. Orion came to Sarah's side and put an arm around her.

She resisted the urge to throw herself at him and sob out her relief that he was there and uninjured, and merely leaned into him instead, hoping that her feelings showed in her eyes when she looked up at him.

"Howdy, ladies," Jubal said. "This here's Private Pete Trenton."

Sarah smiled down at the young soldier who rested on his side. Sweat dotted his forehead, and he grimaced in pain.

"He's got a problem with this arrow in his back," Jubal continued. "We need some hot water and some bandages."

"We also need to get him moved away from these horses so we have room to work on him," Lucy said briskly. "Take him over there by that pine tree." She pointed to a scraggly pine maybe twelve feet high, growing at a crooked angle near a large boulder. "Captain Rutledge, would you please order a fire built and water gathered from the canteens?"

Adam complied, and soon Theodora's sturdy cast-iron tea-kettle steamed over a small fire. Private Trenton was moved to the spot Lucy had picked out and now lay on his stomach on a spread buffalo robe. Lucy and Jubal prepared to work on him, while Sarah and Theodora saw to the other two wounded men, one of whom had a bullet in his thigh; the other had been hit by a bullet that went clear through the fleshy part of his upper arm.

Suddenly the horrible war cries sounded again, followed by gunshots. An arrow embedded itself in the dirt not two feet from Sarah's thigh.

"Take cover!" Colonel Rutledge shouted. "Fire at will!"

The man Theodora was working on pushed her to the ground and covered her with his body. Before Sarah could move, she was knocked over herself, and covered with a man's body.

"Stay still," Orion's terse voice ordered. She lay there, safe under Orion's body, fearful for him, her heart pounding, her cheek pressed into the dirt, and listened to the terrifying sounds of battle rage around her: the shrill cries of the attackers, the screaming of the two children in the rocks above, the squeals of the frightened horses. It seemed an eternity passed before the eerie silence descended again.

Orion moved off of her. "Are you all right?" he demanded.

"Yes." Sarah pushed herself up to a sitting position. She looked into Orion's eyes, saw the fury sparking there.

"I have to find out who they are," he said firmly. "I have to go out there, and then I may need to ride for reinforcements."

The fear spread from Sarah's heart to her stomach and her limbs, until she felt she couldn't move, couldn't breathe. "Orion, no."

He grabbed her arms. "I must," he said harshly. "Perhaps both Jubal and I do. He and I have the best chance of getting through. You must promise that you will do exactly as I tell you, with no argument. There's no time. I need you to obey me, Sarah."

She stared into his green eyes, now flashing with a different kind of intensity than she had ever seen before—a hard determination, a curious pleading.

"You must trust me," he whispered.

His words calmed her, cleared the confusion from her frightened mind. "I do, Orion." She laid a hand against his heart. "I'll do as you ask, and you do what you must."

He kissed her then, quickly and fiercely.

"Come back to me," she whispered.

"I swear it." He sealed his vow with another kiss, then spoke to Jubal in Cheyenne.

Jubal did not look up from his struggles to remove the arrow from Private Trenton's back, but he nodded and responded. Orion stood, and Sarah clutched his hand. He looked down at her, devoured her with his eyes, and moved his hand to caress her cheek. She turned her head and pressed a kiss to his palm, as he had so often done to her. He smiled, then, after speaking briefly to Colonel Rutledge, left. Sure and confident, he went alone, without Thunder, carrying only his rifle.

Never had Sarah known such fear.

Two attacks followed, each leaving a few more wounded and, in the case of the last one, another soldier dead. After Jubal succeeded in prying the arrow from Trenton's back, he, too, prepared to leave. He explained to Colonel Rutledge that the attacks would probably stop at nightfall because of the Indian belief that if a man was killed in the darkness, his soul would get lost on the way to Paradise. After speaking to Sweet Water, the mountain man slipped out of the make-shift fort, on foot as Orion had.

Lucy, Sarah, and Theodora tended to the mostly minor wounds sustained in the attacks, including a gash in little Neville Dillard's cheek caused by a ricocheted bullet. The hysterical Penelope did such a good job of upsetting first Neville and then Clarissa that Lucy finally begged Major Dillard to take his wife away, which the major did. Harriet Rutledge calmed Clarissa, while Libby Gates soon had Neville's tears dried and a tremulous smile on his face as she told him repeatedly what a brave soldier he was.

It appeared that Jubal was right about nighttime attacks, even if some of the attackers were indeed white men, for there were no more. Approximately fifty people settled into an uneasy, cramped encampment in the space they shared with close to sixty horses and mules. Due to the scarcity of fuel, few fires were lit, and those were just large enough to heat water for coffee. Supper, for any who could tolerate the thought of eating, consisted of cold meat, cold beans, and cold bread. The animals had soon eaten every blade of dry prairie grass within the enclosure and were fed small rations of oats. Their water came from the canteens of their masters, poured into buckets that were passed around.

The December night promised to be cold, and people sat

in groups, huddled under blankets and robes around the small fires. Sarah sat alone and stared into the darkness, sick with worry over Orion and Jubal, and Dancer. She felt cheated somehow, and was puzzled by that. True, she had found in Orion what she had always dreamed of in a man, and their future together looked promising and happy. She had found her place in the world, here in this wild, wonderful land, surrounded by Orion and his family—which included Dancer—and by good friends like Theodora, Lucy, Jubal Sage, and Sweet Water.

Now all of that was threatened.

But she wasn't the only one whose dreams for the future were threatened by the band of bloodthirsty renegades lurking in the darkness. Her gaze wandered around the encampment, took in the groups of subdued people hunched around the fires. Did everyone else feel cheated, as well?

"Sarah."

She looked up at the tall man at her side, surprised that she felt no animosity or even wariness. "Hello, Adam."

He crouched down. "How are you?"

"I don't know. Scared, worried, restless, exhausted. How about you?"

"The same. But I've been through this before. Not with Indians, mind you, but during the war with Mexico."

"Do you ever get used to it?"

"No. But maybe it's a little easier for me because I know what to expect."

"What can we expect?"

Adam shrugged. "Another attack, almost certainly. Perhaps many. Some will die; maybe we all will. And maybe we'll get lucky. Maybe we'll get enough of them to make them reconsider and withdraw. We probably have more ammunition than they do, and we have enough food to last for a while. But if it turns into a waiting game, we'll run out of fuel, and water will become a serious concern, especially for the horses and mules. If we lose the animals, we'll be in real trouble."

"Orion said he may go for reinforcements," she said, realizing too late that Adam might not want to hear Orion's name.

"Someone will have to," Adam calmly replied. "He or Sage will have the best chance of getting through alive. No soldier can compete with them in terms of survival skills."

Sarah was astonished; Adam had actually complimented Orion. "How far are we from Fort Laramie?" she managed to ask.

"Maybe twenty miles."

"Then reinforcements can't get here for at least two days, even under the best of circumstances."

"No." He looked at her. "Did you eat?"

Sarah shook her head. "I'm not hungry."

"It would be best if you ate something, if for no other reason than to keep up your strength. You will need it."

"Thank you for your concern," Sarah said sincerely. After all that had happened between them, she was touched by his kindness. She realized, with a start, that she had missed him. Of course she had. Adam had been her best friend all of her life. Why wouldn't she miss him? But all she said was, "I promise I'll try to eat something later."

"Adam, I've been looking for you. Oh." Harriet Rutledge came to an abrupt halt as her gaze fell on Sarah. Her voice rose to a screech. "Why are you talking to her?"

"Aunt Harriet, please." Adam straightened. "I wanted to check on Sarah."

"Let her long-haired scout check on her," Harriet snapped. She stared at Sarah, her fury and hatred palpable. "But he's not here, is he? He and that other one—cowards that they are—skipped out as fast as they could, didn't they?"

"That's enough," Adam said firmly. He took Harriet's elbow. "Where is the colonel? I'll take you to him."

Harriet jerked away from him. "Don't patronize me,

nephew." She pointed a shaking finger at Sarah. "Hunter Beaudine and Jubal Sage led us into this trap, then disappeared. I knew they couldn't be trusted. And to think those men have eaten at my table!"

Sarah was too astonished to be offended. She scrambled to her feet. "Harriet, you can't believe they would betray us."

"Don't defend them! Like all savages, they're lying, scheming vultures, waiting to pick over the bones of our valiant dead!" Harriet's eyes had taken on a strange light. "And God only knows what they will do to the women they take alive, to that precious little girl."

"That is enough!" Adam forced Harriet to turn around. "I'll hear no more of such nonsense. Sarah, please excuse us."

"Good night, Adam." Stunned, she watched as Adam kindly but firmly led Harriet away. Lucy hurried to join them, taking Harriet's other arm, and Sarah realized that many of the people in the crowded encampment had heard Harriet's crazed accusations.

"What on earth was that all about?" Theodora asked.

"I don't know." Sarah stared after Harriet. "I think Harriet may have lost her mind." She glanced at her friend. "Literally."

Theodora's eyes widened. "Even the invincible Mrs. Colonel Rutledge is cracking under the strain," she whispered. "God help us all."

Twenty-five

"We have to get the women and children out."

Sarah looked up at Orion as he spoke, secure once again because his hand held hers. He and Jubal had returned shortly after midnight with disturbing news, which they now shared with Colonel Rutledge and his officers. In the light of the nearly full moon, it was easy to see those gathered together. Theodora stood next to Lieutenant Roe, and Sweet Water listened intently as Jubal translated for her in a low voice. Lucy had left the sleeping Harriet's side to listen. Penelope Dillard and Libby Gates stayed with the children.

"There are more than I first guessed," Orion reported. "This attack was very well planned, and carefully timed. It is no random act. They are well armed, and seem determined to wipe out this company."

"You said many of them are white men in disguise," Adam retorted. "Why would they attack women and children?"

"The women and children make it even more attractive."

"But why?" Colonel Rutledge demanded.

"Maybe to start a war," Jubal suggested.

The mountain man's words startled everyone into silence. His words made sense to Sarah, though. Many people of both races would profit from a war between the white man and the red: renegade white men could steal the supplies and stock from the accosted immigrants; the Indians, through the fear of warfare, could keep the whites out of their land for a little while longer.

Officers could be promoted more quickly during a time of war.

Unbidden, the words flashed in Sarah's mind, and she turned horrified eyes on Adam. Had he not said those very words to her a few months ago, when he was voicing his deep frustration over his duty assignments on the Western frontier?

Orion looked down at her, puzzled, and she realized she had tightened her grip on his hand. Sarah forced her hand to relax.

Surely not Adam. Surely not . . . *Adam.*

"I want to take the women and children to my brother's camp on Elk Tooth Creek," Orion said. "Perhaps if they're gone, the renegades will lose some interest."

Colonel Rutledge frowned. "Captain Beaudine is camped on Elk Tooth Creek?"

"No." Orion met the colonel's gaze. "Gray Eagle and his band of Cheyenne are."

"You want to take them to the Cheyenne?" the colonel asked incredulously. "When we're fighting Indians now? How do you know the Cheyenne aren't involved in this? Didn't you yourself say the arrow you found in that trapper's back was Cheyenne, that the arrows Mr. Sage pulled from your own body were Cheyenne?"

"They want us to believe it was the Cheyenne," Orion said stubbornly. "It wasn't."

"You don't know that for sure," Adam retorted.

Orion stared at him. "Yes, I do."

"You must be mad, Hunter Beaudine," Major Dillard interjected. "You think I would entrust my beloved Penelope and our dear children to the care of *savages?*"

"Would you rather have them dead, Major? In ways you don't want me to describe?"

Major Dillard stared at him, and his mouth snapped shut.

"There's a way up over the rocks," Jubal said quietly. "We can get 'em out tonight. It'll take a few hours of hard walkin', but we'll have 'em safe in Gray Eagle's camp by sunup. Then the Hunter and me'll head for Fort Laramie, by different routes. One of us'll get through for sure. You'll have reinforcements by the day after tomorrow."

Colonel Rutledge's hard gaze bored into Orion. "I trust your brother, Mr. Beaudine, but what about the rest of the tribe?"

"None have any argument with the white man, and they don't want one. They won't harm women and children."

"You're certain this is the best thing to do?"

"Colonel, I am entrusting to the Cheyenne the person who means more to me than life itself." He glanced down at Sarah. "Do you think I would risk her safety unnecessarily? I believe the women and children are in far more danger if they remain here."

"For what it's worth, Colonel," Sarah said softly, "I know Gray Eagle and have no trepidation about going to him now."

"Nor do I," Theodora added.

"Sweet Water is Cheyenne," Jubal put in. "She'll help out."

Colonel Rutledge pursed his lips. "There will be trouble with my wife."

"And with mine," Major Dillard said. "She won't want to take the children to an Indian village."

"It's in their best interests," Orion said. "You must convince them of that."

"Let's do it," Colonel Rutledge said. "I want all the women and the two children to go. That is an order, and it includes my wife." He looked at Orion. "Harriet will be difficult. She is terrified of Indians. Please try to be patient with her."

"I will, sir, as long as she doesn't jeopardize the safety of the rest. You'll have to trust me."

"I do, Hunter Beaudine. Just be certain my trust is not misplaced."

"It isn't, sir."

"What shall they take with them?" the colonel asked.

"Only what they can comfortably carry on a long, rough walk. A little food, a cup for drinking, perhaps a blanket and a change of clothes."

"No water?"

"No. We will see to their water. You'll need every drop you have, and more."

The colonel nodded. "Very well. Lucy, please come and help me with my wife." He strode off, with Lucy at his heels.

Major Dillard stepped closer to Orion. A troubled frown wrinkled his forehead. "I don't like this, Beaudine. I'd much rather have my wife and children here, where I can watch over them."

"I understand your feelings, Major. I'm not going to want to leave Sarah, either. Like I said to the colonel: you'll have to trust me. We'll guard your family as if they were our own, and you'll be free to fulfill your duties here without the distraction of worrying about them. Please get them prepared to leave."

Clearly unhappy, Major Dillard left.

Adam approached, his expression neutral as he faced Sarah and Orion. "You're certain of this, Beaudine?"

"Yes, Captain, I am. I would never risk Sarah's well-being."

Adam looked from Orion to Sarah, then walked away without another word.

"I'd like to come with you," Lieutenant Roe said. When Orion appeared to be about to protest, Roe hurriedly continued. "Mr. Beaudine, there are eleven women to protect in addition to two young children who will no doubt need to be carried the entire way. You and Mr. Sage will need help, and once the women and children are safely ensconced with the

Cheyenne, I can return here and let the men know that all is well."

Jubal rubbed his beard thoughtfully. "That ain't a bad idea, Hunter."

"No, it isn't," Orion admitted. He looked at Roe. "Check with the colonel. If he has no objections, prepare to leave."

"Yes, sir." With a quick glance at Theodora, Roe hurried away.

"Let's get to it," Jubal said.

Orion looked over the group of women assembled before him. Sweet Water, Sarah, Theodora, Lucy, and Libby Gates calmly awaited his instructions. The four laundresses appeared to be nervous, Penelope Dillard, terrified, and Harriet Rutledge, angry and mutinous.

It was going to be a long night.

He spoke quietly. "Ladies, you'll need to tie your bundles at your waists or on your backs; your hands must be free so you can climb." He turned and pointed to the rocky face rising behind him. "We are going up that way."

A few startled gasps were punctuated by an unladylike remark from Harriet.

Ignoring the minor outbursts, Orion continued. "Mr. Sage will lead the way. A ravine cuts down the other side of this hill, one that will allow us to escape the area without being seen, if we're lucky. From there, a walk of several hours will take us to the safety of my brother's camp. You must be as quiet as possible, and that includes the children; all of our lives may depend upon it."

"You can't expect small children to be completely quiet," Penelope Dillard protested. "They are terrified."

Orion thought that Penelope was far more terrified than her children were, but he knew she could easily upset the young ones. "Mrs. Dillard, if I have to, I'll gag your children to keep them quiet."

"Oh!" Penelope squeaked.

"You uncivilized beast," Harriet hissed.

Orion fixed his unrelenting stare on Penelope first, then Harriet. "Let's get something straight. Mr. Sage and I are in charge now, and we are responsible for your safety. Those men out there are murderers—they have already killed two of their own men and three of your soldiers. They haven't given up this attack because they want you women, and if they get you, I promise you'll pray for death long before they kill you." He was pleased to see Penelope pale. Even Harriet seemed to be listening to him now. "I won't allow them to get my woman, and I have no intention of them getting any of you. But I need your help. You *must* do as Mr. Sage or I tell you. Any sign of insubordination, and I'll gag you myself and carry you over my shoulder."

"I am a colonel's wife," Harriet challenged. "You wouldn't dare."

"Mrs. Rutledge, I would take particular delight in gagging you," Orion snapped. "The colonel has entrusted you to my care, and he will not interfere with my methods, so I advise you not to push me. For once, put your personal feelings aside and look around you." He waved at the hushed group of women. "Do you wish to endanger all of them because of your vendetta against me and my family?"

Harriet crossed her arms over her chest and maintained a stony silence.

"I didn't think so," Orion muttered. "Ladies, I know this whole ordeal is frightening for you, but there can be no crying, no hysterics. If you absolutely must speak, do so in whispers."

Jubal stepped forward and scrutinized the group. "Those of you wearin' hoops, take 'em off and leave 'em. Hitch your skirts at your waist while we're climbin' the rocks. Say your goodbyes, and let's get outta here. The sooner we go, the sooner the Hunter and I can get reinforcements back here for your men."

His orders were quickly obeyed. Colonel Rutledge sent

men up into the rocks to offer fire cover if it became necessary, and a few others positioned themselves along the
route Jubal would take up the face of the rocky hillside in
order to offer assistance to the women as they climbed. It
was decided that Jubal would carry Clarissa on his back and
Orion would carry Neville, while Lieutenant Roe would
bring up the rear and guard the back trail.

As Orion watched, Adam approached Sarah. He couldn't
hear the words they spoke, but he saw Adam take Sarah's
hand. A nagging jealousy threatened to rear its ugly head, and
Orion fought it down. He had nothing to fear from Adam
Rutledge. It was only natural that two old friends would want
to say goodbye, to wish each other well in the dangerous situations they both now faced. No one knew what tomorrow
would bring.

The group gathered once again at the base of the rocky
hill. Jubal, with a sleepy Clarissa tied to his back, her little
arms around his neck, started up the incline and, one by one,
the somber women followed. Major Dillard adjusted the rope
that bound Neville to Orion's back, then kissed his son's
blonde head.

"Guard them well, Mr. Beaudine," he whispered.

Orion was touched by the emotion he saw in Dillard's eyes.
"I'll protect them with my life, Major. You stay alive yourself. They need you."

The major nodded, then stepped back, visibly pulling himself together.

Orion turned to Sarah. "Are you ready?" he asked. She nodded, her trust and love shining in her blue eyes. "Then let's go."
He spoke over his shoulder to Neville. "Hang on, boy."

"Yes, sir." The boy's arms snaked around his neck, and
Orion followed Sarah up the hill. His orders of silence had
been obeyed so well that the quiet seemed eerie. He whispered
a prayer to the spirit of the Wolf to watch over them all.

* * *

Sarah marched on, ignoring her weary body's plea for rest. She didn't need the disappearing moon to tell her that they had been walking for hours, for her numb hands and feet sent a clear message that she had been out in the cold for a long time. Surely it couldn't be much farther to Gray Eagle's camp.

Orion and Jubal had allowed only one rest so far, near a spring where all drank and nibbled on a little of whatever food they had brought. The children had been remarkably well behaved, perhaps because they had fallen asleep. Even now, Sarah could see Clarissa's blonde curls resting against the back of Jubal's shoulder. Surprisingly, both Harriet and Penelope had been well behaved, also. Aside from the cold and the exhaustion, the journey had been uneventful. She had watched in vain for a sign of Dancer, but didn't see him. Orion assured her that the wolf was out there somewhere, close.

Jubal called a halt. Orion and Callahan Roe moved to the head of the line as the women gathered around them. Sarah caught the faint scent of wood smoke in the frosty air.

"The camp is over that next hill," Jubal said quietly.

"I'd better go in first. I don't want to startle the guards." Orion worked on the knots in the rope around his chest. "Lieutenant, take the boy." Roe stepped forward and lifted Neville off Orion's back. "I won't be long," Orion said. He touched Sarah's cheek, then was gone, as silent in the tall prairie grasses as the light breeze.

Sarah watched Orion go, amazed that he seemed to disappear. Of course, it *was* dark. Wearily, she wrapped the cape more tightly around her cold body and sank down on the ground next to Theodora. The rest of the group followed suit. Perhaps it was because everyone was so tired, but no one spoke. Lieutenant Roe sat on Theodora's other side, holding the sleeping boy in his arms. Sarah felt a surge of affection for the child, candidly admitting to herself that Neville was much more pleasant to be around when he was asleep. Then she remembered the boy's touching bravery when she had cleaned the cut on his cheek. Perhaps Neville's—and Clarissa's—greatest problem was their neurotic and overprotective mother. She sighed. Poor kids.

"Are you all right?" Theodora whispered.

Sarah nodded. "Just tired and cold. How about you?"

"The same."

They lapsed into silence.

It seemed to Sarah that a long time passed before she heard approaching voices and saw the lights of several torches top the hill over which Orion had disappeared. She scrambled to her feet.

Penelope gasped in fear at the sight of several buckskin-clad Indians moving toward them with torches held high. A strange whimper sounded from her throat. Libby murmured something to her. Sarah glanced at Harriet. The woman's eyes were narrowed, her expression one of loathing. Sarah saw no indication that Harriet was terrified of Indians, as Colonel Rutledge had warned. She merely hated them.

Sarah recognized Orion and Gray Eagle, and hurried to join them, as did Jubal and Sweet Water.

Gray Eagle greeted her affectionately. "Hello, little sister."

"Hello, Mr. Beaudine," Sarah answered, suddenly shy.

"No need for formality, since we'll soon be family," Gray Eagle said. His gaze took in the group of wary women. "Welcome to our village, ladies. Please come. Warmth and rest await you."

The women slowly and stiffly got to their feet. When Gray Eagle offered to take Clarissa from Jubal's back, Penelope protested.

"No. Don't you touch her!" Her voice rose, and it was clear to Sarah that Penelope was on the verge of hysterics.

"Stop it," Libby ordered, grabbing Penelope's arm. "Get a hold of yourself."

Penelope's voice rose to a wail as Gray Eagle cradled her

daughter in his arms. Clarissa started fussing, and Neville awakened, also, and began calling for his mother.

Libby shook Penelope. "Stop it! You're upsetting the children."

Gasping, Penelope fought Libby's hold. "Give me my babies!" she shrieked. Clarissa wailed, and Neville began to cry.

The sound of Libby's hand connecting with Penelope's cheek rang loud in the cold night air. Abruptly, Penelope fell silent, staring at Libby, her eyes wide with shock. The children's crying changed to sniffles.

"You shame yourself and your husband, Mrs. Major Dillard," Libby snapped. "These men are here to help us. Collect yourself and show them the proper respect."

"You struck me," Penelope said accusingly.

"And I will again if I have to. We're all frozen and exhausted, and I'll not put up with any more nonsense." Libby's furious gaze fell briefly on Harriet. "The lives of our dear husbands are at risk, and there is no time for foolishness. Now let's get settled so that Mr. Beaudine and Mr. Sage can be on their way for reinforcements." Libby picked up her skirts and marched to Gray Eagle's side. "Clarissa, stop whining. Mr. Beaudine, we meet again. Please forgive my bad manners the first time I met you at Mrs. Byrd's cabin. I labored under false impressions at the time, impressions which have since been corrected." Again, she glared at Harriet for a moment, then turned back to Gray Eagle. "Please lead the way to your camp. I, for one, am very grateful for your offer of hospitality, and only hope that one day I can repay your kindness."

"Yes, ma'am." Struggling with a smile, Gray Eagle led the way over the hilltop. Libby followed him, as did the four laundresses. Harriet linked arms with a subdued Penelope and marched off, while Sarah, Lucy, and Theodora all exchanged astonished glances.

"She'll make a *fine* Army wife," Lucy said admiringly as they walked. "Even that little one listened to her."

Sarah smiled. Libby would indeed be fine. She reached for Orion's hand and prepared herself for her first glimpse of a Cheyenne village.

"Why did they all stare at us?" Penelope asked in a frightened whisper. She hovered over her sleeping children.

"Because we look as strange to them as they do to us," Sarah explained patiently. The walk into the village *had* been a little unnerving. Cheyenne men, women, and children, wrapped in buffalo robes, had come out into the cold night to observe the visitors. The darkness—deeper now since the moon had waned—and the eerie silence of the villagers, combined with the flickering light of fires and torches and the puffs of white in front of everyone's mouths, had added a mystical, almost fearful element to the experience. Sarah had been very grateful for the comforting presence of both Orion and Gray Eagle. She could understand how intimidated the other women might feel.

Gray Eagle had shown them into a large tipi. A cheerful fire burned in the center, and numerous robes and furs were scattered about the raised earthen sleeping ledge. The tipi was cozy and warm, and now, very crowded. Sweet Water would stay in another tipi with friends, but that still left ten women and two children in the one tipi. And unfortunately, two of the women were definitely hostile. Sarah glanced at Harriet. The woman sat near the fire, her back rigid, her arms folded across her chest. She had not said one word since they had come into the village.

The flap over the door opening raised, and Orion stuck his head in. "Sarah, Theodora, Miss Lucy, and Mrs. Gates, would you please come out here?"

Harriet and Penelope exchanged glances, but neither woman spoke. Those called joined Orion outside. He led

them to another tipi a short distance away and held the door
flap open for them. One by one, the four women ducked
through the door. Several people were inside, including Gray
Eagle, Jubal Sage, Sweet Water, and Lieutenant Roe. A
Cheyenne couple sat behind Gray Eagle, as did a young girl
of about ten.

"Please sit, ladies," Gray Eagle invited.

They all complied. Orion sat last, taking a seat next to
Sarah.

"We need to discuss our plans," Orion said. "Then you
can tell the others." He nodded at Jubal. "Jubal and I are
leaving for Fort Laramie as soon as we are finished here. As
a precaution, we'll go by different routes, and we should
both be there by sundown today." He pointed at Lieutenant
Roe. "You will return to the besieged troops. Gray Eagle
will send a few men along to ensure that you safely reach
the ravine. From there, you should have no trouble getting
back inside the encampment, although they may have you
wait until nightfall. Do as your Cheyenne guides tell you,
and you will live to again call upon the lovely Mrs. Byrd."

Sarah glanced at Theodora and saw that her friend had
blushed and now stared down at her hands clasped in her
lap.

"Yes, sir," Callahan responded. He watched Theodora, his
affection for her apparent in his expression.

"Miss Lucy and Mrs. Gates, we need your help with Mrs.
Dillard and Mrs. Rutledge. Because of their fear and prejudice, they may prove difficult, and must be watched. Under
no circumstances can they be allowed to insult our hosts.
Miss Lucy, I know you can exert some control over Mrs.
Rutledge, and, Mrs. Gates, you were superb with Mrs. Dillard earlier."

Gray Eagle nodded his agreement with Orion, and Libby
basked in the warmth of their approval.

Orion continued. "Use a strong hand with both women if
necessary. You saw how easily Mrs. Dillard upset her chil-

dren tonight. That can't happen here. The Cheyenne teach
their children from infancy not to cry, because a single crying
child could conceivably endanger the entire village if they
were trying to escape an enemy. The Dillard children must
be kept quiet, and if that means removing them from their
hysterical mother's care, do it. Sarah, I want you to be the
spokesman for the group, with Theodora as your second in
command. The women of the village will provide you with
food and water. If you need anything at all, ask Gray Eagle.
He and Sweet Water will help you as much as possible, as
will Sparrow, Gray Eagle's cousin." Orion indicated the child
seated behind his brother. "Sparrow speaks English, so use
her as a translator if Gray Eagle cannot be found."

Sarah smiled at the pretty child as Orion introduced the
four white women to her.

"Orion, I still wish you'd let us return to the besieged
encampment with you now," Gray Eagle said. "We're much
closer than Fort Laramie, and some of our braves wouldn't
mind a battle, especially since the attackers are trying to
make it look like the Cheyenne are behind it all. And I'd love
a crack at Cutler myself. The man's a snake."

"I know, Eagle, but I don't want the Cheyenne involved.
Besides Cutler, I don't know yet who we're dealing with,
and since they attacked the Army, it's better to let the Army
deal with it." Orion cocked an eyebrow at his brother. "In
fact, I suspect some Army people may be involved. If that's
the case, you wouldn't want to spoil Joseph's fun, would
you?"

Sarah stared at Orion, her heart pounding. He suspected
the involvement of Army personnel? Did he suspect Adam?
Her stomach suddenly felt sick, and she turned her gaze to
the fire. Surely Adam could not be involved in something
so heinous, but then, he had changed so dramatically since
joining the Army. Still, the idea of Adam betraying his men,
his company, his country—no, she couldn't believe it. Sarah
sat up straighter. Such an action would be more in keeping

with Lieutenant Fielding's character. In fact, she would mention that to Orion before he left. Fielding had sent Cutler to Theodora's cabin, so she knew the two men were acquainted. And Fielding was now at Fort Laramie.

A grim smile lifted the corners of Sarah's mouth. She would be very pleased if Joseph and Orion caught Fielding at such a serious crime. He would never be free to hurt anyone again.

"Sarah?"

Orion's quiet voice penetrated her thoughts. She blinked and looked up at him.

"Do you have any questions?" he asked.

"Only when we can expect you back."

"I would guess by sundown tomorrow. I'll return to the besieged troops with the reinforcements. When I come for you, the battle will be over."

Sarah nodded. "That is what I expected."

"We'd best be on our way," Jubal said. He stood up, as did everyone except Sparrow and the couple behind Gray Eagle, whom Sarah assumed were Sparrow's parents. Silently, they filed out of the tipi.

After wishing Orion, Jubal, and Callahan good luck, Lucy returned to the tipi where the rest of the women waited. Jubal walked off with Sweet Water, and Callahan escorted Theodora back to the women's tipi. They stood outside, talking quietly for a few minutes. Gray Eagle murmured something about seeing to the horses and left, leaving Sarah and Orion alone.

"What happened in there?" he asked. "It seemed as if your mind wandered off."

"It was your comment about someone in the Army being involved with the renegades." Sarah placed her hand on his chest and fingered the buffalo robe coat.

"It isn't pleasant to consider that a man would betray his fellows, is it?"

"Orion, I must tell you something." Sarah continued to

smooth his coat, refusing to look up at him, until he grabbed her hand.

"What is it, sweetheart?"

She searched his face, finding only kindness and concern there. "Several months ago, Adam told me how he hated the frontier, how he couldn't wait to be posted back East again. He made some comment about how difficult it was to be promoted when there was no war going on." Her fingers tightened on his. "I know him, Orion. Adam would not betray his men. He would not deliberately start a war."

"I don't think he would, either, Sarah." Orion smiled at her. "Captain Rutledge is an insensitive clod when it comes to women, or at least when it comes to you, for which I shall be eternally grateful to him. But he is no traitor."

"Fielding sent Cutler to Theodora's house."

"I know."

Even in the dim light, Sarah could see that Orion's handsome, whiskered face took on a grim expression.

"I'll talk to Joseph," Orion promised. "You just keep an eye on things here."

"I will." Sarah threw her arms around him, and he held her tightly. A surge of love rolled through her, painful in its intensity. "I don't like sending my man off to war," she whispered. "Please come back to me."

"I will, sweet woman." Orion kissed her, softly and reverently. "I promise."

Sarah fought the tears that threatened. "I'll hold you to that, Orion Beaudine. You've never seen me *truly* angry. You will if you get yourself killed." She felt his smile against her cheek.

"I won't get killed, Sarah Hancock. Not when I have you to live for."

His lips found hers, and she clung to him with every fiber of her being. This kiss was different than any they had shared before, for it was one of pure love, one that transcended even sexuality. In that kiss, their souls bonded, and when they reluctantly pulled apart, Sarah knew Orion carried a part of her with him that she would never get back.

She didn't want it back.

"Go with God, my love," she whispered. "Return safely to me."

"I will." He held her a moment longer, then gently set her back.

Gray Eagle waited nearby, holding the reins of a saddled horse. Jubal was astride another mount, ready to go.

Sarah blinked her tear-filled eyes and looked up at Jubal. "Be safe, Mr. Sage."

"I always am, Miss Sarah," he said affectionately. "Don't worry none; this ain't no more'n an early mornin' ride for me'n the Hunter." He nodded in the direction of the lightening eastern sky.

As distressed as she was, Sarah could not help smiling.

Orion accepted the reins Gray Eagle held out to him and climbed into the saddle. "By sundown tomorrow," he said, adjusting his hat on his head.

"We'll have supper waiting," Gray Eagle replied.

"Watch my woman for me, little brother."

In a gesture Sarah found immeasurably comforting, Gray Eagle placed a brotherly, protective arm around her shoulders. "You know I will, big brother," he said. "She will be waiting, too, so don't be late."

"No, sir, I won't." Orion winked at Sarah. "She can get kind of feisty if she's kept waiting. Always says something about making amends."

"You *do* have amends to make, Orion Beaudine," Sarah retorted.

"Yes, ma'am." Orion touched the brim of his hat in a gesture of farewell. "I look forward to it." He touched his lips with a fingertip, then nudged his horse forward and leaned down from the saddle to place that same fingertip against her lips. "I look forward to it," he repeated. His green eyes pierced into her very soul, proclaiming his love for her, then he touched his heels to the horse's side.

Sarah watched him go, clinging to Gray Eagle for comfort as part of her heart rode away with Orion into the awakening dawn.

Twenty-six

Later that afternoon, Sarah made her way back toward the tipi she shared with the other battle refugees, carrying a bundle of soiled clothing. Although the nagging worry for Orion, Jubal, and the besieged soldiers still gnawed at her, she felt more rested and refreshed now. She had managed to sleep for several hours after Orion's departure, and, around noon, Sweet Water and Sparrow had brought a filling meal of buffalo and wild turnip stew. Because of the mildness of the sunny December day, Sarah, along with Libby, two of the more adventurous laundresses, and Sparrow, had just enjoyed the luxury of bathing in a pool naturally heated by a mineral hot spring near the creek. Sarah wore a fresh chemise and petticoats under her wrinkled but clean black skirt, and over her white bodice she wore the gray jacket to her riding outfit. Her unbound hair, freshly washed and almost dry, lay about her shoulders and fell down her back. If only Orion were there, she would be content.

She approached the tipi and was gladdened to see that the other two laundresses and Penelope Dillard had ventured outside into the sun. Perhaps they were beginning to feel more comfortable in their alien surroundings. The children certainly were; Clarissa and Neville sat close to their mother, watching the activities of the respectfully distant Cheyenne with wide eyes, and, Sarah suspected, a little bit of longing, especially when a group of laughing children raced by, chased by a few playful, barking dogs. Lucy and Theodora rested on either side of the door flap, having accepted the duty of surreptitiously watching Penelope and Harriet while Sarah and Libby bathed.

"How was it?" Theodora called.

"Heavenly," Sarah answered. "It seems so strange to climb into an outside pool that is warm. The water smells strange, kind of like rotten eggs, but it feels wonderful. Of course, it's very cold when you get out. Be prepared to dress quickly." She mouthed the word, *Harriet?* Harriet had not spoken one word since their arrival in the Cheyenne camp, and Sarah suspected she had not slept or eaten, either.

Lucy inclined her head in the direction of the tipi. "She wouldn't come out, even though I told her it's very pleasant in the sun."

"I'll check on her." Sarah glanced at Penelope. "The water really is wonderful, Mrs. Dillard. Very soothing and relaxing. It would do you and the children good to take advantage of it." She glanced at the laundresses. "All of you."

"I won't bathe with savages," Penelope said frostily. "And neither will my children." Her disapproving gaze traveled from Sarah's unbound hair down to her skirt.

Sarah shrugged. "Suit yourself. I just thought you might be more comfortable; I know I am. It's heavenly to be clean again."

Penelope merely pursed her lips and looked away.

Stifling an exasperated sigh, Sarah ducked through the opening into the tipi. It took a moment for her eyes to adjust to the dim interior. She finally spotted Harriet sitting off to one side, her back rigidly straight, disdaining even the use of one of the ingenious backrests their hosts had thoughtfully provided. The woman did not acknowledge Sarah with so much as a glance, but continued to stare at the low fire.

"Hello, Harriet." Sarah set her bundle of clothes on the sleeping fur she had wrapped up in earlier. She kept her voice carefully neutral. "Perhaps you might reconsider your decision not to bathe. I really think you'll find the water soothing."

No response.

"Then come outside," Sarah coaxed. "The air is cool, but it is a lovely day. The wind wall they built around this tipi ensures that you will be very comfortable. It will do you good to get out into the sunshine."

Harriet glared up at her but remained silent.

Keeping a rein on her rising temper, Sarah knelt down and examined the contents of the stew pot near the fire. As far as she could tell, the stew had not been touched since the earlier meal, of which Harriet had refused to partake. "Harriet, you must at least eat," Sarah said gently. "You need to keep up your strength. The stew is rather bland, but it's filling." She grabbed the handle of the bone spoon in the iron pot and stirred. "Won't you have some?"

"Don't bring that slop near me."

Harriet's tone was so vicious that Sarah looked up in astonishment.

"All right." Sarah released the spoon and sat back on her heels. "Would you care for something else? I can ask Gray Eagle or Sparrow if—"

"I'll accept nothing from them! Not their food, not their sleeping robes, not their backrests, not their bathing pool! I would not accept their shelter if not for my husband's direct order."

Sarah wondered how dearly and for how long Colonel Rutledge would pay for sending his wife to the protection of the Cheyenne. Despite her best efforts to keep her voice calm, she feared a note of mild scolding came through her next words. "I don't understand your hostility, for these people have shown us nothing but kindness."

The flash of fury in the other woman's eyes should have given Sarah some warning, but she was totally unprepared when Harriet launched herself forward and struck Sarah across the face.

"These murdering savages know nothing of kindness!" Harriet screamed. "Nothing, do you hear me?" She grabbed Sarah's arms and shook her viciously. "They lie and steal and torture and murder, and even then, they don't stop. They mutilate and desecrate and dishonor! They should be exterminated like the vermin they are, every last one of them!"

Stunned, Sarah stared at Harriet's hate-ravaged features, not even recognizing her. There was something there under the hatred, though; a deep anguish, an unrelenting grief. Sarah pried Harriet's bruising fingers from her arms and gently pushed the woman backwards. "What did the Cheyenne do to you?" she asked quietly, rubbing her aching arms.

Harriet blinked, then shook her head, as if trying to shake off a bad dream. She pushed herself farther away from Sarah and once again stared into the dying fire. For a long time, Sarah did not think Harriet would answer her. But she did.

"They killed my son."

Sarah closed her eyes for a moment. She knew the Rutledges' son, Gilbert, had died a few years earlier, just as she knew he had been a lieutenant in the Army. She had not known how he died, for none of the Rutledges—Harriet, Edward, or Adam—would tell her. In fact, Adam had warned her against even mentioning his deceased cousin's name. Now, Harriet's seemingly blind prejudice toward all Indians made sense. Sarah opened her eyes and watched the woman across the fire from her, who now seemed old and caved-in on herself. "I'm so sorry, Harriet." She paused before continuing. "Why wouldn't you tell me when Adam and I were engaged? Why wouldn't you let Adam tell me? Things between you and me would have been so much easier if I had known, if I could have understood."

Harriet raised angry eyes to her. "If you had known, would you have refrained from befriending Jubal Sage and Joseph Beaudine, Indian lovers that they are? Would you have refused to speak to that half-breed Beaudine brother, who is an abomination in the eyes of God? Would you have remained true to my dear Adam, and not forsaken your mother's wishes and your own honor by taking up with that despicable Hunter Beaudine?"

"No." Sarah met Harriet's gaze, fighting for control of her temper. "It would have changed nothing, except that perhaps I could have been a little more patient with you."

With a contemptuous sniff, Harriet turned away.

Sarah tried again. "I know what it is to lose a loved one, and I am very sorry for your loss, Harriet, but surely you can't blame all of the Cheyenne tribe for what some of their men did."

Now Harriet turned on her again. "Yes, I can! My beloved Gilbert deserved better than to die in a godforsaken Mexican desert while searching for a wagon route to California!"

Sarah frowned, remembering a long-ago conversation with Jubal Sage, during which he described some of the various Indian tribes and where they lived. "The Cheyenne don't live as far south as Mexico."

"What is the difference?" Harriet screamed. "They are all the same! Apache, Comanche, Cheyenne—I blame all Indians, damn them to hell! Antoine Leroux, Jubal Sage, Hunter Beaudine—I blame all scouts, who lead our brave troops into danger through their own arrogance, ignorance, or outright deception!" She pounded her hands on the packed earth floor, her eyes glittering with a rage that verged on madness. "And now I am here in the midst of savages, at my husband's misguided command, and his precious life—and my nephew's—rests in the hands of your damnable *scout!*"

"Their lives are in good hands," Sarah said stiffly. "Just as ours are."

"Only with God's help," Harriet snarled.

Someone touched Sarah's shoulder, and she turned to see Lucy's concerned dark face, and behind her, Libby's young one.

"It don't do no good to talk to her when she's like this," Lucy whispered.

Sarah nodded, feeling weary to her soul. So many things now made sense. She glanced at Harriet, who seemed to have fallen in on herself again.

"Let me see to her," Libby said quietly.

Again Sarah nodded, and backed out of the tipi, only to find herself the center of a group of shocked and concerned people. One obvious detriment to life in a tipi, Sarah decided, was the ease with which raised voices carried through the hide walls.

Gray Eagle stood at the edge of the group, tall and proud in his beaded buckskins, his long black hair moving in the wind. Theodora waited next to him. Sarah made her way to them.

"Did you hear?" she asked.

Theodora nodded. "We couldn't help it."

Suddenly embarrassed, Sarah looked up at Gray Eagle's handsome, impassive face, into his kind eyes, eyes so like Orion's. "I'm sorry for the hateful things she said about you and your brothers."

"It's not your fault, little sister." Gray Eagle shrugged. "At least now I understand why she hates my family." His brow furrowed. "She mentioned both Mexico and Antoine Leroux. I wonder if her son was with the Cooke expedition in '46."

"What was that?" Sarah asked.

"After the capture of Santa Fe during the Mexican War, General Kearny sent a captain named Cooke to find a viable wagon route from Santa Fe to San Diego, California. Leroux was the guide—he's one of the best there is—but Cooke didn't follow his advice and instead took what became a longer and more dangerous route in an attempt to save six miles, then accused Leroux of being ignorant of the area."

"Were the explorers attacked?"

"I never heard that they were; over four hundred men went on that expedition, including a battalion of Mormon volunteers. Few people of any race are going to attack a group that size. But that doesn't mean there wasn't Indian trouble along the way—stragglers picked off, wood-gathering parties attacked." Gray Eagle shrugged again. "The expedition went through lands belonging to many different tribes, and some are less friendly than others."

"I'm sorry she lost her son," Theodora said. "But it isn't right for her to blame all Indians and all scouts. Her grief has been twisted into hatred."

Sarah nodded in agreement, and refrained from saying that she feared for Harriet's sanity. No wonder both Adam and Colonel Rutledge were so protective of her. "Nothing is ever simple, is it?" she asked quietly.

Gray Eagle raised an eyebrow. "What do you mean?"

"I viewed Harriet as prejudiced and mean-spirited because of some of her attitudes. Now I know she has what she believes are good reasons for feeling and acting as she does. I don't agree with her, but at least I can understand her a little better. We all have reasons for what we do. Sometimes those reasons just don't make sense to other people."

"Maybe sometimes our own reasons don't even make sense to us," Theodora added.

Both Sarah and Gray Eagle laughed.

"I would agree with that," said Gray Eagle.

"Me, too," Sarah chimed in. She looked up at the man she felt was a brother to her now, just as Joseph was. "I hate how some people react to you, Gray Eagle, yet you seem to take it all in stride."

"One gets used to it."

Sarah eyed him doubtfully. "Truly?"

After a moment, he shook his head, causing his eagle feather to flutter. "No. It's more accurate to say that I have learned to accept it."

"Well, I don't know that I'll be able to," Sarah declared. "I wanted to slap Harriet for how she spoke of you, and I might have, if she hadn't been so pathetic."

"So fiercely protective, just like a Beaudine. You'll fit into the family well, little sister." He smiled at her, then walked away, leaving Sarah with a warm feeling in her heart.

The braves who escorted Lieutenant Roe back to the besieged Army encampment returned to the village late that night, with the report that Callahan had made it safely inside without raising an alarm. Although Theodora and Sarah were relieved, there was still cause for worry, and worry they did until Orion returned late in the afternoon the next day. His arrival was announced by yips and cheers from the Cheyenne and by the excited barking of the numerous dogs.

Sarah stood next to Gray Eagle, watching as Orion approached. Once again he rode Thunder, sitting tall and graceful in the saddle, keeping the excited, prancing stallion at a trot. In one hand he held the lead ropes of the two horses he and Jubal had borrowed. The wind blew his long, uncovered hair back from his face and sent the fringe on his leggings and his buckskin shirt dancing. And even from a distance, Sarah could see the intensity of his green eyes, could feel the heat as his gaze found her, settled on her. Love welled up in her, along with a deep sense of pride and the stirrings of desire. Orion Beaudine was *her* man. And he had come for her. She could not wait to touch him, to feel the vitality of his strength, the warmth of his power, the wonder of his love.

He pulled Thunder to a halt in front of her.

"Greetings, brother," said Gray Eagle.

"Brother." Orion handed the reins of the two horses to a brave, then lifted one leg over the front of his saddle and slid to the ground. He could not take his eyes from Sarah. Did she have any idea what a picture she made, standing there with his brother? She wore a black skirt and the gray jacket from her riding outfit. His beaded necklace lay between the mounds of her breasts. Her hair was pulled back in a simple braid, and dark tendrils curled around her face.

Her eyes, so very blue, seemed to shine. He could feel her love for him vibrating in the cool air. Wordlessly, he pulled her into his arms.

"My beloved," she whispered.

For a moment, Orion could not speak. He rested his cheek against her head, breathing deeply of the sweet scent that was Sarah, and felt their hearts beat as one. His soul had come home.

"The attackers were routed." Orion sat near the fire in the crowded yet quiet tipi, holding Sarah's hand firmly in his. The eyes of the women were riveted on him. "Jubal and I reached Fort Laramie yesterday, and the reinforcements set out in less than an hour. We were waiting for them when they launched their first attack this morning. It didn't take long."

"Did we lose anyone?" Theodora asked, her brows drawn together in worry.

"Altogether, seven dead, over twenty wounded, a few seriously. Lieutenant Roe is virtually unscathed, as is Major Dillard. Lieutenant Gates suffered a superficial head wound, Captain Rutledge was wounded in the left arm, and Colonel Rutledge in the right leg. All are expected to fully recover." He saw tears form in Libby's eyes, Harriet showed no visible reaction, and Penelope closed her eyes, her relief palpable.

Neville pulled on her sleeve. "Is Papa all right?" he asked in an urgent whisper.

"Yes, darling, he is." Penelope hugged the child to her.

"How is Private Trenton?" Sarah asked.

"Still fighting for his life. His wound is among the most serious."

"And the horses?"

"We lost some, of course, but Star is fine, as are most of them. As close to the river as they were, the horses and mules could smell the water, and by this morning it was difficult to control them."

"So close and yet so far," Lucy murmured.

"Exactly. But all is well now."

Sarah looked up at him. "Who were they, Orion?"

"They were not Cheyenne," Orion said firmly, his gaze boring into Harriet Rutledge. "We estimate that, all together, there were between forty and fifty men, most of them wild young Indians from various tribes. Several white men led them, mostly disgruntled fur trappers who, now that the beaver trade has died, have lost their way of making a living. Cutler recruited them—white man and Indian alike—with promises of riches and women." He let that sink in for a moment, because he felt that a few of the women—namely, Penelope Dillard and Harriet Rutledge, who, very uncharacteristically, had not spoken at all—did not appreciate how lucky they were.

"So it was Cutler," Theodora said softly.

"Yes. But you don't have to worry about him anymore. He fell in the final battle, when we had them on the run." He looked around at the silent group. "You'll spend one more night here, and tomorrow, Jubal will bring troops and transportation."

"Why didn't they come with you?" demanded Penelope.

His patience wearing thin, Orion explained, "Because Colonel Rutledge and Captain Beaudine felt it was more important to transport the wounded first. One more night won't hurt you; you've been cared for here."

"Speak for yourself, Mr. Beaudine," Penelope said huffily. "This has been a terrifying ordeal, one from which I shall never recover. Nor shall my poor children."

"Your children will be fine, if you'll leave them alone," Libby snapped. "You are more of a problem for them than the Cheyenne are, Mrs. Dillard. Stop complaining and just be thankful your husband is still alive. Some of those poor soldiers aren't, and it easily could have been one of our husbands."

Penelope gaped at her, stunned into silence.

"Well said, Mrs. Gates." Orion released Sarah's hand and scrambled to his feet, crouching low. "I'm going to clean up. If you have any questions later, please feel free to ask me." He backed out of the tipi and stood up, stretching his stiff body, wondering if Mrs. Rutledge and Mrs. Dillard had made this whole episode miserable for all the others. He suspected they had. With a sigh, Orion started in the direction of the bathing pool. Gray Eagle fell into step beside him.

"How did it go?" Gray Eagle asked.

Orion shrugged. "They aren't happy about staying here one more night."

"Did you think they would be?"

"No, but I still find it annoying. Some of them don't realize how close this came to being a real disaster, Eagle. If those renegades had been better organized and better disciplined, they could have annihilated the entire column the first day. I think the surprise of their initial attack was ruined by a few overeager fools, and that mistake gave us time to find some kind of shelter. And why didn't they use flaming arrows to fire the wagons? The troops had nothing to fight fire with except the water in their canteens. Firing the wagons would have destroyed one protective barrier and panicked the animals into a stampede."

"When he returned from escorting Lieutenant Roe back to the encampment, Running Bear said he was surprised that none of the attackers had circled around the bluff to try to come in the back."

"I know. That's just another example of their overall ineptitude. It doesn't make sense. Bartholomew Cutler was smarter than that. But now he's dead, and I can't ask him."

Gray Eagle eyed him thoughtfully. "Something's eating at you."

Orion led the way through a convenient thicket of willow

bushes that surrounded the bathing pool and offered bathers some degree of privacy. One lone brave rested in the water on the far side of the pool. Orion nodded a greeting at him, then pulled his shirt off over his head. "I think someone in the Army is involved. I suspect it's an officer, one who has access to valuable information, such as when our column was marching to Fort Laramie. And I think that person's only goal was to start a war between the Army and all the tribes, so he could be promoted on the field of glory." Leaning against a rock, Orion removed his boots.

"Any idea who?"

"Fielding." He loosened the knots that secured his leggings to the rawhide band around his waist.

"Can you prove it?"

"Not yet. Joseph will look into it when we return to Fort Laramie."

"Is he coming tomorrow?"

"Yes." Orion removed his loincloth and the rawhide band at his waist, then, with a heartfelt sigh, stepped into the warm water.

"Good." Gray Eagle smiled when Orion groaned in pleasure as the soothing water closed over his shoulders. "I'll leave you to bathe in peace, big brother."

Orion's only response was a weak wave of his hand.

Sarah took a few stumbling steps backwards, her hand over her mouth, her heart pounding wildly. Briefly, she closed her eyes as the familiar and too-long-denied sensual fire again raged in her lower stomach.

Hoping to speak privately with him, she had followed Orion from the tipi. She had not intended to catch him undressing for his bath, but she was not sorry she had. Even now, as she hurried away, she knew that the image of him standing on the bank of the steaming pond—the back of his beautiful, naked body revealed to her—would be branded in her memory for the rest of her life. If Gray Eagle and the other man had not been there, she would have torn her own clothes off and joined Orion in the inviting water.

Frantically, Sarah looked around, searching for a place where she could sit in some degree of privacy. She needed to collect herself.

She needed to be alone so that she could enjoy the images in her mind without interruption.

"Sarah."

Guiltily, she whirled around at the sound of Gray Eagle's voice. "Yes?" she managed to say, refusing to meet his eyes, wondering if he had seen her spying on his brother.

"If you need to speak with Orion, he shouldn't be too long in his bath. I plan to check on him in a few minutes, to make sure he doesn't fall asleep and drown. I'll tell him you're looking for him." Gray Eagle's voice was warm with understanding and a touch of humor.

Sarah gritted her teeth. He had seen her. "Thank you, but it isn't important. I'll see him later."

Gray Eagle reached out to gently lift her chin. "Don't be ashamed because you enjoy the sight of your man's body, little sister. It is part of the gift of love, the pleasure a man and a woman take in each other's bodies."

The fire in Sarah's belly died out and was reborn in her face. Embarrassed and mortified, she could not speak, although the expression on Gray Eagle's face was one of kindness and affection.

"I think you and my brother are long overdue for some time alone," Gray Eagle murmured, almost to himself. A secretive smile curved his lips as he patted Sarah's shoulder and hurried away.

Sarah stared after him in numb amazement.

Twenty-seven

"I'll be glad to leave here tomorrow, if for no other reason than I'll no longer have to listen to Penelope Dillard complain," Theodora said as she tossed a pebble into the creek later that day.

Sarah understood the obvious irritation in her friend's voice. After three days, the crowded quarters of the tipi were getting on everyone's nerves, and Penelope's periodic outbursts and Harriet's petulant, stony silence only made matters worse. In desperation, she and Theodora had gone on a walk after a simple but filling supper of roasted buffalo, even though the sun had gone down and winter's chill was in the air. Sarah pulled her cape more closely around her. "Everyone will be relieved, including the Cheyenne, I'm sure. Someone gave up their tipi for us, you know. They don't keep empty ones available for guests, like a hotel."

"I thought as much." Theodora looked at Sarah. "They are a fascinating people, aren't they?"

"The Cheyenne? Yes. Orion is thinking of spending the remainder of the winter here. I would welcome the chance to learn more of their ways, maybe even some of their language."

"You wouldn't mind living here?"

"No, not for a few months. Think about it, Theo. That tipi is warmer and more comfortable than our little cabin was."

"That's true," Theodora admitted. "It's crowded now, but

it would be quite nice for just two people." She sent a teasing smile in Sarah's direction. "Especially newlyweds."

Sarah waved her comment off.

"So, when is the wedding?" Theodora persisted.

"I don't know yet." Sarah bent and picked up a small rock. Some of her frustration was evident in the strength with which she threw the rock into the water. "We haven't had a chance to talk about it since the battle."

Theodora shook her head in sympathy. "You and the Hunter haven't had a chance to be alone in a long time." She pursed her lips in thought. "Actually, you've never really been alone, except in small snatches of time here and there, usually outside, and in freezing weather."

"I know. Believe me, I know."

"You'd better get married right away, Sarah, just as soon as we return to Fort Laramie. Otherwise you'll both go mad with wanting each other."

"It's too late," Sarah said mournfully. "I'm already mad."

"So am I." Orion's voice came from a stand of trees on the right. He stepped into view. "I didn't mean to eavesdrop, ladies. I couldn't help but hear."

"It's all right, Hunter," said Theodora. She wrapped her arms around herself. "I'm getting chilled. I think I'll go back."

"Theo, you were as anxious to get away from Mrs. Dillard as I was," Sarah protested. "You don't need to leave."

"Yes, I do, Sarah. Your man wants you all to himself." She turned and began to retrace her steps. "Keep her warm, Hunter," she called over her shoulder. "I won't wait up for you, Sarah." She disappeared, leaving Sarah alone with Orion in the quiet, frosty dusk.

"Theodora is a good friend," Orion said as he came closer and put his arms around Sarah. Before she could comment, he lowered his mouth to hers and kissed her hungrily, deeply, until she was clinging to him and gasping for air. "I have wanted to do that for days," he said huskily.

"I've wanted you to do that for days," Sarah whispered.

"Gray Eagle said you were looking for me earlier."

The heat of a blush warmed Sarah's face. Did Gray Eagle also tell Orion *where* she had been looking for him? "I told him it wasn't anything important. I was just curious to know how long you think it will take us to get to Fort Laramie from here."

"Less than a day, because there will be no wagons to wait for. I suspect some of the ladies will be dismayed to learn that they will either ride a horse or walk to Fort Laramie."

"Harriet won't be pleased."

"It can't be helped. There's no trail fit for wagons from here." He caressed her back. "Gray Eagle told me about how the Rutledges lost their son. Now a lot of things make sense."

"I know. It's tragic, isn't it?" Sarah snuggled closer to him. "I feel bad for Harriet, but I don't want to talk about her right now."

"What do you want to talk about?"

Sarah kissed Orion's recently shaved cheek, wondering where he had found a razor. "I can't bear it much longer, Orion," she murmured. Her mouth moved against his lips as she spoke. "I want the freedom to touch you, to kiss you, to hold you, whenever I want to." She nipped his bottom lip with the edge of her teeth. "I feel I shall surely die if I don't soon get that freedom."

Orion moaned, deep in his throat, and took her mouth in a fierce, bruising kiss. Sarah returned his kiss with equal passion, feeling a surge of womanly power like none she had ever known. Rising on tiptoe, she tangled her hands in his long, clean hair, slanted her mouth more advantageously against his, pressed her breasts to his chest with wanton abandonment, slowly rotated her hips in the hypnotic, age-old dance of love. If she could have, she would have crawled into him, body and soul, so deep and complete was her love for him, her desire for him.

Finally, with a visible shudder, Orion pulled away from

her, grabbed her hands when she reached for him and held them to his heaving chest. "Sarah."

For a long moment, they stared at each other. "You started the fire in me again, Orion," she whispered, clinging to his hands. "When are you going to put it out?"

He did not answer her, although something flashed in his eyes, something primal and powerful. She squinted up at him in the fast-disappearing light. "What is it?"

Orion merely looked at her. One hand still held both of hers, but with his other he caressed her cheek. Confused, she pressed her head into his hand. When she opened her mouth to speak, he laid a gentle finger over her lips.

"My brother has given us a gift," he said softly.

Why was he changing the subject? More confused than ever, Sarah repeated, "A gift?"

"Would you like to see it?"

Fighting a sense of disappointment, Sarah replied, "I suppose."

Without warning, Orion swept her up into his arms and started walking in the direction of the village. He didn't say anything, and so neither did Sarah. She looped her arms around his neck, content for the moment just to be near him. They passed several tipis, all lit from inside with the comforting glow of the life-saving fires. Sarah was struck again by the calm quiet of the camp, which must have housed at least one hundred people.

The journey in Orion's arms ended all too soon, for he set her on her feet and stepped back, facing her. He waved an arm behind him, in the direction of a tipi, which she noticed was on the edge of the encampment.

"This is ours for tonight, if we want it."

Sarah looked up at the tipi rising into the night. Like the others, the hide walls glowed with golden, welcoming firelight, and the protective arms of a brush windbreak came around the sides. Her heart started hammering as the full meaning of his words sunk in. "Ours alone?" she whispered.

Orion nodded.

"This was Gray Eagle's gift?"

He nodded again. "Do you want the gift, Sarah? Do you want me?"

She met his gaze, his loving, hopeful gaze, suddenly aware of many sensations. The wind had come up, and now it blew Orion's hair back from his face, just as it pressed her skirts against her legs. Although touched with the scent of wood smoke and roasting buffalo, the chilled, invigorating air smelled clean, and Sarah drew it deeply into her lungs. From far away came the plaintive call of a coyote, which was answered by a quick yip from one of the village dogs.

In that moment, standing in a Cheyenne village, facing Orion Beaudine, Sarah Hancock was more certain of herself than she had ever been in her entire life. Indeed, she felt that everything in her life had happened as if it had been planned, so that she would be led to this moment, in this place, with this man. A deep joy filled her, until she felt she would burst with the wonder of it, or at least cry, as her tearing eyes indicated.

But this was not the time for tears, not even those of joy. Sarah pulled her braid forward over her shoulder and loosened the tie at the end. With her fingers and a quick shake of her head, she freed her long hair from its prison and let it lay about her shoulders and fall down her back. "I want this gift, Orion," she said quietly. "I want you, with all of my heart."

Sarah recognized the answering leap of joy in Orion's eyes as he held his hand out to her. She stepped toward him and took it, loving the feel of his skin as his fingers closed around hers. He led her to the tipi, threw back the door flap, guided her inside, and followed, allowing the flap to fall into place behind him.

Hunched over because of the low roof near the door, Sarah looked around the neat, cozy interior of the tipi and saw that all physical comforts had been provided for. A welcoming fire burned in the fire pit—with extra wood piled neatly to the left of the door—inviting furs and buffalo robes lay about the raised earthen sleeping ledge, a few backrests waited to support the weary. She moved farther into the tipi, circling around the fire to the left, remembering Gray Eagle's explanation of the tradition that, upon entering a tipi, men went to the right and women to the left. Seeming out of place in the native decor, a cast-iron teakettle sat near the fire, next to two carved wooden cups and a tin of tea. Behind the fire, a thin wisp of aromatic smoke rose from something smoldering in a bowl on what Sarah recognized as an altar of sorts.

"What is that?" she asked Orion, pointing at the bowl.

"Sweetgrass. The Cheyenne believe it purifies the spirit." He moved around the fire to the right until he reached the back of the tipi, where, thanks to the clever asymmetrical arrangement of the support poles, he could stand up straight, and held his hands out to the sides. "What do you think?"

Sarah nodded her approval. "It is perfect." She met Orion's gaze. "Everything is perfect."

Orion shrugged out of his buffalo robe coat and threw it aside. "Would you like some tea?"

Was he suddenly nervous? Sarah wondered. She found the idea both touching and amusing, and watched him carefully as she untied her cape. "No, thank you." She held his gaze with her own as she slipped the cape off and dropped it on the sleeping ledge behind her. She started on the buttons down the front of her riding jacket. "I want you."

It seemed that the fire leaped from the pit to his eyes. Again, he held his hand out. "Then come to me," he invited in a husky whisper.

Sarah let the riding jacket join the cape. Her freed hair fell around her, covering her shoulders and arms, sending the faint scent of lavender to her nose. She tossed the dark, fragrant mass back over her shoulders and stepped forward to take Orion's hand.

He pulled her closer, so that he could touch her hair. "I have dreamed of this moment," he whispered, lifting a lock to his lips.

Sarah melted inside at the look of love in his green eyes. "So have I." She leaned forward to kiss him, softly, then turned her back to him, pulling her hair forward over one shoulder so that the row of hooks down the back of her bodice was presented to him. Orion wasted no time in responding to the unspoken invitation. She felt the air on her bared skin above her chemise, and shuddered in pleasure when she realized that his mouth was moving over that same skin. Shivers ran down her body as his hands moved to her shoulders, then down her arms, pushing the bodice off. His arms encircled her waist from behind, and he pulled her back against him.

"Oh, Sarah," he murmured. "My beautiful woman."

He planted a kiss on the side of her exposed neck, sending a new wave of shivers through her. Sarah felt her nipples tighten even before his hands moved up to caress her breasts. A curious heat started in her lower stomach, and curled downward. She reached back to grab his hips and pull him closer.

Orion moaned and whirled her around to face him. His hands fought with the fastening of her skirt. "I'm trying to go slow, but I'm not sure I can," he whispered. "I want to see you naked." He triumphed with her skirt and pushed it down over her hips, then started on the petticoats. "How many of these things do you have on?" he muttered.

"Several," Sarah purred. At his groan of frustration, she added, "It *is* winter." Then she took pity on him and offered her assistance. Soon the petticoats and skirt lay in a pool at her feet, leaving only her chemise, drawers, and boots between Orion and his goal of seeing her naked. She caught her breath at the smoldering look in his eyes as he grabbed the hem of his buckskin shirt. In one smooth movement, the garment was over his head and gone, his gaze once again boring into her. With a trembling hand, she reached out to touch his gloriously naked chest, and fulfilled a dream of her own.

She had felt that incredible expanse of warm skin and powerful muscle before, but Orion had been wounded and she had been filled with guilt. Now, her hand moved over him in joyous freedom, delighting in the feel of the soft dark hair, of the life pulsing within him. She pressed a kiss to the scar on his shoulder, then to the place over his heart, and heard him gasp.

"I'm trying to go slow," he repeated in a tortured whisper as he clasped her to him.

Showing him no mercy, Sarah allowed her greedy hands the same freedom to explore his back. Her wandering fingers found the ties to his leggings, and she toyed with a knot until a thought came to her mind. She glanced uncertainly at the hide walls of the tipi. "Can our shadows be seen from the outside?"

"Yes, somewhat, if we are standing, and if someone wants to step inside the windbreak. A second hide goes about half-way up to help insulate the interior; it's harder to see through that." He held her tight with one arm and pushed against her, using his free arm to break their fall onto the sleeping ledge. "Perhaps we should lie down."

He landed on top of her, and Sarah loved the feel of his weight, of his warmth, of his necklace pressing into her breast, of the intriguing hardness against her leg. She clung to him. "I love you, Orion Beaudine," she whispered.

Orion raised himself up on his elbows, brushed the hair away from her face, held her head between his hands. "And I love you, Sarah Hancock." Reverently, he kissed her, and gradually, the passion grew, until Sarah could stand it no more. She pulled her mouth from his.

"Take these off," she ordered, tugging at the knot of his leggings.

He needed no further encouragement. In a matter of seconds, he was naked beside her, and her boots lay near the fire. His hand boldly searched under her chemise for the tie of her drawers, and when he found it, a simple tug released it, and slowly, he worked the garment down over her hips and legs. Then he pulled her to a sitting position and reached for the hem of her chemise. Sarah helped him by raising her arms, and that garment was gone, too. Now, in fulfillment of another dream, she sat before him wearing nothing but his beaded necklace.

She had not anticipated that she would feel shy. But she did, and, closing her eyes, fought the urge to cover her breasts with her hair, with her hands, with anything she could. Then she felt Orion's tentative touch, his gentle fingers on her skin, his intake of breath when his thumb brushed across an aching nipple. Or was it she who gasped? Sarah's eyes flew open, and she was startled by the expression on his face— love, wonder, desire—they were all there, and any sense of shyness she felt fled.

"You are so beautiful," he whispered. As she watched, he slowly leaned forward and touched the tip of his tongue to the nipple his thumb had just left, and an agony of pleasure shot through her, so intense that she feared she would faint. Unable to bear it, she fell back on the furs, and he followed, his mouth latching onto her nipple. She cried out, softly, and it was as if something in him broke, some kind of restraint, for suddenly, his hands were everywhere, his mouth was eve- rywhere, caressing, teasing, tormenting, his long hair follow- ing the touch of his lips with its own soft, erotic whisper against her quivering skin.

Now it was he who showed no mercy.

While his ravenous, talented mouth explored her breasts, one hand stroked the length of her legs, parted them, and explored the wet warmth between them. At his shocking, maddening touch, Sarah instinctively raised her hips, inviting him nearer, inviting him in. But he only moved his fingers over her, giving her feelings she had not known existed, feelings and sensations that grew, and grew more, and more, until she exploded in a burst of ecstasy. Again, she cried out, and clung to him, stunned. At last his maddening fingers stilled, and he whispered loving words to her, words she could not make out over the sound of her heated blood pounding through her veins.

Then he was between her legs himself, his male hardness begging for permission to enter. Sarah heard the silent entreaty of Orion's body, of his heart, and she opened herself up in every way, pulling him in. He plunged deep, caught her surprised gasp of pain with his mouth, apologized to her for hurting her by planting gentle kisses all over her face. But her body grew used to his presence, and, impatient now, she tightened around him, bucked against him, urged him on, and all gentleness between them was gone.

She welcomed his powerful thrusts, reveled in his strength, wondered at the pleasure he was building in her again. In that moment, Sarah loved being a woman, loved Orion for being a man, loved the gift nature had given them in the urge to mate. Never had she been so alive. She was so alive that when he again took her over the edge, Sarah felt that they were flying across the sky. The tears of joy threatened again, and she clung to him, heard his soft cry of pleasure, felt the pulsing of his body deep within her. And she knew she had glimpsed heaven.

Orion looked down at the woman nestled next to him and wondered what he had done in his life to deserve being so blessed. Sarah's head rested on his shoulder, her arm curved over his stomach under the protective covering of the buffalo robe he had pulled over them, her soft breath caressed his chest as she dozed. His necklace still encircled her neck; he could feel the beads pressing into his side. She had awed him tonight with her unrestrained love, with her innocent and enthusiastic acceptance of his touch and his body. She had welcomed the gift he had made her of his heart and soul, had reciprocated by giving him her heart and soul, and now they were one. They were bound together forever.

Throughout the long night, they loved, and slept, and loved again. Orion made tea, which they sipped while he explained that he had asked the tribal council for permission to spend the winter with the Cheyenne, if she was agreeable. Sarah was, and they discussed their plans for acquiring their own tipi and other necessities. When the tea was gone, they snuggled together under the buffalo robe and shared their dreams for the future, until sleep claimed them again.

Sarah awakened early in the morning, feeling warm and content, relishing the warmth of Orion at her side. She never wanted to move from his embrace, not ever, not for the rest of her life. The ridiculous thought brought a smile to her face, one that fled when she suddenly realized that there was a dark form lying in front of the door opening. She stiffened.

"What is it?" Orion asked sleepily. His hand took a lazy journey over the curve of her hip.

"Someone's in here."

In a flash, Orion was on his knees in front of her, knife in hand. Sarah pulled the robe over her breasts and fearfully peered around him. A furry head raised, revealing two golden eyes.

"Dancer!" she breathed.

Orion stepped down from the sleeping ledge and circled the fire pit, apparently unconcerned with his graceful nudity. Just watching him move stirred the fires of desire in Sarah's belly again, and she wondered if she would ever get enough of him. To pull her mind back from the path toward which it was veering, she asked, "How did he get in here?"

"He pushed the flap over with his nose." Orion scratched

between the wolf's ears. "Dancer can be very creative when he wants something badly enough."

"I'm so glad he's all right. I hate it when I don't see him for days. A part of me is afraid I may never see him again."

"That might happen some day." He took pieces of wood from the pile.

"I know." A curious sadness settled over Sarah's heart as she watched her lover—her *lover!*—build up the fire. She didn't want to tell him that she felt the same fear for him when he left on a scouting mission, that she knew there was always the possibility he would not come back, that he would die in the wilderness he so loved, as he almost had not so long ago. But she could not ask Orion to stop being a scout any more than she could ask Dancer to stop being a wolf.

Orion straightened from tending the fire. "What's wrong?"

"Just a bit of reality creeping in." Sarah took in his naked splendor and trembled, then flung back the buffalo robe in invitation. "Help me keep it at bay for a while longer."

She saw the first stirrings of his fascinating manhood and felt again a surge of feminine power. Orion paused to pet the dozing Dancer once more, then joined her on the sleeping ledge. As he took her in his arms, she said, "I guess now we'd better get married as soon as we reach Fort Laramie."

Orion pulled her on top of him, pulled her legs apart over his hips, pulled her hair back behind her shoulders. She nestled against him, thrilled to feel his hardening length grow against her stomach.

"Well?" she asked, nibbling on his lip. "What do you think?"

"According to the Cheyenne, we're already married."

Sarah's eyes widened in surprise for more than one reason, for as he spoke, Orion grabbed her hips and lifted her slightly, then positioned himself and settled her down again, filling her as he did. Slow and sure, he began to rock under her, into her. "How are we . . . already . . . married?" she whispered as her eyes drifted closed.

"By sharing this tipi." He grazed on her neck, sending shivers down her body and causing her nipples to tighten.

"That's . . . it?"

"Well, there's usually a little more to it." Orion grabbed her shoulders and eased her up into a sitting position, an action which allowed his necklace to hang down between her breasts and, as Sarah discovered, had other interesting consequences, as well.

First, her breasts, aching for his touch, were now exposed, a situation Orion quickly and mercifully took advantage of, putting his hands to good use.

No, Sarah decided after further deliberation. To *wonderful* use.

Another consequence—her legs naturally spread farther, giving her greater movement and control, allowing her to draw him deeper, so deep that she felt he touched her soul.

And another, one in which Sarah took particular delight—Orion's breathing suddenly seemed, well, labored. And he apparently had lost his train of thought.

"Pray continue with . . . your description of a . . . Cheyenne wedding," she encouraged.

"The groom brings . . . horses."

"I get a . . . new horse?"

"And there is a . . . feast." As if to make his point, Orion pushed himself up on his elbows and feasted on her nipple.

"I . . . like a feast."

He pushed up farther, so that he was sitting, which freed his hands to grab her hips.

"What . . . else?" Sarah urged.

"Uh . . . gifts."

"I can . . . have gifts?"

Orion's grip tightened and his thrusts took on an added urgency. "You can have . . . anything . . . you want. Oh, Sarah!" Her name ended with a low cry and he strained against her as his seed pumped into her, sending her over the edge with him.

Sarah clung to him, drowning in wave after wave of pleasure. Orion fell back on the bed furs, taking her with him, pulling a buffalo robe over them. They lay together, their hearts pounding.

When her breathing calmed enough for her to speak, Sarah whispered, "I already have everything I want."

Orion's arm tightened around her while his other hand stroked her hair. "Then I guess we're already married." He kissed her forehead. "Wife."

"Husband," Sarah murmured against his chest. She pressed another kiss over his heart.

They were married.

Twenty-eight

"I'm sure going to miss that pool," Lucy said with a sigh of contentment as she, Sarah, and Theodora approached the women's tipi following their bath the next morning.

"That's for sure," Theodora added.

Sarah said nothing, for she was going to have the use of the pool through the rest of the winter. She feared she was in danger of becoming addicted to the soothing waters.

Orion had sent her off to bathe with the women, and she had gone, even though she had longed to share the pool with only him, to fulfill yet another dream, but she doubted the opportunity would arise while they lived with the Cheyenne. The pool was simply used too often, and the Cheyenne followed strict rules of etiquette. Young boys and girls bathed together, but never men and women. Someday, Sarah had vowed as the healing water eased the unfamiliar but satisfying soreness between her legs, she and Orion would bathe together—make love together—in a heated pool.

Still, she had enjoyed her visit with Theo and Lucy, neither of whom appeared to consider odd her announcement that she and Orion were now married. They had both expressed their disappointment that she would not be traveling with them to Fort Laramie, but they seemed to be genuinely happy for her. However, as she approached the women's tipi, Sarah suspected others would not be as understanding.

The women at the tipi were involved in a flurry of activity, preparing for their journey later that day. Their relief at the impending departure was pathetically visible, even though Sarah doubted the soldiers would arrive for several hours yet. Little Neville and Clarissa raced about, excited beyond measure, and completely ignored their harried mother's admonitions that they sit quietly.

Even Harriet Rutledge had ventured forth from the tipi and now sat on a tied bundle of clothing, her breath visible in the chilled morning air. Sarah was shocked by the woman's appearance, for Harriet's complexion was deathly pale, with the exception of the dark half-circles under her eyes. There was nothing pale about her eyes, though, which grew dark with hatred when she saw Sarah.

"You dare show your face here, among decent women and children?" she demanded.

"I have done nothing to be ashamed of," Sarah responded. On the contrary, she felt proud and joyous, which, she mused, probably added to Harriet's sense of outrage. "Orion Beaudine and I are married."

"How wonderful!" Libby came forward to give Sarah a quick hug. "Congratulations."

Over Libby's shoulder, Sarah caught a glimpse of the startled laundresses, of Penelope Dillard's shocked expression, of Harriet's disbelieving one.

"Thank you, Libby," she said.

Harriet jumped to her feet. "You aren't married," she spat, wagging an accusatory finger in Sarah's face. "You and that man are fornicators!"

Sarah caught Harriet's waving hand in hers and stepped very close to the woman. "You are wrong, Harriet," she said, her voice low and quiet. "But I'll not argue with you again. For the sake of the children, please keep your thoughts about my marriage to yourself."

If it were possible, Harriet's face turned even whiter. Her mouth abruptly closed on whatever she was going to say, and, with a glance at the two now-very-quiet and obviously fascinated children, she sank back down on her bundle of clothing.

Sarah looked down at the woman who seemed to be a shadow of her former formidable self. Lucy had confirmed earlier that Harriet still refused food, still refused to sleep. A wave of pity rose up in Sarah. "There's no reason for this battle between us to continue," she said gently. "Everything is over. I am no threat to you, to Adam, or to your way of life."

Harriet merely turned her face away.

"Here are your things." Libby handed Sarah the tied bundle of clothing she had left in the tipi the night before.

"Thank you." Sarah managed a smile. "I'll come and see you off."

"You're not coming with us?" Libby asked, frowning.

"No. Orion and I are going to spend the winter here. We'll come to Fort Laramie in a week or so to get my things, and to stock up on some supplies. I'll call on you then." She smiled at Theodora and Lucy, then turned and left.

Outside their tipi, Orion greeted her with a loving kiss and an enveloping hug. "I missed you, Mrs. Beaudine."

All of Sarah's negative thoughts and feelings fled in the warmth of his love, and she dropped the bundle of clothing to wrap her arms around him. "I missed you, too, especially in the pool."

"In the pool?"

"Someday I want to bathe with you in a heated pool."

"Mm." Orion nibbled on her ear. "Sounds like fun."

Sarah closed her eyes at the shivers that raced down her body. "It will be." She swatted his rear. "But you'd best get to your own bath, before I drag you back inside."

"That sounds like fun, too."

With a laugh, Sarah pushed him away. "Go, you insatiable man."

"All right," Orion grumbled.

"Where is Dancer?" Sarah called after him.

"He took off a while ago, when the village really started stirring. He'll be back."

"Who'll be back?" Gray Eagle asked as he approached.

"Dancer," Orion replied.

Sarah stared at Gray Eagle, at the imposing, beautiful Cheyenne warrior who was now her brother. Love and gratitude welled up inside her, and she went to him and took his hands. "Thank you, my brother," she said sincerely. "Your gift to us was priceless."

A pleased smile lit his handsome face. "Welcome to the family, Sarah Beaudine." He drew her into a warm embrace, which she gladly returned.

"Thank you," Sarah said again, deeply moved. "I always wanted a big family."

"You have one now," Orion said. "A husband, two brothers, two sisters, and a mother. Come spring, I'll take you to St. Louis so you can meet the rest of the clan."

"I can't wait." Sarah stepped back. "But you'd best get to your bath, or I'll follow through with my earlier threat."

"All right, all right." Orion looked at his brother. "We've been married for less than a day, and already she's bossing me around."

Gray Eagle shook his head in mock regret.

"I'm off to the pool," Orion added. "Want to come along?"

"Sure."

The brothers turned away.

"What was her earlier threat?" Gray Eagle asked.

"Something about dragging me back inside the tipi if I didn't get to the pool."

Gray Eagle stared at him. "And you're going to take a *bath?*"

Sarah laughed and waved them away, then ducked into the tipi herself. As she straightened the bed furs and buffalo robes, the memories of the night she had shared with Orion washed over her—memories of the things they had done to each other, of the pleasure and, most importantly, the love each had given and received. "Lord have mercy," she muttered. "I'll never get anything done if I don't put that man out of my mind." She gave herself a mental shake and turned to tend the fire.

The tipi was neat and organized, the water supply replenished, and a pot of stew, brought as a gift by the smiling Sweet Water, simmered on the fire when Orion stuck his head through the door opening. "The soldiers are here."

Sarah patted her hair, which she had pulled back into a neat braid, and tried to calm her suddenly nervous stomach. What was she afraid of? she wondered.

She left the tipi and, at Orion's side, walked to the edge of the village. The Cheyenne were watchful and quiet, and it occurred to Sarah that they might be uncomfortable with the soldiers knowing the location of their winter camp, of actually coming to the camp. Many people had been inconvenienced and imposed upon in order to offer sanctuary to a group of white women and children, and it irritated Sarah that some of those women were rude and ungrateful.

The approach of the twin lines of uniformed cavalrymen was impressive. Flags waved in the crisp morning air, and the men kept their mounts in formation, even though some led saddled horses. Jubal Sage and Captain Joseph Beaudine led the column. Joseph gave the command to halt and dismount a short distance from where Gray Eagle, Orion, and Sarah stood.

"Greetings, brothers," he said. "Miss Hancock."

Orion placed an arm around Sarah's shoulders. "It's Mrs. Beaudine now, Joe. You have a new sister."

Jubal Sage whooped his approval in Indian fashion, while Joseph jumped down from the saddle and caught Sarah up in a bear hug.

"Well done!" he cried. "Well done!" He pumped Orion's hand.

Sarah basked in the love and acceptance of her new family.

Then her gaze fell on Adam Rutledge. Her smile faded when he deliberately looked away from her.

A clamor behind them announced the arrival of the rest of the white women. Lieutenant Callahan Roe hurried by, making a bee-line for Theodora. He grabbed her outstretched hands and pulled her into his arms for a quick hug, then, his young face bright red, released her. Sarah could not hear what they said to each other, but her heart swelled with gladness for her friend.

"Oh, thank God!" Penelope Dillard cried as she rushed forward with Clarissa in her arms and Neville racing behind her. "Where is my husband? Captain, where is Major Dillard?"

"He's with Colonel Rutledge, ma'am, and the rest of the company," Joseph answered. "He'll be waiting for you at Fort Laramie." He looked at Libby. "The same with your husband, Mrs. Gates. You probably know he was injured."

Libby nodded, her young face tight with worry.

"He'll be fine, ma'am," Joseph assured her.

As the others gathered around Joseph and Jubal, Sarah turned to Orion. "I'll be right back," she said, with a quick glance at Adam. Orion's brow knitted with concern, but he nodded. She walked over to where Adam waited on his horse, stiff and proud, his left arm in a sling, his jaw clenched under his blonde beard. "I heard you were wounded," she said. "I hope not badly."

"Not badly." He looked down at her then. "Did I hear correctly? Did you marry him?"

"Yes."

Adam's mouth tightened. "I didn't know there was a minister here."

"We were married by Cheyenne law."

His disapproval was evident, "Convenient, but not legally binding. You'll have to have a Christian ceremony when you return to the fort."

"There's no reason to. Orion and I are married as surely

as if we stood before God himself." Which Sarah felt they
had done, but she was certain Adam would not understand
that any more than Harriet had.

The ever-rigid Adam seemed to sag in the saddle. When
he looked down at her, Sarah saw in his blue eyes some
rekindling of the old friendship. "Do you love him, Sarah?
Does he love you?"

"Oh, yes." Sarah reached for his hand. "Be happy for me,
Adam," she begged.

"I'll try." Adam took her hand in his gauntleted one. "I
still think you've made a terrible mistake, but you have to
do what you think is best. I wish you good luck, old friend.
I fear you will need it."

Sarah shook her head. "No more than anyone else starting
out in marriage."

A strange pain flashed in Adam's eyes and was gone. "For
what it's worth, Sarah, I think Beaudine is a lucky man."

A lump formed in Sarah's throat as she stared up at the
man who had been her dearest friend for most of her life.
"That is the nicest thing you have ever said to me," she said
quietly. "Thank you."

Adam released her hand. "How is my aunt?"

"Not well."

His eyes widened in alarm, and he stepped down from the
saddle. "What's wrong with her?"

"She told me what happened to Gilbert, Adam. Feeling
as she does about Indians, this was a terrible ordeal for her.
She has refused to accept their food, refused to sleep."

"My uncle was worried about that," Adam admitted.
"That's why he sent me to fetch her. With his leg wound, he
could not have ridden this far, although he desperately
wanted to. He still feels it was for the best, though."

"I think everyone does, except Harriet and Mrs. Dillard."
Sarah turned and walked with Adam toward the group of
excited women. "Prepare yourself for her appearance." She

glanced up at him. "I fear her mind may be unsettled. She needs care."

Adam nodded wearily, and Sarah suspected the news did not surprise him at all.

At that moment, Harriet Rutledge pushed her way through the crowd of women and soldiers. Her frantic gaze fell on Adam, and she rushed toward him. "We must go, nephew, quickly, before the savages attack!" She turned on Sarah. "Get away from him, you traitor! You Indian-loving *harlot!*"

Adam caught Harriet's flailing fist and held her as best he could with only one arm. Lucy and Libby hurried forward to assist him, while Orion pulled Sarah out of the way. Even though she was supported, Harriet sagged to the ground, sobbing piteously.

Sarah turned her face to Orion's shoulder and drew strength from the feel of his loving arms around her.

It broke Sarah's heart to say goodbye to Theodora. Both women fought tears as they embraced.

"I'll see you in a week or so," Sarah promised.

Theodora nodded and brushed a tear from her cheek.

"I hate leaving you," Sarah admitted. "I'm worried about you, about how the others will treat you."

"No need, Sarah. Some of the other laundresses have warmed up to me over the last few days. Things will be better in that regard, but no one can take your place." Her lips curved in a watery smile.

"No one can take yours, either, Theo." Sarah paused. "And what of Lieutenant Roe?"

Theodora's large brown eyes took on a thoughtful expression. "If nothing else, he is my friend."

"It's a good start."

Lucy and Libby Gates approached.

"We wanted to say our goodbyes, Mrs. Beaudine," Lucy said.

"I'll miss you, Miss Lucy," Sarah said affectionately, holding out her hand, surprised when Lucy took it. "You have been a good friend to me."

"Don't start with the thank-yous," Lucy warned.

Sarah laughed. "All right." She gazed into Lucy's warm brown eyes, took in her attractive dark face, the neat, colorful scarf wrapped so intriguingly around her head, and realized how much Lucy had given with her honest if reserved friendship. She could not resist the impulse to hug her.

Lucy seemed startled, but she did not pull away. She patted Sarah's shoulder awkwardly. "You made the right choice, Mrs. Beaudine," she whispered. "Like I always told you, you'll be fine."

"I know." Sarah released her and stepped back.

"I'd best get back to the Mrs. Colonel." Lucy walked away.

"Have a safe journey," Sarah called after her. She waited a moment, then added, "Thank you!"

Lucy glared back over her shoulder and waved in annoyance, but Sarah saw the smile on her friend's face before she turned away again.

"I wish you the best of luck, Sarah," Libby said.

"Thank you, Libby." Sarah felt a surge of affection for the young woman. "You take care of that baby now."

Libby smiled down at her slightly rounded stomach and placed a hand there. "I will."

"You were a great help over the last few days."

"You sure were," Theodora added.

A frown puckered Libby's forehead. "I'll probably get in trouble when we get to Fort Laramie, for the way I talked to Mrs. Major Dillard. I don't mind her being nasty to me, but I hope she doesn't take it out on my husband somehow."

Sarah shook her head. "She can't do much damage, because everyone knows her for what she is. If word gets around about what you did, they'll probably give you a medal."

A smile teased the corners of Libby's mouth.

"Besides," Sarah continued, "Mrs. Colonel Rutledge has much more influence, and she is your ally."

"But she's ill, Sarah. Really ill. I'm worried about her."

"I know, but I think she'll feel a lot better when she is safely back at Fort Laramie, and with her husband. Remember, she has Adam, too. The Mrs. Colonel is a strong woman, Libby."

Libby nodded. "Well, it looks like we're about ready to go." She held her hand out to Sarah. "I'll never forget you."

Ignoring Libby's hand, Sarah gave her a quick hug. "Nor I, you, Libby Gates. You'll do just fine as an Army wife and as a mother. Never lose faith in yourself."

"All right. Goodbye." She hurried off.

"I'd better go, too." Theodora nodded toward Callahan Roe, who stood holding the reins of two horses. The women embraced again, and Theodora left.

Orion came to stand at Sarah's side. "Any misgivings?" he asked quietly.

"None." Sarah watched the lines form. "Ironic, isn't it? Harriet has steadfastly refused all offers of assistance from the Cheyenne, and now she is forced to lie on one of their travois if she hopes to reach Fort Laramie and her husband." She nodded in the direction of the patient horse to which the travois poles were tied. "She is so ill. I wonder if she will ever completely recover."

"From her son's death? Probably not." Orion draped his arm around her shoulder. "I'm not certain any of us ever completely recovers from what we view as a great loss. It's part of being human. Of course, most don't lose their minds."

Joseph rode toward them, pulling his mount to a halt in front of them. "I'll start the investigation into Lieutenant Fielding's possible involvement in both the attack against you and the one against the column as soon as I get back," he said.

Orion nodded.

"See you both in a few weeks." He touched the brim of

his hat and smiled at Sarah. "Be happy." He turned his mount's head and cantered away. The sound of his strong voice giving the order to move out echoed over them, and the column began to move.

Sarah stood with Orion's arm around her and watched until the column disappeared over the top of a small rise. The cold wind blew her skirt against her legs and moved Orion's long hair against her cheek. The sounds of the village behind her reached her ears—dogs barked, horses whinnied, children laughed and shouted in a language she did not yet understand. With the disappearance of the Army column, a phase of her life ended.

As she turned with Orion to go back to the village, she saw Dancer on another hill, watching. Gray Eagle stood a distance away with Jubal, Sweet Water, and Sparrow, waiting. Sarah looked at the man who walked beside her, holding her hand. Her husband.

She had made the right choice.

Twenty-nine

Sarah adapted easily to life in the Cheyenne village, with the help of Orion, Gray Eagle, Sparrow, Sweet Water, and Jubal Sage—who now insisted that she call him "Jubal" rather than "Mr. Sage," since they were practically kin. She learned that her husband was an accepted and honored member of the tribe, and the news of his marriage was well received. Because she had no family, Sarah had been somewhat disconcerted to learn that the bride's family traditionally provided a newly married couple with most of their domestic necessities, but Orion assured her there was nothing to worry about. Sweet Water and Sparrow had worked with other women in the tribe to construct a tipi for the newlyweds, and now, only a week later, Sarah and Orion had their own home.

Sarah stood inside that cozy home now, imagining how it would look when she brought some of her things from Fort Laramie in a few days. Her trunks and most of her belongings would remain in Joseph's care until the spring, when she and Orion would make the decision about where they would live, but a few things would definitely come in handy now, like cooking utensils and a few more clothes. Sarah looked down at her skirt. As the days went by, she was finding that she felt more and more out of place because she was the only person in the village who wore white man's clothes. She had taken to wearing her hair in a single braid, except when she left it unbound for Orion, and found that much more comfortable than pinning the heavy masses up on her head. Perhaps, rather than bring clothes from Fort Laramie, she should ask Sweet Water and Sparrow for help in making a buckskin dress.

"Sa-rah."

Sarah recognized Sparrow's young voice and distinctive accent. With a smile, she stepped through the door opening and allowed the hide flap to fall back into place. "Hello, Sparrow. Thank you for offering to go with me to gather wood."

"No trouble." Sparrow looked up at the sky. "The Hunter was right about a storm coming in, though. We can't go far."

"You're the boss."

"What is 'boss'?"

"Someone who tells other people what to do, and they have to do it."

Sparrow grinned. "I think I like this 'boss.' "

Sarah laughed and caught Sparrow in a quick hug. She had quickly grown to love the girl, who was Gray Eagle's niece through his mother's side of the family. Sparrow was maybe ten years old, slender and occasionally awkward, as growing children tended to be, with long, gorgeous black hair restrained in two neat braids, and a pretty face that held the promise of great beauty. She wore a buckskin dress, leggings, and moccasins, over which she had draped a buffalo robe. With absolute confidence, Sparrow led Sarah out of the village.

Thankful for the warmth of her wool cape, Sarah trudged along behind Sparrow. She would have known a change in the weather was coming, even if the dark, ominous clouds over the western mountains and Orion's prediction hadn't told her so, for she could feel a difference in the air, could smell it. Perhaps she was becoming more sensitive to the world around her, she mused. She hoped so; she would like to be more at home in the wilderness Orion knew so well.

"Do you think Orion and Gray Eagle and the rest of the men had any luck with the hunt?" Sarah asked.

"Of course." Sparrow glanced back over her shoulder. "All the men of my tribe are good hunters, but your man is the best. You will never go hungry, Sa-rah."

Sparrow led her to a stretch of low-lying land near the creek. A long-ago flood had deposited several uprooted trees of varying sizes around the area, trees that were now seasoned perfectly for firewood. Sarah could not help but think how much more beneficial a lumber saw would be than the small hatchet she carried. But the Cheyenne did not have a lumber saw, and even if they did, the men of the village would not use it to cut the huge tree trunks into manageable size. Collecting firewood was woman's work, a duty in which the women of the village took great pride.

Orion had tried to explain that the division of labor was very exact in the Cheyenne culture, that men and women had clearly defined areas of responsibility, and that their way of life was very successful. He had cautioned her not to look at the Cheyenne ways with white man's eyes, which Sarah had found to be easier said than done. She tried to understand, to refrain from judgment. Still, she thought as she chopped at a stubborn branch, a saw would come in handy.

Before long, she and Sparrow had gathered a good amount of branches, and a few lazy snowflakes had begun drifting down. From experience, Sarah knew they would tie the wood in bundles and either carry it on their backs or drag it behind them, just as she knew the large pile of branches would not be that heavy.

"I will rope the pile," Sparrow announced.

"Let me get this last branch and I'll help you." Sarah struggled with the long branch, trying to force it into position so she could use the hatchet. She finally succeeded, and was in the process of collecting the smaller pieces when she heard a strange thunking sound behind her.

Sarah turned and, to her horror, saw Sparrow face-down

on the ground. A man wearing a matted, oversized buffalo robe coat stood over the girl with a rifle in one hand, a knife in the other.

"No!" Sarah screamed. She raced toward the man, mindless of the fact that he raised his rifle to her, mindless of anything except the still girl on the ground.

"Stop right there, Sarah Hancock!"

How did he know her name? Why did his voice sound naggingly familiar? Sarah slowed to a cautious walk, strongly tempted to pull out the hatchet that was tucked into the waist of her skirt and hidden under her cape. She decided she was too far away, and so continued with her slow steps, staring at the man, desperate to figure out who he was. He was disheveled and dirty, his hat rode low on his head, and several days' growth of beard covered the lower half of his face. With a start, she saw a yellow stripe down the side of his trousers, almost completely obliterated by dirt. Not only was the man a soldier, he was an officer. Recognition dawned in her mind, as did very real fear.

"Why are you here, Lieutenant Fielding?" she demanded, her voice deliberately heavy with scorn. "Other than to kill children?"

Fielding glanced down, the contemptuous look on his face a clear indication of his opinion of Indians. "I've come for you."

Sarah forced a laugh. "You must be mad. I'm not going anywhere with you." She darted a look at Sparrow. Blood covered the side of the child's head, evidence that Fielding had clubbed her rather than stabbed her. A head wound versus a stab wound. Sarah didn't know which was worse.

It was as if Fielding hadn't heard her defiant remark. "That damned Captain Beaudine figured out my connection to Cutler. He was going to have me arrested and court-martialed!" He sounded truly affronted. "But I outsmarted them, and now I'm on my way to California, with you along as insurance."

The falling snow had increased in volume, and Sarah wondered if her flippant remark about him being mad was closer to the truth than she had at first realized. "You can't leave for California in December and expect to make it there alive," she pointed out. "Especially with the Beaudines on your trail. You won't get as far as South Pass."

"The Beaudines will back off when they learn I have you." Fielding's lip curled in derision. "If they don't, the Hunter will have to bury his little bride before he even had a chance to plant another Beaudine bastard in her."

"You fool," Sarah spat, ignoring his chilling words. The rage in her boiled up over the fear. "You're already a dead man. That child at your feet is the beloved niece of the Beaudines. Even if you do no more here, if you leave me and run away now, they'll still track you to the ends of the earth for what you did to Sparrow. If you tangle with one Beaudine, you tangle with all of them. You should know that, Lieutenant. As I recall, Captain Beaudine made it very clear on at least one occasion."

Fury flashed in Fielding's eyes. "We'll see who's right in the end, missy." He tightened his grip on the wicked-looking knife. "As soon as I slit this brat's throat, we'll be on our way."

"No!" Sarah cried. "She's already dead. You can tell by looking at her. Let me cover her face, and I'll go with you peacefully." She took a tentative step forward, praying that, by some miracle, Sparrow still lived. When Fielding said nothing, she took another. He backed up, keeping the rifle trained on her. After a few more steps, Sarah was close enough to kneel at Sparrow's side. The handle of the hatchet dug into her hip, and Sarah welcomed the pain. With bated breath, she pulled a glove off and felt the child's neck, and her shoulders sagged in relief when she found a faint pulse. She wanted to shout with joy, but was careful to hide any reaction.

Sparrow moaned and her eyes fluttered.

"I told you she was dead," Sarah said loudly, placing gentle fingers over Sparrow's eyes to hold them closed. "She was only a child. There was no reason to kill her." Her fingers slid down to Sparrow's mouth as she silently begged the girl to lie still. Whether Sparrow understood the message of Sarah's fingers or again lost consciousness, Sarah didn't know, but the child remained motionless.

Knowing that to go with Fielding would mean almost certain death, Sarah decided upon a desperate plan. She pulled the buffalo robe from Sparrow's shoulders over the girl's face with one hand, while her other hand worked the hidden hatchet from her waistband. With a cry of fury, Sarah launched herself over Sparrow's body and, fearing that the small hatchet would not penetrate the heavy coat he wore, hacked at Fielding's leg. Grim satisfaction roared through her when she felt the blade sink into flesh, heard Fielding's scream. Then a terrible pain crashed through her head, and everything went black.

About a mile from the village, Orion, Gray Eagle, and the rest of the hunting party waited for a lone rider coming from the north to join them.

As the uniformed man approached, his arm raised in the Plains sign language gesture for greeting, Orion was surprised to see that it was none other than his brother, Joseph.

"Joe!" he called gladly. "What brings you out here?"

"Trouble. What else? Eagle." Joseph nodded at his brother, then to the other men in the party.

"Hello, Joseph," said Gray Eagle.

Joseph pulled the collar of his Army-issue wool coat up around his neck. "I need your help, Orion." He nudged his horse into place between Orion and Gray Eagle, and the group continued on toward the village.

The grim expression on his brother's face bothered Orion. "Tell me about it," he invited.

"You were right about Fielding. He was involved with Cutler up to his eyebrows. When Captain Rutledge tried to arrest him, Fielding shot him point-blank and escaped."

Orion stared at him. "How is Rutledge?"

"Hurt bad—shot in the chest. But he isn't dead yet, so he may pull through."

"I don't like Rutledge much, but I hate to hear of that. Sarah will be upset."

"I know." Joseph looked up at the gray sky. "Snow's starting already. Damn."

"Are you tracking Fielding?" Gray Eagle asked.

"Not yet. Fitzpatrick is."

Orion whistled in surprise. "Old Tom? I thought he retired."

"He did this as a favor to me, until I could get you on the trail." Joseph's voice turned ugly. "I want the bastard, Orion. I want him bad. He's a traitor and a murderer, just as responsible for the deaths of those soldiers from Fort St. Charles as if he shot them himself."

"Let me tell Sarah and gather my gear, then we'll get on it." Orion urged Thunder to a gallop, and a few minutes later led the group into the village. He went directly to the new tipi he shared with Sarah and called her name as he jumped down from the saddle. When she didn't answer, he ducked through the door opening. The interior was as neat as a pin, and chilled. The fire had burned down to almost nothing.

"Orion."

The ominous tone of Joseph's voice caused a knot to form in Orion's stomach. He pushed back through the door and straightened. What he saw started a terrible fear drumming through his veins.

His old face a mask of sorrow and fury, Jubal Sage slowly approached, carrying Sparrow in his arms. She hung limp, like a little broken bird, her pretty young face covered with blood.

Gray Eagle stepped forward and brushed the blood-matted

hair back from Sparrow's face. "What happened?" His voice was raw with grief.

"Hunter's wolf come for me, took me out to where the little one was gatherin' wood."

A terrible cry echoed through the village, the anguished cry of a mother whose child had been hurt. Little Leaf, Sparrow's mother, came running, as did Raven's Heart, her father. With great care, Jubal gave the injured child to Raven's Heart. Then he faced Orion.

"She weren't alone out there, Hunter."

Orion knew what was coming even before Jubal held out Sarah's glove. His heart slammed down to his stomach. "Sarah," he whispered. It was just as well that Joseph took the glove from Jubal, because Orion couldn't move. He could barely breathe.

"The little one said it was an Army man, 'cause Sarah called him 'lieutenant.' He hit Sparrow first, from behind, and Sarah made her play dead so he wouldn't finish the job. Then Sarah went after him with this." Jubal held out a small, bloody hatchet. "She must've got him, 'cause Sparrow heard him yell."

"But he got her, too." Orion bit out the words.

"Reckon so. Someone was drug to where a horse waited, and from the depth of the tracks, there's two on that animal." Jubal stared helplessly at Orion. "Who'd do this?"

"Fielding," Joseph answered. "He was in it with Cutler. He shot Captain Rutledge and took off."

"The sonovabitch!" Jubal looked up at the sky. "We'd best get after him; this snow's only gonna get worse."

The strange immobility left Orion's limbs and was replaced with a furious energy. He strode over to where Raven's Heart stood with his daughter in his arms. At their side, Little Leaf quietly sobbed. Orion bent and placed a gentle kiss on Sparrow's cheek. "My brave girl," he murmured in Cheyenne.

"Hunter." Sparrow gasped his name and grabbed at his shirt.

"Shh." Orion caught her cold, frantic hand. "It'll be all right, little one. I'll find Sarah."

"Cal-y-forny."

He leaned forward. "What did you say?"

"The bad man . . . he take her to . . . Cal-y-forny."

"California?"

Sparrow nodded, then grimaced with pain.

Orion looked at Raven's Heart, saw a father's anguish and rage in the warrior's eyes. "Take her home. We'll wait for you here."

Raven's Heart nodded and carried his daughter off, his wife trailing after them.

"He's going to California?" Joseph repeated. "In December? I expected him to head east."

"That's why he's going west." Orion retraced his steps. "Like I told Raven's Heart, we'll meet back here." His voice sounded harsh and rough, even to himself. Without another word, he pushed back into the tipi he shared with Sarah.

It now seemed so empty. And cold.

Orion fell to his knees and reached blindly for the branches stacked to his left, then set the wood on the glowing embers in the fire pit.

Sarah had gone for more wood because of the coming storm. She was trying so hard to be a good wife, a good Cheyenne wife. Orion swore she would never gather wood again.

A thick branch snapped in his hands as an agonized cry welled up from his very soul, a cry he screamed only in his head.

Sarah!

Had she seen him, Orion knew that Sarah would not have recognized the face of the painted man who stepped from their tipi a short while later, nor would she have immediately known that the painted war-horse was Thunder. Orion looked at the men gathered in front of him and nodded his approval. Gray Eagle and Raven's Heart both wore war paint, as he had expected. To his surprise, so did Joseph and Jubal.

He eyed Joseph. No sign of the Army captain remained. His older brother was dressed in buckskin and a buffalo robe coat, his face painted for war. Only his mustache indicated that he was a white man. "This is no longer an Army problem," Orion warned. "Fielding will not live to be court-martialed."

"Right now I'm not in the Army," Joseph said firmly. "I'm a Beaudine, first and foremost, and that bastard attacked our family, our *women*. He hurt my niece and took my sister. You're damn right he won't make it to a court-martial."

Orion grabbed his brother's forearm in a show of solidarity, then turned to Jubal. With his wide-brimmed hat and gray beard, the war paint streaked on the top half of Jubal's face looked almost comical. But there was nothing comical about the murderous expression in the old man's eyes.

"I'm family, too, Hunter Beaudine," Jubal growled. "I love your gal like she was my own daughter, so don't even think of tellin' me I gotta stay here."

"That thought wouldn't enter my mind." Orion gathered Thunder's reins and vaulted into the saddle. "Let's go get my wife." He raised his rifle over his head and let out a furious war cry. Joseph took it up, as did Gray Eagle, then Jubal and Raven's Heart. The cry echoed over the village as men came from their tipis and joined in. Women wailed, children yipped and shouted, dogs howled.

As he rode his prancing stallion through the village, Orion was overwhelmed by the approval and the support of the Cheyenne people. He felt their power, felt the fury and the glory of their collective spirit. He felt the power of the Wolf fill him, strengthen him. He would return with Sarah, warm and alive, riding Thunder with him as she had the first day they met. He would return with her, or die in the effort.

How long had they been riding?

Too long, for certain. Sarah's gloveless hand ached with cold, and her left cheek was stiff with what she suspected was dried or frozen blood from the swollen wound on her scalp. The pain that pounded inside her skull would not go away, adding to the threat that her stomach would revolt again, even though she knew there was nothing left in her.

Sarah was trapped in the saddle with Roger Fielding's arms around her, his knife pressed to her throat, and every step the weary horse took carried her farther away from Orion. Every snowflake that fell—and now there were many—would help bury the tracks. She knew Orion was a good tracker; the best, many said. Was he good enough? Was he back there even now, reconstructing what had happened, filling in the pieces Sparrow couldn't provide? Was little Sparrow still alive to be able to help him?

A sob caught in her throat. She would never forget the horror of seeing the child lying on the ground with blood pouring from her head.

Behind her, Fielding groaned. Sarah glanced down at his wounded thigh. The hatchet blade had indeed gone deep; the blood had long ago soaked through the piece he had torn from her petticoat for use as a bandage. Perhaps, if he lost enough blood, he would also lose consciousness.

Sarah hoped so. Like the image of Sparrow's bleeding, injured body, she would also never forget the rage and hatred in Fielding's eyes when he promised that she would pay dearly for what she had done to him. She would die, he swore, no matter what Hunter Beaudine did, and by the time he was finished with her, she would beg him to kill her. Sarah believed he would keep his evil promise, if he got the chance. But he would fail. He would not have the pleasure of killing her. She would take her own life before she allowed him to take it.

The mare stumbled.

Sarah's heart ached for the valiant animal, enough so that she risked speaking. "You must let the horse rest, or we will all die in this storm."

"I told you to shut up!" Fielding pressed the knife more firmly against her neck. Instead of allowing the horse to stop, he kicked it. "Faster, you worthless nag! Faster!"

The mare squealed her protest.

"She can't!" Sarah shouted.

"Yes, she can." Fielding moved the knife from Sarah's throat, and before Sarah's horrified eyes, slashed at the mare's shoulder.

Sure enough, the animal broke into an uneven trot. Sarah had heard of the unbelievably cruel tactic of inflicting small wounds on a dying horse so that it would continue to run until it literally dropped in its tracks. Until now, she had considered the tale a horror story, akin to those told to frighten young children into behaving. Now she knew different.

The mare slowed to a walk, her sides heaving. With a vicious curse, Fielding jabbed the animal again. But this time, the horse screamed and reared up, giving Sarah the opportunity she had been waiting for. As Fielding struggled to keep his seat, she deliberately pushed out of hers. The horse lost its balance and fell. Sarah threw herself from the saddle as the mare went down. She hit the ground hard, with her right leg bent under her and the breath knocked out of her. The pain in her hip, in her thigh, in her back, was extreme, but she managed to scramble out of the way of the flailing hooves. She lay on her stomach with one side of her face in the snow, and watched as the plucky mare struggled to her feet.

"Good girl," Sarah muttered. She wanted to just lay still

for a minute, to learn to breathe again, but she had to find Fielding.

He found her first.

"You bitch!"

Through the falling snow, Sarah saw him coming, staggering, actually, the knife held high. She fought to push herself up to a sitting position.

Then she felt it.

The Power of the Wolf.

She heard it. The low, warning growl.

"Dancer." She whispered the wolf's name, prayed his name.

Fielding came closer, his eyes seeming to glow with evil fury, with Death.

Sarah felt an incredible peace steal over her even before she saw the tall figures materialize from the storm. Like ghost warriors they came, their moccasined feet silent in the snow, their faces painted, some with arrows notched, some with rifles aimed. The wolf growled again, this time in her ear, and Sarah knew that Dancer stood beside her.

Fielding lurched to a stop, his eyes now wide with fear. He stared at her, at the wolf, at the man behind her who laid a comforting hand on her shoulder. Fielding turned, saw other figures, and started to shake.

Joseph gathered Sarah in his arms and carried her toward the trembling mare, away from the evil that had threatened. He held her carefully, tightly, his relief and love evident in his brown eyes. Sarah rested her head against her beloved brother's shoulder.

"It was your woman he took, Orion," Joseph said. "It's your call as to what we do with him." He repeated the words in Cheyenne for the benefit of the warrior Sarah recognized as Sparrow's father. Raven's Heart nodded his agreement, although he did not lower his bow with its drawn arrow.

Fielding backed up, limping, the knife waving in front of him, a worthless weapon against rifles and arrows.

"I say we all shoot him on the count of three." Jubal pulled back the hammer of his ancient and deadly Hawken. The ominous click sounded loud even in the snow-muffled air.

Sarah saw that Gray Eagle stood with a drawn arrow aimed, that Dancer waited, alert and ready. They all waited for Orion's command.

Orion stood as still as a statue, his rifle at his shoulder, his aim steady and unerring. He knew they waited.

Powerful, conflicting feelings warred within him. His throat ached to give the command to fire, his finger itched to pull the trigger. If ever a man deserved to die, it was Roger Fielding.

But did he want to kill a man in front of Sarah? Did he want her to see that vicious, violent part of him, the part that could kill a man who deserved killing and sleep like a baby that same night, with no regrets, no remorse, no sorrow? Did he dare risk the possibility of seeing disgust and horror in her beautiful blue eyes when she looked at him?

No. Nothing was worth that. Not even the killing of Lieutenant Roger Fielding, traitor and murderer.

Orion eased the hammer back into place and lowered his rifle. "I'm going to give you a choice, Fielding, which is more than Cutler gave Enos Foster, which is more than you gave those murdered soldiers from Fort St. Charles, or Adam Rutledge, or that sweet little girl whose head you bashed, or my beloved wife, whom you have injured and terrorized."

"What do you mean, a choice?" Fielding sneered, his voice heavy with suspicion.

"Me or the storm. Take your pick."

"You mean all of you or the storm."

"No. Just me. Unlike yourself, these are honorable men." Orion waved a hand. "They will give their word to stay out of it."

"Even if I kill you?"

"Even then, if it were possible for you to kill me, which it isn't."

"Not with a gash in my leg, it isn't. That bitch hurt me good."

Orion steeled himself against a surge of anger. Under the circumstances, name-calling was a minor offense, one not worth losing his focus over. "I could have warned you not to upset her," was all he said, very mildly. "Sarah has a temper."

Fielding hedged, shifting his weight back and forth from his injured leg to the other.

"Look, in light of your injured leg, let's even up the odds a little more," Orion said conversationally. "My brother Joseph—you know him as Captain Beaudine—he's well traveled. He told me once about an Apache way of fighting, where a man's ankle is tied to a six-foot length of rope, which is in turn tied to a stake. I'd be willing to do that. I'll be tied, you can move freely, and we fight with knives to the death. If you win, you go free. What do you say, Lieutenant?"

Sarah stared at her husband, unable to believe her ears. She clung to Joseph and whispered, "He can't be serious."

"He is," Joseph assured her. "Dead serious."

She shuddered at Joseph's unfortunate choice of words, then held her breath, waiting.

"Choose, Fielding," Orion ordered. "The storm is worsening."

Fielding stared at Orion. Whatever he saw in those green eyes, or in that hard facial expression, evidently helped him choose. "Give me the horse."

"Nooo," Sarah moaned against Joseph's shoulder.

Orion laughed, a harsh, humorless sound. "If I do, you'll have her dead within ten minutes. And you're mad if you think we're going to give you one of ours."

Raven's Heart spoke rapidly in Cheyenne.

"What did he say?" Fielding demanded.

"He says to make up your mind or he'll let loose with that arrow and be done with it," Jubal snarled. "And my own arm's gettin' real tired. My trigger finger just might slip. The

Hunter give you a fair choice, which is more'n you deserve and a hell of lot more'n you'd get from me if'n I was callin' the shots here. Sorry for swearin', Sarah."

"You're out of time, Fielding." Orion tossed his rifle to Gray Eagle—who lowered his bow and effortlessly caught it—and pulled his knife. "Which will it be?"

"Damn you all to hell!" Fielding shouted. "Can I at least have my rifle?"

"Sure." Orion jerked his head toward the mare.

Jubal lowered his Hawken with an audible sigh of relief and hurried to retrieve Fielding's weapon from its case. "I wouldn't waste your only shot on one of us, if that's what's on your mind," he advised as he handed the rifle to Fielding barrel first. "You might need it later to fend off a bear, or maybe some Sioux, if you get that far on your trip to California." He shrugged. " 'Course, your powder's prob'ly wet, so that rifle's gonna be of no use, 'cept for maybe as a club, which is prob'ly how you struck down that little girl. Maybe you'd better get goin' before I get mad all over again."

"I'll see you all in hell!" Fielding swore. He turned and limped off into the storm. In a matter of seconds, he was gone from sight.

"I look forward to it, you sonovabitch!" Jubal shouted after him. "I'll kill you all over again, you and that damned Linus Harley, 'cause he's there for sure. Sorry, Sarah."

Orion replaced the knife in its sheath as he hurried toward Sarah. She reached for him, clung to him, as he took her from his brother's arms.

"Oh, Sarah," he whispered, holding her close.

The hood of her cape fell back off her head. "How is Sparrow?" she asked fearfully.

"Alive. She could talk. We all hope she'll be all right."

"What did you mean about Fielding not giving Adam a choice, Orion? What happened?"

"Fielding shot him when Rutledge tried to arrest him. Joseph said he's in bad shape, but he's still alive, too."

Sarah closed her eyes against the fear and pain that washed over her. So many people hurt, some badly, some killed, all because of one man's cruelty and evil ambition.

"Can you get up on Thunder's back, sweetheart?"

"Yes." With Orion's help, she made it into the saddle, then noticed the colorful markings on Thunder's face. "What happened to him?" she asked in amazement.

"He came ready for war, as we all did." Orion swung up behind her. He brushed the snow off her head and kissed her ear before he pulled her hood into place.

Joseph handed the lost glove up to her, which Sarah gratefully accepted. "How is the mare?" she asked as she forced her stiff fingers into the softness of the fur-lined leather.

"She's in bad shape. Jubal and I will put her between our horses and take it slow going back. If she makes it to the village, I may be able to save her." He looked up at Orion. "Get your woman home, little brother."

"Yes, sir, Captain Beaudine." Orion reached around Sarah and gathered the reins. "You look like hell, Joe. That paint ran down into your mustache. Sorry for swearing, wife."

Smiling, Sarah leaned back against the warmth and security of her husband's chest as Thunder started after Gray Eagle and Raven's Heart.

"Yeah, well, you're no picture yourself, Orion Beaudine, unless it's an ugly one," Joseph called after him. "The snow ruined your masterful artwork, too."

Orion laughed and waved. Sarah looked back until the falling snow obliterated Joseph and Jubal from view. A wolf—Dancer?—howled, the sound both eerie and beautiful.

They rode in silence for a distance, then Sarah spoke. "Why didn't you kill him?"

"I didn't want to in front of you."

"Had I not been there, you would have?"

"At one time, yes. But not now."

Sarah tilted her head and looked back at his painted face. "Why not?"

"I wasn't sure how you would feel about me if you saw me kill a man, even one who deserved it, and I wasn't willing to do anything that might risk the love we share." He positioned her hood more securely on her head.

Stricken, she looked down. "You are more noble than I, Orion. I would have killed him if I could have, after he hit Sparrow. I thought he was going to kill me. The only reason I went for his leg instead of his black heart was because I feared that little hatchet wouldn't go through his coat, and I figured I didn't have a chance of reaching his neck before he struck me down."

"You figured right, my bloodthirsty woman."

She frowned. "Don't tease me. How would you feel if I had killed him?"

"Honestly?"

"Of course honestly. That was our agreement long ago, remember?"

Orion tightened his arm around her. "I would have been terrified, and furious, that you were even put in the position of needing to defend yourself. If you had actually been forced to kill, I would worry about how you took it—emotionally, I mean—because it is no easy thing to kill, even someone who deserves it. And I would have been proud that you had the courage and the brains to do what needed to be done."

"You would be proud?"

"Yes."

Sarah snuggled against him again. "A part of me wanted you to kill him."

"A part of me wanted to. A big part. And had the situation called for it, if we were engaged in an ongoing battle or if you were in immediate danger, I would have. I have killed when necessary, and will again if I have to. I just felt it wasn't absolutely necessary to kill him in front of you."

"Do you think he'll survive the storm?"

"No. Fielding may be crafty and conniving, but he's not smart, not when it comes to the wilderness. Rather than running his horse near to death, he should have found shelter, holed up for the storm, cared for his animal. Stupidity is one thing the wilderness does not forgive. He'll die out there, and it will be his own fault, because of the choices he made."

"He hurt a lot of people."

"The world is better off without him."

"I know." Sarah yawned.

"I should warn you that someone's waiting for us at home."

"Who?"

"An old friend of my father's, a man named Thomas Fitzpatrick. He tracked Fielding from Fort Laramie. We met up with him at the place where Fielding attacked you, and I took over. Fitz was worn out, so I told him to wait at our place."

"That makes sense." Sarah yawned again. "Orion, I think I'm falling asleep. How far are we from home?"

"Too far." Orion's arms tightened around her. "I wish I could fly you there." There was an obvious note of worry in his voice.

"I'm fine, as long as I'm with you."

"You'll be with me forever."

She rubbed her head against his shoulder in a weary, loving gesture. "Then I'll be fine forever."

Sarah awakened to see Orion seated cross-legged near the fire, examining a paper he held in his hands. For a long moment she watched him, allowed her hungry gaze to roam over his shining black hair, over his scrubbed, paint-free face, over his bare, broad shoulders, inviting chest, muscled arms, and long fingers. She sighed with longing, and relived their earlier homecoming.

When they had arrived back at their tipi, after a noisy welcome from the people of the village, darkness was falling and the storm was rising. The kind, white-haired man Orion introduced as Thomas Fitzpatrick had the fire burning high and the stew pot bubbling. Mr. Fitzpatrick offered to help Gray Eagle see to the horses and had disappeared, leaving them alone. Orion had insisted upon helping her out of her clothes, his mouth drawn tight at the sight of her bruised body and bloodied head, his expression appearing even more fierce than it actually was thanks to the fearsome streaks of war paint on his face.

Over her protests, he had wrapped her in a warm buffalo robe and carried her to the pond, where her dream of bathing with him was fulfilled, but not in the manner she had envisioned. He had carried her into the warm water, washed the blood from her hair, massaged and stroked her aching muscles, cleaned the war paint and sweat from his own body. Then he had bundled her up and carried her back to their tipi without so much as one sensual word. No, their first bath together was not as she had dreamed.

Sarah stretched in lazy contentment, enjoying the feel of the bed furs against her naked body, grateful that her aches had eased. Perhaps it was the herbal poultice Gray Eagle brought for the wound on her head, or the willow bark tea Sweet Water had made for the ache *in* her head, or the dried mint leaves Orion had soaked in warm water and applied to her bruises. Perhaps it was the soothing mineral bath, or the long nap she had just awakened from, or the fact that both Orion and Dancer were here with her, safe and warm, while a snowstorm raged outside. Whatever the reason, she felt better. She rolled over on her stomach and reached out to caress Orion's shoulder. He looked up at her with a smile.

"What is that you are examining so closely?" Sarah asked.

"You and Dancer." He handed her a piece of thick paper.

Amazed, Sarah examined the sketch of her in a sitting position with Dancer at her side, her arm draped around the wolf's neck. The artist's angle was from the side, showing their heads in profile. Both she and Dancer had thoughtful expressions on their faces. She wore her riding hat, and the black gauze scarf around the crown floated forever on a long-gone breeze. The sketch was lovely. "Where did you get this?"

"From Joseph. He drew that after he took you riding one day when we were all at Fort St. Charles."

"I remember that day." Sarah stared at the picture. "He's very gifted."

"Yes, he is." Orion reached out to brush a strand of hair away from her cheek. "I treasured that sketch when I was away from you, just as I treasured this." He held up her black lace shawl.

"I wondered if you still had that."

"Of course I do, just as you still have my necklace." He glanced up at the necklace, which hung from the support pole where he had placed it while helping Sarah undress.

She held out the sketch. "Put this in a safe place. I'm afraid I'll wrinkle it."

Orion took the paper and slipped it into a leather *parfleche* with the shawl. He stroked the sleeping Dancer's back, then rose and removed his leggings and loincloth. Sarah scooted over to make room for him.

"Joseph stopped by while you were sleeping," Orion said as he gathered her in his arms. "The mare made it this far."

"Thank God," Sarah breathed. She rested her head on Orion's shoulder. "That poor creature. Do you think Joseph can save her?"

"If anyone can, he can. Not only is the horse his spirit animal, but he has a gift with them, just as he does with a pencil and a sketchbook."

"You have a few gifts from the gods yourself, Orion Beaudine."

A pleased smile lit his face. "You think so?"

"Definitely. You've been blessed with an incredible wolf, a wonderful horse, an indescribable wife . . ." Her voice broke off in a shout of laughter as Orion tickled her ribs.

"You dare to mock me, wife?" he growled, rolling on top

of her, pinning her hands near her head. "I do indeed have other gifts, talents, if you will," he nibbled on her neck, "which I would be happy to demonstrate."

Sarah's laughter faded under the force of a rush of desire. She searched for his lips, gratified when he raised his head from her neck so their mouths could meet, his hair falling around their faces like a dark curtain. How she loved the feel of his chest pressing down on her breasts, of his hips covering hers, of his stirring manhood, of their entwined legs.

How she loved him.

"I love you," she breathed against his lips

"And I love you." He raised up on his elbows, pushed his hair to one side, and looked down at her. Desire and concern warred in his green eyes. "I want to show you my love." He gently rocked his hips against her, letting her feel the hot, hard evidence of his passion. "But you are battered and sore. I don't want to hurt you further."

Tenderness welled up in her. "You couldn't hurt me, Orion." She caressed his cheek, his neck, his shoulder. "Especially if you go slow and easy."

Orion groaned. "I've never done well with slow and easy, woman, not with you. Every time I try, you drive me mad with wanting you."

Sarah's wandering hand trailed down his chest, down his stomach, worked its way between them, seeking. Orion stilled when she found him. When her fingers closed around him, his eyes closed. His breathing stopped as she slowly explored, stroked, guided him home.

"Slow and easy," she whispered, her hands pulling his hips forward with gentle pressure, her body opening for him, taking him in to the hilt.

"Sarah." Her name was all Orion could manage to say. Somehow, the very subtlety of her movements heightened his desire to an almost unbearable level. He fought the urge to move faster and harder.

As if she sensed he needed the encouragement, she whispered breathlessly, "That's it. Slow and easy You'll do fine."

Orion looked down at her, watched in awe as the golden firelight played over her lovely face, sparkled in her dark hair spread over the furs, showed him that her lips parted as her breath came faster. Her eyes drifted open, shined up at him, revealed in their blue, blue depths the sweet, powerful love she felt for him.

Unable to look away from those beautiful, honest eyes, Orion moved against her, in her, with her, and knew that together, both he and Sarah would do just fine.

Epilogue

Spring came to the plains, bringing with it warm days and the promise of new life, both in the land and in Sarah. The chokecherry bushes along the creek bed blossomed, their delicate white flowers fragrant and short-lived, and the mild morning sickness that had plagued Sarah for two months eased.

It was time for the Cheyenne to begin their nomadic wanderings of summer, following the roving buffalo herds, and it was time for Sarah and Orion to leave the Cheyenne.

The women showed Sarah how to dismantle her tipi, helped her pack, and made her a travois, which Orion hitched to the gentle mare Joseph had saved and given to Sarah as a gift. The leave-taking had been poignant and painful, but Sarah took comfort from the fact that Orion promised they would visit again, perhaps winter with the tribe every year, much as his father had done during the summers so many years ago.

Gray Eagle accompanied them on the journey to Fort Laramie, for the dual purpose of seeing Joseph and picking up supplies. It took them a full day to travel the twenty-five miles to the fort, for they went slowly, due to the travois and Sarah's condition.

Close to sundown, as they approached the bustling fort, all were astonished to see the improvements which had been made in the four months since their last visit. Gray Eagle commented on the circled wagon train north of the fort. The new wave of travelers had started early.

A few minutes later, Orion lifted Sarah down from her saddle outside Joseph's modest quarters. "This place is really beginning to look like something, Joseph," he commented. "Are they going to build a stockade around the entire compound?"

"Lieutenant Woodbury, the engineer, would like to, but I don't think Congress will fund it."

Sarah shaded her eyes and gazed at the deteriorating adobe walls of old Fort John to the south, which had been the first fort built on the site. "What will they do with the old fort?" she asked.

Joseph shrugged. "It's so far gone now that there's no point in trying to restore it. Eventually I think it will be torn down." He looked at her closely. "How are you feeling?"

"Fine." Sarah smiled at him as her hand automatically strayed to her slightly curved stomach. "The ginger tea Miss Lucy sent back with Jubal last month did wonders. I rarely feel ill any more, and when I do, the tea does the trick. I think the worst is over." Sarah glanced at Orion and saw the now-familiar look of joy mingled with pride on his handsome face. She fought a smile as she wondered if he would actually strut about. He was so proud of the coming baby, of her, of his role in creating the new life that was unfurling inside her. She found it touching.

"Theodora is over at the laundry," Joseph said, taking up Sarah's reins. "She and Callahan Roe have been waiting to marry until you could be here, so I guess there'll be a wedding in the next few days. Roe resigned his commission, and they plan to hook up with one of the wagon trains heading for Oregon."

"That's wonderful news!" Sarah cried. "Oh, I can't wait to see her!"

Joseph continued his litany. "Mrs. Gates is probably at the officers' quarters. She's due to have her baby any day now.

And Miss Lucy is at the Colonel's quarters." He pointed to two obviously recently built adobe buildings as he spoke. "Have you heard that Colonel Rutledge has been posted back East? He and the Mrs. Colonel are leaving within the week, I believe."

"How is Harriet?"

"Better. Nursing Captain Rutledge back to health after Fielding shot him last winter seemed to do her a lot of good, almost like it gave her a reason to get better. Captain Rutledge is fully recovered," he added, answering her unspoken question.

"Good."

Orion kissed her cheek. "Go visit your friends, Sarah. I'll find you later."

"All right." She walked away in the direction of the laundry. Before she got there, however, a sight befell her that stopped her in her tracks.

Adam Rutledge was strolling across the parade ground with a lovely woman on his arm, a woman whose hoopskirts swayed gracefully as she walked, whose pert hat and pretty face were shaded by a fringed parasol. Sarah could only stare. Never had Adam looked at *her* with such an expression of interest and devotion on his handsome, bearded face. A rush of happiness for her old friend filled Sarah's heart. She picked up her skirts and hurried toward the couple.

"Adam!"

He looked up. "Sarah!" A wide smile lit his face. He stepped toward her and caught her up in a warm embrace. "How are you?"

"Very well," she assured him. When they separated, she grabbed his forearms. "How are you, Adam, truly? I was so upset to hear you had been wounded."

"I'm fine now. Captain Beaudine told me of your own adventure with Lieutenant Fielding. I wanted to kill the man for what he put you through."

"That was a popular sentiment," Sarah said. "But justice

has been served. A Cheyenne hunting party found his remains when the snow melted."

"Good." He looked at her closely. "You look beautiful, Sarah, and so happy. I hear a little one is on the way. Congratulations."

"Thank you." Sarah *felt* beautiful, but she wondered how beautiful she actually *looked* in her simple skirt and jacket, with her hair pulled back in a long braid and covered with a practical wide-brimmed felt hat, when compared to the lovely creature who waited patiently behind Adam. She discreetly nodded toward the woman.

"Where are my manners?" Adam exclaimed. He released Sarah and turned toward the woman. "Miss Pendragon, please forgive my rudeness. My joy at seeing my dear friend is the only excuse I can offer." He gallantly held out his hand, which Miss Pendragon accepted. "Sarah, may I present Miss Emmaline Pendragon of Boston? Miss Pendragon, this is Mrs. Beaudine of New Haven and, more recently, points farther west."

"How nice to meet you, Mrs. Beaudine. Captain Rutledge thinks highly of you, as I'm certain I shall." A genuinely sweet smile curved Miss Pendragon's bow-shaped pink lips.

Sarah was charmed. Emmaline Pendragon seemed as sincere and as kind as she was beautiful. "I'm certain we'll get along famously, Miss Pendragon."

"Sarah, I hate to rush off, but if I am to return Miss Pendragon to her father's quarters so that I may participate in the retreat dress parade, we must go." Adam shrugged in apology.

"I understand. Orion and I will be here for several days. We'll find time later for a nice chat."

Adam leaned forward to kiss her cheek. "You made the right choice, for both our sakes," he whispered.

"I know," she whispered back.

He winked at her, then led Miss Pendragon away.

"Miss Sarah."

At the sound of her name, Sarah turned to find Lucy standing not far away.

"Miss Lucy." Sarah held out her hands as she walked toward her friend. She was surprised and pleased when Lucy pulled her into a quick embrace.

"It's good to see you," Lucy said gruffly.

"Oh, it's good to see you, too," Sarah replied. "I was on my way to visit Theodora. Would you like to walk with me?"

"Yes." Lucy fell into step beside her. "You look well. The Hunter must be taking good care of you."

"He is. Thank you for the tea you sent; it helped a lot."

Lucy shrugged. "It was nothing."

"Joseph told me the Rutledges are going back East. How soon will you leave?"

"They're leaving next week. I'm not going with them."

Sarah stopped walking and stared at her friend. "You quit?"

"Not yet, but I will." A smile played around Lucy's full lips.

"There's something you're holding back," Sarah said, her eyes narrowed with curious suspicion. "Something good. Tell me."

Lucy looked at her, her dark brown eyes filled with wonder. "I'm going to Oregon."

"How wonderful! With Theo and Lieutenant Roe?"

"Not with them exactly, although they're going, too. I met a man."

"Lucy!" The name slipped out without the title. *"Tell me!"*

"The first wagon train of the season came last week. There's a few Negro families on it, free men, on their way to a new life in Oregon and California. They've invited me to go with them."

"You mentioned a man."

Lucy smiled again. "Samson Channing. He's the one who did the asking. We're going to marry before we leave."

Sarah looked at her. "A week isn't a long time to know a man you plan to marry."

"It's long enough for me," Lucy said firmly. She pierced Sarah with her knowing gaze. "And you're a fine one to talk. You knew with the Hunter real soon, too, probably within a week. In fact, it was only days. After that morning ride you took with him, you were never the same. You just took your own sweet time admitting it."

"You're right," Sarah admitted with a rueful laugh.

The two women resumed walking.

"Will I get to meet your Samson?" asked Sarah,

"Of course. Since you're here, I was hoping you and the Hunter would honor us by coming to the wedding."

"It is we who would be honored, Miss Lucy."

Lucy was quiet for a moment. "I think we should drop the 'miss' now, if it's all right with you."

A happy grin split Sarah's face. "You know it is. What changed?"

"I'm not a servant anymore. I'm going to be a wife, same as you, same as Theodora." Lucy shrugged. "Of course, I'll be doing the same chores, working just as hard, but it's different working for your own family, for your own man."

Sarah hooked her arm with Lucy's, pleased when Lucy did not pull away. "I'm happy for you, Lucy, happier than I can say. Does Theo know?"

"Not yet."

"Then let's go tell her."

As they walked, it occurred to Sarah that her two dear friends were going to move far away. There was a very real possibility that once Theodora and Lucy left for Oregon, she would never see them again. As happy as she was for her friends, a pensive mood fell over her.

It seemed all of life was a series of beginnings and endings, of continuing seasons and cycles, of good times and bad. And perhaps that was as it should be.

Her hand fell to her stomach, to where another cycle of

life was just beginning. A sense of peace came over her. Yes. All was as it should be.

"Sarah looks wonderful, Orion," Joseph said admiringly as he pulled the saddle from Star's back. "So happy and healthy, almost glowing. Life with the Cheyenne agrees with her, as does impending motherhood, apparently."

"What about life with me?" Orion demanded.

With one eyebrow raised, Joseph eyed him over Star's back, as if he were giving the question serious thought. "Personally, I wouldn't want to wake up next to you every morning," he finally said, his brown eyes twinkling with humor. "But there's no accounting for some people's taste. Especially women. They can be easily led by what they consider a pretty face." He peered at Orion. "Nope, I don't see it."

"You're just jealous, big brother."

Surprisingly, Joseph sobered. "No, I'm happy for you. Truly. I have to admit to some envy, though. I want what you found with Sarah."

Suddenly sober himself, Orion nodded. "I'm a lucky man."

"You sure are," Gray Eagle put in.

After a moment of silence, Joseph started brushing Star. "Have you and Sarah decided where to settle down?"

Orion shook his head. "Not yet. We're going to go to St. Louis first. I promised Sarah a visit with Ma and the girls."

Gray Eagle spoke. "Orion and I have talked it over, Joseph. I don't like them being back there and us being out here any more than you two do. The idea of bringing Ma and the girls out pleases me."

"I thought I'd spring it on them when Sarah and I are back there, see how they feel," Orion said.

Joseph nodded his agreement. "Good. See if you can at least get them to come for a visit. Maybe they'll like it enough to stay."

"What are you going to do, Joseph?" Gray Eagle asked.

"I've written the letter resigning my commission, but I haven't turned it in yet."

"So you're going to quit."

"I have to." Joseph led Star into the corral and released her. "Changes are coming, Eagle. A wagon train bound for Oregon rolled in here last week, and it's only the beginning of May. This year will be worse than last year, and next year will be worse yet. Trouble is coming with the change. I can feel it. I want to be in a position where I can help. In the Army, there are too many restrictions." He looked at both of his brothers. "Tom Fitzpatrick sees it coming, too. I think maybe I'll work with Fitz and see what happens with the Indian tribes, and train horses to make a living. I'd like to track down the man who trained Thunder, Orion. I've been hearing more about him; it seems he has a way with horses."

"Eagle says he's way to hell and gone up in the mountains somewhere, Joe. I'd love to go with you, but I won't be able to until Sarah and I get back from St. Louis, which might not be until the end of the summer."

"The tribes let him and his children live up there in peace because they think he's crazy; you know, touched." Gray Eagle tapped his head.

"So I've heard." Joseph sighed. "The end of the summer will suit me, Orion. I'm probably just enough of a fool to stick it out with the Army until this next wave of immigrants passes."

Orion released Thunder into the corral. "You'll find what you're looking for, Joseph."

"You think so?"

"No question. Trust me, big brother. You'll be fine." He looked at Gray Eagle. "You both will."

Gray Eagle punched his shoulder. "Thanks for telling us, big brother."

"You're welcome, *little* brother. Now let's go find my wife."

As the sun sank behind the mountains to the west, painting the sky with brilliant streaks of red and gold, the three sons of Jedediah Beaudine crossed the now-deserted parade ground. And on a hill to the south, overlooking the fort, a lone wolf sat. He raised his nose to the sky and howled, his haunting song in perfect harmony with the ancient land and the endless sky.

Dear Reader,

Hunter's Bride is the first book I have written set in 1849, and it required research for an era I had not studied thoroughly before. As always, I found the research fascinating and exciting. My descriptions of Fort Laramie are accurate to the time; however, Fort St. Charles is a figment of my imagination. I got the idea for my imaginary fort from an actual fort that was built south of Fort Laramie by a Spanish-speaking crew from New Mexico in 1841. That fort never offered real competition to the trade at Fort Laramie, nor was it ever manned by the U.S. Army, and it was eventually abandoned, as were most of the military forts in the American West, some after only a short life. For example, Fort Phil Kearny was built on the Bozeman Trail in Montana in 1866 and abandoned a mere two years later as part of an agreement with the Sioux. All of the hard work of the soldiers who built the fort was for naught, as the Sioux burned the fort to the ground immediately after the troops pulled out. Even the important Fort Laramie was abandoned, in 1890. The soldiers rode out and literally left the fort to the elements. Fort Laramie, located in eastern Wyoming, is now a National Historic Site. I went there on a hot summer day and wandered through the buildings—some restored and reconstructed, some still in ruins. I stood on the long-deserted parade ground and looked out at the Laramie River, at the surrounding grass-covered hills, and at the mountains in the distance. The hot wind blew against me, and I felt the spirit of the past. It was a powerful and moving experience.

I have also felt the Power of the Wolf. One glorious summer day at the summit of Mount Evans, high in the Rocky Mountains of Colorado, I had the opportunity to meet three wolves. One allowed me to pet her, to scratch her ears and massage her neck. We were literally face to face, nose to nose, and I saw in her incredibly beautiful eyes the gentle wisdom of the ages. Just as Dancer kissed Sarah, that wolf kissed me, and it was a deeply moving, almost mystical experience, one I will never forget as long as I live, for our spirits connected. I also one time heard a captive pack sing at the full moon as dusk was falling. The lovely, haunting sound touched my soul. There really is such a thing as the Power of the Wolf.

Although it had died out by the time of the War Between the States, the quaint custom of addressing officers' wives with their husbands' ranks was common in the first half of the nineteenth century. A woman's position in the social hierarchy of a military post was directly related to her husband's rank, and that may explain why the custom was first developed. Mrs. Colonel Rutledge did not exaggerate the impact—positive or negative—a woman could have on her husband's career. On a military post, social hierarchy as well as social rules were usually unwritten and always very rigid.

My next book, *Joseph's Bride,* is, perhaps obviously, the story of Orion Beaudine's older brother, Joseph. He searches for a legendary old man, hidden in the mountains, who is reputed to have a special way with horses. This man also has a beautiful granddaughter, one who has been blessed with special gifts of her own. *Joseph's Bride* is scheduled for an October 1997 release.

I have come to love the Beaudine family, and will not rest until all of their stories are told. I feel like they are part of my own family, and I hope you are drawn to them, too. I also hope that my books leave you with a sense of satisfaction and enjoyment. At least in these pages, good overcomes evil, justice is served, and love conquers all. Perhaps one day our real world will reflect those values. Until then I will continue to read and write romance novels. Happy reading!

Jessica Wulf
P.O. Box 461212
Aurora, Colorado 80046
(An SASE is appreciated if you write to me.)

ABOUT THE AUTHOR

Jessica Wulf is a native of North Dakota and has spent most of her life in Colorado, where she now lives with her husband and two dogs. She has a B.A. in History, as well as a passion and fascination for it, and often feels she was born in the wrong century. *Hunter's Bride* is her fourth novel.